A Regency

Earl's Pleasure

ISABELLE GODDARD

MILLS & BOON

Published in Great Britain 2016
by Mills & Boon, an imprint of Harlequin (UK) Limited,
Eton House, 18-24 Paradise Road, Richmond, Surrey, TW9 1SR

A REGENCY EARL'S PLEASURE © 2016 Harlequin Books S.A.

The Earl Plays With Fire © 2011 Isabelle Goddard
Society's Most Scandalous Rake © 2012 Isabelle Goddard

ISBN: 978-0-263-91770-3

052-0616

Harlequin (UK) policy is to use papers that are natural, renewable and recyclable products and made from wood grown in sustainable forests. The logging and manufacturing processes conform to the legal environmental regulations of the country of origin.

Printed and bound
by CPI Group (UK) Ltd, Croydon, CR0 4YY

**ROM
Pbk**

The Earl
Plays With Fire

ISABELLE GODDARD

Isabelle Goddard was born into an army family and spent her childhood moving around the UK and abroad. Unsurprisingly it gave her itchy feet and in her twenties she escaped from an unloved secretarial career to work as cabin crew and see the world.

The arrival of marriage, children and cats meant a more settled life in the south of England, where she's lived ever since. It also gave her the opportunity to go back to 'school' and eventually teach at university. Isabelle loves the nineteenth century and grew up reading Georgette Heyer, so when she plucked up the courage to begin writing herself the novels had to be Regency romances.

Chapter One

London—1816

'Have you heard the latest?' The voice came out of nowhere.

Christabel Tallis, aimlessly fanning herself, stopped for a moment and glanced at the mirror which hung on the opposite wall. She knew neither of the women reflected there. Perched uncomfortably on one of the stiffly brocaded benches that lined the Palantine Gallery, she had been wondering, not for the first time that morning, why she'd ever agreed to her mother's suggestion that they meet Julian here. Lady Harriet had insisted they attend what was billed as the show of the Season, but for Christabel the delights of London society had long ago palled. The salon was overheated and far too crowded, and her delicate skin was already slightly flushed.

'About the Veryan boy, you mean?' one of the women continued.

The name hovered in the air, menacing Christabel's shield of calm detachment. The buzz of inconsequential chatter faded into the distance and every fibre of her body became alert.

'He's hardly a boy now, of course.'

'Indeed no. How long has it been? Lady Veryan must be overjoyed that he is returning home at last.'

Suddenly Christabel longed to be far away from this conversation, away from this room. A shaft of sunlight streamed through the gallery's long windows, breaking through a lowering sky and burnishing her auburn curls into a fiery cloud. The warming light was gone almost as soon as it appeared, but to her it seemed to beckon escape. Escape to where, though? To a country of grey slate and blue seas, a landscape of moor and rocks? To Cornwall, to home? But that could not be; she knew well that her future lay elsewhere.

'One can only hope that he actually arrives,' the woman opined in a hushed voice.

The other shuddered theatrically. 'I understand the journey from Argentina is very long and most dangerous.'

'My dear, yes. You must remember *The Adventurer*— just a few years ago. It sailed from Buenos Aires…'

The women moved away and she heard no more. That was sufficient. Richard's name reverberated through her mind. After all these years—five, six it would be—he was coming back. Her deep green eyes stared into the distance and saw only memory.

She was seated on a stone bench in the garden of the Veryan town house, the lush fragrance of rose blossoms tumbling in the air. Richard was standing straight and tall in front of her, his mouth compressed and his face white and set. She had just told him that she could not marry him and was offering his ring back. She could not marry him because she was in love with Joshua. And Joshua just happened to be one of Richard's closest friends. What a wretched business that had been. She and Richard had drifted into an engagement, more to please their parents than from any passionate attachment, and Joshua was the result. The family estates bordered each other and she'd known Richard all her life. It felt natural to be planning to spend the rest of it together. But her visit to London to buy bride clothes had vouchsafed a different perspective: Cornwall and their shared childhood vanished in a sea mist. Instead there was a thrilling round of parties, balls, picnics, assemblies and, at the end of it, Joshua. No, she couldn't marry Richard. She was too young and too passionate and friendship was not enough.

'Miss Tallis, please accept my sincerest apologies for arriving so late.'

A well-dressed man in a puce tailcoat and fawn pantaloons stood before her. He took her shapely hand in his, kissing it with elaborate courtesy, and bowed politely to Lady Tallis, who had broken off her conversation with a chance-met companion just long enough to smile benignly at the man she hoped would become her son-in-law.

Sir Julian Edgerton's pleasant face wore a rueful

smile. 'I fear the Committee took longer than expected. There is always such a deal to do for the Pimlico Widows and Orphans. I hope you'll forgive me.'

'Naturally, Sir Julian, how could I not? You lead a truly benevolent life!' Christabel's musical voice held the suspicion of a laugh, but her face was lit with the gentlest of smiles.

'Now that I am here, may I get you some refreshment?'

'What a good idea! It's so very hot in this room. Lemonade, perhaps?'

'It will be my pleasure,' he said gallantly, 'and when we are once more comfortable, would you care to make a quick tour of the paintings with me? I am anxious to hear your views. You have such a refined sensibility.'

She sighed inwardly, but nodded assent while her mother beamed encouragement. She knew Lady Harriet was counting on Sir Julian's proposal. At nearly twenty-five Christabel was already perilously close to being on the shelf and she could no longer delay the decision to marry. Sir Julian might not be the most exciting man of her acquaintance, but he was solid and dependable and would make a restful husband. More than that, he would be an adoring one. And she could trust him. After the bruising experience of her girlhood, such a man was surely worth any amount of excitement.

If she made this marriage, it might help repair some of the destruction she'd wreaked all those years ago. Her parents had loved Richard as a son and his dismissal had hit them very hard. As for Richard, she was sure he'd remained heart whole. He'd never loved her with the passion she had craved. Instead he'd been angry and humiliated. It was the gossip he had loathed, being on everyone's tongue, the jilted suitor. Within a sennight he'd escaped England and was on a boat to Argentina. Lord Veryan had told the world it was needful that his son administer the family's growing estates in South America, but the world had known the real reason for Richard's sudden departure. So he'd escaped, but she'd paid the price for her indiscretion. Jilting a man three weeks before the wedding was the height of bad *ton* and scurrilous gossip had swirled around her head for months. It was difficult to recall six years later just how vulnerable she'd felt. Today she was an acknowledged leader of fashion, an ice-cold beauty who'd remained impregnable despite countless suitors. But then she'd been a raw, passionate girl, in the throes of a thrilling infatuation, and unable to dissemble.

'I'm afraid the lemonade is as warm as the salon.' Sir Julian had emerged from the crush and was at her elbow, proffering the glass he'd procured with some difficulty.

For a moment she looked blindly up at him. Past distresses were crowding in on her and, for the second time that morning, she looked for escape. She needed distraction, needed to be on the move.

'I think I would prefer to view the pictures after all, Sir Julian.'

She rose from her seat as she spoke and, smoothing the creases from her amber silk walking dress, took her suitor's arm. They began slowly to stroll around the gallery. As always her elegant figure drew glances of frank admiration from those she passed and Sir Julian, feeling pride in his possession, held her arm even more tightly. While they walked, he spoke sensibly about the paintings they inspected and she tried hard to conjure interest in his carefully considered opinions. He was a good man, she told herself severely, and she must not hanker for more. That way lay disaster. She had learned that lesson well. It had taken little time to discover that Richard was worth twenty times the man who'd displaced him. The relationship with Joshua had petered out, destroyed by her guilt and his inevitable betrayal.

'I must say that I find these colours a little too forceful. They jangle the nerves rather than soothe.'

Sir Julian was standing before a group of canvases whose landscapes pulsated with lurid crimsons and golds, an anarchic depiction of the natural world.

'What do you think, Miss Tallis—am I being old fashioned?'

'Not old fashioned precisely, Sir Julian, but perhaps a little traditional? One needs to open one's mind to different possibilities,' she hazarded, thinking that just one of the pictures on her bedroom wall would be enough to keep her awake at night.

'As always you are right. I will look with your eyes and endeavour to see these canvases anew.'

Why did he always have to agree with her? Richard would have mocked her pretensions, laughed openly at her and they would have ended sharing the joke together. But Richard's companionship was long gone. How strange to think that he would soon be in England, but this time returning as the new Earl Veryan. It was three months since Lord Veryan's life had been brutally cut short by a riding accident. Richard would have left for home the minute he'd received the dreadful news, but a long and treacherous journey meant his father had been buried while he was still on the high seas. At the funeral Lady Veryan had been beyond grief; it was certain to be a very sad homecoming for her son. Her escort continued to talk, but Christabel's thoughts were elsewhere, straying inevitably towards a lone man adrift on a distant ocean. With a great effort she forced herself to return to Sir Julian and his enthusiastic recital; the small successes of Pimlico's deserving poor had never seemed less riveting.

A few hundred miles away, the new Earl Veryan gazed blankly over the sea as it threaded itself swiftly past the ship. He was deep in thought and not all of it was pleasant. The last image of his father played through his mind, the stocky figure waving from the dockside, a bright red handkerchief in his hand, growing smaller and smaller as the ship made its way to the open sea. He had been away from England for too long; he had not been there for his father when he needed him. Now at last he was returning home, but to an unknown life. The Great Hall would no longer echo to Lord Veryan's greeting and the task of administering a large estate was now his. He knew himself well capable, but he was sorry to be leaving Argentina behind. The country had been good to him. A rugged outdoor life had taught him authority and decisiveness. It had honed him physically and created an inner strength he'd not known he possessed. And life there had not been all hard work. The social round was lively and largely free of the stifling conventions of London society, and the tall, handsome Englishman was a popular guest. There had been music and laughter and plenty of beautiful women happy to engage in a light flirtation or more. He'd enjoyed their favours freely and indifferently, determined to consign love to the vault of history and simply enjoy the physical pleasures of the moment. It had become a way of life for him, demanding little emotion and no commitment.

The moon cut a path across the surface of the small waves so bright that it made him blink. His eyes focused on the expanse of ocean, at the different shades of silver and black stretching to the horizon, then to the lanterns which hung above him, swinging comfortingly to the rhythm of the ship. The crew were engaged elsewhere and he had the deck to himself. He wondered if he dared to smoke a cigar, a disastrous habit he'd contracted in Argentina, but decided that he'd better keep that delight for later. Dinner would be served soon and he did not want to escort Domino to the table smelling of tobacco.

The boat gave a louder creak than usual with the sudden swell of the ocean, but the vessel soon recovered its peaceful passage. A sailor appeared from the deck below and waved a greeting.

'Fine weather, sir, and the forecast's good. Should be a quiet landfall, I'm thinking.'

It had not always been so calm; they had suffered tempests aplenty since leaving Buenos Aires and there had been times when he'd wondered if they would ever make it to land again. But it was tranquil now and he had leisure to think. The grey eyes were expressionless, his dark straight brows furrowed. The meeting with his mother would be painful, he knew, but there would be joy too. To be home again; to feel Cornish air on his skin once more and to awake to the sound of Cornish surf breaking on the rocky cove below Madron Abbey. He saw in his mind's eye the winding path from the house across the green headland and then the sudden dramatic fall of cliffs tumbling into the wild seas. He'd walked that pathway so many times in memory. In just a few weeks he would be walking it in reality.

Immediately the ship berthed in Southampton, he would post up to London and ensure that Domino was safely consigned to the care of her aunt. The sooner he could do this, the sooner he could travel on to Madron.

'There you are, Richard. I've been looking everywhere for you.'

The speaker was a diminutive brunette who barely came up to his chest. She raised a pair of soft brown eyes to his hard grey ones and smiled sweetly. Richard smiled back in response.

'Not quite everywhere, it seems. I'm not exactly invisible.'

'I didn't expect you to be behind the lifeboats! Were you thinking of leaving the ship without telling me? Or, more like, you were just about to smoke one of those noxious cigars of yours.'

He looked guilty and she crowed with delight,

clapping her hands together and doing a little dance around him.

'You see, I know you so well.'

He doubted that, but it would hardly be surprising if she thought so. They'd been cooped up together in this small vessel for nigh on a month. When he'd first been asked to escort the Spanish ambassador's daughter to London, he'd been aghast. His mind was beset with worries over his mother and grief for his father and he had no wish to assume the responsibility of a seventeen-year-old girl.

But Señor de Silva had been persuasive. Domino had been invited by the English branch of her family to spend a Season in London and then to make the journey on to Spain and her paternal home in Madrid. Alfredo de Silva was insistent that his daughter should experience something of European society.

'Argentina is pioneer country, you know, Richard, not the place for a young girl.'

'She seems to have thrived on life in Buenos Aires,' Richard protested, trying to escape the fate he saw coming.

But Señor de Silva was adamant. Domino must be launched on society and not in a rough-and-ready place like Buenos Aires. As a considerable heiress, and charmingly pretty, his daughter could look to the highest for a husband.

'It's a very long journey for a young girl. There are dangers.' Richard made a last attempt, but to no avail.

'Yes, yes, I have considered well,' Señor de Silva reassured him. 'The time is right—Napoleon is captive and confined on the island of St Helena where he can do no further harm. Domino will be able to travel in safety to England and then on to Spain. And you will be with my darling to protect her on the long journey.'

And so he'd agreed with reluctance to chaperon the girl aboard ship. He would see her safely on land and delivered to an aunt in Curzon Street, but after that his role would end.

Domino was speaking again. 'When we get to London, Richard, will there be many parties and balls?'

'Almost certainly,' he smiled teasingly. 'Otherwise why would you leave all your admirers in Buenos Aires and come to London?'

'My father says I must make good use of my time there. I can have fun, but I must make sure that I meet lots of gentlemen too. Eligible gentlemen.' She rolled the syllables off her tongue and pulled a face.

'That will be for your aunt to decide. She is your chaperon and she'll tell you who is eligible and who is not.'

'Are you eligible, Richard?'

'For you, no. I'm far too old and a deal too worn.'

'How old are you?'

'Twenty-eight.'

'That's not old. My father was ten years older than my mother. And I like the way he looked in his wedding pictures. Worldly and experienced.'

She looked up at him trustfully, the melting brown eyes smiling a clear invitation. He was taken aback. This was one outcome he had not foreseen. He'd no wish to be part of any emerging adolescent fantasy. He knew too well the pain which could accompany the insubstantial dreams of youth.

The image of a pale-faced girl with a torrent of red curls and glinting green eyes swam suddenly into his vision. He was startled. It was years since he'd thought of Christabel, really thought of her. It must be that he was nearing England, coming home after so many years. She would be settled amid the London society he hated, probably married with a pair of children to her name.

He didn't know for sure. His parents, mindful of his feelings, had never kept him informed of her whereabouts or her doings. And he had not wanted to know.

It had been enough to know that she had betrayed him, and with a man he'd considered one of his closest friends. That moment when he'd realised, known for certain that he'd been blind and a fool, came rushing back to him. The whispers which he'd ignored, the sympathetic looks which he'd refused to see, and then the two of them—Christabel and Joshua—a secret smile on their faces, secret murmurs on their lips, emerging from the darkened terrace into the lighted ballroom, walking side by side, bound together as one. The sharpness of that moment still cut at him. He'd looked around the room and realised that every pair of eyes was fixed on him, wondering what he would do, what he would say. He'd left the ball abruptly, incensed and distraught in equal measure. The next day she'd told him. A little late, he'd thought bitterly, just a little late. Three weeks to their wedding and she was sorry, she loved another.

Sorry! Sorry for betraying him with a fly-by-night, a professional second-rater who'd pretended friendship only to get closer to his prey. And she, she'd been willing without a second thought to betray people she had professed to love and to expose him to the most shameful tittle-tattle.

He had drifted into the engagement with Christabel. Their two families had been friends for as long as he could remember and as youngsters they'd been constant companions. It wasn't difficult to do what their parents had been dreaming of, not difficult to imagine a life lived with each other in the Cornish homeland they shared.

But in the end it had not felt that way. He had begun the affair in nonchalance and ended in love. He had wanted to marry. He had wanted her: her russet curls tickling his chin as they walked together in the gardens, the sensation of her body moulding to his as they dared to learn the waltz together, the softness of her skin to his touch, the softness of her mouth to his lips when he'd first ventured to kiss her. It had been a revelation. Now standing on this weathered deck, the empty ocean spread before him, her beautiful sensual form seemed to envelop him once more and he felt himself grow warm and hard with longing. He cursed silently. To feel passion after all these years was ridiculous. Surely it was only an image of the past that aroused such feelings, only an image, not reality that still had the power to hurt.

'Are you all right, Richard? You look quite angry.'

Domino's eyes held a troubled expression and he pulled himself back abruptly to the present.

'I'm fine,' he replied easily, 'I'm not at all angry. But we mustn't stay on deck any longer—it's grown far too cold for you.'

'But I love it here. The moonlight is so beautiful, isn't it?'

He had to agree. The moon had risen fully now and the world was bathed in silver. Against his will his mind refused to let the memories go, for it had been a night like this when they'd gone swimming in the cove. Forbidden, thrilling, an intimation that Christabel was no longer the child she'd once been. And he had gloried in it. The water contouring itself around her slim form. The long shapely legs glimmering through a gently rippling surface. All he'd wanted to do was wind himself around her and stay clasped, fast and for ever.

'Dinner is served, Lord Veryan, when you're ready.'

Neither of them had heard the captain as he approached from the saloon behind. They had been caught up in their own thoughts, standing motionless before the beauty of the ocean.

'Thank you. We'll come now,' Richard replied swiftly and offered his arm to the petite young lady beside him.

'Lord Veryan? That sounds so grand, Richard.'

'It should do. Take heed and obey!'

She giggled and made haste to the table that had been prepared for them. The smell from the kitchen was not encouraging. She pulled another face and her eyes glinted mischievously. Her aunt would have to stop her showing her feelings quite so evidently, he thought. It would not do to be too natural in London society. In his experience the Season involved nothing but artificiality and sham. He heaved a sigh without realising he was doing so.

'Something troubles you, Richard? You're not looking forward to going home?'

'Indeed I am. I'm going to the most beautiful place on earth. How could I not be looking forward to it?'

'More beautiful than Argentina?'

'To my mind, Domino, but everyone thinks their own home is the best in the world.'

'Tell me about Cornwall.'

'Let's see, what can I tell you? It's wild and free. Its colours are green and grey—granite cliffs and slate-roofed houses, but rolling green fields. Above all the sea is blue within blue and never still. I can hear the sound of the surf breaking on the beach from my bedroom window and smell the salt on the air.'

'You make it sound a paradise. And what about your house?'

'The Abbey is very old and built of grey stone. It has mullioned windows and a massive oak front door studded with iron. Every room is panelled in the same dark oak.'

'That sounds a bit gloomy—but perhaps abbeys always are?' Domino puckered her forehead in disappointment.

'It could be, but in the summer the garden is a cascade of colour—some of the flowers as vivid as those in the tropics because Cornwall is so warm—and in the winter, the rooms are lit by the flicker of open fires and the house is filled with the sweet smell of burning apple wood.'

'Ah, then it does sound wonderful after all. And do you have many friends there?'

'A few.' His tone was indifferent.

'No one in particular?'

'No one,' he reiterated, this time with certainty. And the image of flying red hair and shining emerald eyes was once more banished from his conscious mind.

Christabel returned early that night from a supper party and sat quietly in front of her mirror while her maid carefully untangled the knot of auburn curls. The evening had been insipid and she'd been glad of the excuse of a headache to leave for home. Although her face had maintained a calm detachment throughout the day, her mind was troubled. Ever since hearing his name that morning, she'd not been able to put Richard out of her thoughts. There'd always been a part of her, buried deep, that held his memory, but the passage of the intervening years had soothed the raw pain of his departure and the collapse of the world she'd trusted. She'd done all she could to forget him. Now a random conversation between two unknown women had brought his memory throbbing back to life.

She scolded herself. He would be so changed that she would hardly know him, nor he her. In all probability he would sail into Southampton with a new Lady Veryan on his arm. They were bound to meet again at some time in the future, given the proximity of their homes, but not for many months. He would be certain to post down to Cornwall as soon as he could, to be with his mother. And she, where would she be? No doubt by the end of the Season preparing to be Lady Edgerton, and packing her valise for a protracted stay at Sir Julian's Berkshire estate. She sighed involuntarily and Rosa stopped brushing her hair for a moment, thinking that she had hurt her mistress. Christabel was smiling at her reassuringly when the bedroom door opened.

'I'm so glad I've found you still up. I wanted a brief word with you, my dear.'

She nodded dismissal to her maid and looked warily at her mother. She knew well the likely nature of the brief word.

'I was so pleased today at the gallery to see you on such good terms with Sir Julian. You do like him, darling, don't you?'

'Yes, of course, Mama, what is there not to like?'

'I mean,' her mother said doggedly, 'that it's not simply a case of not holding him in aversion—you do *positively* like him?'

'I think so.'

Lady Harriet tried to restrain her irritation with this lovely but obdurate daughter. 'You don't sound very certain.'

'That's because I'm not. Sir Julian is kind and charming and obviously a very good person, but perhaps he's just a little too good for me.'

'Stuff,' her mother exclaimed unexpectedly. 'How

can you talk so, Christabel! You deserve the very best.'

Her daughter remained silent, gazing gravely at her reflection in the mirror.

'Are you still thinking of that business with the Veryans?'

Even her mother, she noted, did not dare to speak Richard's name. Lady Harriet came close and put her arms around her daughter.

'Bel, my darling, that's over and has been for years. It's nonsense to let it determine the rest of your life. It was a bad affair at the time, but you must put it out of your mind and make a fresh start.'

Whether it was her mother's hug or simply because she'd had a jarring day, she couldn't say, but Christabel found herself dissolving into tears.

Lady Harriet soothed her lovingly and then spoke to her as if to a weary child. 'The time has come, Christabel, to make a sensible decision which will affect the rest of your life. You have received many offers of marriage and have refused them all. In a few months you will be twenty-five and in our society that is not a good age to be single still. If you really dislike the idea of marriage to Sir Julian, you know we will not try to persuade you otherwise. Your father and I have profited from painful experience. But if you feel you could live comfortably with him, then I would urge you not to wait too long. He is obviously deeply in love with you and you have only to "throw the handkerchief"—a vulgar saying, I know, but a perfectly true one none the less—and he will pick it up with alacrity.'

'I know, Mama.' Her daughter's woebegone expression raised a smile on Lady Harriet's face.

'Do not look so miserable about it. You will have a splendid life. You will never want for anything and will have a man by your side whose only wish is to make you happy.'

How to tell her mother how she felt? How to explain it even to herself? Her head told her that a tranquil life with Sir Julian was the best possible compromise she could make, but her heart murmured traitorously that tranquillity would not satisfy. What did she want, then? Gaiety, exhilaration, adventure even? But she knew her mother was right. She was a mature woman and she must behave like one. That meant making a sensible decision about her future.

Thinking that her homily had gone home, Lady Harriet continued. 'Promise me, my love, that when the moment comes you will listen to whatever Sir Julian has to say and consider his words favourably.'

'I promise, Mama.'

She made the undertaking in good faith. She must try not to disappoint Sir Julian, nor let her family down again.

Her pledge was put to the test the following Saturday morning. She was quietly engaged with Rosa, selecting dresses from her wardrobe that needed attention and listing the new gloves and slippers she must purchase now that the Season was well advanced, when the second footman appeared at her bedroom door.

'Milady would like to see you in the drawing room, Miss Christabel.'

She wondered what was toward and made haste downstairs. Her heart sunk when she saw Sir Julian perched rather unsafely on one of the decorative but spindly chairs her mother had recently hired for the drawing room.

'Miss Tallis, how good to see you. And how well you look in that ensemble.'

She looked blankly at the old dress she was wearing and wondered if her potential spouse needed glasses. 'But then,' he continued, 'you always contrive to look amazingly elegant.'

Her mother beamed appreciatively. 'Sir Julian has been speaking of the new floral exhibition in Hyde Park. It sounds truly magnificent and has been especially designed as part of the celebrations arranged for the French Royal Family.'

'In fact,' Sir Julian interjected eagerly, 'they are actually to celebrate the Prince Regent's own assumption of power, but since his father is so very ill, it would be bad form for him to broadcast it, I dare say.'

Christabel looked from one to the other in some puzzlement, wondering where she fitted into this conversation. Her mother was at hand to help.

'Sir Julian has very kindly called to discover if you would care to see the display. I know you have no engagements this morning, my dear.'

Sir Julian added his voice to the petition, 'I hope I do not importune, Miss Tallis, but I would welcome your company. And I am sure you will be charmed, knowing your highly developed sense of beauty. The southern tip of the park is a sheer blaze of colour.'

Christabel had no alternative but to agree, only stopping to change her gown and unpack the new bonnet which had just been delivered by Celeste, her favourite milliner. It was a charming confection, a light-green cottager style tied beneath the chin with an enormous chiffon bow. It set off to perfection a gown of pale primrose silk. If she was to be wooed, and she had no doubt that this was Sir Julian's plan, she would at least look the part.

Hyde Park was unusually busy for a Saturday morning and for some time they had little leisure to converse, their attention distracted by the need to avoid a constant parade of slowly moving barouches and their elderly occupants, baby carriages with their nursemaids and schoolboys bowling their hoops. It seemed the whole world and his wife had come out to play this early April morning. And it wasn't hard to see why. The sun streamed down from an almost cloudless blue sky and spring was in the air.

Richard was also in the park that morning, carefully shepherding Domino through its north gate towards Rotten Row, which was already busy with riders. It would be a good opportunity, he thought, for the young girl to experience one of the more popular pursuits of London life. Annoyingly he had been forced to kick his heels in the capital for some days while legal papers were being prepared for his signature. But he could at least enjoy this heaven-sent morning.

He glanced sideways at his companion, an amused expression on his face. She was in high gig now that he'd unexpectedly remained in town and her aunt had agreed to his chaperonage. Lady Blythe's horror at the notion of a male escort the younger side of thirty had evaporated the moment Richard presented himself in Curzon Street. His manners were excellent and he showed an avuncular affection for Domino that not even her worst nightmare could translate into any threat to her charge. She was only too pleased to accept his protection for her young niece whose company she was already finding exhausting.

They had hired hacks from the stables around the corner from Aunt Loretta's house, but had almost instantly regretted it. Neither had any hesitation in characterising their respective mounts as out-and-out slugs. Domino had already begun to feel irked by the restraints her aunt had found it necessary to place on her; after weeks of confinement on board ship, she was restless for the kind of unfettered gallop she had been accustomed to in Argentina. Her horse was unlikely to provide that. Yet the morning shone with perfection and the greensward stretched invitingly in front of her. She could not resist the attempt, and before Richard could stop her she had dug her spurs hard into the horse's flanks. Startled out of his wits, Firefly was for once in his life true to his name. He shot off across the park at breakneck speed to the shocked outrage of those sedately taking their morning promenade. Forced to ride sidesaddle, Domino crouched low over the horse's neck in order to keep her seat, with her hair streaming inelegantly behind. After a frozen instant of shock Richard urged his mount into an unwilling gallop and rushed after her, fearful for her safety and intent on stopping her from creating the kind of scandal of which she had no notion.

Firefly hit the dust of Rotten Row, choking nearby strollers and scattering them to the winds as they leapt for safety, just as Sir Julian had worked himself up to the point of a declaration.

'I shall be leaving for Rosings in the morning, Miss Tallis, and had hoped to depart with one very important question answered. It is a question dear to my heart and only you can settle it. I do not, of course, require an immediate answer, but I would be truly grateful if you would agree to think over what I have to say. You see, Miss Tallis, Christabel—'

He was forced to break off mid sentence and take drastic action as Firefly thundered towards him and his lovely companion. In a trice he had swept Christabel up and literally jumped her out of harm's way. A second later another horse galloping headlong in pursuit caught up with the runaway and grabbed hold of Firefly's bridle.

'Never, ever do that again!'

Richard's voice expressed his cold fury. Badly jolted by the headlong flight of her horse and realising that she had committed a serious social sin, Domino slipped from the saddle, her face white and frightened. She had never seen Richard so angry and she wasn't certain whether she should shout or cry. He gave her no chance to decide. Turning to the couple who had narrowly escaped Firefly's thundering hooves, he bowed in apology. Sir Julian inclined his head at the irate stranger before him. He had no idea of his identity for he had been travelling on the Continent when Richard Veryan had first come to the capital.

'Please forgive my companion,' Richard offered stiffly. 'She is a visitor to London and unaware of the rules governing riding in Hyde Park. I trust that you have received no harm.'

'I'm glad to say that we haven't,' stuttered Sir Julian, now very shaken by the incident, 'but your charge—for I take it that she is your charge—needs to be given a summary lesson.'

'She shall have it,' he said crisply, glaring at Sir Julian with annoyance. Domino had put him in the wrong and he did not like it.

He turned to apologise to the woman he had only glimpsed from the corner of his eye and for the first time in the encounter was struck dumb. For what seemed endless time, he stood motionless and without expression, absorbing the picture before him, hardly believing what he saw.

He had not visualised the moment when he would meet Christabel again. He'd made quite sure that his imagination never strayed into such dangerous territory. But if he'd been tempted to speculate, it would not have felt like this. He would have felt nothing—the meaningless liaisons of years would have done their work—and any carefully suppressed images that still remained in the recesses of his memory would have, should have, shrivelled in the cold light of reality. He ought to feel nothing. But that, it seemed, was not so. He stood and looked and his heart received a most painful jolt.

She was even more beautiful than he remembered. The glinting green eyes and the sensual tumble of red locks against translucent skin were arousing all his senses. He looked searchingly at her ungloved hand. Astonishingly she was not married, at least not yet. That popinjay with her was no doubt the intended.

Christabel had known him immediately. He was still the same tall, athletic man that he had always been, but he seemed stronger now, more muscular, his face lean and tanned. There was an authority about him that had not been there before. His grey eyes as they fixed her in an unwavering stare beneath black, straight brows were lacking in all emotion. There was no warmth, no answering response to her tentative smile.

His voice was as indifferent as his expression. 'Miss Tallis? Your servant, ma'am.'

How hateful of him to speak to her thus, stiff and formal as though they had met for the first time only yesterday. Sir Julian looked questioningly between the two of them and Christabel forced herself to perform the social niceties.

'Sir Julian, may I introduce Earl Veryan. Lord Veryan, Sir Julian Edgerton.'

The two men eyed each other askance, instinctively hostile. Domino, abandoned at a distance, walked her horse towards them and Richard was compelled to make her known to her erstwhile victims. She smiled sunnily at them.

'I'm so sorry, please forgive me for frightening you.'

Her accent was marked as though she hoped that this might produce a swifter forgiveness.

'I don't know the rules,' she continued, 'and Richard never told me, did you, Richard?' And she smiled up at him, her eyes glowing with affectionate entreaty.

But Richard was still looking at Christabel and saw those extraordinary green eyes half-close. Was that perhaps unhappiness at Domino's youthful adoration, an attempt to erase a discomfiting image? It seemed unlikely given her ruthless rejection of him. Yet undoubtedly she'd flinched at Domino's display of fondness. The girl meant nothing to him, but Christabel was not to know that. He hoped that she was suffering at least a little of the agonising jealousy that he'd once known.

He was shocked by the vindictive thought, shocked that his emotions were surging out of control. That he should be so susceptible, so easily disturbed, after six long years was dismaying. He schooled his face to remain expressionless as he bowed his formal farewell, but his mind was deep in tangled thought. He walked swiftly away and Domino had almost to skip to keep up with his long stride.

The unexpected meeting had unnerved him. He'd felt his body invaded by unwanted desire and his mind battered by conflicting impulses. He was bewildered by his reactions for they made no sense. But of one thing he was certain. He could not allow himself to be drawn to Christabel again; he had to overcome a weakness that had come out of nowhere. As he walked a vague sense grew upon him that if he could prove to himself, prove to the world, that her beauty was only skin deep, she would cease to bother him. The veriest shadow of an idea began to form in his mind.

Chapter Two

Christabel allowed herself to be escorted home, Sir Julian steering her expertly along the pavement while remonstrating at length on the licence given the very young these days. She hardly heard him for her mind was in turmoil. The unexpected meeting with Richard would have been difficult enough but his cold aloofness had at first amazed her and then upset her deeply. Years had passed since she'd broken their engagement and she'd imagined that whatever anger he'd felt towards her would have cooled long ago. But it was clear that it was not so. Those steely grey eyes had expressed— what, indifference, aversion, even enmity? Richard, of all people, the boy who had meant most to her for most of her life.

Sir Julian continued his monologue as they made their way through the busy crowds that thronged May-fair that morning.

'I am only glad, Miss Tallis, that you sustained no lasting injury. How I could have reconciled myself to that I do not know. It was I who invited you to view the floral display—if it had not been for me, you would never have been in danger.'

She roused herself to reassure him. 'Please don't blame yourself, Sir Julian. The incident was in no way your fault. You could not have foreseen such a thing happening.'

'That is true, but I still feel a heavy responsibility. And tomorrow I must go away. I cannot delay my visit to Rosings any longer. I have already put it off once and my bailiff remains most anxious to consult me.'

'Of course, you must not delay. Why ever should you? As you see, I am perfectly unharmed. My nerves may be a little jangled, but they will soon recover.'

'Miss Tallis, you are a pearl among women. Others would have had hysterics. You are so cool and admirable under adversity.'

Sir Julian's fussing was becoming an irritant. She might well have succumbed to hysterics, but not from the possibility of being crushed by a runaway horse. She could hardly admit that the shock she'd sustained was in encountering Richard's hostility, and she was desperate for her well-meaning companion to drop the topic. Thank goodness he was to journey to his estates tomorrow and she would be free of his company for the next few days. But how dreadful that she should feel this way about the man she was considering taking as a husband.

'I shall be back very shortly—' he had almost read

her mind '—and then, Miss Tallis, I hope to renew our conversation which was so violently terminated.'

They had reached the house in Mount Street that Lady Tallis rented every year and Sir Julian bounded up the white stone steps and knocked sharply on the front door with his cane. Christabel wasn't sure if this was to impress since there was a perfectly good door knocker. However, he was beaming down on her with a gentle kindliness and she tried to look suitably grateful for his care. As soon as she could, she would send him on his way and seek refuge in her bedroom. She needed time to think, time to digest all that had happened that morning.

The bright blue door of Number Six finally swung open after an unusual delay and the two of them made to enter, but were pulled up sharply on the threshold by a scene of rampant confusion. The hall was overflowing with trunks, cases, holdalls of all kinds and a decidedly sulky-looking parrot in a white ironwork cage that Christabel recognised instantly.

'Sophia? Sophia is here?'

'Yes, Sophia *is* here.'

A strident voice emanated from behind the furthest stack of parcels. The young lady who emerged, smiling triumphantly at her sister, was not ill favoured, but against Christabel's pure beauty she appeared unexceptional.

'What on earth are you doing in Mount Street? Why have you left Cornwall?' Christabel exclaimed.

Before her sister could answer, a cheery male voice

called out from the adjoining library, 'Hey, Sophy, you could hang the bird here.'

'Benedict? He's here too?'

Christabel was dumbstruck at this sudden eruption into her life of the two siblings she had supposed to be fixed at Lamorna Place for the next few months. Lady Harriet floated into the hall, waving her hands ineffectually over the assorted baggage as though by doing so it would miraculously order itself and march away.

'Christabel, my darling, I'm so glad you're back. The servants are being amazingly slow at sorting this mountain and I need your help.'

'I'm not surprised they're slow—why on earth is there so much?'

Sophia drew herself up with an indignant puff and was just about to launch into an impassioned response when she spied Sir Julian hovering just behind her sister. Christabel had not introduced him immediately and he took the chance to excuse himself, saying in a rather nervous voice that he could see the family was extremely busy at this time and he would take his leave.

'May I call on my return, Miss Tallis?'

'Yes, of course, you may.' It was her mother who replied so readily.

Sir Julian bowed himself elegantly out of the door and down the steps, but not before he heard Sophia's accusing voice. 'Why didn't you introduce us to your fiancé, Christabel?'

The door shut behind him.

'He is not my fiancé.'

'That's very strange. We understood that you were engaged. That's why we're here, isn't it, Benedict?'

Benedict smiled in a superior fashion. 'It may be why you're here, but I'm here to have fun,' he returned.

'Mama, may I speak privately with you for a moment?' Christabel asked in a tight voice as she ushered her mother into the library.

Lady Harriet looked flustered. 'Shouldn't we get the hall cleared first, my dear? The house is at sixes and sevens and the staff really do not like it.'

'In a minute, Mama. This is more important.'

Once in the library, she wasted no time. 'Why are Sophia and Benedict here?' she asked, fixing her mother with a minatory look.

'They are family. It is quite natural that they should come to stay with us,' her mother responded defensively.

'But why now, Mama? You know that it was decided they would both remain in Cornwall for the next few months.'

'That was certainly the initial plan, but things have changed a little.'

'What things precisely?'

'Sophia is eighteen and should have the opportunity to partake of at least some of the Season.' Her mother appeared unwilling to answer her directly.

'She was eighteen when we left Lamorna, so I ask you again—what has changed?'

'Sir Julian has changed.'

'What do you mean by that?'

'I mean that he is ready to make you an offer,

Christabel. You cannot deny it and if, as I hope, you will see fit to accept him, Sophia must be introduced to the *ton* at the earliest possible moment so that she, too, has the chance of contracting an eligible alliance.'

'But it was agreed that she would come out officially next year.'

'That was before we knew about Sir Julian.'

'What do we know about Sir Julian? Sophia said that he was my fiancé. Why should she say that?'

'He is—almost,' her mother ventured.

'He has not asked me to marry him.'

'But he will. And I cannot think why he did not do so this morning. It was clearly what he intended.'

Christabel ignored this and pursued her own enquiry relentlessly.

'Have you told Sophia that I am engaged?'

'I may have mentioned in letters to your father that it was possible you were on the point of accepting a proposal.'

'And Papa has repeated this to Sophia?'

'He may have mentioned it.'

'May have? He obviously let it slip and, knowing Sophia, she will have plagued him to death until he agreed that she could come to London. Isn't that so?'

Her mother hung her head guiltily.

'I thought so. And I am to be coerced into agreeing to this marriage so that my sister can have her way.'

'No one is talking of coercion, Bel. You know that you must be married, if not to Sir Julian, then to someone else. We've had this conversation a hundred times before. And it's only fair to Sophia that she be allowed her place in the sun.'

'And is Benedict also to be allowed his place in the sun?'

'Don't be foolish. Benedict is still a stripling and only just down from Oxford. Your father thought it wise to let him gain some town bronze before he settles to learning the management of the estate.'

'What you mean is that he also plagued Papa until he was allowed to come.'

'He will be here only a month, my dear, and someone had to escort Sophia. I cannot understand why you are so cross.'

Christabel took a deep breath and said with deliberation, 'I am cross because I feel my hand is being forced. I understood that we would be here on our own for this Season and expected to have time and peace to consider my future. Now I have virtually the whole of my family breathing down my neck and pushing me into a marriage I don't want.'

'You don't want it!'

Her mother looked scandalised and Christabel felt stunned. She hadn't meant to acknowledge such troublesome feelings so starkly, even to herself, let alone express them aloud. She tried to recover her composure as best she could.

'I understand my position, Mama, and I will do what is expected of me. But don't demand that I am glad.'

And with that she turned on her heel and threaded her way swiftly through the still-cluttered hall and up the stairs to her room without another word. Brother and sister, still standing amidst the clutter of baggage, looked after her in surprise.

Once in her room, Christabel flung herself down on the satin counterpane and closed her eyes. The morning had been full of shocks and she was not coping well with them. She needed to pull herself together. Sophia was an unfriendly presence that she could have done without, but nothing more. As for Benedict, he would be filling Mount Street with noise and disturbance. Maybe that would be beneficial; it would help to distract her from the reality of her life. Which was what, exactly? Marriage to a man she did not love and hatred from the man she had once loved. The near-fatal accident, her siblings' unwelcome arrival, her mother's pretence, could all be forgotten. It was Richard's undisguised hostility that stayed with her.

Early the next morning she woke to a household already on the move. She'd slept badly and wanted nothing more than to stay curled in bed. But very shortly Sophia bounced into her room, more than happy to explain the bustle.

'Mama has said that I am to go shopping and you are to accompany me,' she announced peremptorily.

Christabel blinked sleepily and reached for her cup of chocolate. 'Don't you already have enough clothes?'

'No, I don't. I shall need a completely new wardrobe to make a splash in London. *You* have a rail of exquisite dresses, so don't be selfish, Bel!' Her sister was at her most indignant.

She flounced out of the room only to be replaced by a second morning visitor.

'Bel, my darling, I know you're not happy about accompanying Sophia, but I would count it a great favour.'

'I will go, of course, Mama, but I won't be able to stop her buying the most dreadful clothes. She will listen to your advice far more readily than to mine.'

'My dear, Sophia listens to no one, as you well know. And you have such elegant taste—I'm hoping some of it will rub off on her.'

Christabel did not share that hope, but felt it only right she attempt to help. Her mother was looking unusually tired and harassed by the sudden eruption of two youthful and demanding offspring into her hitherto peaceful household.

Within the hour they were in the carriage and on their way to Lady Harriet's favourite modiste. The morning that followed was one Christabel never wished to repeat. Again and again she sought to dissuade the younger girl from unwise purchases: heliotrope was not on the whole an immensely flattering colour; a bonnet sporting six ostrich plumes and a cluster of brightly coloured gemstones might be thought a trifle vulgar; a dress of gauze worn over a transparent petticoat was unlikely to ingratiate her with the most illustrious members of the *ton*. But she was helpless against the onslaught of Sophia in full cry and could only watch in despair as the carriage gradually filled with an array of packages containing the most unsuitable attire.

The clothes had been costly and eaten up most of the very generous allowance bestowed by Lord Tallis and still they had not purchased gloves, slippers, reticules— all the myriad accessories necessary for a young lady about to embark on a social whirl. Christabel's tentative suggestion that they go to the Pantheon Bazaar where she'd heard there were bargains to be had was received with surprising enthusiasm and they drove immediately to Grafton House. Very soon they found themselves immersed in stalls displaying an abundance of coloured muslins, ornate trimmings, silk stockings, fine cambric handkerchiefs, all at astonishing prices. The bazaar was not generally visited by ladies of high fashion, but within minutes of entering the emporium Sophia was exclaiming loudly over the bargains to be had. The only drawback to the shop was its popularity for by noon it was completely full and shopping had become a tedious business of jostling elbows. Both young ladies were heartily relieved when the last piece of lace and the last pair of kid slippers had been chosen. Their relief was short-lived, however, for the increasing crowds made it necessary to wait a considerable time to pay at the final counter.

Sophia had at last reached the head of the queue when Christabel heard a voice that was faintly familiar. She turned her head and caught a glimpse of a stylishly gowned woman holding in her hand a collection of colourful loo masks.

'They will be just the thing, Aunt Loretta, if we go to Vauxhall—and you did promise!' The woman's younger companion was almost jumping with enthusiasm.

'I think you're stretching the word promise, Domino. I said we *might* go.'

But Domino had lost interest in the masks and was staring instead at Christabel. She darted forwards eagerly and offered her hand.

'Miss Tallis, isn't it? How are you feeling? I'm so sorry about the accident yesterday—I was worried about you.'

'Thank you for your concern, but I'm perfectly well.'

'Richard said that you would be fine and he's always right. He said that you were the coolest of women and unlikely to suffer any disordered feelings. You see, I've remembered his words exactly.'

'What accident, Domino?' her aunt interjected.

'Only a small one, Aunt, a little frightening at the time, but over in a moment.'

She looked from one to the other, a pleased expression on her face. 'I must introduce you immediately. Aunt Loretta, this is Miss Christabel Tallis—I have it right?—such a difficult name for my tongue! Miss Tallis, this is my aunt, Lady Blythe.'

'How do you do,' Christabel responded in her musical voice, 'I'm very happy to meet you.'

Lady Blythe smiled anxiously as she shook hands. 'Domino said nothing to me of an accident.'

'Please don't be concerned—I have taken no harm from yesterday's adventure, as you see.' And she smiled reassuringly at aunt and niece. She had no wish to get this vivacious young girl into any further trouble.

'Is not this shop the most wonderful you've ever seen, Miss Tallis?' Domino's eyes were lit with pleasure.

She glanced around her rapturously and Christabel glimpsed a uniformed footman standing a few paces away already loaded with packages. Lady Blythe saw the direction of her glance and said wryly, 'As you see, Miss Tallis, we have had a busy morning.'

'You know you've enjoyed it as much as I,' Domino protested. 'And I did need to add to my wardrobe, didn't I? I've been invited to so many parties.'

Her aunt smiled indulgently as her niece, still prattling happily, turned to Christabel.

'I've been in London only a very short while, Miss Tallis, but already I must have been to a dozen entertainments. It's been splendid. And Richard has been a wonderful escort. He's been wonderful, hasn't he, Aunt Loretta?' and she turned impulsively to the older lady, her cheeks glowing.

'Lord Veryan has certainly been a good friend to us,' her aunt agreed.

The girl's soft brown eyes were smiling and she looked the picture of happiness. She obviously revered Richard and just as obviously knew nothing about Christabel. He had not told her of their shared history. It was as though he wished to wipe the slate clean and obliterate that part of his life. The Christabel he'd known in his youth had ceased to exist for him. Instead a callous and unfeeling woman, a woman whose emotions were never disordered, had taken her place.

She was saved from making any further conversation by Sophia, who had finally finished paying for her goods. Before Christabel knew what was happening, her sister had seized her hand and was dragging her towards the entrance of the shop without a glance at the couple standing nearby.

'Come, Bel, or we'll be late for luncheon.' Christabel had time only to execute a hasty bow before she was bundled outside.

'Really, Sophia, there is little point in buying smart dresses and clever fripperies if you lack manners to match,' she remonstrated, as they emerged into the fresh air and once more climbed into the waiting carriage.

'I had to get out of that shop. It was so hot that I thought I'd melt. And I must go home this minute and try on all my new outfits.'

Her sister demurred. 'Before we return to Mount Street I'd like to call in at Hatchards to collect the book I ordered. *Mansfield Park* is being spoken of everywhere and I'm most anxious to read it.'

'You can pick the book up tomorrow,' her sister complained. 'At this hour of the day Piccadilly will be blocked with traffic and it will take an age to get home.'

Christabel remained unmoved. 'I particularly wish to begin Miss Austen's novel today and we'll only be in the shop a few minutes. You owe me a little time after this morning, don't you think?'

Sophia looked sulky, but did not dispute further. The traffic was lighter than expected and very soon they were standing outside Hatchards's impressive bow windows. The smell of leather greeted them as Christabel trod briskly across polished wood to a large counter where a stack of volumes of different shapes and sizes was awaiting collection.

Already bored with the errand, Sophia began an immediate prowl around the lines of high-sided bookshelves in the hope of seeking out possible acquaintances. Soon she had disappeared from view so completely that when Christabel went to look for her, she was nowhere to be seen, even in the furthest recesses of the shop. A carriage full of new dresses had been too much of a temptation, Christabel thought, and Sophia must have ordered the groom to drive her home and left her sister to make her own way back. It was a nuisance, but not a disaster. Mount Street was a ten-minute walk away and she had no fear of undertaking the journey on her own.

She began to make her way to the shop entrance, zigzagging around the rows of tall shelves, and was just turning the corner of one particularly high stack of books when she looked up to find Richard Veryan barring her way. For a moment she froze. He was the last person she expected to see. He wore a drab riding cape over a tightly fitting coat of blue superfine and what looked to be a recent purchase, a cut Venetian waistcoat and the palest of fawn pantaloons. His air of elegance was subtly enhanced by the powerful muscularity of a body long hardened by physical activity.

He smiled sardonically as he swept her a bow. 'Good morning, Miss Tallis. I trust I find you well. I hope that you haven't suffered unduly from yesterday's unfortunate incident.'

For a moment she was mesmerised, unable to speak,

unable to take her eyes from the figure who stood in her path. It was as though she were seeing him for the very first time. Yesterday his sudden appearance, when she'd imagined him still on the high seas, had sent her mind into disarray. She had been conscious only of those crystal-hard eyes raking her down. Now the full force of his masculine attraction hit her hard. She struggled to find words.

'I'm well, Lord Veryan, thank you, and have suffered no lasting effects,' she managed at last.

'I'm very happy to hear that. I would not have anyone injured because of my lack of foresight. But I could not have anticipated Miss de Silva's actions—it was sheer recklessness, I fear, on the part of my young companion.'

'This is her first visit to London and she can surely be excused,' Christabel returned gently. 'She would not know the regulations governing riding in Hyde Park.'

'She does now, however, and will in future follow them strictly. Then we should go on well enough. Rules are a necessary part of civilised society, don't you think? Myself, I've always placed a good deal of trust in observing them, but I imagine you must know that.'

Christabel said nothing. He was clearly intent on upsetting her.

'You're silent—perhaps you're unwilling to criticise the young lady in question? Rest assured that I've already done so. She's received a trimming she'll not forget. But she has youth on her side and youth has one great advantage, I find—it can learn from its mistakes.'

'I'm sure Miss de Silva will. No doubt you are a proficient teacher, sir,' she replied sharply.

'I trust so. I certainly should be. I was lucky enough in my own youth to have an equally proficient teacher who taught me to learn from my biggest mistake.'

His face was grim and she had an overpowering desire to flee, but he was barring her way and escape was impossible. She steadied her nerves and refused to be intimidated.

'I hardly know the young lady, of course, but she seemed well able to manage her own affairs.'

'She gives that impression to the uninitiated, but to those who know her well,' he said meaningfully, 'the case is otherwise. Her spontaneity is certainly entrancing, but is like to run away with her. She needs someone to exercise a firm control.'

'I hope she sees the situation as you do.'

'And if she does not?'

'Then she will reject that control and simply be herself,' she threw at him.

'Naturally I should have expected you to say that, Miss Tallis. But for the moment I'd forgotten that you are an arch advocate of self-expression, no matter what the cost.'

His smile was belied by the frost in his cold, grey eyes and she felt her stomach twist into knots. It seemed he'd accosted her quite deliberately in order to bait her, but she could not let him ride roughshod.

'You misunderstand me, sir. I was not encouraging

Miss de Silva to break rules, simply proposing that everyone must have the freedom to make some mistakes.'

'Ah, yes, you would know a deal about such freedom. Dare I suggest that restraint is a more admirable quality?'

'Restraint and youth do not sit easily together,' she retorted.

'Yet for most they can be negotiated. Dishonour is a powerful deterrent, would you not say?'

She was weary of the cat-and-mouse game he seemed to relish and made to walk forwards. 'If you will excuse me, I am meeting my sister here and would not wish to keep her waiting.'

He made no move to allow her to pass, but instead looked around him mockingly. 'I don't see her. She is certainly nowhere in the shop. Are you sure you were supposed to meet her here?'

'Yes, indeed. She will no doubt be outside.'

'And if she is not, you will have no companion to accompany you home. May I offer my escort?'

'I thank you, but no,' she said hastily, 'I have my carriage.'

'I fear you're out of luck. There was no sign of a carriage on the road when I entered the shop. It must have left without you—but then perhaps Sir Julian Edgerton is close by to take you home?'

She shook her head.

'No? I made sure that he would be. From our meeting yesterday, he seemed a most attentive gentleman. Our untimely descent on you perhaps interrupted an important conversation. I do apologise if this was so—I wouldn't want to frighten him away. Where is he now?'

She was angered by his insinuations and also bewildered. How had he known that Sir Julian was about to propose?

'He is visiting his country estate,' she said in a ruffled tone. 'If you wish to see him, I suggest that you call at his town house in a few days' time. It is in Brook Street, I believe.'

'There you are, Bel. I've been looking for you everywhere.'

Sophia bounced suddenly into view, almost running around the adjacent bookcase and only just preventing herself from cannoning into Richard. He turned round with annoyance; the interview had just been getting interesting. He'd followed Christabel into the shop on impulse, feeling an overpowering need to confront her with the words he'd kept suppressed for so long. Even more compelling had been the need to protect himself from her, to keep her at a safe distance, by wielding ugly recriminations.

'Good gracious, are you who I think you are?'

Sophia had been just twelve when Richard quit England and had only a vague memory of her sister's former fiancé.

'Whatever are you doing *here*?' Sophie continued a trifle too bluntly.

Christabel intervened. 'Lord Veryan is newly arrived in town. We met yesterday in Hyde Park when there was a slight accident. He has been kind enough to enquire how I am, but I think it's time for us to go.'

Richard glanced at Sophia with disfavour. She had never been an appealing child with her insistence on frills and furbelows and the constant preening in every mirror she could find. To his jaundiced eye she looked very little improved. Christabel as a child had been so different—a skinny, reckless tomboy of a girl with a tangle of red hair and freckles to match. She had always been ready for adventure and just as always ready to drag him into whatever trouble she had been brewing.

Looking at her now, a slender vision in eau-de-nil silk, a matching ribbon threaded through those wonderfully fiery curls, he smiled inwardly, forgetting for the moment his purpose in accosting her. No greater contrast between past and present could there be. He remembered the day he'd returned from Oxford to find his one-time playmate transformed, a butterfly fluttering the hearts of all the local beaux. He had gazed at her in wonder, drinking in her beauty, spellbound.

His reverie came to an abrupt end as he became aware of Sophia still scowling at him from a few feet away. With a brief bow, he moved aside for the sisters to make their exit.

'Where were you? I've been an age looking for you,' Sophia scolded as she marched forcefully towards the glass-paned doors. 'The carriage was causing an obstruction and Stebbings has had to move it. We'll have to walk the whole of Picadilly now.'

Christabel made no reply, but moved swiftly along the flagged thoroughfare in deep thought. Richard had appeared in Hatchards at the very time that she'd chosen to call at the shop. It was as though he'd been shadowing her, waiting for an opportunity to confront her. And it had been a confrontation. She recalled the ice in his eyes and the anger in his voice, as he sought to remind her of her crime.

And he'd been at pains to emphasise his new-found intimacy with Domino de Silva, while a few hours earlier the young girl had made it clear that she admired Richard greatly and that in her eyes he could do no wrong. Christabel didn't blame her for that idolisation. Richard was the perfect hero for an adolescent dream—a honed body, a handsome face alight with intelligence and an air of innate strength, which more than matched his elegance. And, if she were honest, he was a hero for more than adolescent girls. When he'd appeared so suddenly before her, polished and powerful and blocking her escape, she'd felt a charge of pure sexual magnetism. But it was momentary and quickly evaporated as it became plain that he intended only to distress her. She must not dwell on his beautiful form and face, nor on his seeming desire to exact some kind of retribution. Her life would soon resume its normal peaceful rhythm. Sir Julian was returning and, she told herself severely, she would look forward to that. By dint of repetition she was sure she would come to believe it.

Chapter Three

'You've not forgotten that Lady Russell is to collect you at eleven o' clock?' her mother prompted the next morning, whisking through the hall on her way to consult with the housekeeper.

'Lady Russell?' Christabel grappled with the name for a moment.

'Sir Julian has arranged it, has he not? The tickets for Montagu House?'

'Ah, yes, I remember now,' she said heavily, 'He was keen that we view the Marbles that Lord Elgin has brought back from Greece.'

'A stuffy museum *and* Lady Russell all in the same morning,' interjected Sophia as she emerged from the breakfast room in one of the eye-opening ensembles she had purchased yesterday. 'Rather you than me!'

Her mother rounded on her sharply. 'You're becoming far too pert for your own good, Sophia. You must learn to keep a check on your tongue or you will fare badly in society.'

This was an important consideration for an aspiring belle and Sophia looked suitably contrite. 'I'm sorry, Mama, but, from what I hear from friends who are already out, Lady Russell is a gorgon.'

'That's as may be, but you had much better keep your opinions to yourself. And, Christabel, you must hurry. You will need to dress in something a little more demure.' Christabel glanced down at the low neckline and French trimmings of the apricot sarcenet and sighed. Her mother was right. Lady Russell was a stickler for correctness and only a simple day dress of sprigged muslin with a high neck and a matching spencer would satisfy that matriarch.

It was weeks ago that she'd agreed to the visit. At the time she'd been feeling more guilty than usual at her lack of enthusiasm for Sir Julian's company and he'd been so touchingly anxious that she become better acquainted with what small family he possessed that she'd felt forced to consent. Since then she'd acquired a genuine interest in the marble wonders that had travelled all the way from Athens and, were it not for Lady Russell, she would be looking forward to the morning's expedition with pleasure.

Sir Julian's sister was punctual to the minute, an erect figure in a heavy but serviceable barouche, awaiting Christabel outside the Mount Street house with scarcely concealed impatience. The severe grey kerseymere gown and dreary poke bonnet that she wore did nothing to lighten the atmosphere. Her greeting was perfunctory. She was not at all sure that this young woman was a suitable wife for her brother. She was altogether too beautiful, and beautiful women usually meant trouble. And there was that unfortunate business years ago when her name had been bandied around the town as a tease and a jilt by every wicked rattlejaw. Her modest behaviour since had done much to redeem this unsatisfactory reputation, but still one never knew when old habits would surface.

You only had to look at that hair—wild to a fault. But Julian was evidently head over heels in love with her and you could hardly blame him. Men could be very stupid, never seeing beyond what was in front of their eyes.

'Are you looking forward to viewing the Marbles, Miss Tallis?' she eventually asked her companion as the barouche rolled smoothly forwards. Her smile was one of gracious condescension.

'Indeed, ma'am, I am. I have been reading a good deal about them and my interest has been greatly stirred.'

Lady Russell unbent slightly. At least the girl had some intelligence, which was all to the good. It was necessary that Julian marry a woman who was serious enough to understand and tolerate his charity work. As far as Lady Russell was concerned, her brother's projects for the labouring classes remained wholly inexplicable.

'I have learned,' she remarked magisterially, 'that a special gallery has been built for these statues at a vast cost so we must hope that they warrant such expenditure.' The faltering conversation was effectively closed down.

Once the carriage left Mayfair and was bowling towards Bloomsbury, the roads became a great deal clearer and they reached the entrance of the British Museum only a few minutes later than expected. It did not stop her ladyship tutting loudly at her groom, who had made the journey to Montagu House in record time and was even now negotiating a difficult manoeuvre to bring the carriage exactly to the bottom of the flight of steps which led up to the impressive panelled entrance.

A steep staircase, a spacious entrance hall and they were upon the Marbles almost before they realised. Two long whitewashed galleries had been constructed for the purpose with exhibits laid out on either side. The monumental size of many of the statues was staggering and both ladies paused on the threshold to adjust their perspective. Then they began a slow inspection of the initial gallery, first down one side and then the other, with Lady Russell insisting on reading aloud every handwritten label the curators had provided.

During this prolonged examination, the room had been gradually filling up and by the time Christabel was ready to tackle the second gallery a considerable crowd had gathered. She looked across at Lady Russell, who appeared weary and a trifle disenchanted, and was not surprised to hear her excuse herself, saying that she would await Christabel in the spacious hall beyond.

The carriage, she reminded her severely, would leave promptly at one o'clock.

Christabel nodded assent, happy to be rid of the older woman's irksome presence. With a new sense of purpose she crossed into the adjoining room; almost immediately her attention was caught by the statue of a woman, a large sculpture of Iris which had once decorated the west pediment of the Parthenon.

She stood enthralled, marvelling at the precision with which the intricate folds of the goddess's dress had been carved—the marble seemed to sing out life. The harmony of the carving and the sheer exuberance of the goddess was a joy. Lost in thought as she was, the voice at her elbow startled her.

'It's so sad, isn't it, that she has lost her legs *and* her arms?'

She turned to her questioner. It was Domino, looking freshly minted in primrose-figured muslin and carrying a matching frilled parasol.

'She may not be complete,' Christabel agreed, 'but it doesn't seem to matter. She possesses such enormous vitality, don't you think?'

Domino gave a small laugh. 'What must she have been like as a whole woman, Miss Tallis!'

'Very powerful, I imagine, particularly as she enjoyed such a prominent position on the top of the Parthenon.'

'Poor thing, she must find it very cold in London.'

'No doubt.' Christabel gave an answering smile. 'But if she'd been left to bask in her native sun, we wouldn't have been able to see her today in all her glory.'

'I don't think I would have minded too much,' the younger girl divulged. 'There are so many statues to see and some of them are just fragments. I don't find them particularly inspiring.'

'You didn't wish to come to the exhibition?'

'Not really, but Aunt Loretta said I should as all of London is talking about it. She said that if I'd seen the statues I would be able to join in conversations and not sound too silly.'

'Aunt Loretta has a point.'

'I know, but to be honest I would much rather have gone to Astley's,' she confided naïvely. 'I've heard they keep troops of horses there who can re-enact scenes of war and that there are daring equestriennes who perform the most amazing acrobatics on horseback!'

'I believe so,' Christabel answered her seriously, though she was amused by the young girl's enthusiasm for the less-than-refined pleasure. 'The equestrian ballet of Astley's is famous.'

'A ballet on horseback?' Domino's eyes grew round with amazement. 'I *must* see that.'

'What must you see?'

A man's voice broke through the female weavings of their conversation. It was Richard. He bowed unsmilingly at Christabel. He was looking exceedingly handsome in a claret-coloured waistcoat and light grey pantaloons, which fitted to perfection. The folds of his snow-white cravat were precisely arranged and held in place by a single small diamond stud.

'Miss Tallis says there's an equestrian ballet performed at Astley's. Can we go, Richard?' In her eagerness Domino tugged hard at her companion's immaculate coat sleeve.

'You must ask your aunt to take you. In the meantime, where is your taste for higher culture?' and he waved his hand carelessly towards the statues on either side of them.

'Aunt Loretta will never agree to go to Astley's. It will be much too vulgar for her. Now she is even saying that she doubts we will go to the fireworks at Vauxhall.'

'Then you must be content with more refined pastimes, child.'

Christabel was disconcerted by his tone. He sounded almost like a parent. The surprise she felt must have shown on her face because almost immediately he sounded a softer, even caressing note.

'By all means put Astley's on your list, Domino, and we will make every endeavour to get there.'

She clapped her hands in pleasure watched by Richard, an indulgent expression on his face, but his words were for Christabel.

'Books yesterday, statues today, Miss Tallis. You appear to be an avid follower of cultural pursuits.'

'I partake in them only as much as any other rational woman, Lord Veryan.'

'But then how many women are as rational as you?'

She made no answer, but his eyes remained fixed on her. 'Very few, I make sure,' he continued sleekly.

'I bow to your vast experience, my lord.'

'Hardly vast, but enough—sufficient to suggest

that logic and reasoning are not always becoming to a woman.'

She felt herself being forced into another confrontation and when she spoke, her tone was cold but measured. 'I cannot imagine why you should find fault with rationality. My sex is usually criticised for precisely the opposite.'

'In general it's an excellent quality for a female to possess, I agree, but taken to extremes rationality can destroy a woman's natural affections.'

'I think that unlikely,' she retorted.

'Do you? Then consider the case of a woman who decides "rationally" to prefer one man to another on the grounds that he is likely to be a bigger matrimonial prize. When logic leads, a woman's heart is prone to wither.'

Fire began to simmer within the green depths of her eyes and her whole body tensed for combat.

'By that reasoning, sir, only women who are witless can know affection.'

'That's a trifle crude, but the sentiment is not entirely without merit. I think it likely that many men, including Sir Julian Edgerton, would agree with me. By the way, does he accompany you this morning?'

'He is still out of town.'

'Dear me, he appears to spend an inordinate amount of time away from London.'

Christabel took a deep breath and replied as levelly as she could, 'Rosings is a large estate and takes a good deal of his time.'

'Of course, he *would* have to have a large estate.' His expression was sardonic, a trace of a sneer on his unyielding mouth.

Domino looked from one to the other, aware of the tension which crackled between them, but bewildered as to its cause.

'As you appear interested in the trivialities of my life, sir, you may wish to know that I am accompanied this morning by Sir Julian's sister.' Christabel's perfectly sculpted cheeks were flushed an angry pink. 'She is waiting close by so I must beg you to excuse me.'

And with a hasty bow to them both, she walked briskly towards the entrance hall, her mind seething and her form one of unexpressed anger. The frills on her muslin gown tossed as though caught in a tempest and the wayward auburn curls began to tumble out of the restraining satin bandeau she wore. It seemed she was to be followed at every opportunity and forced to submit to any taunt or goad he wished to aim. It was insufferable. She was truly reaping the whirlwind she had sowed all those years ago.

Still standing beside the figure of Iris, Domino wore a puzzled look and her tone was one of concern.

'Do you not like Miss Tallis, Richard?'

'I neither like nor dislike her.'

'I think you made her angry.'

'I would be sorry to give offence, but if she was angry, it was quite unnecessary.'

She frowned at this. 'She was offended and I don't think it was unnecessary. I think she had good reason. You seemed to want to upset her. But why?'

Richard contemplated pretending ignorance, but then said, 'It's an old story and not for your ears.'

'Then you knew her before you came to Argentina—from when you were last in England?'

'I've known her all my life.'

'How is that possible?'

'Her family's estate runs alongside mine in Cornwall. We played together as children—like brother and sister,' he ended drily.

'Then you should be friends.'

'Oh, we were, very good friends.'

'So what happened? Why are you so unhappy with each other now?'

'A betrothal.'

'A betrothal? Whose?'

'My betrothal to Miss Tallis. We were to be married.'

'You were betrothed to Christabel Tallis!' Domino gaped with surprise. 'What happened?'

'We decided that after all we did not suit each other.'

'But if you were both agreed, why are you still so unhappy with her?'

Richard sighed. 'It's complicated.'

'It doesn't seem that complicated to me,' she said with decision. He saw that he would have to tell her the full story or at least enough to satisfy her.

'I was away at Oxford for three years,' he began, 'either at the university studying or staying with friends in the holidays, so I didn't see her for a long time. When I finally returned home to Cornwall, I found her very changed. She'd always been a tomboy, a thin, gawky girl with her dresses usually torn and her hair in a tangle. But now she was this amazingly beautiful young woman. I could hardly believe my eyes the first night I saw her again. She was the toast of the county, worshipped by Cornish manhood from Penzance to St Austell—and that's a long way, Domino.'

He paused for a moment, remembering that evening when he'd walked into the drawing room at Lamorna and found her waiting, a slender vision of cream lace and gold roses. When she'd glided forwards and laughingly put her arms around him in welcome, she'd taken his breath away.

'I suppose I was irritated,' he continued. 'Whenever I visited Lamorna Place I tripped over some lovesick swain clutching a posy of flowers or reading her the latest bad poem he'd written in her praise. It was comical, but also annoying. She'd always been my particular friend and now I was supposed to share her company with all the fops and dandies from miles around. So I decided to woo her myself, win the prize and delight my parents—it was what they'd been hoping for since we were children.'

'And Miss Tallis?'

'I think she was flattered by my sudden interest. I was a welcome diversion from the cloying attentions of her local admirers, but only a diversion—until her come-out at the next London Season. But she never did come out that year. Her mother couldn't leave the younger children to travel to London, so she deputed the task of presenting Christabel to a relative. Then the relative became ill quite suddenly and the plans were cancelled. Christy had to resign herself to staying in Cornwall and it was then that she agreed to marry me.'

'So when did you find out that you had both made a mistake?'

'When she made love with another man.' Richard had not been able to stop his bitter denunciation.

Domino looked shocked.

'His name was Joshua,' he said acridly, discarding any hope now of keeping the full story from his young admirer. 'My mother had accompanied Christabel and myself to London to buy bride clothes. Instead Christabel purchased a very different item—the attention, for I cannot call it love, of a man I'd thought a friend. She confessed that she'd fallen in love with him. Perhaps she had: he was clever and handsome and the sole heir of a very wealthy uncle. She said that she could no longer marry me. I left for Argentina shortly afterwards. The rest you know.'

Domino considered his story for some time. Christabel Tallis had not seemed the kind of woman who would treat a man so shockingly, but there was no doubt Richard had suffered hurt.

She turned impulsively to him, but her question was tentative. 'It happened such a time ago, Richard, can you not forgive her?'

'There's nothing to forgive,' he said in a breezy voice. 'It's over.'

But it wasn't, he thought, as he escorted his young companion to Gunter's for her favourite elderflower ice.

It was far from over. Christabel had come back into his life and the world he'd built for himself had begun to shatter. He remembered how in those early months in Buenos Aires, he'd walked around a stunned man. He'd lost so much, not just the girl he loved, but his entire life. Early one blisteringly hot morning, he'd walked on the beach when the world was still asleep and he was alone. Looking out over the limitless ocean, he'd willed himself back to his beloved homeland. But friends and family had gradually faded from view and he'd been helpless to recall them. He'd borne the rupture calmly, stoically, never allowing a hint of trouble to show, and he'd grown to love Argentina. He'd put down new roots, made new friends, taken new lovers. So why was he allowing such furious resentment to seep into his life and destroy the pleasure of his homecoming? After his scourging from the Tallis affair, he'd become adept at sidestepping deep feeling and for the first time in years strong emotions were crowding in on him. Ever since he'd seen Christabel. His constant need to provoke her, to disturb her, was a signal that he'd never truly overcome her betrayal. He'd simply shut it away. Seeing her afresh had reawakened feelings that he'd thought dead.

His anger was directed as much at himself for still being in thrall to her. If he were to know any peace, he must exorcise that demon and do so as quickly as possible. The lawyers, he'd learned, would be ready within a fortnight and last night he'd written to his mother to expect him shortly. But how to free himself of this unwanted legacy from the past? In the heat of their first unexpected meeting, he'd entertained some wild thoughts. But were they that wild? If he could prove Christabel unchanged, prove that she was the same inconstant woman, surely that would get her from under his skin.

Instinctively he knew that she was not wholly indifferent to him. Her face might remain immobile, but her eyes gave her away. He had the power to rouse this cold and remote woman to strong feeling—anger and love were bedfellows, after all. There was a lingering tie between them, he was sure, and he'd taken every chance to play on whatever jealousy Christabel might feel towards the young girl who walked beside him. He had done so in the hazy belief that he might force her into showing her true colours. But there had to be more. He would have to entice her into his arms, tease her, goad her, until she was ready to say she loved him, ready to be disloyal. Ready to betray Sir Julian Edgerton as she'd betrayed him. The man who had taken her arm so proudly would be forced to recognise her for the jilt she was. And if he could learn the same lesson himself, her power to perturb would be over. He would be free of her—for ever.

The Tallis family ate an early supper, for Christabel and Lady Harriet were engaged to attend Almack's. Christabel felt no joy at the prospect. This morning her pleasure in viewing the Marbles had been spoiled by Richard's antagonism and an evening spent at the exclusive club was no compensation. It would be a tedious few hours although largely effortless. Several glasses of lemonade, a number of country dances, a nod or two at acquaintances and then they would be free to return home. She'd never understood what made the place exceptional, but her mother always held it to be good *ton* to attend regularly and made a point of escorting her elder daughter every week. Sir Julian, too, was a frequent visitor and Christabel derived some comfort at least in knowing that tonight he was safely lodged at Rosings many miles away and she would be free of any threat of a marriage proposal.

She had dressed with some care for the evening. After the unsettling events of the last few days she felt the need to look her best. The emerald silk gown opening to an underdress of the palest green gauze was a stunning creation, her hair flaming in contrast and the green of her eyes reflected in its deepest tones. A low bodice revealed the pale perfection of shapely breasts and shoulders as smooth as alabaster. Without immodesty, she knew from experience that she would attract the attention of most of the men there. Not Richard's, though. He would certainly not be at Almack's. Even in his youth it had been a place he'd always refused to attend, though she had often begged him to be her escort.

She looked across the table at her sister who was drinking soup with exaggerated care, intent on preserving her gown. With a start she realised that Sophia was dressed rather too elaborately for dinner at home and wondered why. The conundrum was soon solved.

'Sophia will be coming with us,' her mother announced with studied carelessness.

'To Almack's?' Christabel asked blankly.

'Yes, of course, to Almack's.'

'But what about vouchers?'

'I have managed to obtain some. Lady Jersey was kind enough to bestow them on me at short notice. She understood the position and wanted very much to make Sophia's acquaintance.'

'Nobody gets tickets for Almack's that quickly, Mama, so you must have known for some time that Sophia was coming to London.'

Her mother made no reply and the ruthless interrogation continued. 'I thought you said that you and Papa had decided only recently that she should visit—in fact, you must have been plotting it together for weeks!' The net seemed to be closing in on her ever more tightly.

Her mother's telltale blush revealed her unhappiness at the deception while Sophia's face was one of untroubled victory.

'Hardly plotting, Bel. Sophia's coming to stay was certainly not part of any grand plan. But when Sir Julian began to grow ever more particular in his attentions to you, it seemed sensible to introduce Sophia to *ton* society a little earlier than we planned. I heard only last week that your brother and sister were on their way, but said nothing. I knew you had a lot on your mind and thought it would be a delightful surprise.'

'Delightful,' Christabel offered drily. 'But do you feel that the dress is quite right for the occasion?'

'And what, pray, is wrong with my dress?' Sophia asked combatively.

Lady Tallis, who had unsuccessfully tried to direct her younger daughter to one of the more modest creations hanging in her wardrobe, interjected gently, 'Christabel has such refined taste, my dear, and she is familiar with what is most suitable for Almack's. Why don't you reconsider the magenta? The rose chiffon would become you so well.'

'The rose is boring and I have no intention of being boring.'

'You won't be that,' Benedict put in unhelpfully, 'the whole world will see you coming at fifty paces.'

'You have no notion of female dress, so hold your tongue,' she spat.

'I have no notion of going to Almack's either so I won't be the one who has to hand out the sunshades,' her unrepentant brother grinned.

'What is this, Benedict, of course you are to come with us,' his mother chided. 'You will need to put on evening dress. I assume that you brought it with you.'

'But not to do the pretty at Almack's,' he grumbled.

After a good deal more in this vein he agreed reluctantly to squire his mother and sisters. Almack's he stigmatised as being the waste of a good evening and issued a cryptic warning that he would be leaving pretty promptly as he had far more interesting prospects in view.

* * *

Almack's was always crowded even at nine o'clock in the evening. The doors shut promptly at eleven and anyone arriving after that time, no matter how important, was barred. The patronesses controlled every aspect of the club with iron fists and Lady Jersey's vouchers had been hard won. In the entrance hall Sophia stopped to preen herself in the Venetian mirror, which hung at the bottom of the red-carpeted stairs, but not for long. Her mother was soon ushering both girls upwards into the main salon, ablaze with a thousand candles hanging from crystal chandeliers and tucked into the wall sconces. People looked curiously at the small party, finding it difficult to believe that this new young woman was Christabel's sister. There could be no greater contrast, one tall, willowy, an ice maiden with flaming hair, the other shorter, rounded and an undistinguished brunette. No wonder the gown had to be magenta. It was Sophia's way of seizing some of the attention that always fell so unfairly to her sister.

In the event neither girl lacked for partners. For some Sophia's was a new face and a likely diversion while for others she promised to be the means of an introduction to the peerless Christabel. Happily she had no notion of this and smiled benignly on the world as she passed down the rows of the country dance on the arm of one partner after another. Benedict had discovered a few choice spirits who had also been coerced into escorting family members and was content for the moment to bide his time. The evening was young and he felt sure that it could only get better.

Only Christabel felt depressed. This night was one like so many others. She smiled gracefully at her partners and diligently performed each dance. Between cotillions and quadrilles she sipped lemonade and made kind conversation with those young damsels sheltering by the wall and too shy to talk to anyone else. But there was emptiness in her heart. Soon it would be time to call the carriage and return home, but for what? In two days' time Sir Julian would return and her future would be decided for ever. If she accepted him, this was one engagement that would have to stick.

A sudden flurry at the top of the stairs made her look up. A small brunette, her dark curls glistening in the candlelight, had just made it through the doors before they were locked. The girl looked around her with animation and then turned to her companion, grasping his arm and pointing out the glittering chandeliers and frescoed ceilings. Christabel drew a sharp intake of breath. It was Richard, of course. Richard, who had never before set foot in this hallowed place, now dancing attendance on the little Spaniard. She watched as though in a dream as he presented Domino first to Lady Sefton, one of the patronesses present that night, and then on to Mr Davenant, Lord and Lady Wivenhoe and the Misses Newcombe. The girl had an entrancing smile, Christabel thought, and though she beamed happily on everyone she met, it was clear that she smiled for Richard alone. *She loves him*—the thought struck her with explosive force. Her stomach began to churn sickeningly, but why she could not understand. Richard had been dead to her for six years. Why should it matter who his fancy now alighted on?

At that moment she was claimed for a country dance. Somehow she managed mechanically to perform the steps without making a mistake. Out of the corner of her eye, she saw Richard and Domino take the floor. He'd always been a graceful dancer and she noticed that in this respect he hadn't changed. Throughout he kept up a lively conversation with his partner and it was evident that he was delighted to be with her. Social rules dictated that they could not stand up together for more than two dances, but when they were not on the floor he talked to her; when she partnered other men, his gaze was never far away. And so it went on, dance after dance, while Christabel watched the clock and prayed for the carriage to arrive. She felt she could not bear to look at them a minute longer and yet her eyes were instinctively drawn in their direction. They made a handsome couple and it was clear that others thought so too. There were many admiring glances and much chatter behind opened fans.

When the orchestra struck up for a waltz she was relieved to be sitting out the dance. For some years she'd been permitted by the patronesses to waltz at Almack's, but Sophia was not in that fortunate position and she had no desire to irritate her sister any further. She had deliberately kept her dance card free so that she could keep Sophia company.

'Miss Tallis, I believe you waltz?'

Richard Veryan stood before her, immaculate in white ruffled shirt and black long-tailed coat. The crisp white folds of his silk neckcloth were tied in a perfect *trône d'amour*. Well-fitting black-satin knee breeches did nothing to disguise the muscular thighs beneath. His attire was that of the most fashionable of London gentlemen, but the lean, tanned face hinted at another story.

Christabel found herself once again struggling to maintain her composure.

His grey eyes, flecked with flint, were fixed penetratingly on her and without speaking he held out a hand and with the other gestured to the dance floor.

'Thank you, sir,' she said, recovering her wits a little, 'but I do not care to waltz while my sister does not dance.'

Richard glanced indifferently at Sophia, who stared haughtily back at him.

'I'm sure Miss Sophia Tallis would not wish to keep you from enjoying a dance she must know you love.'

It was true. Ever since she'd learned to waltz, she'd treasured the joy of floating light as thistledown across the ballroom, her feet skimming the floor and her whole body responding to the rhythm of the music. Her sister pursed her lips angrily, but said nothing. Richard was still holding out his hand, his cold eyes seeming now to blaze with something akin to fire. Christabel could not understand his persistence, but found herself mesmerised into accepting his invitation.

A slight pressure on her waist and he had led her into the dance. His arms encircled her body lightly at first, as, twisting and pirouetting, they became familiar with each other's paces. They had always danced well together and soon they were in tune, step by step, movement by movement. The music's lush strains trembled through her limbs and she lost herself to its rhythms.

Gradually his arms tightened around her and she was acutely aware of the warmth of his body pressing her close. The heady smell of his scent enveloped her as she was held ever more nearly, his face almost bruising her cheek. Carelessly his mouth brushed the top of her hair and without thinking she melted more closely into his embrace. They were dancing now as one, their bodies a rhythmical caress which shocked those who witnessed it. Yet the power of Christabel's beauty held them spellbound. She looked magnificent, almost otherworldly in her splendour, the green silk of her dress swishing across the floor, little emerald slippers on her feet and that haze of red curls cascading downwards to meet her wonderful white skin.

Her mother, sitting on one of the small gilded chairs reserved for chaperons, looked up and caught her breath in distress. That was surely Richard Veryan!

She had no idea he had returned to England. And Christabel was dancing with him and in a fashion that could only be described as provocative! Richard's hand was curved around Christabel's waist and his face so close to hers that he could, if he'd wished, nuzzle and caress the soft skin almost touching his.

And he did wish. He felt his body hard against this woman he'd loved so well. He felt her soft pliable form fusing with his and rejoiced in the sheer physical exultation that was pulsating through him. He could have danced with her all night and then—no, he could not think like that. It was his mission to entice her and the dance must be part of that. His delight in her proximity was something he must not acknowledge.

The music stopped and for a moment they stood dazed. Then he led her back to the row of chairs, every eye in the room upon them.

'Thank you, Miss Tallis, for a most enjoyable dance,' he said formally.

'It was a pleasure, my lord,' she replied, equally formal.

'We must waltz more—I hope to see you at Almack's again very soon.'

'I fear that is unlikely. I shall not be in London long and I imagine that you will be leaving shortly yourself.'

'Why are you so sure?' and he looked over to where Domino was standing, wide-eyed and apprehensive.

'I beg your pardon, but I thought you would be returning to Cornwall to be with your mother.' Christabel sounded puzzled.

'One can return, and return again—if one has something worth coming back for,' he replied smoothly.

Once more he looked meaningfully across the room at the young girl waiting patiently for his return. Christabel was bewildered. Seemingly he wished her to understand that Domino de Silva was the woman who held his heart, yet just seconds ago he had been dancing with *her* in so intimate a manner that together they'd shocked the assembled company. They'd danced as one body, man and woman, merged in a sensual unity. She'd felt his warm breath so close she could have reached out and tasted it. And now this.

'I do believe that finally I have something to come back for,' he continued, making it impossible to mistake his meaning.

She gathered up all her reserves of dignity and faced him with a studied calm. 'You are indeed fortunate.'

'I think so, Miss Tallis. And I trust that you too will know such good fortune.'

'You are all kindness, sir.'

His answering bow was mocking. With a kiss of her hand, he turned around and walked across the room to Domino, who greeted him with a shy smile and outstretched hands.

'Well!' Sophia was at her elbow. 'You're a sly one. You seem to make a habit of meeting Richard Veryan— you must have known he would be here, but you never said a word. And to see you dancing with him! It was shameless! What would Sir Julian say?'

'It really is none of your business,' Christabel snapped.

'It will be if you disgrace the family again by breaking a second engagement,' her sister retorted.

'There is no second engagement,' she muttered though clenched teeth, 'and rest assured that you would be the last person I'd ask for advice on my conduct.'

'You could do worse. At least I haven't made myself an object of scandal.'

She had an insane desire to scream at Sophia for her spitefulness, but, constrained by the hallowed portals of Almack's, she kept silent, biting her lip so hard that she drew blood.

'What *were* you thinking of, Christabel?' Her mother was at her side, throwing more coals on a fire which was already burning brightly. 'To dance in that fashion with a man, and with Richard Veryan of all people. What would Sir Julian have said?'

Her mother's echo of the earlier taunt breached Christabel's iron control. She broke free from Lady Harriet's clasp and said in a stifled voice, 'I'll not wait for the carriage. I will walk home.'

'But you cannot…' Her mother's words were lost in the distance as she turned swiftly and made for the door.

Richard watched her go. He had been badly disturbed by their dance. It had thrilled him to take Christabel's glacial beauty in his arms and mould it to his desire. The feeling of her body against his still resonated. While they'd danced, the ardent girl of yesterday had broken through that frozen surface—and he had been the one to melt her. She was a magnificent creature and he had gloried in the moment. What was she doing contemplating a mediocre marriage with a milk-and-water nonentity? But he must think objectively, he told himself, and objectively his plan was working. He should be pleased. He had stirred the embers of passion in her and soon he would awake such a frenzy of feeling that she would be desperate to know his love. He would have proved her inconstancy and be free to walk away. That moment was a little way off, but he should be satisfied with what he'd achieved that night. He wasn't sure why the victory felt forlorn.

Chapter Four

'It's time I took you home, Domino.'

Richard's tone was decisive. Once Christabel had left, he had no inclination to remain at Almack's and was anxious to return the girl to her aunt's care. Loretta Blythe had been suffering from a chill for some days and this evening had finally succumbed to a fever and taken to her bed. It was inconvenient. He'd hoped to dispense with his escort duties before now, not least because Domino showed no sign of tiring of his company. He'd expected that once fully launched into the delights of London society she would cease to have an interest in him. Instead, the wider she spread her acquaintance, the more she seemed to cling.

Having reached Lady Blythe's house, Richard stepped into the hallway and made ready to wish Domino goodnight, but instead of taking the hand he held out, she raised herself on to her toes to reach his cheek and planted a gentle kiss. Seriously disconcerted, he remonstrated with her.

'You mustn't do that, Domino. Remember that I stand in your aunt's place. You must think of me as a friend—an elder brother, if you will.'

'I don't see why,' she exclaimed rebelliously. 'You're by far the most attractive man I know!'

'I thank you for the compliment, but I'm not a suitable partner for you.'

She shook her head as if to block out his words. 'I don't believe that. You think me too young to love truly, but you're wrong.'

'I am eleven years older than you and my situation is not a happy one.'

'You mean that you're still in love with Christabel Tallis.'

Surprise rendered him silent.

'You see, I have her name at my fingertips. How could I not? She is a truly beautiful woman and I can't blame you for caring for her still.'

There was a sparkle of tears and her voice was that of a chastened child. He felt a deep sympathy for her.

'My relationship with Miss Tallis should not concern you,' he rebuked her gently. 'The situation I referred to was my father's death. In a very short while I must return to Cornwall. My mother needs support and I have to get to grips with the management of the estate. It's been allowed to drift since my father's death and that can't continue.'

'I understand,' she breathed eagerly. 'Of course you

must go to your mother. But I can wait until you're settled. Then perhaps you'll invite me to Madron Abbey. I would love to see your home.'

'It will be a great pleasure to show both you and your aunt around. But you will come as a guest, Domino, not as a future bride.'

The girl lowered her head, a mulish expression on her face. Baffled by her obstinacy, Richard spoke more bluntly than he intended.

'I am truly sorry that you have feelings I cannot reciprocate, Domino, but you must be sensible. You're no longer a child. You have built a fantasy and started to believe in it. For your own sake, you must dismiss it from your mind. In time you will find the man that is right for you.'

'I have found him,' she said, gulping down unshed tears, 'but he is too stupid to see.'

He strode to the front door, but before he could open it, she called out to him from the marble balustrade above, 'Will I see you at Richmond Park tomorrow?'

'Richmond? Ah, yes, the Wivenhoes' alfresco lunch, otherwise known as a picnic.'

'I believe the Park is charming—such a large space of countryside and so near the city. You *are* coming?' she asked anxiously.

He didn't answer directly. 'I'm sure you'll find your aunt a great deal better in the morning and she'll be looking forward to accompanying you to Richmond.'

He felt too unsettled by their conversation to return immediately to his hotel. He had decided from the outset that he would put up at Brown's rather than opening the house in Grosvenor Square. A solitary stay amid its lonely expanses did not appeal and the few days he planned to be in London would have meant unnecessary disruption for its skeleton staff. But tonight the hotel looked just as uninviting and he needed to clear his head. He would walk a while in the evening air and then look in on one of the gentlemen's clubs that lined St James's Street.

He'd been scrupulous never to suggest that he could be more than a friend to Domino, but he still felt guilty for causing her unhappiness. It hadn't helped that he'd been her constant escort since they'd arrived in London. If he'd not spent so much time with her, what had been an incipient affection on board ship would have been nipped in the bud. But Lady Blythe had shown herself only too willing to delegate her duties whenever possible and now the wretched woman had taken to her bed. Surely she would be better in the morning.

Richard's resolve that he would no longer be Domino's escort was broken almost as soon as it was made. A loud banging at his door early the next morning woke him from a deep sleep. It seemed as though he'd hardly been to bed and his head ached from too much brandy the night before. But the hotel porter, breathing heavily in the doorway from his climb up the stairs, was waving a badly folded sheet of paper under his nose and clearly expected an answer.

'Who brought this?' Richard asked blearily.

'A groom, my lord.' The porter was disapproving.

'Whose groom?'

'That I couldn't say, my lord.' The porter held his face aloof, expressing in no uncertain manner that Brown's Hotel thought poorly of such early morning intrusions.

Richard pulled back the curtain better to read the note and groaned as the morning light flooded the room.

'Get me some coffee, for heaven's sake.'

'Certainly my lord. Shall I tell the groom to wait?'

'If he wants an answer. But get me that drink.'

He spread the crumpled note out and saw at once that it was from Domino. He knew almost without reading that it would be a plea to accompany her that morning to the Wivenhoes' picnic. It seemed that her aunt was still not feeling well enough to undertake a long drive. And Domino wanted so much to see Richmond Park. Could Richard please come and this would be the very last time she would ask, she promised. Aunt Loretta had signalled her willingness for Richard to be her escort.

I have no doubt she has, he thought savagely. He hardly knew Domino's aunt, but from his few meetings with her she seemed to be the sort of woman for whom ill health, as long as it were not too severe, was entirely beneficial.

In an hour he had washed, shaved and dressed, and presented himself in Curzon Street complete with hired curricle. Domino had evidently been watching at the window for she appeared almost immediately, tripping lightly down the front steps, her face glowing with pleasure. Her patent delight in going on the expedition almost reconciled him to the prospect of attending an event he'd hoped to escape.

For Christabel there was no escape: she would have to join the family party. She sat at the breakfast table, listlessly toying with a piece of toast and looking tired and pale in the harsh morning light. Her mother had accepted the Wivenhoes' invitation on her behalf weeks ago and at the last moment her siblings had been hurriedly included. Her heart felt leaden. She was certain that Richard would be there, squiring his new love and flaunting his happiness. She would have to endure their close proximity for hours without giving the slightest hint of discomfort. It would be necessary to put on a guise not only for her fellows, but also for her family.

Her mother was worried, she knew. Late last night after Sophia had danced her fill at Almack's and the two had returned home to Mount Street, Lady Harriet had tiptoed into the bedroom. Christabel had pretended sleep and not answered her mother's anxious query. Instead she had lain silent and still, the tears pricking at her eyes and her heart a confusion of pain. She didn't understand what Richard was doing nor even why she felt so deeply upset by his conduct. It was evident that he'd not forgiven the broken engagement. But surely his humiliation could not still be so raw that he needed to wage a war against her. Yet that was exactly what was happening. One minute he was angrily haranguing her for past crimes, the next he was caressing her—with his smile, his voice, even his body. When last night she'd danced with him so freely, she had been careless of gossip, careless of her reputation. She had given no thought to guarding her feelings and she'd allowed herself to desire. She'd allowed him to stir emotions within her that she'd schooled herself never to feel again and now today she would have to face him once more. She would have to put on the performance of her life.

'Where's the ham?' Benedict demanded as he breezed into the breakfast room and searched the side table anxiously. He looked fresh and full of energy, despite having slept little.

'Bel, where's the ham? Sophy, you've eaten it all,' he accused as his younger sister appeared in the doorway, elaborately dressed in a bright green-velvet spencer over daffodil-yellow silk.

'I've had a great many things to do other than eating breakfast, you stupid boy. If you want ham, ring the bell for more.'

'Who's stupid? At least I don't look like a parrot,' he said, gesturing to Sophia's preferred apparel for driving in Richmond Park.

'Someone should have told you that making personal remarks is offensive.'

'Someone should have told you that dressing like a pantomime is even more offensive.'

'Do stop, both of you!' Christabel's quiet voice intervened, the steely tone surprising them into silence.

'Hoity-toity,' said Benedict half under his breath. 'By the way,' he offered as he sat down at the table, his plate groaning with devilled kidneys and a couple of eggs he'd unearthed, 'd'you know what they're saying in the clubs?'

'The rubbish that men bandy amongst themselves is of no interest to us,' Sophia said haughtily.

'It might be since it concerns a very close neighbour of ours.'

Both sisters looked at him, Christabel's face devoid of expression, but even paler than before.

'Rick Veryan, Richard. You saw him last night at Almack's?'

'Of course we saw him.' Sophia was impatient.

'He was with that pretty, dark-haired girl. She's from Argentina.'

'We know.' Sophia's tone was getting dangerous.

'Bet you didn't know that the odds are mounting on his marrying the girl within the year. Can't be any earlier—he's in mourning—bad *ton*.'

'What do you know of bad *ton*?'

'It might surprise you, Miss Superior, just how much I do know. Anyway a lot of money was changing hands last night, betting on the marriage. Lucky old Rick, eh? Comes back from some outlandish place and walks straight into a title and now a fortune.'

His sisters looked blankly at him.

'Loaded,' he said succinctly. 'That's the word. Full of juice and a good looker too. What more could a man ask? I talked to her myself last night. Introduced by the *grande dame*, Mrs Drummond-Burrell. I think she thought Domino—what a name—was in need of younger company.'

'She certainly got it with you,' Sophia said derisively.

'And she enjoyed it, may I say.' He ruminated for a

while, chewing thoughtfully on the last kidney. 'Taking
little thing, I thought, though she never quite mastered
the steps of the cotillion.'

'And you, of course, are the supreme exponent of the
dance.'

Christabel got up swiftly, unable to bear her siblings'
bickering a minute longer. Benedict's words had washed
away her earlier resolve. How could she possibly keep
an impassive countenance when she knew for sure that
Richard was planning to marry? She would make her
excuses. The family must go without her.

'What's the matter, Christabel?' It was Sophia stopping her at the door. 'Can't face seeing your old beau
getting wed? Why should it matter to you? After all,
aren't you marrying Sir Julian?'

Benedict gaped. He knew little of the events of six
years ago, having been away at school, and had not realised the effect his news might have. But it was Sophia's
words that cut Christabel most deeply. In her spite, her
sister had arrowed straight to the question which was
causing her such agitation. Why *did* it matter so much
to her that Richard was to marry? She must prove that
it did not. She must prove Sophia wrong. There would
be no evasions—she would go to the picnic.

It seemed that the Wivenhoes could not have chosen
a better day for their alfresco party. An almost cloudless sky and an unusually warm April sun enabled their
guests to view the beauty of the park from open carriages. Herds of red and fallow deer grazed undisturbed
in a pastoral landscape of rolling hills, grassy slopes

and woodland gardens. The fresh untouched green of springtime already clad most of the ancient trees and beneath their light shade shimmered daffodil gold. The company drove leisurely through this sylvan setting before arriving at a central pagoda where they were to be served refreshments.

Christabel, her mother and sister were soon ensconced on its terrace, sitting comfortably on a padded *chaise* and gratefully sipping tea. Servants bustled to and fro, some bringing additional cushions and blankets for the older members of the group, and others plates of dainty sandwiches and small iced cakes. Sophia made ready to plunder the dish of madeleines left temptingly on their table.

'What a beautiful place,' her mother murmured to her hostess as she passed by. 'And such a wonderful day!'

'Indeed—it seems that summer is already with us!' Lady Wivenhoe happily mingled among the knot of people gathered on the terrace.

Christabel hardly heard them. The cream muslin gown she wore, trimmed with delicate chartreuse lace, might pay homage to the season, but her spirits remained locked in winter. She felt frozen in time, yet her mind was never still, never at peace. She thought she might be going mad. For the hundredth time she tried to understand why in that faraway summer she'd acted as she had. Richard had meant so much to her and yet, with hardly a thought, it seemed, she'd returned his ring and thrown herself at a man who even then she'd suspected was not to be trusted. Why, oh, why had she done that? Only the intoxication of first sexual awakening could explain the wilful breaking into pieces of the jigsaw of her life. But it was not quite the first awakening, was it? There was that evening in Cornwall when she and Richard had thrown themselves into the sea together. They'd been just a little crazy and the swim had sparked something deep and elemental between them, or so she'd thought. But almost immediately he'd turned away. He'd not wanted that intimate bond and she'd been left bewildered, ashamed of the physical ache that had taken hold of her. And then the trip to London with all its glamour, all its glories, had pushed everything else out of her mind. Joshua had swum into her presence, a man who was more than willing to set her body alight. She had loved him dreadfully. No, she corrected herself, she had lusted for him dreadfully. And lust had its own shameful penance. She thought she'd paid that price, but now, it seemed, she must continue to pay.

In the distance she could see Domino laughing and prattling with Richard. On occasions he responded in a similar vein, but there was a serious expression on his face which seemed at odds with the frolicking of his younger companion. At length the girl seemed to grow tired of entertaining him and turned to Benedict, who had just then emerged at her side and was making ready to reintroduce himself. When the two young people began to stroll together across the greensward towards King Henry's mound, the highest point of the park, Christabel thought that Richard looked almost relieved. How strange. But she'd probably imagined it.

Sophia, meanwhile, was maintaining a critical commentary on her fellow guests as they strolled along the intersecting pathways which met at the pagoda.

As each new costume passed beneath the balcony, it duly received the full force of her disapproval. Her own ensemble had attracted a mixed response and she was still smarting from some of the remarks she'd overheard. Her mother, anxious to restore her to good spirits, extended a comforting arm but in doing so caught her hand in the intricate pattern of the lace tablecloth and spilled the contents of her teacup on to the disputed outfit.

'Mama, just look what you've done—how clumsy!'

'I am sorry for the accident, Sophia, but your rudeness does you no credit,' her mother reproved.

For once Sophia looked abashed. Her nerves were on end. She had dreamed of making her mark in *ton* society, but so far society had shown an entire lack of interest. This morning she had tried particularly hard with her *toilette*, but it appeared that this effort was still not enough. To add to her misery her elder sister sat next to her, seemingly serene and unruffled, but looking effortlessly lovely and attracting frequent glances of open admiration from the other guests.

'Come with me,' Lady Tallis urged, making for the small cloakroom at the rear of the pagoda, 'we must sponge your dress immediately.'

Sophia trailed miserably behind her and Christabel was left alone with her thoughts. But not for long. The sound of firm footsteps on the stairway leading to the balcony made her look up.

'I trust I see you well, Miss Tallis.'

'Thank you, Lord Veryan, I am most well,' she answered curtly.

'And how are you enjoying Richmond Park?' he pursued.

'It is very beautiful.'

'You have seen it only by carriage? It is even better viewed at close quarters.'

She nodded briefly, but said nothing, averting her glance. His shapely legs encased in well-fitting breeches and riding boots of dazzling gloss were an unnecessary distraction.

'If you would care to take a stroll, I would be happy to escort you.' He was smiling and for once the grey eyes smiled with him.

'Thank you, but I have already walked a distance around the park,' she lied.

'Then you are before me.' A slight flush crept into his lean cheek as he recognised the snub.

'It would appear so.'

He had been studying her from a distance, seen the sadness in her face and felt his determination waver. But her flagrant rejection of courtesies hardened his heart again and spurred him once more into attack.

'I'm surprised by your energy. I would have thought you had little left after last night's magnificent display of dancing.'

'I am not such a poor creature.' And the flash in the emerald eyes was unmistakable. He remembered well that indomitable spirit and once more his heart softened a little.

'You were never a poor creature, Miss Tallis,' he said quietly. 'Far from it, as I recall. I still have the scars to prove it!'

She looked at him, surprised.

'I spent my childhood following you,' he offered. 'Jumping rocks, climbing trees, hacking my way through woods. It was a tough training.'

Her face broke into the shadow of a smile, the troubles of the present for the moment cast aside.

'And were you always the follower?'

'Always. I rarely saw more than a tangle of red curls in the distance.'

Her smile broadened. 'I was always that far ahead?'

He looked quizzically at her. 'There were times when I got to see the back of two skinny brown legs, but never much more.'

'Why did you follow me if it meant suffering scars?'

'Why wouldn't I? Life was a daily adventure and the scars were simple ones. Childhood was the easy part. It was growing up that was difficult.'

Her smile vanished. 'How sad it is that we cannot stay children,' she almost blurted out.

'Unfortunately we cannot. Nor can we undo life.'

'But surely we can start again.' Their reminiscence had emboldened her and her voice now held a definite plea.

'I fear not,' he said sternly. 'We are prisoners of the life we make and we must live with that knowledge.' His face had entirely lost its earlier warmth.

'I cannot agree,' she said vehemently. 'That would be to underestimate the human spirit and its capacity for change.'

'I have never underestimated *you*, Miss Tallis.'

His words were oblique, but she knew well their meaning. Nothing had altered and she felt sick to her stomach. He was still her implacable enemy.

'Nor I you, Lord Veryan,' she managed at last.

'It seems that we are agreed on one thing at least.'

'It matters not to me whether we agree or disagree. If you will excuse me...'

And with that she rose in one fluid movement, pushed back her chair and was tripping down the steps before he realised her intention. The breeze caught her mane of red curls and tangled them wildly into a fiery haze. He felt a momentary madness to rush after her and take hold of that hair, smooth it, caress it, cover it in kisses. It deserved to be worshipped.

'Richard? I thought it must be you. I am very pleased to see you again. You were at Almack's last night, I believe, but there was no opportunity to speak to you.'

Lady Tallis had appeared from the rear of the pagoda and was now standing beside him looking, despite her words, not at all pleased. She had glimpsed the figure of Christabel in the distance walking rapidly away towards the lake and drawn her own conclusions. In her short absence the sky had begun to cloud alarmingly.

'Lady Harriet! How good to see such an old friend.' Richard felt genuine pleasure at meeting the woman who for much of his life had been a second mother to him.

'I have to admit some surprise at seeing you in London,' Lady Tallis returned. 'I had no idea you were in the country.' Her tone verged on reproof. 'But naturally I am delighted that you have returned safely. I make no doubt that the voyage was a testing one. Your mother must be overjoyed.'

He looked a little self-conscious, but felt there was no point in dissembling.

'She will have learned only recently that I landed safely.'

Lady Tallis raised her eyebrows. 'Forgive me, but should you not have apprised her of that fact immediately?'

'I've been a little delayed in London, but intend to leave for Cornwall within the week. By now she will have had my letter telling her to expect me shortly.'

'I see,' she said thoughtfully, though in truth she did not. Whatever could have kept him in London? She had heard gossip about a young woman from Buenos Aires, someone he had supposedly escorted to England, but that surely would not have prevented him making for home as soon as he was able.

She fixed him with a severe expression. 'Anne will be waiting in some anxiety for you.'

She felt strongly that he should be with his mother in Cornwall and almost as strongly that he should not be in London upsetting Christabel. Particularly not at this delicate moment when she was poised to accept Sir Julian.

A sudden clap of thunder shook the pagoda roof and in seconds shattered the gentleness of the April morning. A moment later shards of rain were beating on the woodwork and bouncing off the grass. The party on the balcony hastily decamped to the back of the pagoda for shelter, but Lady Tallis bethought herself of Christabel, under the open skies and without protection.

Richard was before her. He grabbed one of the umbrellas presciently provided by Lady Wivenhoe for her guests and ran down the steps, striding rapidly in the direction he had last seen Christabel heading. On the way he passed a furious Benedict and a joyful Domino. The rain had obliterated Benedict's carefully crafted hair style *à la* Brutus to the huge amusement of his companion. Despite being severely buffeted by the sudden tempest, her peals of laughter rang out across the park.

Richard ignored the noisy pair and hurried on. He found Christabel in minutes, standing motionless by the waters of the storm-tossed lake. She was drenched, her skin translucent and gleaming beneath the downpour, and the curves of her lithe figure apparent through the sodden muslin of the once-beautiful dress. She turned at that moment and her face wore such a look of unhappiness that he wanted to take her into his arms there and then and put a stop to the nonsense he had started. But he knew well that beyond the fragility lay pure steel. The deep-green eyes flashed anger at him and bade him keep his distance just as surely as if she had spoken.

Mutely he offered the shelter of the umbrella. Even

she had to smile at that ineffectual gesture. She could not become any wetter.

'Thank you for the thought, Lord Veryan. I fear, though, that you are a little late in coming to my rescue.'

There was more meaning to her words than the social nicety she expressed. He looked at the rain-soaked figure before him, his gaze lingering unwillingly on her form. The long shapely legs and the soft swell of her breasts were clearly visible through the transparent muslin and he knew desperate desire. He moved towards her as though in a dream.

She remained where she stood, unflinching. She saw his arms slowly reaching out towards her and then her long, cold fingers were held tightly within his, sending a warmth coursing through her body until she was tingling from head to toe, from her saturated slippers to the riot of wet curls framing her face. They stood, body to body, for what seemed an age. She felt her pulse beating tumultuously and her limbs tremble as the hard planes of his body pressed against soft flesh. Wave after wave of flaming heat swirled through every small part of her, melting resistance, dissolving protest. His hands were on her waist, pulling her urgently towards him, his body even closer, even harder against hers. Now his hands were sliding upwards and over her breasts, cradling them, brushing at their fullness and sending swirls of shocked pleasure spiralling through her. Onwards and his hands were cupping her cheeks, tipping her face to meet his. She looked into his eyes and drowned, drowned in pools of molten grey.

'Christabel,' he began, the soft whisper of his voice flowing through her and reaching to her heart. 'Christabel, I—'

'Christabel! Come quickly.' It was her mother's urgent tones. 'We must get you home immediately or you will become ill.'

Lady Tallis was hurrying towards them, waving yet another umbrella. The moment of intimacy was at an end, diffusing itself amid the misty rain.

Christabel's hands slipped from his and she walked away, leaving him to curse her power and his weakness. This was not what he intended, to be caught in the web of his own spinning. He must subdue this wretched, uncontrollable desire that once more threatened to tear him apart. He must stay aloof even while he continued to entice her into betraying herself. There were only a few days left to accomplish his plan and every one of those must count.

By now Lady Tallis had reached his side and was observing him with disapproval.

'Miss de Silva is ready to leave, Richard. I understand that you are her escort?'

'You are right to remind me of my duties, Lady Harriet,' he replied stiffly and began to make his way back to the pagoda.

Christabel caught his words on the air and was deeply puzzled. Could he really be speaking of his future wife when he talked of 'duties'? And if he were promised to Domino de Silva, why had he allowed himself just now to hold her so long, to touch her so intimately? During their scandalous dance at Almack's she'd imagined for a moment that he felt the same attraction as she. But only for a moment. His hurtful rejection had soon disabused her. This time, though, she could not be mistaken. There had been a charge so powerful between them that she was left dazed. Naked desire—that's what she'd felt. Not even the errant Joshua, in her days as a green girl, had aroused such fervour in her. And it was Richard, a man she'd once dismissed as worthy only to be a friend, who'd provoked it. Nothing made sense. Richard today must be a very different man to the one she'd once known—or maybe she'd never really known him. Perhaps she'd been too young, too inexperienced, to recognise what might have been. The irony of the situation hit her hard. It seemed that she could feel passion for this man, a passion that shook her to the very core, but only now that he was promised to another woman.

She thought back to the moment when she'd first seen Richard on his return from the university. He had grown into a dashing young man, a figure far superior to any of her local suitors and she was no longer the skinny, freckled tomboy he'd known from the past. She'd watched with amusement his stupefied expression when he'd first caught sight of her and knew instantly that she had captivated him. His jealousy of the gaggle of admirers who daily haunted Lamorna was evident and she thought guiltily of how she'd enjoyed playing one man off against another. In her defence she was hardly more than a child and the game was a heady one. The distant cousin who was to present her had fallen seriously ill and her planned come-out had not materialised. The excitement of having young men vie for her favours was a pleasing compensation. Richard's courtship had been swift. He'd capitalised on their long childhood friendship to infiltrate her life with ease, and in no time he'd succeeded in banishing his rivals and filling the centre of her world. Suddenly she was engaged and unsure of quite how it had happened. It seemed natural to be promising to spend the rest of her life with him, but also something of an anticlimax. She'd been exhilarated by the excitements of the chase and revelled in the handsome and vigorous man he'd become, yet she knew him almost too well. There were no secrets, or so it seemed, no concealed feelings, no hidden fire.

Until, that is, that one evening in the cove. In her memory she retraced their steps that night. They'd walked out together after an early dinner, escaping the last frenetic preparations for the morrow when they would travel to London in company with Lady Veryan. Christabel was to stay at the Veryans' town house and Richard's mother was to supervise her purchase of bride clothes, her own mother being unable to leave her younger siblings for any protracted period.

It had been a beautiful evening in early summer and they'd sauntered at dusk towards the sea along a lane already heavy with hawthorn. Very soon the granite rocks and soft white sand of their beloved cove came into view. The sea was flat calm and Richard had begun to skim stones along the surface of the water. She had joined in, trying to make her stones bounce further. It was an old game of their childhood. The competition between them grew fierce and he shouted with delight when he finally made an unbeatable shot. Beneath the newly polished surface, he was still not much more than a boy. With mischief in her eyes, she'd challenged him to another contest from their childhood: who could swim out the furthest without pausing for breath. He'd demurred; they were not dressed for the water and in any case it hardly seemed proper. In answer, she'd stripped off her clothes down to her chemise, leaving Richard staring in wonderment at the lithe, willowy figure standing so close to him. Then he had been seized by the same madness and was stripped and plunging into the cool water before she had time to reach the sea's edge. They had swum out until they were both exhausted and then drifted lazily back towards the shore, the waters around them silvered by the moon newly risen in a clear sky. She was floating beside him and on impulse it seemed he'd caught hold of her, encircling her waist with his arms and tangling his face in her salt-soaked curls. The feel of his hard, male body against hers took her breath away and she knew a frantic desire to hold him close to her, to meld her body to his. Her legs looped around him and their flesh met in a mutual caress. Even now she grew hot thinking of it.

But the moment was over almost as soon as it arrived, the spark extinguished, and they were scrambling up the beach and into their clothes as though pursued by the Furies, ashamed it seemed of that instant of burning connection. The next day they had left for London and a round of parties, routs, ridottos, balls, such as she'd never before encountered: a kaleidoscope of pleasure which took over her life. As an affianced woman she'd enjoyed the freedom it conferred, freedom to talk unchaperoned with other men, freedom to dance and even to flirt with them, and freedom to meet a Joshua.

A magnificent rout was to be held that evening at the Seftons' London mansion, a short distance from Mount Street. Sophia, insatiable as always for *ton* society, was greatly excited at attending such a prestigious event. It was sure to afford her a splendid hunting ground for potential partners. The torrential rain had done Christabel little harm other than a ruined dress, but she was grateful that it served as an excuse for staying home that night. She was more than happy to spend a quiet evening by herself when the alternative was the painful spectacle of Richard and Domino together. She was lying curled on her bed, flicking through back numbers of *Lady's Magazine*, when her mother slid quietly into the room.

'Have you seen these extraordinary models, Mama? They must be at least ten feet tall,' she said with an attempt at gaiety. The emaciated females depicted were so long and thin as almost to disappear off the page.

Her mother smiled slightly. 'Extraordinary indeed! They would be quite terrifying to meet in the flesh.'

She sat down on the bed and took her daughter's hand. 'I came to say, Bel, that I won't be going to the Seftons' rout tonight. There is little need for my presence: their house is within easy walking distance and Benedict can act as escort to his sister for the evening. It won't do him any harm to take on a little responsibility while he's enjoying his holiday. And it will give us the chance to have a comfortable coze.'

Christabel's heart sank; an evening spent alone with her mother was the last thing she wanted. Pressing her hand to her forehead in a gesture of pain, she hoped that she looked convincing.

'I'm so glad you're staying home, Mama, I'm not feeling at all the thing. I must have caught a chill in that downpour.'

Her mother looked suspicious and glanced pointedly at the magazines her daughter had been devouring. Christabel redoubled her efforts.

'I've been trying to distract myself with these,' she murmured, leafing through them with a weary motion, 'but without much success. I feel so hot—I think I may be developing a fever. It's best if I retire to bed early and try to sleep it off.'

Her mother's expression remained sceptical, but without another word she turned to go, quietly shutting the door behind her. It was unlikely that Lady Harriet would believe in her illness, but Christabel was beyond caring. After the day's events, her mother's gentle enquiries would be the last straw. Until Richard arrived in London, her future path had been clear, if uninviting. The time had come for her to step out of her sister's way and there had been a simple choice: wed a good man who loved her or remain a spinster without consequence or respect.

For years she'd kept at bay even the most determined of suitors. A glacial reserve had served her well, but now it had been ruptured. She had begun to feel again.

The dance at Almack's, the encounter by the lake, had begun an unstoppable thaw which threatened to trigger an avalanche of feelings she must not entertain. Today by the lakeside she had known no reserve. She had responded ardently to her body's impulses, she had throbbed with desire for Richard to possess her. How truly shocking! But *his* conduct was even more shocking. He was not hers to be possessed and yet he'd sought her out, danced with her as though he could have danced her into bed—she blushed deeply at the thought—embraced her, caressed her, imprinted her with his passion. And at the very same time he'd used every possible opportunity to taunt her with his new-found love, the girl it appeared he was ready to make his wife. It had to be part of his plan to pay her back for betraying him—there was no other explanation. No matter how softly he spoke or how enamoured he appeared, he was intent on exacting a penance from her. The thought overwhelmed her. She felt as though a giant hand had descended out of nowhere and squeezed every vestige of life from her heart and her body. She was no longer the woman who had bid Sir Julian farewell just a few days ago and she dreaded meeting him again.

Sir Julian, meanwhile, was looking in vain for his beloved at the Seftons' rout. He had despatched his business at Rosings as swiftly as he could and returned to London in time to attend the evening event. He knew that Christabel had been invited and was hoping that he would have the chance to talk privately with her.

He had unfinished business and was anxious to

settle it as soon as possible. He had no doubt of her answer—she had made it plain that he was her preferred suitor—and had not her sister called him Christabel's fiancé, making it clear that the Tallis family expected an imminent betrothal. But he wanted their relationship to be made firm and public. He was a man who liked an ordered life and was looking forward to planning their future together.

'How good to see you back so soon, Sir Julian!' It was Sophia, looking a little less exotic this evening in rose-pink lustring.

Sir Julian searched his memory, for he was sure he should know this young woman.

'Sophia Tallis, Christabel's sister,' she helped him out.

'Why, of course. I am very pleased to make your acquaintance again, Miss Sophia.' Sir Julian sounded genuinely glad to see her. If she were here, then Christabel would not be far away.

'And how was your visit to Rosings?'

'Busy, very busy,' Sir Julian mused, 'but nevertheless restful. I find the house has an aura of great tranquillity about it.'

'Indeed, yes,' she said encouragingly. 'I understand that its atmosphere is most mellow. I read in *Ackermann's Repository* that it is one of the oldest houses in England.'

Sir Julian's interest increased. 'I knew that certainly but I had not realised that Rosings had been featured in such a well-known journal.'

'You are too modest, Sir Julian. You must know that you own a most famous property,' Sophia cooed.

Feeling that the subject had now been exhausted, Sir Julian was eager to discover his beloved's whereabouts.

'Christabel?' Sophia responded carelessly. 'She's not here this evening.'

'How is this? Surely she was invited?'

'Naturally she was invited, but she didn't care to come.'

Sir Julian's well-bred eyebrows rose slightly and Sophia saw her chance.

'You must know that Christabel is invited everywhere, Sir Julian. She is the toast of the *ton*, I believe. She picks and chooses as she wishes.'

'I must admit I am a little disappointed. I returned from Rosings today on purpose to see her and was sure she would attend the rout.' He breathed a small sigh and looked slightly wounded.

'She probably didn't give a thought to your being here tonight. She isn't the most reliable of people.'

'Miss Tallis has always been most scrupulous about keeping appointments,' Sir Julian said a trifle sharply.

Sensing that she might have gone a little too far, Sophia carefully backtracked. 'Ah, now I recall—she was not feeling too well earlier this evening. She must have thought it best to stay at home.'

'Not well? How is this? She was perfectly well when I last saw her.'

'There's nothing to worry about, I assure you. The

family attended a picnic today in Richmond Park and we were all caught in the rain. It meant nothing to me, of course, I'm built of stronger stuff, but Christabel is a little fragile.'

'Yes, indeed, almost ethereal, I sometimes think.'

This was not the effect that Sophia had hoped for, but she recovered quickly. 'I'm sure her decision to stay home was right. She would not have wanted to attend with blotched cheeks and a red nose.'

Sir Julian looked aghast at this unimaginable picture of his loved one and sought reassurance. 'I trust that Miss Tallis is not seriously unwell.'

'She will be greatly improved in the morning, I'm sure. She is some years older than me, you know, and needs a little time to recover her spirits. And if she had come tonight, I doubt she would have had the energy to dance,' Sophia finished pointedly as the orchestra struck up for a country dance.

The Seftons had decided that though refreshments and conversation were normally deemed sufficient for a rout, their guests would be treated to a little informal dancing if they so wished. Sir Julian, mindful of his duties as a gentleman, immediately begged Sophia to grant him the favour of a dance. She accepted primly and only spoilt the effect by scowling at her brother who was leading Domino de Silva down the opposite line of country dancers.

'Is that not your brother I see, Miss Sophia?'

'Yes', she admitted in a bored voice, 'he's supposed to be my escort though he chooses rather to dance attendance on some foreigner.'

* * *

The foreigner was putting on a good show of enjoying herself despite an aching heart. Ever since the evening at Almack's, when Richard's lack of interest had been made so brutally clear, her happy spirits had been slowly and surely evaporating. The dance came to an end and Benedict, tired of having his feet crushed by an inattentive partner, said hopefully, 'You don't want to dance any more, do you?'

She shook her head and looked around the room in search of her aunt. Even her chaperon appeared to have deserted her.

Sensing her dejection, Benedict tried a diversion. 'Have you ever gambled?'

She opened her eyes wide. 'My father used to gamble sometimes in Buenos Aires, but he said the clubs were not fit for young girls.'

'There are clubs like that in London too—' Benedict grinned '—but you don't have to go to them to gamble. There's usually the chance at most parties.'

'Really? You can gamble here?' She was genuinely taken aback. To be offered gambling in what seemed the wealthiest and noblest of settings was curious.

'Let's find out. I think they've set up a hazard table or maybe faro in the next room. Would you like to watch the game?'

It was a distraction. She would go and watch until her aunt found her. They strolled into the adjoining card room and saw that a game of faro was in full swing. The bank had already amassed what looked like a fortune in rouleaus and the expressions on the players' faces ranged from boredom through irritation to downright vexation. It took little time for Domino to understand the simple rules with Benedict as her willing tutor. As she watched card after card emerging from the spring-loaded faro box, heard the click of tokens changing hands and felt the building tension as losses and wins followed in quick succession, she began to forget about the interview with Richard. Gambling, it seemed, was the perfect antidote for a broken heart.

'I want to play too,' she whispered.

Looking into her glowing face, Benedict stifled any misgivings and deftly inserted her into the circle. Very soon she was in the thick of the play. Her flushed face and sparkling eyes spoke of pleasure, but Benedict began to feel uncomfortable. She had taken to the game rather too enthusiastically, he thought, and now, looking around the table at their fellows, he didn't like what he saw. To Domino they appeared unexceptional. The women perhaps were showing too much *décolletée*, but they were sumptuously and fashionably dressed and hardly differed from their sisters dancing just a few yards away; the gentlemen were very correctly attired in evening dress and treated each other with a jokey politeness that spoke of long-term intimacy. But from Benedict's limited knowledge some of those gathered around the table were hardened gamesters and whispers of compromised virtue swirled around a number of the women. There was at least one wholly disreputable rake in the room.

Lord Moncaster lazed at the head of the table in charge of the faro bank. It was customary for the wealthiest of patrons to take turns in running the bank and Leo Moncaster enjoyed riches enough to run a hundred faro banks and still have plenty left to indulge his every whim. At that moment his whim was turning to Domino. His weary eyes rested gratefully on her, savouring her youthful beauty and unsophisticated delight in this novel entertainment. As his eyes ran over her assessingly, she looked up from the table and caught his glance. She wasn't sure what to think of him. He certainly made a splendid figure, looking as though he could have stepped straight out of one of Byron's poems, but there was something in his glittering gaze that disconcerted her and she looked quickly away. Benedict had seen that gaze too.

'Let's go back to the salon and find a cold drink,' he suggested.

'Not yet, Benedict. Just one more wager. Next time I'm bound to win.'

'That's what everyone thinks, and you won't.'

'How do you know that? Just because you always lose.'

'I don't always lose—well, not all of the time,' he finished lamely.

'There you are, then. It's my turn to win.'

'I should take you back to the salon. Your aunt will murder me if she knows I've brought you in here.'

'If you're afraid of my aunt, you'd better go.'

He was getting heartily bored with this recalcitrant girl. Perhaps if he upped and left she would follow. 'I'm going, then, and if you're wise you'll come too,' he whispered rather too loudly.

Lord Moncaster raised a quizzical eyebrow, causing Benedict to flush with annoyance and make haste to leave. Once out of the room, he shrugged off any qualms at deserting the girl. She wasn't his responsibility and he wanted to enjoy the rest of his evening.

Chapter Five

Christabel came down to breakfast the next morning still looking pale, but unruffled. She'd spent a difficult night, unable to sleep with any ease. Her mind had for hours refused to stop its constant churning of the past week's events, but finally she had found some repose. Her decision was made. She had allowed herself to be manipulated, to be too easily swayed by feelings she should never entertain. From now on she must ignore Richard's behaviour and concentrate on her own. With great severity she reminded herself that she was the only person responsible for her actions. If she could hold to that determination, she would cope with what lay ahead. Sophia's chatter had alerted her to Sir Julian's return to town and she knew that it would not be long before he renewed his proposal. She must be ready.

She saw that her mother had taken note of her pallor and was looking at her with gentle concern. 'Bel, are you well enough to pay that morning call on Lady Blythe?'

'I feel a good deal better, thank you, Mama, and I will be happy to go.'

It was a lie, for Domino was likely to be present and the thought of meeting the girl so soon after the disasters of the picnic troubled her. But she needed to appear unconcerned and calm in the face of any suspicions her mother might harbour.

Lady Harriet looked relieved. Her daughter seemed not to have been so badly affected by yesterday's events as she had feared. And she had a mountainous collection of letters awaiting her attention. Christabel's offer to attend on Loretta Blythe was most welcome.

'Perhaps Sophia would care to accompany you?' her mother suggested tentatively.

But Sophia instantly forestalled that notion; she was far too busy this morning organising her steadily increasing wardrobe. Christabel was more than happy to go attended only by her maid, and a walk to Curzon Street would be a pleasant escape from the house. The rain clouds, which yesterday had appeared out of nowhere, had vanished entirely and in their place was the deepest blue covering and a spring sun already climbing the sky and warming the world it shone on.

She sauntered slowly along the tree-lined pavements with Rosa by her side. The slightest of breezes washed over her, catching at the primrose ribbons in her hair and twisting them in and out of the soft tendrils of auburn that framed her face. With each step on this glorious day she felt herself walking away from discord and entering a place of deep calm. The night had brought counsel. Whatever the truth of Richard's relationship with Domino, it was their affair, not hers. It was immaterial, too, whether the passion he'd poured on her was genuine or simply feigned as part of his plan to punish. Certainly those moments by the lakeside, moments scorched into her consciousness, had not appeared feigned. He had seemed as fevered, as impassioned, as she.

'Curzon Street is the third turning on the right, Miss Christabel,' her maid reminded her. 'What number is Lady Blythe's?'

'Number Twelve, I believe,' she answered absently.

No, it wasn't important whether or not he'd meant the caresses he'd lavished on her—what was important was how she reacted to them. And so far her reactions had been far from laudable. Twice in the last few days she'd been overcome by desire for a man who should mean nothing to her. The old Christabel, rebellious and passionate, had risen again and exploded into the ardour of yesterday's embrace. But she was no longer the girl she'd been and instead must be true to her new life. How could she have allowed herself to behave in that fashion when she was as good as promised to another man? And such an upright man who would never give her cause for concern. *He* would never find himself locked in a fervent embrace with a lover from his past! The unlikely image made her smile.

'This day is meant for smiling, is it not?'

A male voice cleaved through her thoughts. Richard was there, in front of her, doffing his curly-brimmed beaver, grey eyes smiling and flecked by the sun's rays. As always his Hessians were polished to a blinding finish, complementing a pair of immaculate, close-fitting cream pantaloons clearly designed to display his legs to advantage. She forced herself to remember the vows of just a few minutes ago.

'It is a most beautiful morning,' she agreed, trying to keep her voice steady and her gaze neutral. Trying very hard not to think of their last encounter, their last few minutes together.

A difficult silence began to develop.

'At least we can be certain that today we won't receive a soaking,' he said mildly in an attempt to break it. 'I trust you suffered no ill effects from yesterday's downpour.'

'Indeed, no,' she responded quickly, relieved at this unexceptional topic of conversation, 'though I felt very sorry for the Wivenhoes. They had taken so much trouble over the arrangements only to see their plans ruined.'

'Forces of nature can't be gainsaid.'

His remark had been lightly meant, but it was not the most felicitous, he thought. A force of nature had destroyed the icy reserve which for years had defended Christabel, and he was responsible. He was not proud of that. In the night watches he'd argued himself into never-ending circles. It was essential that he prove her base, yet she was the woman who warmed him, excited him, entranced him. His plan was a clever strategy, he told himself, yet he felt shame in its tawdriness.

The image of Christabel's abject unhappiness

haunted him, knowing that he was its architect. It turned out that her unhappiness was his also. Yesterday by the lakeside he'd wanted to take her into his arms and kiss the tears away one by one. And he *had* taken her in his arms. More than that, he'd felt every beautiful curve of her and his heart had sung. When he'd caressed her, she'd responded as ardently as he could ever wish. He could have taken her there and then, he was sure—hotly, urgently, beneath the sheeting rain. What was that but inconstancy! He had surely proved what he'd set out to, proved that she was incapable of being true. By rights he should feel free, released from her spell, so why did he not?

In truth, in the deepest recesses of his heart, he could not believe her a false woman. She had been disloyal once, in a lifetime of loyalty. So why had she behaved so much out of character and to such devastating result? During the endless night, watching the shadows darken into unrelieved blackness, watching the dewy light of dawn creep gradually into the four corners of his room, he too had come to a decision. He had to know why she'd betrayed him. He had to hear it from her lips. If he could understand that, then he was certain that he would finally be able to lay the past to rest.

Silence stretched between them once more and again he was the one to break it.

'Are you on your way anywhere in particular? May I escort you?'

'Thank you, but I'm very close to my destination. I am to pay a morning call on Lady Blythe.'

'Then let me offer you my arm,' he said briskly,

nodding dismissal to Rosa. 'You may return home, your mistress will not need you.'

Before Christabel could protest, her maid had begun retracing her steps to Mount Street.

She did not take his arm, but stood facing him on the narrow pavement.

'That was high-handed, Lord Veryan. It is my prerogative to dismiss my maid.'

'I'm sorry if you disapprove. I have no wish to quarrel with you.'

'That would certainly be a change,' she returned acidly. His arrogance had helped her regain her poise.

'I hoped that I might speak with you alone.' His tone was level, giving no hint of what he might be feeling. And for a moment he appeared unwilling to go on, unable to find the words he needed to broach the topic burning so brightly in his mind.

'Shall we walk on?' The movement seemed to act as a release. 'After yesterday, you see, I've done some thinking,' he continued quietly. 'In fact, a good deal of thinking.'

He paused again and Christabel waited, her composure once more in danger of slipping away. What was he about to say? That he loved her after all? That after their impassioned lovemaking, he still cared deeply for her and could no longer consider marrying Domino de Silva? What traitorous thoughts, what stupid thoughts, she chastised herself.

'I wanted to apologise,' he began again. 'I wanted to tell you how deeply sorry I am for any upset I've caused since my return to London.'

'Any upset? You must know that you deliberately set out to distress me.'

'I won't deny it, but I am still sorry.'

He was looking contrite, unusually so, and she felt emboldened to question him.

'I cannot understand why you have been so intent on hurting me. Why?'

He shook his head. 'I'm afraid I can't answer with any truth. I don't know myself. When I disembarked at Southampton, I thought the past was dead and buried for me.'

'But it wasn't,' she said flatly.

'No, it wasn't.' He paused and then said with deliberation, 'I've behaved foolishly, I'm willing to admit, but if I could understand the past, then I think it would finally die for me.'

She wore a puzzled expression and he turned towards her, looking at her directly, his gaze searching and serious. 'If I knew, if I could understand, why you did what you did.'

She gave a small, uncertain laugh. 'I could echo your own words. I can't answer with any truth, I don't know myself.'

They rounded the corner of Curzon Street and, with an effort, she tried again. He deserved that at least.

'Put it down to naïvety, youthful stupidity, if you will. When you are young and untried, it's easy to be dazzled by surfaces. I was living in a world I'd never known before, a world heady with excitement.'

'But to be taken in by a creature such as Joshua,' he protested.

'You were equally taken in,' she reminded him sharply. 'He was your friend.'

'And that surely makes it worse. It makes me more stupid and you more venal.'

She flinched at the word. 'He made me feel special,' she said defensively.

'And I didn't?'

'I was just part...' and she strove to find the phrase which would adequately convey her sense of his indifference '...I was just part of the furniture of your world.'

'Never!' He felt stunned. He had been drowning in love for her and she hadn't noticed! 'How could you not know—?' He broke off, biting back the words of passion he'd been about to utter.

But Christabel, deep in that distant past, had hardly noticed. 'Joshua made me feel that I mattered to him, really mattered. I know now that I was a fool.' Her voice was barely more than a murmur and she glanced down at the delicate kid sandals she wore, as though hoping she might be absorbed into the pavement. 'In fact, I knew that almost immediately.'

'You parted very soon? I never knew.'

'Why would you? I can't imagine you wanted to hear any news from home.'

He grimaced at the truth of the observation.

'It was never going to work.' She sighed. 'Joshua was charm itself, but he was an opportunist.'

'A here and thereian?' It was doing Richard good to hear how miserably the affair had ended.

'If you like.'

'But someone who wreaked destruction wherever he went,' he pursued, his tone now one of quiet sympathy.

'I won't make him an excuse,' she said robustly. 'I caused damage to everyone who cared for me. I recognise that. But as you were happy to remind me just yesterday, I can't undo it. Any of it.'

'But you don't need to compound it.'

'What do you mean?'

'Don't make another bad choice.'

She bridled. 'And how might I do that?'

'I'm hardly the right person to give advice, but you must know that the future you're proposing is wrong—for you, for everyone. You've earned your freedom, so live free.'

'You're quite correct,' she responded tartly, 'you *are* hardly the right person.'

They had reached the door of Number Twelve and with this parting shot, she climbed the front steps. His face, as he raised his hat in farewell, was blank of all expression. He turned around and walked away down the road and Christabel was left bewildered. He'd shown himself sorry for his conduct, sorry for the distress he'd caused. He'd conversed seriously, dared to talk about the past with her, and amid the barbs of resentment there had been sympathy. It seemed that he'd had a change of heart. But why? And what did he mean, that she should live free? How dared he presume to tell her how to shape her life? It was well enough for a man to say 'live free'. He had the luxury of choice but, as a woman, she did not.

The door opened and she was ushered into Loretta Blythe's drawing room. She knew most of the faces gathered there and it was an easy matter to smile sweetly and murmur the necessary vacuous compliments. But while she observed the social niceties, her mind was roving through every detail of the recent encounter. Was it just luck that she'd met Richard where and when she had? She thought not. It was clear to her that he'd been visiting at Curzon Street. And he would have come, not to sit drinking tea with Lady Blythe and her intimates, but to see Domino. He'd been visiting Domino, the girl he intended to marry. Naturally they would have wedding plans to discuss for when his period of mourning was at an end, even now perhaps arrangements to make for the girl to visit Madron. Christabel quailed at the thought, but that was something she must grow accustomed to. It was possible that his forthcoming marriage had contributed to a new generosity of spirit, his willingness finally to forgive and forget the past. She should feel grateful for that, she supposed.

That night she slept better than she had for days. Whether it was sheer exhaustion or the fact that she and Richard were no longer enemies, she didn't know. But his interference in her life appeared to be at an end. So did his interest, another voice whispered unkindly. But that voice was swiftly squashed. She must bury the past as Richard was doing, bury it and move on to a new and different existence. That evening she'd had plenty of time for reflection, the family for once spending it by their own fireside, and by the time she'd crawled into bed, she was ready to fall into a deep and dreamless sleep. Not even Benedict's noisy return with the dawn had the power to waken her.

Benedict's mission to enjoy himself to the full had been so successful that when the next day, bleary eyed and slumped over the breakfast table, his mother reminded him that he'd agreed to escort his sisters to St James's Park, his only answer was a heartrending groan.

'We really don't need him, Mama,' Sophia chirped. She was in fine form, still bubbling from the two long dances she'd managed to extract from Sir Julian at the Seftons' party. To add to her pleasure, Christabel appeared of late to have lost her usual bloom.

'Stebbings will be with us and that will be sufficient. In fact, Bel can stay home too. She still doesn't look at all the thing,' she added solicitously.

'What nonsense. You cannot possibly go driving with just a groom for company.' Lady Harriet looked anxiously across the table at her elder daughter, 'You will go with Sophia this morning, I trust?'

'Yes, of course, Mama, it's arranged that we meet the Misses Banham at eleven.'

She couldn't remember exactly why she'd agreed to drive with two sisters she privately considered bird-witted in the extreme, but managed to finish brightly, 'It's another beautiful day for a drive in St James's.'

She went quickly upstairs after breakfast to complete her *toilette*. Sophia was already arrayed in midnight blue and she had no wish to challenge her sister's colourful palette. Instead she donned a robe of figured cream lace over an underdress of soft amber silk. Her hair was brushed into shining auburn curls and threaded through with a simple cream ribbon. She felt instinctively that this was an important day and she wanted to look her best in meeting it head on. A newly discovered sense of purpose had brought back colour to her face and the porcelain cheeks now sported a delicate glow. She looked as fresh and as young as the spring morning into which the sisters now ventured.

Sophia glared at her in annoyance. A resurgent Christabel was not what she wanted. Sir Julian had mentioned at the rout that though he must give immediate attention to business brought back from Rosings, he would be riding in the park this morning and hoped to see both herself and her sister there. Sophia was under no illusions as to whose company he really sought and had hoped to intercept him before Christabel once more entered his orbit. She was anxious to exploit their friendship of two nights ago in any way she could and her sister's radiant presence would hardly further her plan.

Once out of the house Benedict suddenly remembered a prior engagement and swiftly excused himself. He had made a casual promise to Domino to ride with her this morning and this was likely to be more entertaining than plodding dutifully after his sisters' carriage. He was also feeling a little guilty at having abandoned the girl so cavalierly at the Seftons'.

Sophia was pleased to see him go. If she could only

think of a pretext to lose Christabel too, she would be free to seek out Sir Julian and fascinate him as she knew she could. But Christabel was going to be difficult to evade; her sister had opted to take the reins, the groom by her side, and further frustration swiftly followed when they encountered the Misses Banham waiting for them at the north gate of the park. Annoyingly they had remembered the arrangement to meet and while Christabel held the horses steady, they were soon clambering noisily into the carriage. They were arrayed in matching dresses of sprig muslin and each carried a frilled parasol in a contrasting colour. They positioned themselves on either side of Sophia, like two chattering bookends. Laughing and giggling their way into the park, they exclaimed at Christabel's skill at driving the carriage through such busy thoroughfares and asserted with loud squeals their complete confidence that she could be trusted to tool them around the park without mishap. Most of what passed for conversation between them—the latest scurrilous *on dits* circulating in town—went unanswered, but since they needed no audience but each other, they were not disconcerted by their hosts' silence.

When they'd finally exhausted current gossip, they turned their attention to their companions. They complimented the Tallis sisters on their looks, their dresses, their carriage. Everything that could be praised, was praised. Unusually for Sophia she seemed not to notice their flattering remarks even when they were particularly lavish in their admiration of her blue satin. Christabel thought she seemed disturbed, almost excited, looking nervously from right to left and then behind, sometimes even hanging over the side of the carriage to gain a better view. It hardly seemed likely, but was it possible that Sophia had made an assignation with someone?

'There's Lucy,' the elder Miss Banham suddenly shrieked. 'And with Petronella!'

'Our cousins,' the younger sister explained to the startled Tallises. 'Miss Tallis, Miss Sophia, would you mind awfully if we were to get down? It's an age since we've seen our cousins and there's so much to tell!'

The Tallis sisters readily assented. They were both heartily weary of the clamour that had accompanied their drive around the park. Sophia's face became intent. She had now only to free herself from her sister's company and she could at last seek Sir Julian alone. But nothing happened to aid her plan and just a few minutes later they saw him riding towards them.

He hailed them with pleasure, reining in his horse by the carriage to greet Christabel for the first time in nearly a week. For a while he sat silently gazing at her. He had forgotten just how beautiful she was and was suffused with eagerness to make his declaration and possess her as his wife. Belatedly he remembered her sister's presence.

'Good morning, Miss Sophia. I trust you suffered no ill from your exertions at the rout?'

Sophia smiled a little sourly. Sir Julian seemed not to notice and immediately turned his attention back to Christabel.

'I was most sorry to hear of your indisposition, Miss

Tallis, but I see from your looks that you are now fully recovered. I had hoped to see you at the rout but in your absence your little sister kept me on my toes.'

'So I understand, Sir Julian.' Christabel smiled, her green eyes warm and welcoming. 'And how did your business at Rosings prosper?'

'It went well, plenty to do, you know, as always, but also plenty of time to plan.' He looked suddenly serious. 'I am most pleased to find you here this morning. There is something particular I wish to discuss with you. I wonder if you would do me the honour of walking a short way with me?'

She knew that this was the moment that had threatened for so long. Now that it had finally come, she felt calm and resigned. This was something she must do for herself and her family. It was no good thinking that a dashing white knight was going to ride to her rescue. Those were the foolish daydreams of an immature girl. This was the reality—a comfortable life with a comfortable husband. She allowed Sir Julian to hand her down from the carriage and stood waiting for him. He was about to join her when Sophia indicated that she also wished to alight. Sir Julian was surprised by this lack of tact, but, polite as always, he carefully handed the younger girl down and they began walking together over the luxuriant carpet of grass from which the dew had only just disappeared.

At that moment Benedict and Domino were manoeuvring their horses through the busy West End traffic. Pedlars, carts, every kind of carriage thronged the roads leading to St James's and all their attention was taken up with gaining a safe passage through the maelstrom of noise and bustle. Twenty long minutes later they finally reached the safety of the park and trotted smartly through its eastern entrance. Benedict glanced briefly at his companion. He was not the most acute observer, but she seemed unusually subdued. At first he had put it down to the late nights and this morning's early rising, but as they rode, he became increasingly aware of tension within the slight figure alongside him. After a few abortive attempts at conversation he gave up talking and they rode in silence.

The air was still and cool and shafts of sunlight filtered through the newly leafing trees overhead. As they pushed their way further into this small island of nature, Domino decided to make her confession. Her frustration at Richard's continued blindness had been replaced at the rout party by a new fascination. In that hot, enclosed little room she had been captivated by the ebb and flow of changing fortunes, the excitement of placing her stake, the rush of adrenaline as the cards sped from the faro box and the thrill of delight when the pile of rouleaus in front of her began to grow.

Not so delighted, though, when they began to disappear. But then Lord Moncaster had come to her rescue, had advanced her some of his own rouleaus for no more payment than her handkerchief. In the thrill of the game it had seemed perfectly normal for her to hand over this small personal possession. But the sly looks the other players exchanged alerted her to the fact that his lordship's offer was hardly usual. He'd behaved impeccably, though, even advancing more tokens without demanding anything further from her. At least for the moment. He'd said that he would think of some way she could repay him, but that she wasn't to worry her pretty head. He was a rich man, a few losses meant nothing to him. At these last comments Domino's immediate neighbour, apparently so correct and punctilious, had smirked knowingly. She caught both his grimace and Leo Moncaster's answering smile and a vague discomfort became a pressing anxiety to leave.

'What do you know of Lord Moncaster?' she asked suddenly.

Benedict looked at her cautiously, trying to gauge how much he should say. 'Not a lot,' was his unhelpful reply.

He saw her biting her lip and relented a little, 'Why do you ask?'

'Only that I'm interested in the people I met at the Seftons'. I understand it was Lord Moncaster who held the faro bank.'

'He often does. He's a very rich man.'

'Is he married?'

Where was this leading? thought Benedict. 'No, not married.'

'Yet he's quite old.'

'He's not that old and he doesn't exactly lead the kind of life that goes with being married,' he added bravely.

'What kind of life?' came the inevitable question.

'Pretty rackety.' Better to be brutal to be kind if the girl had any idea of snaring Moncaster.

'Benedict, I lost money to him,' she disclosed in a sudden rush of words.

'We all lost money to him.'

'I mean, I lost more—after you left.'

'You couldn't have lost much more. You only had enough rouleaus left for one more stake.'

'I borrowed more.'

'Borrowed? From him?' He whistled under his breath.

'It was not a good idea?'

'Definitely not. What did you pledge?'

'Pledge?'

'What did he ask for?' Benedict was getting seriously alarmed.

'My handkerchief, first, but then he gave me rouleaus for free.'

'He never gives anything for free.'

'That's what I'm thinking now,' she said miserably. 'What will he do, do you think?'

Benedict hardly liked to put his thoughts into words. The vague feelings of guilt that had previously visited him found vent in scolding.

'Whatever made you do such an idiotic thing?'

'I didn't realise it was wrong until later. You were not there to advise me,' she accused him.

'It shouldn't be me advising you. It should be your aunt. You must tell her what you've done and she must repay Lord Moncaster his debt.'

'I can't do that. She will be so angry with me and despatch me immediately to Spain.'

'I wouldn't blame her. You're too much of a

responsibility. Anyway, you're leaving for Spain at the end of the Season, so why not now?'

'I have my reasons,' she said gravely, the image of Richard hovering close. Then, following her train of thought, she asked in a falsely bright voice, 'Is Miss Tallis riding here today?'

'She's out driving with my sister. I'm supposed to be with them, but Sophia's screeching sends me insane. I thought you were the better bet!' He grinned.

She ignored the witticism. 'Is she here right now? Perhaps we should go and find her.'

'We won't have to look too far.' He raised his arm to point ahead. 'She's there, just to the right of that clump of trees.'

They reined in their horses. A carriage had been drawn up beneath the trees and to one side they saw Sir Julian Edgerton talking animatedly to Christabel. He had her hand raised to his lips and then, as they watched, slipped what looked like a ring on her finger.

'Perhaps not the right time to interrupt,' Benedict commented drily.

Domino felt considerable surprise, but also a warm pleasure. If Christabel were pledged to another man, it might mean Richard would look more kindly on her. 'They are to be married?'

'My mother's been waiting an age for this—Bel must have finally decided to put the man out of his misery.'

'It's a very happy day, then. Let's go and congratulate them.'

'I don't think I will right now,' he prevaricated. 'Just look at Sophia!'

They looked across from the betrothed couple and saw a figure in bright blue satin some distance from the carriage, standing rigidly with averted head.

'Like I said, perhaps not the best time to interrupt.' He gave a mischievous smile. 'Come on, let's have a gallop. No one's around to tell tales.'

'I must not, Benedict. I'm already in trouble for that.'

He set himself to persuade his companion that a gallop was just the thing to blow away her megrims when a large black stallion cut across their path and Richard Veryan was hailing them with a smile.

'Good morning to you both. I'm very glad to see you, Domino, though I must admit I didn't expect to meet you so early in the morning.'

'It's such a beautiful day that I couldn't lie abed. Did you particularly want to see me, Richard?' Her tone was eager, almost breathless.

'I was worried that I might miss you, knowing what a crowded social calendar you have,' he teased. 'I wanted to tell you that I'm leaving for Cornwall very shortly.'

'Cornwall? But why now?' Her dismay rang out clearly.

'Why not now?' he said bracingly. 'I've tarried too long in London—my mother deserves better. I should be at her side, don't you think?'

'Yes', she stuttered, 'of course, but it seems a sudden decision.'

'Hardly sudden. It's taken time to organise my

affairs, but everything is now in a fair way to being settled. There's no need for me to remain in London any longer.'

Benedict saw her face and knew instantly that his supposition over Moncaster was false. But this relationship didn't look much more promising. There was an awkward silence and he felt it incumbent to oil the social wheels.

'I'll be returning to Cornwall myself pretty soon, Rick. We must make sure to ride out together—if you can spare the time.'

The other man smiled his assent. 'There's always time for a decent gallop.'

Domino had been following her own thoughts and blurted out abruptly, 'But won't you stay for the Vauxhall spectacle, Richard? It's only a few days away.'

'I think not, but you're sure to enjoy yourself. I remember seeing the fireworks for the first time when I was about your age and they were truly spectacular.'

Domino dug her nails into her hands and screamed inwardly. Wanting to hit out, she said as casually as she could, 'If you're leaving so soon, you'd better make haste to congratulate Miss Tallis. She is close by, I believe.'

Benedict looked at her with surprise, wondering what her game was. Not for the first time he felt completely out of his depth in trying to fathom females.

'Congratulate Miss Tallis?' Richard was questioning.

'We've just seen her with Sir Julian Edgerton in a most romantic situation, haven't we, Benedict?' Her companion looked suitably revolted. 'Benedict tells me that the betrothal between Sir Julian and his sister is something the whole family has been expecting, and it looks as though today it's finally happened,' she added helpfully.

Richard was far too self-controlled to betray his feelings, but his face grew austere and the light went out of the smiling grey eyes.

'I had better do as you suggest, then, and seek Miss Tallis out.'

He wheeled his horse sharply around and rode away. His face might be an impassive mask, but inside he was incandescent. She was going to marry the man! How could she even consider it? Just a few days ago she had kissed him, caressed *him*, laid herself open to *his* lovemaking. The thought almost tore the breath from his body. Only yesterday in Curzon Street he'd felt certain that he could leave behind the old history at last. He'd been shocked to discover that Christabel had never known the depths of his youthful love and begun to understand just how easy it had been for Joshua to mislead her. The familiar, nagging hurt hadn't disappeared completely, but he'd felt better able to contemplate the past with some serenity. Now, though, the wound had opened again and laceratingly. Yet another man was to smile into those startling emerald eyes, to run his hands over that beautiful, lithe body, to laugh and tease and fun with her. No, *that* he wouldn't do. Sir Julian Edgerton was not a man made for fun. Nor was he a man made for love, not the kind that she needed at least. If *he* were still in love with her... But he wasn't, was he? Her betrayal might have been an act of youthful folly, but she had damaged him too badly for him to trust her again. And now she was to marry this dull do-gooder and be lost to him for ever. How could she? The question thrummed blindly through every particle of his flesh.

Behind a veil of tears, Domino watched his figure as it grew slowly smaller in the distance. Riding alongside, Benedict maintained a discreet silence. He trusted that he would not be called upon to become a confidant and waited for her to recover herself. With a great effort, she turned to him with a show of enthusiasm.

'That was exciting, wasn't it, but can we return to my problem? I need to win back the money that I lost to Lord Moncaster. Will you help me do that?'

'You want me to win it?'

'Of course not, I want to win it. It's my debt. But I need you to introduce me to a place where I can do that.'

'You're asking me to take you to a gambling den?'

'Yes.'

'I won't,' he said flatly.

'Why not? If you're scared we might be recognised, I could go in disguise.'

'It gets worse.'

'No, it doesn't, I can disguise myself very well as a boy and go as your friend.'

He looked at her slim figure appraisingly. 'I'm sure you can, but I'm not taking you to any gaming hell.'

'I don't want to go to a hell, just a place where I can win back the money.'

'That's a gaming hell.'

'Please, Benedict.'

'No, no and definitely no.'

'Then you won't help me.'

'I've told you what to do. Go to your aunt and confess. The worst she can do is to pack you off to Spain. Would that matter so much now?'

She flushed at the implication, but knew that he was right. She supposed that she must find the right opportunity to tell Lady Blythe what had happened. But then her aunt would be sure to tell her Spanish relatives of her disgrace and from the moment she arrived in Madrid, they would be watching her every movement. She wished she'd never left Argentina.

In the distance Richard had ridden up to the small group standing beneath the trees. Sophia had joined her sister and Sir Julian near the carriage, as anxious now to leave as she had been earlier to find him. She scowled even more ferociously as she recognised the man seated astride the glossy black horse picking its way towards them.

Richard Veryan slid from the saddle as Christabel turned. He came forward and bowed just a little too deeply.

'I understand from your brother that felicitations are in order.' His voice was harsh, slightly disdainful. 'May I take the opportunity, Miss Tallis, to congratulate you and Sir Julian, on your forthcoming marriage,' and here he bowed extravagantly towards the other man. 'I wish you both all the happiness you are capable of.'

Christabel flushed, knowing the double edge of those words, but executed a dignified bow in response. Her fiancé smiled happily and without guile.

'Thank you, Lord Veryan. Your good wishes are most welcome. I consider myself to be blessed indeed to have won this remarkable lady for my future wife, a gift beyond anything I deserve.'

Richard's expression was sardonic. 'You must not sell yourself short, Sir Julian. I'm sure Miss Tallis would be the first to agree that your honesty and loyalty are qualities to aspire to.'

Sir Julian blinked at this sentiment, but his smile broadened even further. He felt supremely happy and nothing was going to spoil this wonderful day for him. Sophia stood close by, an interested observer. Richard's comments appeared to be coming from between gritted teeth and offered a small hope. She might yet salvage something from the plans that had gone so badly awry.

Pinning on her most enticing smile, she turned to the happy lover. 'I believe, Sir Julian, that you were involved in plans for the canal which has been constructed to feed the lake. I would love to see it and understand exactly how it works. Would you be good enough to take me?'

If Sir Julian felt this was a strange request coming at the very moment of his betrothal and from a girl who had hitherto not shown the slightest interest in engineering, he was far too polite to show it. Willing to do anything for anybody on this glorious morning, particularly a close relative of his beloved, he immediately agreed.

'It appears we must leave you, sir,' and he bowed his farewell. 'Thank you again for your good wishes.'

He began to walk towards the Chinese bridge with Sophia in tow, already beginning a complicated discourse on his understanding of the water-management system. Equally bewildered by her sister's request, Christabel turned to follow them, but was stopped in her tracks by Richard roughly grabbing her arm. He hardly waited for the others to be out of earshot before grinding out, 'You can't really mean to marry that man!'

'I beg your pardon!' She was genuinely shocked.

'I think you understand me, but, just in case, I was questioning your sanity in agreeing to marry Julian Edgerton.'

'How dare you presume to question whom I marry!'

'I dare to presume because I seem to know you better than you know yourself. But even you must be aware of how unsuited you are to each other.'

The red cascade of curls trembled with anger. 'You are insulting, sir!'

'I would call it honest rather than insulting, but it's better to be insulting than concur in this charade.'

'You are misinformed, my lord. There is no charade. Sir Julian and I have known each other for many months and have agreed that we will suit admirably.'

She wondered why she was defending her choice of husband to Richard of all men but she felt compelled to continue and found herself declaring, 'Sir Julian is a man of the highest honour and integrity.'

'I'm sure he is. He's also a gudgeon if he thinks he can control you.'

'No man controls me and Sir Julian is far too wise to wish to do so.'

'But not wise enough to refrain from marrying you,' he retaliated.

She glared furiously at the tall, elegant figure in front of her and responded in a voice crackling with ice, 'This is mere ranting and I will listen no more. I bid you good day, sir.'

Her cream skirts swished to one side as she made to walk away. But Richard would not concede. Ignoring her cold fury and the summary nature of his dismissal, he called out, 'If you value his happiness as much as your own, don't do it.'

She retraced her steps and stood looking directly up into his eyes, now dark and glittering.

'If we are to give each other marital advice, I would suggest that wedding a child fresh from the nursery is unlikely to guarantee success. I, at least, intend to marry a man of my own age and one I have known for many months.'

Brushing aside his supposed alliance with Domino, he coldly countered her logic. 'But how much of a guarantee is that? You once agreed to marry another man of your own age and one you had known a *very* long time, but that alliance wasn't too permanent, was it?'

He smiled derisively at her. 'At the moment Sir Julian is living in his own little paradise, but how long do you give him? He would be well advised to grow steel armour in the very near future, say three weeks from his wedding day.'

'You have been as offensive as it is possible to be, Lord Veryan, but nothing you say can touch our happiness.'

He grimaced. 'How charming! And how strange that there was a day when I felt that too. I looked deep into your green eyes, touched your luminous skin, tangled my hands in that wild red hair—and what a premonition that was—and believed that I was as happy as it was possible to be, that nothing could ever touch that happiness. How wrongly can a man judge!'

Christabel swallowed hard. 'Yesterday you assured me that you considered the past dead. Can you not accept that we made a mistake and forget?'

'*You* made a mistake, Miss Tallis. For myself, the past is nothing. But I find it difficult to forget those others for whom the pain still lives. But then you never cared too much about them—friends, parents, all could be sacrificed. All that mattered was that you had your desire, a desire, it seems, which died almost as soon as it flickered into life.'

He was being unjust, deliberately stoking his anger against her, but he found himself powerless to stop.

'You are unfair to accuse me of not caring for the pain I caused. You must know otherwise. It has been an open wound for all these years.' Her voice faltered and unshed tears stung her eyelids. She steadied herself and tried for a calm she was far from feeling.

'In my youth I made a mistaken attachment—I have

freely confessed it—and I have paid for that mistake. If you once cared anything for me, can you not find it in your heart, if not to wish me well, at least not to wish me ill.'

For a moment he felt an overpowering weariness. Had he not made the decision just hours ago to put this anguish behind him? So why was he continuing to haunt this woman, to pile hurt upon hurt? She saw the trouble in his shadowed eyes and the frown that appeared between the dark brows and pushed her advantage.

'Because *our* betrothal did not succeed, that is no reason to suppose that my marriage to another will not.'

'If so, that other will need to be a very different man from the one you have chosen. He will need to be a man who matches you in strength of character and depth of feeling. For all his honour and integrity, Sir Julian is not that man.'

He spoke the words slowly and deliberately, his fierce gaze searching, seeking, tugging at her soul. For a moment she forgot they were antagonists engaged in cruel conflict and flamed beneath his regard. For what seemed an age they devoured each other with their eyes, neither speaking. Then recovering a frigid poise, she snapped back her response.

'And who would you suggest, Lord Veryan? Where is this model of manhood I must aspire to? Surely not yourself?'

'I would never again willingly endure such an ordeal.' His tone held a bitter intensity. 'You say *you* have suffered. I hope so indeed, for my years have been every bit as painful.'

His voice sliced through her skin like a scalpel. She could only murmur, 'I know nothing of your life in Argentina, but I cannot imagine it was devoid of all pleasure.'

'Argentina?' he questioned bleakly. 'I refer not to life there, but to the constant pain of living with betrayal.' And then in a searing aside, 'Naturally you would know nothing of that.'

'On the contrary, I am no stranger to betrayal,' she said in a low voice, 'though you would judge it well deserved.'

She found herself moving towards him, drawn by the warmth of his body and a strange need to offer comfort. She resisted the urge to take his hand but could not stop herself pleading, 'I thought we had agreed, Richard, to put injuries aside. I wish you well in the alliance you are doubtless about to make. Can you not wish the same for me?'

His eyes found hers and for an instant there was an answering warmth. The taut lines of his face relaxed and his mouth softened in the way she remembered so well, a prelude to his kiss. She waited, hardly daring to breathe. But then his whole body visibly tightened and his face resumed its hardened expression. When he spoke, it was clear that anger had reasserted itself.

'My relationship with Miss de Silva has nothing to say in the matter,' he ground out. 'The truth remains that the man you propose to marry is not worthy of you.'

She took a step back as though he had slapped her

in the face, and observing her shock, his anger flared again. 'Good grief, can you not see what a travesty this marriage is? Have we suffered so much for so little?!'

His wrath was answered by a newly awakened fury in her. 'Allow me to tell you, sir, that I find your sentiments abhorrent and your conduct highly improper.'

They stood facing each other so close they could taste one another's breath. Both had been shaken by the intensity of their anger. Both had felt the familiar throb of desire, which neither could acknowledge. Christabel drew her slim figure erect and confronted him with eyes which glinted like green glass.

'I have borne much in this interview, sir, but will not do so again.' Her voice was brittle with feeling. 'Leave me now, please, and ensure that you never again approach me.'

His face expressionless, Richard turned on his heels and scooped up the reins of his mount grazing quietly nearby. Without a backward glance, he flung himself into the saddle and dug his heels into the flanks of the startled beast. Christabel remained where she stood as the horse bounded forwards, her face equally impassive, but her heart beating tumultuously.

Sir Julian, having by this time exhausted his knowledge of canal engineering, was in time to see Richard ride furiously away. Clearly there had been an altercation.

'Let us make haste, Miss Sophia,' he said in a worried tone, 'I fear all may not be well with your sister. That man—Lord Veryan—appeared extremely angry and I am concerned that she may have suffered some mischief from him.'

'That man has known Christabel all her life, Sir Julian, and is hardly like to prove a threat. In fact, he knows her so well...' and here Sophia produced her trump card with a fitting display of naïve innocence '...that they were once promised to each other.'

'Betrothed?' Sir Julian looked bewildered. 'How is this?'

'Oh, I do beg your pardon. You didn't know? How stupid of me. I assumed that Christabel would have told you or that you would have heard mention of it—it was the town's biggest *on dit* for many weeks. But perhaps you were away from London at the time?'

'What happened exactly?' he asked weakly.

Sophia was admirably succinct. 'She jilted him three weeks before the wedding.'

'Good gracious,' was all he could utter before Christabel joined them. He managed to smile solicitously down at the lovely face, trying to blot out Sophia's last words.

'My dear...' he patted her hand ineffectually '...I do hope all is well.'

Still reeling from the encounter with Richard, she withdrew her hand with a little shrug of impatience. 'Naturally, Sir Julian. What could be wrong?'

'Then shall we continue our stroll in the park? The weather looks as though it will hold for some hours.'

His face was hopeful, but she longed for solitude and the latter won. 'Will you forgive me if I cut our walk a little short today? There are things awaiting my attention at home.' It was a feeble excuse, but it would have to do.

'Sophia, are you coming?' Christabel was already climbing into the waiting carriage.

Her sister was equally quick with her response. She would return to Mount Street on foot and Sir Julian would escort her. 'For I don't doubt that he could do with some company,' she said repressively.

Christabel stared hard at her sister, but the bland face gave nothing away. Beside her Sir Julian stood looking dazed, even shocked. She knew that she could no longer bear to be in his company. Richard's strictures rang ceaselessly in her ears and she had to get away. She gave a sign to Stebbings that she wished him to take the reins and in a moment the carriage had jolted forwards.

The journey to Mount Street was accomplished in less than a quarter of an hour, but she hardly noticed. She should be used to Richard's animosity by now. From the moment they'd literally bumped into one another in Hyde Park, it had been plain there was to be no truce between them. Yesterday's interlude was simply a pause in hostilities. His conduct had swung between indifference, discourtesy, even aggression, intermingled with moments of rekindled desire. But whatever extremes he'd loosed upon her, they seemed always to proceed from a deep-seated antagonism, a fierce desire to make her regret what she'd done.

Yet even when she was thinking the worst of him, she'd sensed a kindness that he couldn't quite suppress, some feeling for her from the past that he couldn't quite dismiss. And today he'd confessed that she had hurt him badly. That must mean that he'd loved her once, not as a sop to parental wishes, nor as a trophy, but deeply and heartfelt. If that were true, she had judged him very wrongly. If that were true, it would explain why he could not overcome his anger, why he was still her enemy.

And now his love was no more: he'd made that plain. He didn't want her for himself, but he had no intention of letting her go quietly into a new life. He was seeking to destroy even that solace. Until this morning she had never truly grasped the power of his ill will. This morning he'd made a mockery of her wish to consign the past to oblivion. It would always be with her. Despite the warmth of the sun that flooded through the open carriage, the thought made her hands shake and her teeth start to chatter as though she suffered a severe chill.

At home she climbed to her room with a bone-weariness, her feet dragging from stair to stair. Once in the safety of her chamber, she flung herself on the bed and lay there in a state of utter fatigue. The day's events—Richard, Julian, even Sophia—rushed past her unseeing eyes in a chaotic blur. Even Sophia! Her sister's behaviour was not the least odd thing that had happened. She wondered what ailed the younger woman.

An hour later the front door slammed and purposeful steps sounded outside her room. Sophia jerked her head around the door, looking unbecomingly flushed, but with a smug expression on her face.

'I'm sure you'll be pleased to know that I more than compensated for your absence,' she taunted.

Christabel stared at her uncomprehendingly. Her head had begun to ache. 'What are you talking about, Sophia?'

'I'm talking about your fiancé. Well, I presume he still *is* your fiancé. I've just returned with Sir Julian and it's clear to me that he's deeply upset by your behaviour. I've tried to smooth things over but I can't be sure how successful I've been.'

Christabel sat up swiftly, her indignation banishing the incipient headache.

'I don't understand what right you think you have to speak to me in this fashion or indeed to discuss me with Sir Julian, but be very sure that I have given you none.'

Sophia remained in the doorway, her arms crossed in defiance. 'I know nothing about rights,' she declared truthfully, 'and of course I don't possess your rather obvious enticements, but I think I know a little better how to treat a man. And it's not with the contempt you deal out.'

'What nonsense you talk.'

She laid her weary head back on the pillow once more. There was a grain of truth in Sophia's pronouncement, but only a grain. And why was her sister so exercised on Sir Julian's behalf?

'Contempt!' Sophia reiterated ringingly. 'You become engaged to an honourable man and immediately begin consorting with your old lover. You accept Sir Julian's ring and then refuse to spend time with him.'

Christabel no longer seemed to be listening, but this did not deter her sister. Sophia was becoming ever more agitated, her face working furiously.

'How do you think that makes him feel?' she harangued, taking angry strides into the room and pointing dramatically at her guilty sister. 'You don't deserve his love!'

'And you do?' Christabel suddenly understood the drift of her sister's conversation. It made sense of her earlier conduct. She had evidently been on the look-out for Sir Julian, hoping to meet him alone in the park.

'More than you at any rate,' Sophia snapped back. '*I'm* not made of ice!'

And with that she banged the bedroom door behind her, leaving Christabel to wrestle with this new and unwelcome development.

Chapter Six

Sir Julian had made elaborate preparations for an evening's visit to Vauxhall. It was not a venue he would ordinarily have patronised—the Gardens had a reputation for encouraging wanton behaviour—but the Prince Regent himself was to sponsor a fête there and nothing else had been talked of among the *ton* for days but the magnificent firework display to be mounted in his honour. So it was that Sir Julian planned with great care every detail of the evening's entertainment. His carriage was to call at Mount Street at seven o'clock and take up Christabel and her siblings. Lady Harriet had cried off at the last moment, citing the burden of preparations for Sophia's ball. The party would drive to Westminster Pier and from there take a boat over the Thames, approaching the Gardens by the water entrance. Sir Julian had already hired one of the hundred supper boxes available in the central amphitheatre and looked forward to serving his guests the wafer-thin ham for which Vauxhall was famous, washed down with the very best champagne. A fifty-strong orchestra would entertain them throughout the meal, but their box was sited far enough away for conversation not to be unduly disturbed. Reserved places at the fireworks arena were also secured. Nothing had been left to chance; he was determined to make the evening a fitting celebration of his recent engagement.

To his dismay the expedition got off to an uncomfortable start. Christabel was already waiting in the hall when he arrived at Mount Street, looking voluptuous in a low-cut silk robe of the deepest gold worn over a flimsy underslip of ivory gauze. He had never before seen her dressed so seductively and after his initial surprise, felt himself falling ever deeper under her spell, the perplexities of their last encounter well and truly forgotten. His enchantment, though, was soon fractured by the sounds of a stormy dispute above.

'You foolish boy, look what you've done!'

It was Sophia, thumping down the main staircase in an unladylike fury. Hardly able to speak, she glared at the two of them patiently waiting and pointed a trembling finger at the hem of her dress.

'Do you see that? It's torn beyond repair! And all because he can't keep his clumsy feet to himself. He's not content to stand all over my dress, oh, no, he has to tear it to shreds.'

'If you hadn't got into such a temper and pulled against my foot, it would never have torn.' Benedict arrived down the stairs two at a time, looking as cross as his sister.

'I didn't pull it, idiot. I was trying to free it. Why did you stand on it in the first place?'

'Why does the sun shine? Why do you wear ridiculous frocks? There's no answer.'

She was just about to loose another tirade at him when Christabel intervened, 'You could change into your lilac silk, Sophia. It will be perfect for the Gardens and then tomorrow you can ask your woman to restitch the hem.'

'How can she mend such a huge tear? And why should I wear the lilac? It's completely insipid and I hate it. I shan't go to Vauxhall and it will be your fault.' She rounded angrily on her brother.

Sir Julian, ever more aware of the advancing hour, thought it time to try his own hand at peacemaking. 'Miss Sophia, you have a wardrobe of beautiful dresses from which to choose. Please do so and favour us with your company this evening.'

Benedict snorted derisively, but his sister allowed herself a glimmer of a smile in Julian's direction before she retraced her steps to the bedroom. Sophia's infatuation was still in place, Christabel noted. Her sister's passions had a tendency to disappear almost as quickly as they erupted and she hoped that this would prove to be the case with Julian. If she made sure that Sophia knew their engagement to be happy and secure, she was hopeful that her sister would shortly transfer her affections elsewhere.

* * *

They had been late for the boat and Sir Julian had had to pay a hefty waiting charge, but was relieved simply to have got all of them to the Gardens. Sophia and Benedict kept up a low-level sniping for most of the journey but Christabel blocked her ears to their wrangling. She was determined to make the evening a success, to make amends for her earlier dudgeon and show Julian that she appreciated the considerable thought he'd expended on the evening. And she was enjoying herself. She had never before visited Vauxhall, even though it was a popular pleasure haunt of the *ton* between April and June, and when they stepped from the boat and began to make their way along the Grand Walk, she was entranced. Tree-lined promenades and gravelled pathways led off from the main route and everywhere fountains, statues and even artificial ruins dotted the landscape. The evening light had by this time darkened and they walked in a fairyland of thousands of lanterns hanging in festoons from the trees and between the cast-iron pillars of the vaulted colonnade which ran alongside the Grand Walk.

'What a magical place!' she breathed, her eyes in the shadowy light deep pools of turquoise, 'and how good of you to think of this excursion.'

Sir Julian, suffused with happiness, smiled benignly and tucked her arm tightly into his. Benedict had disappeared almost as soon as they'd reached dry land, and although Sophia maintained a forbidding frown, a degree of peace was restored. Lavish praise of a particularly fetching loo mask that she had bought for the occasion mollified her sufficiently to consent to explore the Gardens with her sister and future brother-in-law.

For an hour or so the three of them strolled along the walkways, listening to the bands of Pandean minstrels which played on platforms scattered around the Gardens. Even Sophia was intrigued at some of the innovations that had been placed to interest visitors, marvelling for some time at the mechanical Cascade which played endlessly at the centre of the South Walk, another stately avenue spanned by three triumphal arches. Eventually they made their way to the two central semi-circles around which supper boxes provided places to eat, to listen to the orchestra or simply to watch the strolling crowds.

Sir Julian, all attention, made his two guests comfortable. A shawl here, a cushion there, and a hovering waiter despatched to fetch the supper he had previously ordered. Dozens of waiters ran from box to box, bringing platters of chicken or ham with salads for the guests to mix themselves and bowls for them to brew their own very potent arrack-punch. This was already having some effect in a few of the supper boxes, their inhabitants masked and feeling free to conduct themselves with abandon. The masqueraders were laughing immoderately at their own jokes or cavorting to the music which played nearby. A few of the women were already looking a little dishevelled. Their own box was slightly set back from the majority and Sir Julian felt relieved that the ladies under his charge would not be incommoded by such improper behaviour.

'What curious murals!' Christabel pointed to the rear wall, hazily illuminated by the globe of light hanging from the roof and covered with paintings.

'I believe they were done by a Francis Hayman in the last century,' Sir Julian intoned, 'but they have to be constantly repaired because so many people examine them a little too closely!'

'I do believe you've been researching this information for us,' she teased.

He smiled and admitted as much while Sophia scowled and ostentatiously yawned with boredom. It was fortunate that a distraction soon materialised in the form of supper and with it Benedict, who appeared out of nowhere to eat his share. He didn't stay long, however. As soon as the chicken and ham had been despatched he excused himself with the words that he thought he might try a little jaunt around the dance floor. At this Sophia scowled even more ferociously and began pointedly to tap her feet. Christabel was by now wholly out of patience with her sister though she knew well the cause of her bad temper.

But Sir Julian, blissfully ignorant of the tension, offered his arm to the younger girl, saying genially, 'I think it must be time for us to repeat our efforts of the other evening, Miss Sophia—that is, if your sister has no objection.'

Christabel was only too pleased to be left in peace. There was now quite a crowd of people dancing to the infectious music of the orchestra and she enjoyed watching them twirling and spinning beneath the trees, the lanterns dusting the moving figures with sprinkles of light. A carnival spirit was abroad, many of the dancers dressed in full disguise. She thought she saw Domino and her aunt among the crowd of harlequins, cavaliers, jesters and shepherdesses. She could have been mistaken, but it was possible that Lady Blythe had been persuaded after all to bring her charge to this den of iniquity. If so, it was strange that Richard was not with them. She fell to wondering why she and Richard had never visited Vauxhall when they were a betrothed couple. But those had been awkward weeks in London when her decision to marry had begun to seem hideously wrong. The growing influence of Joshua had seen to that. He, of course, would have leapt at the chance of meeting her at Vauxhall. Masked and disguised, it would have been a perfect opportunity for the kind of underhand lovemaking he was so good at. But Richard would have shrunk from it. He was too upright, too conscious of what was deemed proper conduct. Or had been, she amended. The Richard she'd encountered in the past few weeks was anything but proper. He was unpredictable and passionate and his tirade in the park just a few days ago had gone well beyond the bounds of correctness. Had he really changed so much and Argentina made him literally into a new man? Or had that streak of dissent, of recklessness, of fervour, always been there just waiting to be lit? Six years ago she had chosen not to apply the flame, but instead had turned away to Joshua. It was a sobering thought.

'All alone, sweetheart?'

She looked up, startled. A man dressed in a scarlet domino had suddenly appeared at her side. She had been so deep in thought that he must have leapt over the wooden barrier without her hearing a thing.

'We can't have that, can we, not on a night made for merrymaking?'

The man let out a harsh guffaw and breathed fumes in her face. Repulsed, she rose from her seat, thinking to escape down the staircase at the side of the box, but he was too quick for her. Grabbing her arm, he pulled her close and began to rub his face against her cheek. With a mighty wrench she snatched herself away and desperately made for the stairs, but her flimsy slipper caught in the table leg and he was on her again almost immediately. His arms encircled her waist and dragged her into a clumsy embrace. She shrank back against the wall of the box as his fleshy mouth hovered over her lips. Then a hand alighted on the man's shoulder and jerked him roughly backwards. He let go in surprise and turned to face the cause of this intrusion. Dark grey eyes gleamed behind a black velvet mask and a steely voice commanded him to leave immediately. Christabel knew the voice and the figure instantly.

'Who d'you think you are to tell me what to do?' the man in scarlet protested.

The grim figure stood tensed. 'You'll find out soon enough unless you leave now.'

The man put up his arms in readiness for a brawl. Dreading the scene to come, she looked wildly around for Sir Julian and her sister. Even Benedict might be of use in this situation. Then quite suddenly it was over. The intruder had been picked up bodily and tossed over the barrier he had earlier jumped. At the first sounds of the quarrel people had begun to emerge from the neighbouring supper boxes to see what was amiss and now a small crowd gathered around the prostrate man. Those revellers who had imbibed most seemed to think the whole thing a drama put on for their entertainment and were loud in their praise of the acting. But the more sober were plainly concerned with this breach of the peace and began to mutter ominously amongst themselves.

In response the black-masked figure grabbed Christabel's hand and propelled her swiftly down the stairs and out of the box. He carved a ruthless path for them through the now restive crowd, always holding to her tightly, and a few minutes later she found herself running with him up the Dark Walk. No lanterns hung here and the only light was that of a crescent moon filtered through the rags of lowering clouds. The air was heavy with the scent of lilacs now in full bloom, their abundant foliage casting inky shadows on the gravelled pathway. She could hardly see a foot in front of her, but her rescuer's firm hand kept her from stumbling. The crowds gradually dwindled and the sounds of music faded into the distance. Breathless, they came to a halt outside a small rustic shelter cleverly hidden within a clearing in the mass of surrounding trees. It was invisible, except to those standing immediately outside. Richard pulled her into its sanctuary, hardly allowing her to catch her breath before he began to berate her.

'Where the hell is your fiancé?' he uttered explosively.

She bridled immediately. 'How dare you use such language in my presence?'

He ran his hand through his already dishevelled hair and attempted to gain control of his rage.

'I apologise for my intemperate speech, but I repeat— where is your supposed fiancé?'

'He is not supposed, he *is* my fiancé,' she retorted icily.

'Then why isn't he taking care of you?'

'Sir Julian has taken every care of me. He was absent for a short time only while he danced with my sister.'

'And while he placates that bad-tempered little vixen, he leaves you exposed to the attentions of any rake on the cut.'

'You exaggerate. The man was a nuisance, no more.'

There was silence while they glared furiously at each other. Then in a challenging voice she said, 'I thought I'd made it clear that I never wished to speak to you again.'

'And I'm most happy to concur, but what am I to do when I see a woman, any woman, menaced by a scoundrel?'

'You make too much of the incident—there was no cause to intervene.'

'Really? Then why were you cowering in fear?'

'I was not cowering, nor did I wish to become embroiled in an unseemly wrangle. Did you have to be quite so brutal?'

'Would you have preferred to be ravished?'

'That was hardly likely. The man was clearly drunk.'

'But sober enough to see the prize he was winning.'

She said nothing and again a long, tense silence filled the air between them. The moment of danger had passed and they were both acutely aware of their isolation from the crowd and their proximity to one another. He could not resist looking at her, his gaze growing rapt as the seconds passed. He longed to unpin her curls and bring the burnished curtain cascading down. The sensuality she radiated was engulfing him and the soft contours of her body seemed to cry out for his touch. Exerting all his self-control, he expunged the expression from his face and when he spoke his voice was heavy with irony.

'Evidently I misjudged the situation. The man was no threat to you and I have done him ill. I'll leave you to convey my apologies to our unfortunate friend,' and he gestured back the way they had come. 'You'll doubtless make a better job of it than I.'

She followed the direction of his hand and looked quickly behind her. 'Has he come after us?'

He shook his head. 'There's no one there.' He knew he should leave it at that and walk away, but his frustration impelled him to carry on the fight.

'You can relax, you're quite safe,' he jeered, 'but then you always have been with me, haven't you? A little too safe.'

He looked down at her with a cynical smile. 'For

someone who despises the familiar, it's strange how little you enjoy excitement when it comes knocking!'

The energy drained from her. It wasn't enough that she'd been forced to brave the unwanted attentions of a stranger; now she must rekindle her strength for yet another battle with Richard. The knowledge caused her to shiver in the warm night air.

He saw and said tauntingly, 'Perhaps you should have worn just a little more this evening. Or was this a special treat for Sir Julian?'

She ignored the gibe, but a growing anger rippled through her body.

'Or perhaps,' he continued to harass, 'this is just the old Christabel resurfacing, the one that likes to give everyone a special treat!'

The blood whipped her cheeks pink and she turned savagely towards him, her hand raised. She hardly knew what she was doing. This was more than justified fury; all her suppressed desire fuelled the flight of her hand. He caught her arm mid-air and pulled her towards himself.

'What happened to the ice maiden?' he goaded, his eyes dark and brooding.

Then his hands were in her hair, tangling the wild red curls in his fingers and kissing them fervently. Unresisting, she allowed him to liberate her carefully fashioned locks until they tumbled across the smooth swelling of her breasts.

She knew that she was a lost woman. She wrapped her arms around his neck and offered her face to his. Hungrily her lips sought his mouth. She needed his touch with a desperation she had not thought possible. His mouth fastened on hers and she took in the full taste of him. His lips grazed her cheeks, her neck, and glided downwards to the smooth whiteness of her breasts.

Then his fingers were undoing the tight bodice, slowly exposing the yielding flesh of her bosom, slowly but firmly stroking her into ecstasy.

Cupping her breasts in both hands, he brought his mouth to them, one after another. Slowly and expertly he savoured her, until her whole body was swept by a coruscating fire.

She moaned with the intensity of her pleasure and he pushed her against the warm wood of the shelter, fitting himself to her body, moving against her until she felt her legs would collapse beneath her. She tore at his shirt, burying her face in his bare throat. She wanted only to feel his naked skin, to feel the hardness of his body against her. Neither heard the footsteps running up the Dark Walk.

'Christabel? Christabel?' Sir Julian's plaintive cry echoed along the deserted path.

Then Sophia's impatient tones. 'She will hardly have walked here alone in the dark.'

'She may have fled this way. I shall never forgive myself if anything has happened to her.'

'Nothing will have happened, Sir Julian. My sister is well able to take care of herself.'

'We should not have left her alone. I had no idea of such a dreadful event occurring.'

'How could you? You must not blame yourself. She

was alone for only a few minutes and we were dancing close by.'

'But not close enough. We should have waited until Benedict returned to the box.'

'Benedict!' she snorted. 'We would have been waiting until the Gardens closed.'

The two stood motionless in the dim shadows of the shelter, their pulses racing and their breathing irregular. She was the first to emerge from the sultry haze, fumbling with the ties of her bodice and desperately trying to smooth the creases of her skirt. She made a monumental effort to regain her calm. Richard was still gazing down at her with a look that turned her knees to water but she gave him an agitated push towards the entrance and with a last, lingering glance, he gathered up his loo mask and slipped out of the shelter into the darkness beyond.

'Christabel!' They were still calling as she stepped out on to the Walk.

'I'm here, don't worry. I'm safe.'

Sir Julian almost ran to her side. In his agitation his cravat had become untied and his carefully styled hair was ruffled beyond repair. He clasped her hands tightly. 'Thank goodness, my dear. Thank goodness we've found you. I have been out of my mind with worry.'

'I'm sorry to have caused you such concern, but I had to leave the supper box unexpectedly.' There was hardly a tremor to her musical tones.

Sir Julian still wore a worried expression. 'You gave us a serious fright, my dear. When we returned to the box, it was upside down—plates broken, tablecloth askew and chairs strewn everywhere. And you had vanished. Whatever happened?'

'Just a little unwanted notice from someone who'd drunk too much punch, but a passing gentleman intervened. I've come to no harm so let us forget about it.'

'But why did you choose the Dark Walk?' Sophia asked curiously. 'It's so gloomy and there's no one around.'

'I didn't choose the Dark Walk, Sophia,' she replied with a touch of asperity, 'I wasn't thinking where I was going. I was trying to escape.'

'Of course,' Sir Julian soothed. 'And thank heaven you were able to. This unfortunate business has been entirely my fault. I was most remiss in leaving you without an escort.'

'Are you all right, Miss Tallis?' Lady Blythe and Domino were hurrying up the gravelled pathway to join them. 'We heard Sir Julian and your sister searching for you and thought we should help.'

'How kind you all are. There was a slight incident, but nothing too troublesome.'

'What a relief! I told you that these Gardens were not at all the thing, Domino. I hope you will believe me now.'

Domino hardly heard her aunt. She was looking around her uncertainly. 'Are you sure everything is well, Miss Tallis? I thought I saw a figure among the trees just now.'

'I don't think you can have. I'm certain that I outran the man who was pestering me.'

'If he's lurking nearby, I will find the blaggard.' Sir Julian was feeling a lot stouter now that his beloved was safe.

'There's nobody here except myself. I expect you saw the shadow of a tree, Domino. There's so little light.'

The girl looked unconvinced, but remained silent. The firework display was imminent and she wanted to find Benedict and speak to him urgently under cover of all the noise. Another bruising encounter with Lord Moncaster that evening had made it urgent that she exact help from her only friend.

Sophia, too, was anxious not to miss the pyrotechnics and said grumpily, 'I think we've spent long enough in this miserable spot. For goodness' sake, let's find our places for the display.'

She had enjoyed two whole dances with Sir Julian before he remembered that they'd left Christabel alone. Surely that proved his love was weak. He might be enthralled by her sister's beauty—men could be unbelievably stupid—but he didn't truly love his fiancée, Sophia was sure. It was only a sense of duty that had prompted him to return to the supper box.

Christabel took her place in one of the front rows of chairs. Her heart was still hammering and the promised spectacle held little appeal after the tumult of the last hour. She noticed Domino seated a little to the right. The girl must have seen Richard as he made his way back through the wood; she was attuned to him and must know his form by heart. How truly dreadful! How could Richard, how dared he, make such abandoned love to her even as his betrothed was walking close

by. And after all her promises to herself, she had succumbed without an instant's hesitation. They had both
behaved disgracefully.

She would never have come if she'd known he was
to be here this evening. And surely he should have
escorted Domino and Lady Blythe. Instead he'd chosen
to come alone and in disguise, and there could only be
one reason. His motive had to be the freedom it gave
him to act badly, the chance to continue her punishment.
His fury at her betrothal was still fresh in her mind
and it would be easy for him to find an opportunity to
torment under cover of darkness. Not that he'd had to
search very hard. She'd offered herself, all of herself,
without restraint. Willingly, eagerly. She could still see
the deep grey of his eyes, glowing and intense in the
shadows, the strong curves of his face sculpted out of
the dark by the silvery haze and then the feel of his skin
on hers, the feel of his touch as he skilfully explored her
body for the first time. But in the warm darkness he had
seemed as caught up in the moment as she, in thrall to
this intoxicating passion that had flamed between them.
Even so she knew this could not be. She lived in daily
expectation of reading the notice of his forthcoming
marriage. Once he had confessed this new love to Lady
Anne, he would publish it to the world.

A few seats away Domino had already forgotten that
shadowy figure in the Dark Walk. She had more pressing matters on her mind. As soon as the first cluster of
fireworks was tracing its multi-coloured path through
the sky she slipped quietly away, leaving her aunt

looking skywards. Benedict wasn't hard to find. He was on the outer circle of people, laughing and talking with some choice spirits he'd managed to befriend during the evening. She recognised his slim, rangy figure immediately. He hardly need have bothered to don his loo mask.

The touch of Leo Moncaster's hands earlier that evening was still on her and she felt slightly sick. She knew that she'd brought this trouble on herself. She'd set out to win back the favour that Moncaster possessed and free herself of his presence for ever. Instead she'd ended up in even deeper debt and he now held her vowels for a sum of money she could never hope to repay.

Tonight when he'd tracked her down and skilfully detached her from her aunt, she'd been forced to submit to his caresses. Under cover of darkness and in the midst of the boisterous crowd, he'd taken liberties that Domino was desperate to blot from her mind. It was a piece of great good fortune that at that moment Sir Julian had raised the alarm. Moncaster had melted away and she'd been reunited with Lady Blythe.

But not before he'd whispered his very clear threats in her ear. A handkerchief was but a poor return for the friendship he'd extended. She owed him money and he would be paid one way or another. The time for settlement had come, but this was by far too public a place. His house would prove a much cosier love nest. They were both bid to Sophia Tallis's come-out ball on Friday. He would see her there and when the dancing was at its height would send a signal to her to slip away and meet him outside. A carriage would be waiting to take them to his town mansion for an intimate dinner *à deux* followed by...well, he would no doubt think of something. He would deliver her back to the ball in time for Aunt Loretta to take her home and no one would be the wiser.

Domino was in despair. When she'd first met Leo Moncaster he'd seemed a dashing, handsome, experienced man of the world whom she'd managed to attract despite being little more than a schoolgirl. But very soon she'd been forced to confront the frightening reality that she was at the mercy of a predator with a perverted taste in young girls. She knew herself to be too naïve and inexperienced to deal with the situation alone and she could only hope that Benedict would prove her saviour.

'You must come away with me at the ball,' she announced to him, hardly waiting to exchange the customary pleasantries.

He gaped. 'Come away with you! What are you talking about?'

'At your sister's ball! I'll be there and so will Moncaster. You must take me away or I'll be forced to go with him.'

'Are you crazy? Have the fireworks fried your brains?'

'I'm serious. He'll make me go with him if I don't escape.'

'Don't be so bird-witted. He can't force you to do anything if you don't wish it.'

'He has my handkerchief—you know that—and now he has my IOUs too.'

'What!'

She hung her head, not daring to meet his gaze. 'You wouldn't help me and I tried to win back the handkerchief and lost even more money. If I don't do as he says, he will go to my aunt with my vowels and tell her how dreadfully I've behaved.'

He shook his head in disbelief. 'Then speak to her yourself before he can. I told you before that your best hope is to be honest with her—throw yourself on her mercy.'

'But now it's worse. It's not just the money—she'll suspect that I've behaved, well…not very properly,' she finished lamely.

'Of course you haven't behaved properly,' Benedict exploded. 'But she must know what kind of fellow Moncaster is and she won't judge you too harshly, I'm sure.'

'She'll send me to Spain immediately and I'll be travelling there in disgrace. When I arrive, they'll say I've brought shame on the family. They might even lock me up!'

'And how will going away with me be less shameful?'

'I won't really go away with you, or at least not far, but I need you to make arrangements for me. A carriage to Dover and then a passage across the Channel.'

'You can't travel all that way alone, a chit of a girl like you.'

'I'm not a chit.'

'You're seventeen and the biggest wet goose I've ever met.'

The conversation was not turning out the way she'd hoped and Domino could see her chance of securing his help fading away.

'Benedict, please, please, help me. If you don't think I should travel alone, come with me as far as Paris. My father has friends there and I could stay with them. They'll help me travel on to Spain.'

The pleading in her soft brown eyes was having its effect, but he still couldn't understand what she would gain from her plan.

'But don't you see,' she said trying hard to remain patient, 'I can leave a note for Aunt Loretta saying that I've left London because I'm so unhappy. Someone I met has hurt me.' That at least was true. 'I'll ask her to keep my confidence and not discuss with anyone why I've left. She won't know about the debts and neither will my relatives in Spain. They'll just think that I've arrived a little earlier than they expected.'

'And when Lord Moncaster knocks at your aunt's door with your IOUs after you've left?'

'Do you think he will?' A scared look had returned to her face and Benedict relented.

'Probably not. It's you he wants, not the money. Once you've fled, there won't be much point in trying to harass Lady Blythe.'

'There, you see, I'm right. All we have to do is to get to Paris and then everyone will be happy.'

'Oh yes, everyone,' he said acidly. 'And how do you propose that we get to Paris? Hiring a carriage to Dover costs money and if you think I'm travelling with you on the common stage, you can think again.

And when we get to the port, there'll be money needed for a boat ticket and you might not get a berth straight away. That will mean laying down more blunt to pay for accommodation.'

'I don't think I'll stay overnight in Dover,' she said hurriedly.

There would be little point in rescuing her reputation from Leo Moncaster's clutches only to have it shredded by another man.

'We'll go on board straight away.'

Benedict wasn't at all sure that would be possible; he imagined that berths on ships crossing the Channel had to be booked some time in advance, but Domino seemed to know what she was talking about. He'd never travelled beyond England before and the girl's assurances that she still had a large sum of her father's money intact and that she spoke passable French finally convinced him. He was still feeling guilty that her troubles had begun when he'd introduced her to gambling. He cursed that evening heartily. If he'd had a clue what she would do, he would have kept dancing that night until his feet dropped off. Wearily he agreed to ride with her the next day and make their detailed plans for her escape on Friday evening.

Christabel heard her brother coming in a few hours later. He made no attempt to be quiet, banging the front door behind him and thudding loudly up the stairs to his room. Presumably his night at Vauxhall had gone little better than hers. Her evening had been ruined. Not by the drunken intruder, for her fear of him had been fleeting; almost as soon as she'd realised that he could be a real danger, Richard had knocked the man down and thrown him over the barrier. Then in swift succession their escape from the crowd, the breathless journey up the Dark Walk and finally those moments of sweet delight. Once again he'd set her body alight and left her yearning and confused. Once again she had known no caution. Consumed by raw desire for him, she'd matched him kiss for kiss, caress for caress. The soaring pleasure she'd felt as their naked skins fused still had the power to set her heart pounding all these hours later. Surely she must believe she was loved.

But, no, he was playing with her—his affections lay elsewhere. He was simply intent on proving her unfaithful, especially now that he so abhorred the marriage she was about to make. He wished to expose her as a woman who accepted one man while making impassioned love with another. Her betrothal should have protected her from folly, but once again she had betrayed Sir Julian. While he was frantically searching for her, she was being caressed into ecstasy by another. She had wanted Richard as badly as she would ever want a man and had shown him just as plainly. If they'd not been interrupted, she knew she would have given herself to him completely. He had proved her forthcoming marriage was nothing more than a sham, proved she was the inconstant woman he'd always thought her. He had won their battle of wills.

Chapter Seven

If Christabel wondered why her old lover had chosen to roam the gardens of Vauxhall alone, masked and in disguise, Richard was asking himself much the same question. He'd refused Domino's invitation to escort her to the fête and with good reason. Accompanying her to a masked revelry was unlikely to wean her from her infatuation and he'd already been at pains to bid her goodbye. The legal papers he'd tarried for were now signed and stamped and while Domino was enjoying the party, he was supposed to be well on his way to Cornwall. Yet last night he'd lurked in the shadows, eager to avoid detection, his cloak and loo mask a flimsy disguise. Why on earth had he done so?

The news of Christabel's betrothal had fallen on him like a bludgeoning hammer. He'd felt himself disintegrating from the force of his anger and had needed immediate action, immediate distraction, to free himself from the fury that had him in its grip and was literally shaking him. He'd ridden swiftly from St James's to the livery stables, then marched straight to Jackson's Boxing Saloon where half-a-dozen rounds with the Gentleman himself had left him physically bruised and battered, but feeling a good deal better. At least for a while. But then the old haunting refrain began once more and a fervent need to see her swept over him. She'd been adamant that he stay away and he dared not risk another open confrontation. The temptation to grab her there and then and show her just why she shouldn't marry Sir Julian would be irresistible. Yet the need to see her was like a drug. It had him in its grip and would not let go. The fireworks at Vauxhall had been talked about for weeks and he knew she would be there.

In the event he'd been reduced to watching her from afar. He'd seen her take her place in the supper box with her irritating sister and that stuffed shirt Edgerton. She had looked magnificent—her wayward curls framing a pellucid skin had seemed almost alive and ready to spill into a cascade of fire. And the fall of her gown, its rich, gold silk, had transformed her slender figure into voluptuous beauty. He'd stood transfixed, desire touching every one of his senses and almost sweeping them away. He'd felt himself galvanised into action, urged forwards to leap the barrier and pull her into his arms. Almost, but not quite. Self-discipline had some-how prevailed and he'd continued to watch from the shadows.

But when the intruder had suddenly appeared and threatened her, caution had been thrown to the winds.

There'd been immense satisfaction in taking out his frustration on the miserable unfortunate who had dared to frighten this goddess. And then the whirlwind run with her up the Dark Walk to elude the attentions of the gathering crowd. Looking back, he recognised their flight had been more than a response to menace. It was an attempt to escape with her, to run away and leave behind the mess they had jointly made and just simply be together. The memories of their tryst were still with him: the soft rustle of foliage, the sweet odour of lilacs and her body inviting and responsive beneath his hands. He was her prisoner and the ferocious desire she aroused in him was causing as much suffering as he'd ever inflicted.

For she belonged to another man. She could not break the engagement she had entered—the label of jilt would not be so easily shrugged off this time. She would have to marry Sir Julian. Already she was progressing steadily towards the altar, preparing herself for a calm and uneventful life with a calm and uneventful man. That was the choice she'd made and, for her sake, he must stand back and let her follow it. Wasn't true love selfless?

Somehow the injuries he'd suffered had dissolved to nothing. She'd failed him, yes, but he was sure that her heart had been honest and true. She'd been the victim of a master seducer against whom her inexperience was no match. And he was partly to blame. He'd been her betrothed, her lover, but he'd not shown her the love she had craved. He'd been stiff, awkward, shy almost. She hadn't guessed, maybe couldn't guess, the depths of his feelings for her. He saw her now in his mind's eye, a young, vital girl, saw her at the very moment that she'd agreed to marry him. They'd stood on the cliff top, the waves thundering beneath, random spray misting the very air between them. She'd gazed up at him, her face warm with happiness, and said yes. Then she'd reached for his hand and tugged him along the path to the cove, her smile urging him on, her eyes laughing with pleasure. She had been honest and true, he was sure.

After years in which he'd kept the past under lock and key, meeting her again had released a great dam of emotion. He'd thought he would never feel so deeply again, but he'd been wrong. And why was that? He could pretend no longer. Without a doubt, he knew that he loved her. It seemed that he'd always loved her from the days of callow youth through the years of exile to this very moment. His clumsy plan to teach her a lesson and free himself from her power was simply hurt love. He longed for her, burned for her, but he must subdue those feelings. Tomorrow there would be a ball at Mount Street in honour of her tiresome sister and he had been invited. He would bid her farewell in a crowded room and bow out of her life as gracefully as he could. His luggage would be packed and waiting for him at the inn. Early the next morning he would be on his way to Cornwall.

Number Six Mount Street was a house in upheaval and if Christabel were tempted to dwell on her transgressions at Vauxhall, the preparations for the ball effectively banished all such remorse. For days the housemaids had been dusting and sweeping every corner of the house, shining silver and polishing chandeliers. Every spare glass had been unearthed and washed until it sparkled.

The house was a modest size and to hold a ball for up to fifty people, though small by the Season's standards, was an immense undertaking. The two first-floor salons were to be made into one and act as the ballroom by the simple expedient of sliding back the wooden partitioning.

'We must roll up the carpets,' Lady Harriet instructed three panting footmen, early on the Friday morning. 'They will have to be taken to the cellar, I fear, but the parquet floor will be excellent for dancing.' The men, perspiring down three flights of stairs, did not appear overly impressed by this information.

'Bel,' her mother called urgently to her from the drawing room, 'do you think the quartet we've hired could be stationed at one end of this room?' She indicated the window enclave.

'That would mean that we can't open the windows behind them, Mama,' Christabel warned, 'and it looks likely to be a very warm day.'

Her mother's brow wrinkled. 'The room is already uncomfortably stuffy, I admit, but I cannot see where else to put the musicians.' She sighed. 'It will have to do.'

'It might not matter,' her daughter comforted. 'We can fling the windows wide at the far end of the other room and if people get too overheated, they can step out on to the balcony to refresh themselves.'

'Not too many people,' her mother said wryly. The ironwork balcony which overlooked the gardens to the rear of the house was no more than six feet wide.

As the day wore on, Christabel became aware of her mother's increasing anxiety. The evening's event had been planned as a modest introduction of Sophia to the *ton*, but somehow it had escalated. More invitations had been issued than Lady Harriet had bargained for and some of these to the most fêted in society. Refreshments had been ordered from Gunter's in addition to those being produced in the kitchen by Cook and her willing helpers, and the best champagne had been ordered at a ruinous cost.

What should have been a simple occasion had been transformed into a major undertaking. Lady Harriet could not decide just how this had happened, although Christabel could have enlightened her. She knew her sister had been busy. Sophia had not been content with what she'd described privately as a paltry affair and refused to be put off with the promise of a much grander ball in her honour the following year. She was partaking of London society now and she wanted her official launch to be talked of for weeks to come. She had been unable to persuade her mother to hire a more prestigious venue but she was determined that everything that could be done to make the party memorable would be done. It was she who had chosen the champagne and ordered the additional delicacies and she who had ensured that invitations had gone out to the very highest of the *ton*.

That was her sole contribution to the evening's success. Her day was spent in her room preparing for her grand appearance. The dress she had originally chosen for this momentous occasion was deemed that morning to be commonplace and she was engaged in a frantic and increasingly bad-tempered search for the perfect ensemble. It was left to Christabel to assist her flurried parent in the hundred-and-one tasks that had to be accomplished. Had the flowers arrived and how were they to be arranged? Was there going to be sufficient room for the musicians in the window enclosure and what should the order of music be? Where were the dance cards ordered at least three weeks ago and why had the ices been delivered so early that they were bound to melt well before they could be served? So it went on as the hours of the day ticked by, Christabel and her mother scurrying from ballroom to dining room to kitchen to hall, solving problems, settling disputes, until they were both so fatigued that all they wanted was to retire to bed and let everyone else dance the night away.

In the confusion that permeated the house, they hardly noticed Benedict. He had quickly been pronounced useless in preparing for the ball and advised to lose himself for the day. That suited him perfectly. He had plenty to do if he were to carry off Domino early the next morning and his family's abstraction meant that his constant comings and goings went unremarked. It struck Christabel that he looked unusually serious, but she was too busy to enquire further. Meanwhile upstairs Sophia continued to drive her maidservant to distraction until finally she had decided on the outfit which would eclipse all others and the entire house breathed a sigh of relief.

At nine o'clock Sophia, primped and pampered, took up her place in the entrance hall at the head of the family, waiting to greet her guests. Christabel, standing slightly behind her, hoped that her own appearance was not too disordered. She had completed her *toilette* with only a few minutes to go, scrambling into her dress as the first of the carriage wheels were heard rumbling across the cobblestones outside. She need not have worried for her beauty was undiminished. In the short time available Rosa had given up any idea of achieving the latest elaborate style known as *à la Méduse* and decided on a simple arrangement of soft curls around the face with the rest of her mistress's unruly hair pulled back into an orderly chignon. Diamond clips on either side softened any severity and matching diamonds sparkled from her ears and nestled in the curves of her bosom. The Pomona-green gauze she wore over a paler under-dress accentuated the emerald of her eyes and the small diamond fastenings to her bodice made her seem alive with light whenever she moved. She had made little attempt to appear anything other than acceptable, yet she easily outshone every other woman in the room. Those daring young damsels who had worn gauze dresses over damped and transparent petticoats in order to attract attention looked frankly tawdry in the face of such transcendent beauty. Fortunately Sophia was so immersed in her own absorbing bubble of pleasure that she had no eyes for any of her family, least of all the sister she hoped to supplant.

Domino and Lady Blythe were among the first to arrive and Christabel noticed how very pale and quiet the young girl was. Something ails her, she thought, but what? Leo Moncaster followed close behind, suave and debonair as ever, but exuding a sense of threat, subtle and unexpressed. She was at a loss to understand why he'd come since he was not a particular friend of the family, but seeing Sophia's blush as she curtsied to him, she knew immediately who had pushed for his invitation. Lord Moncaster's attendance at one's coming-out ball was a fine prize to win. She had little time to contemplate the oddities of the guest list before Sir Julian was before her, splendid in black satin knee-breeches and long-tailed coat, and reverently taking her hand.

'How good to see you, my dear. And looking breathtaking as always! I seem hardly to have managed a word with you of late.'

She looked guiltily up at him. 'I'm sorry. This week has simply sped by—there's been so much to do for Sophia's come-out and Mama is without my father's help.'

'I know how busy you must have been, my dear Christabel, and that is only right. Your mother needs your support and I would expect nothing else from such a loving daughter. But when this evening is over, I hope we will have the chance to spend time together.'

'We will, of course,' she reassured him hastily.

'I am very much looking forward to taking you to Rosings as soon as ever it is convenient with you—and your mother, of course. I'm sure that you will both enjoy the country air and I hope it's not too boastful to say that you will be well pleased with the home that you find there. Every member of my staff is ready and eager to welcome the new Lady Edgerton.'

She brushed aside this reference to their marriage, but tried to sound enthusiastic about the forthcoming visit.

'I'm looking forward to seeing Rosings as much as you are to showing it to me.' This was only half a lie at least. 'But until Sophia and Benedict return to Cornwall, you must see that it is impossible.'

Sophia, who had moved towards Sir Julian as soon as she saw him enter the room, caught the tail end of the conversation and looked thunderous. Only the arrival of a new dance partner prevented an outburst. Instead she smiled extravagantly at the young man who stood before her and made a play of ticking off his name on her dance card. With a withering look at her sister, she allowed herself to be swept back on to the ballroom floor.

It was halfway through the evening before Sir Julian caught up with his beloved again. Her duties had not stopped with the arrival of guests; she and Lady Harriet had constantly to mingle, to introduce, to smooth the social waters. He finally ran her to ground just as she had finished giving instructions to one of the footmen to begin opening the final crate of champagne.

'Christabel—' he pounced '—this dance must be mine!' The musicians were just tuning up for the first quadrille of the evening.

She found herself having to apologise yet again. 'I regret I cannot, Julian—there are a hundred-and-one things I should check before I can think of dancing.'

His face fell and she glanced wildly around. 'I see Sophia is temporarily without a partner. It would be most kind of you to ask her to join the quadrille.'

Sir Julian gave a resigned smile. 'If you wish it, my dear. It's well that your sister dances so creditably.'

He moved obediently to where Sophia stood disconsolate. The name on her card had failed her and she was without a partner at her very own party, but Sir Julian's arrival transformed the miserable situation. Seeing the genuine smile of warmth directed at him, he felt that his sacrifice had not been in vain. They were soon dancing easily together, chatting almost as old friends, Christabel noted. She was satisfied. The better Sophia knew Julian, the less likely she was to continue to weave fantasies around him.

By eleven o'clock the ball was in full swing. Almost every guest who had been bidden to the party had arrived and those who were planning to go on to other and grander events had not yet left. The dance floor was crowded, a kaleidoscope of jewelled shades as the women twirled and pirouetted in interweaving patterns of colour. If the musicians felt stifled in their embrasure, they did not show it, playing without pause for the eager dancers. The temperature of the room had been rising all the time and the copious banks of flowers which decked the walls on either side were beginning to wilt. The starched shirt points of the gentlemen showed a definite tendency to limpness and even the most elegant of the women had recourse to their fans as the evening wore on. The call to partake of refreshments when it came was greeted with some relief.

Supper was a sociable event. The Tallises' dining room had been cleared of furniture and in its stead trestle tables set up, covered in starched white linen and furnished with white porcelain and silver cutlery. Small crystal bowls of deep pink roses dotted the length of the buffet and a splendid centrepiece of mauve-and-white lilies towered majestically over the whole. The table groaned with every conceivable dainty that the combined efforts of Cook and Gunter's could produce. It was an intimate space and people gathered in groups around the table or arranged the few chairs still remaining in small clusters. The flushed, happy faces and the buzz of chatter was evidence that the event was deemed a success and Christabel could relax.

At last she had leisure to look around her. Sophia was in high gig, sitting with Sir Julian and two of her female confidantes. She was evidently pleased to have netted the man she clearly considered the beau of the evening. Benedict hovered in the background, a jumpy look on his face. Christabel watched him for a while, feeling concerned, but unsure why. She saw that he was staring rather too fixedly at Domino, who seemed to be involved in some kind of altercation with Lord Moncaster. How extraordinary! Leo Moncaster rose from his seat at that moment and made for the door. Immediately she sped to the hall to bid him goodbye, her brain teeming.

'Are you leaving us already, Lord Moncaster?' she said lightly.

He turned, smooth as always, his face giving no inkling of his thoughts.

'I regret, Miss Tallis, that I have business elsewhere. Do accept my thanks for a most enjoyable evening.'

His tone was genial, but there was a metallic ring to his voice and his smile was tight and controlled. What could have upset him so much that he would risk gossip from an angry dispute and an early departure? She noticed that his antagonist, too, was making her way to the door. Domino, still pale faced, must have persuaded her aunt to leave betimes.

The musicians struck up again and the ballroom filled with couples still determined to enjoy the evening. Christabel had just decided that this might be an opportune moment to offer Julian the dance he desired when a tall and striking figure was ushered through the door. The man wore the black satin knee breeches of the gentleman of fashion and a black tailcoat which fitted him to perfection. A white frilled shirt set off the lean, tanned face and a single diamond stud held in place a neckcloth tied in the intricate Oriental style. It was Richard and he looked superb. She could hardly believe her eyes. Richard! Who on earth could have invited him? Her sister's cunning smile told the story. Of course, Sophia would hope to cause trouble if she could and this was her master stroke. Well, she would not succeed.

'Good evening, Lord Veryan.'

Christabel's voice strove to remain unhurried and calm. The remembrance of their last encounter came rushing back; her eyes were held captive by the figure before her, lingering on the seductive picture he presented. She gave herself a mental shake; she could not afford to show any sign of the feelings he aroused in her.

'Good evening, Miss Tallis, I hope I see you well?' His tone was crisp and businesslike. It helped to steady her.

'Yes, my lord, very well,' she responded formally.

They stood, unable to continue the conversation, unable to stop their eyes from feasting on each other. He was the first to recover.

'I'll not be staying long. I came only to say goodbye.'

'Goodbye? You are leaving London?'

'I've always had the intention of returning to Cornwall as soon as I could, but circumstances have made it difficult.'

'Really?' There was a challenge in her voice. 'I imagine Lady Anne must be very glad that *circumstances* now allow you to return home.'

He bowed his head, acknowledging her hit. She looked at him again. His eyes held a wistfulness that she did not remember before and the intensity of his gaze made her limbs begin to weaken, her strength dissolving as she stood there.

'Won't you stay to dance a little while?' she managed. 'Unfortunately Miss de Silva has just left—she could not have known you were attending—but there are many others who would be delighted to partner you.'

He blinked at the mention of Domino's name but then recalled that Christabel still believed in the fiction of their relationship, a fiction he had been at pains to foster.

'I need no other partner, but if *you* will dance with me, I would be delighted. A waltz is just beginning.'

Mindful of having refused Sir Julian earlier in the evening, Christabel demurred. If she accepted, he would feel justifiably offended and she had no wish to snub the man she was soon to marry. More truthfully, she knew that dancing with Richard was likely to unleash a tumult that would crack open the social façade she wore.

'I am not dancing this evening, Lord Veryan.'

'Come—a few steps only and then I'll leave.'

She hesitated; the temptation to find herself in his arms again and for the last time seemed overwhelming. But she must not succumb to this insistent longing; such feelings were inadmissible and must be put behind her for good. Her hand was trembling as he took it and raised it to his lips.

'A few minutes of the waltz should not take up too much of your time.'

As if in a dream she allowed herself to be swept on to the dance floor. He held her tightly, his form fitting hers, two halves making a whole. Swaying sinuously to the strains of the music, they moved as one. They heard and saw nothing other than themselves: two bodies locked in hot intimacy. Their fever mounted inexorably, licking them with its flames, consuming them with its ardour. They could not bear to keep dancing. And so it was that as they neared the far window, Richard pulled the curtain swiftly to one side and danced her on to the balcony.

She gasped. 'Whatever are you doing?'

His eyes glittered in the moonlight which lapped the ornamental balustrade; when he spoke, his voice was rough with desire.

'I came to say goodbye, Christabel, but I find I can only do so in private, just you and I alone together for a few moments.'

The soft evening air washed over them, the smell of Albertine roses on the wall below drowning them in a sweet perfume. A slight breeze flicked her curls across her cheek and his hand went automatically to brush them back. He stopped himself.

'I came to say goodbye,' he repeated, 'and to wish you well for the future.'

The sincerity in his voice was unmistakable. His anger had gone. He had accepted her betrothal and whatever schemes he'd been devising were finished. This was the outcome she'd craved during the past days of misery. Yet she was filled with the greatest sorrow— in just a few minutes she must watch him walk from the room and out of her life for ever.

As if reading her mind, he said gently, 'You deserve

to live happily. I should not have hurt you, you of all people.'

She could see this sentiment came from deep within his heart and wondered what other feelings might lie beneath that calm, elegant exterior. It took her a while to answer and when she did, her voice sounded barely above a whisper.

'As we both know, my own past has not been free of blame.'

'We were young and foolish, and there I should have left it. But when I saw you again…' He shrugged his shoulders expressively. 'It was all up with me. The old grievances began to live once more and I seemed powerless to slay my demons.'

'And now?'

'I haven't exactly slain them, but they're back under lock and key.'

His smile was awry, his face shadowed despite his best efforts. She had a crazy urge to take him in her arms and kiss him back into happiness. The shocking thought rendered her silent for a moment.

'You need fear no more intrusions from me,' he said, thinking she required reassurance. 'You will have a splendid future, I'm sure, and I wish you all the happiness that is possible.'

'You were always a generous spirit, Richard,' she whispered.

'And you were always a loving girl, as I'm sure Sir Julian will find. He once said that he considered himself blessed to have won you for his wife and he was right to think so.'

His face moved closer to hers, his eyes hungrily devouring her delicate beauty. She felt herself tremble and move instinctively closer to him. His fingers touched her hand lightly and trailed their way up her bare arm. Then they were in her hair winding, stroking, caressing the fiery curls. Both hands moved to cup her face and he gazed intently into her eyes, absorbed in their emerald depths.

'One last kiss,' he whispered.

She raised her face to his, her mouth soft and yielding beneath the hard pressure of his lips. His arms were round her pulling her body into his, moulding her to himself.

'Christy,' he groaned, 'what have we done?'

His use of her pet name demolished any remaining resistance. His mouth once more fastened on hers, his lips insistent, and then his tongue was gently pressing her lips apart, delicately exploring her mouth until she wanted nothing more than to feel him, all of him, close to her and for ever. For long minutes they were oblivious to everything. They did not see the curtain being quietly lifted and two pairs of eyes staring at them, Sir Julian's in horror and Sophia's in jubilation. When they emerged from the enclave, shaken from their encounter, neither observer was to be seen. Sir Julian had taken a hasty leave of Lady Tallis and Sophia, the picture of innocence, had joined a new set for the country dance which was just then striking up.

For the few hours that remained of the ball, Christabel was glad to have plenty to do. There were still refreshments to be ordered from the kitchen, damsels to partner, coats to be retrieved and farewells to say; almost anything would do to keep at bay the deep throb of pain which threatened to crush her. Richard had gone. Those words danced blackly in her mind's eye and had constantly to be repressed. It was only when the last person had been escorted to the last carriage that she could no longer hide from her grief: Richard was gone and his leaving was for ever.

There was no sign of Benedict, but her mother and sister were in the hall, looking tired from their individual exertions, but both pleased with the evening's success.

'Thank you, Bel, for all your hard work today.' Lady Harriet clasped her hand warmly. 'Without you things would not have gone so smoothly. I'm sure Sophia is most grateful,' and she looked meaningfully at her younger daughter.

Sophia did not respond and there was an uncomfortable silence.

'What happened to Sir Julian, Mama?' Christabel asked lightly. 'He seemed to disappear in a puff of smoke.'

Her joke fell lamely on the air, but her mother smiled and said mildly, 'He left shortly after supper, my dear. I'm not entirely sure why. He said something about another engagement. It seemed rather odd to me, but I thought you might know.'

'No, indeed, I understood he would be present for the whole evening. How very strange!'

'He seemed a little distressed,' Lady Harriet said thoughtfully, 'but I could be wrong.'

'You're not wrong, Mama. He *was* distressed.' Sophia had come instantly to life and was ready for the kill.

'Why, whatever has happened?' her sister queried in astonishment.

'I don't know how you have the nerve to stand there and ask that!' Sophia was almost jumping with fury.

Her mother looked questioningly at a bemused Christabel, but no help was forthcoming.

'Explain yourself, Sophia,' Lady Harriet commanded crossly.

'If you really want me to I will, but I would think Bel should be the one to do the explaining. She's the one who's engaged to Sir Julian, but can't seem to stop kissing other men.'

'What!' Christabel and her mother exclaimed in unison.

But it was Christabel who turned pale. Sir Julian must have seen her kissing Richard and naturally it was Sophia who had led him to that window and ensured her disgrace. Her sister must have been watching them all the time and seized her golden opportunity the minute it came.

'What is this, Bel?' her mother was demanding.

'Richard came to say goodbye, Mama,' she began calmly. 'He was bidding me farewell.'

'Hmph!' Sophia interrupted crudely. 'Some farewell! You were in his arms and he was kissing you in a quite scandalous way.'

'Christabel, is this true?'

She did not answer her mother, but turned away and began to climb the stairs in silence. She was sick at heart and there was nothing she could say in her defence.

At eleven o'clock the next morning Sir Julian Edgerton presented himself at Mount Street and asked to speak to the eldest daughter of the house. He was in a chastened mood, but also determined. He had sat up late into the night, thinking through his predicament, and had come to a decision. He must see Christabel Tallis immediately before he changed his mind. He only hoped that meeting her again would not throw him off track.

When the maidservant scratched at Christabel's door with Sir Julian's name on her lips, she braced herself for what she knew would be a distressing interview. She had been up and dressed for many hours; in fact, she'd hardly slept, going over the events of the previous evening in her mind and preparing herself for the likely outcome. Now the moment had arrived. She walked slowly down the stairs, her serene expression and graceful carriage masking her discomfort. Sir Julian, looking towards the staircase, saw a vision of the palest pink tulle descending towards him. He drew himself up resolutely.

'Good morning, Miss Tallis.' No Christabel now, she reflected.

'Good morning, Sir Julian,' she responded equally formally. 'You wished to speak privately with me?' He was grateful that she had come straight to the point.

'Would that be possible?' He cleared his throat nervously.

She led the way into the library, a room normally deserted for most of the day. The servants had already cleaned and they were unlikely to be disturbed. In any case she imagined the discussion would not take very long.

'Miss Tallis,' Sir Julian began, clearing his throat again. 'We have known each other for many months now and you must be aware that I have grown to esteem you highly…and to love you.' He almost mumbled these last few words. Christabel inclined her head slightly.

'I had hoped,' Sir Julian began again with difficulty, 'that we were well enough suited to contemplate making our future lives together. When you accepted my proposal, I was the happiest man alive. However…' and he appeared to be choosing his words carefully '…it would seem that you were not of the same mind.'

She bowed her head. She must say something to this honourable man who was clearly struggling to make sense of a world turned upside down. The future he had so blithely anticipated lay now in ruins.

'Sir Julian, please believe me when I say that I also shared that hope.'

'Then I do not understand what has occurred.' His face lost its fixed expression and collapsed into a bewildered sadness; he looked hopelessly out of his depth and Christabel's heart smote her.

'I fear it will be no comfort for you to learn that I am as confused,' she offered. 'However, you should know that the painful situation that has arisen is no reflection on you. You have been wholly generous in your conduct. This is entirely my fault.'

'You are most kind, Miss Tallis, and it relieves me to know that I could not have done anything more to make our betrothal a success. But it leaves us with a problem.'

'There is no problem, Sir Julian. In the circumstances it is impossible for us to marry and I imagine you came here today to tell me so. The notice of our betrothal has not yet been sent to the papers and only a few people know of our plans.'

Sir Julian looked pained. 'I regret that you are right in your surmise. After what has occurred I feel that neither of us could give ourselves wholeheartedly to a marriage. But what shall we say to those people who have been told we are to wed?'

'We will simply say that we found that after all we were not suited to each other.'

Sir Julian turned this over in his mind and then smiled faintly. 'That sounds pleasantly vague. And people can pick it over at will and make what they wish of it.'

'Exactly.'

'As always, Miss Tallis, you have the perfect touch.' He looked regretfully at the beautiful woman who stood before him.

'Not always, Sir Julian,' she reminded him gently.

'Quite so,' he said and hurriedly turned towards the door.

The interview was at an end. They had survived it and without permanent scars on either side. Christabel breathed a sigh of relief. Now that it was done, a burden seemed to have been lifted from her. Her future life would be difficult, but she was no longer living a lie.

She followed him out into the hall and almost fell over the figure of Sophia, who had clearly been loitering outside the library door, agog to see what had happened and ready with sympathy for Sir Julian.

'Miss Sophia, good morning,' he said without much enthusiasm. The strident tones of violet silk hit him in the eyes and he winced. He had been hoping to escape from the house without having to encounter any other of the family.

'How nice to see you, Sir Julian,' Sophia chirruped gaily as if nothing of any import had happened. 'Are you intending to walk in the park? It's such wonderful weather again, it's a waste to spend it indoors.'

He had been planning to return to his own home and lose himself in paperwork. He needed to obliterate this most painful meeting of his entire life. But Sophia was smiling encouragingly at him and shafts of sunlight flooded the hall from the transom over the door. Perhaps after all a walk in the park with a congenial companion might be beneficial. Sophia had shown great enthusiasm for his latest project, the foundation of an orphanage in Shoreditch, and her opinion on a number of pressing issues which had emerged since their last discussion might be valuable.

'If you would care to accompany me to Hyde Park, I would be delighted, Miss Sophia,' he responded obligingly.

She snatched up her bonnet from the chair and was

at his side in an instant. It was clear that she was well prepared for this moment and Sir Julian was flattered that she had planned to devote herself to keeping him company. At least one of the Tallis sisters held him in esteem. He reflected on how much time he had spent with Sophia lately when Christabel had been unable or unwilling to be by his side. In hindsight those frequent absences were significant. And he had grown to like the younger girl. Admittedly her taste in dress was a little unusual, but she seemed willing to listen to whatever small suggestions he made. Above all he felt flattered by her interest in his affairs: she always gave him her full attention. There was merit attached to a girl who was not the most sought-after belle in society. And merit, a small whispering voice added, to a girl who was not prone to sexual flirtation.

Lady Harriet had come into the hall as the pair left. She looked questioningly at Christabel still standing with her hand on the library door.

'Mama, I have to tell you that Sir Julian and I have decided that we do not after all suit.' The phrase ran glibly off her tongue.

'Do not suit!' her mother parroted. 'What can you mean?'

'Just that. The betrothal is over.'

Lady Harriet sighed heavily. 'After what occurred last night, I suppose that Sir Julian could do little else.'

'It was a mutual decision.'

'Precipitated by your reckless conduct! Whatever were you thinking?'

She ignored the reference to her encounter with Richard and said soothingly, 'It's for the best, Mama.'

Lady Harriet looked bewildered. 'But why in heaven's name, Christabel? Everything seemed to be going so well between you.'

'"Seemed" is the right word. We were never really suited. I fear that for a short time I persuaded myself otherwise.'

'And now you have a second broken engagement to your name. I hope you realise what that signifies in the eyes of society.'

'If you mean that I have no earthly chance of ever finding a husband now, yes, I do realise. But believe me, Mama, there are worse things in life.'

Lady Harriet groaned and twisted her hands. Her beloved daughter had committed social suicide and there was nothing she could do to rescue her.

'Don't be too upset—' Christabel warmed to the task of rallying her mother '—you might just catch Sir Julian for another Tallis!'

Lady Harriet's expression was fiercely indignant and it was well for her daughter that a servant appeared at that moment with a note in her hand. The maid was unable to read, but was clearly agitated by having found the paper prominently displayed on Lady Harriet's small writing desk. Irritated, her mistress snatched the note and dismissed the maidservant. She scanned the brief message and her face drained of all colour; she looked as though she were about to crumble to the floor. Christabel stepped swiftly forwards.

'Mama, what is it?'

Chapter Eight

❦

She took the note from her mother's trembling hand and read it quickly. 'I don't understand. He's gone to Paris? Benedict?'

'How could he?' her mother wailed. 'What more will befall us?'

'But what is this about Domino?'

'It's evident, isn't it? They've eloped.'

'Forgive me, Mama, but that has to be a nonsense. Benedict eloping? He's never shown the slightest interest in females.'

'I am not at all sure that's so. He seems to have spent a great deal of time with this girl lately.'

Christabel thought back over the last few weeks and had to agree: Benedict meeting Domino at Almack's, laughing with her at the picnic, the regular rides in the park and then last night at Sophia's ball, his fixed concentration on the girl. But her lover? That still appeared unlikely.

She said as much to her mother, but Lady Harriet refused to be comforted.

'If he is not her lover, then what is he doing going to Paris with her? It's clear to me that they are eloping.'

'Mama, even if they wished to marry each other, why would they elope? Wouldn't it be more rational for Benedict simply to ask Domino's guardian for permission to wed her?'

'That's just it!' her mother produced triumphantly. 'He must know there would be little chance of obtaining permission to marry. The girl is only seventeen and, I understand, a great heiress. Benedict hardly figures as the most eligible suitor.' A sudden dreadful thought struck. 'Do you think that he's eloping for her money?'

'How can that be? Benedict has lacked for nothing in his life.'

Her mother did not reply immediately, but began an agitated walk up and down the hall, her mind beset by this new enormity.

'I haven't said anything to you, Bel,' she began finally in a faltering voice, 'but I've become worried over some of his activities. I suspect that he has begun to gamble more seriously than we know. What if he's plunged himself into debt, huge debt, and hasn't wanted to tell us?' She shook her head in despair at the thought and her tears began to gather.

'Not even Benedict would be foolish enough to think

he could elope with an under-age girl and then make free with her inheritance!'

Her mother appeared deaf to these rousing words. She sank into the large leather chesterfield that stood against the wall and stared blindly into space. When her daughter bent down and tried to hug her, she began to rock backwards and forwards, keening quietly; she seemed to have disappeared into a nightmare world of her own conjecture. Christabel was alarmed. Her mother's self-possession was renowned and had survived countless family troubles. But this new tragedy to strike Mount Street, coming so quickly after the events of the previous evening, had clearly overwhelmed her.

She came to a decision. 'Mama, I'm going to see Lady Blythe. She may know more than us.'

'No!' Galvanised by these words, her mother sat bolt upright. 'We cannot allow this news to be made public.'

'It won't be. Lady Blythe will be just as eager as us to hush things up. Together she and I may be able to put together a rescue plan.'

'Rescue? How can you rescue them? Benedict left the house before dawn. They could be anywhere by now.'

'We have the advantage of knowing where they're headed. If we could reach them within the next few hours, nobody except ourselves need know a thing.'

Particularly Richard, she thought. For his sake, if for no one else's, she must do her utmost to rescue Domino from this foolish journey.

'And who is to follow them?' her mother was saying querulously. 'Your father is hundreds of miles away in

Cornwall and you have managed to alienate the fiancé who might have lent us his support.'

Before her mother could renew this still-raw grievance, she rang for Lady Harriet's dresser.

'Her ladyship is feeling unwell, Mitford. She needs to rest. Could you ensure that she is made comfortable and then bring her some sweet tea?'

Once her mother had been safely despatched to her room, Christabel donned her bonnet and walked swiftly to Curzon Street. She had dismissed her mother's suggestion that Benedict had eloped because of money troubles, but the thought that he might have become seriously infatuated with Domino could not be so easily lost. It was true that he had hitherto shown little interest in women, but she could not deny that he had been dancing attendance on the young girl in recent weeks in a way that was quite foreign to him. What if Domino returned his feelings? Where would that leave Richard? Her heart ached for him that he should be treated so shabbily by the two women he had asked to marry.

The moment she was ushered into Lady Blythe's presence, she saw that the older woman, too, had received an unwelcome missive. Her face was unnaturally pale and she seemed to have difficulty rising from her seat. She came towards her fair young visitor and offered an unsteady hand. Once they were alone, she silently passed a single sheet of paper to Christabel. The note her niece had left proved much longer and far more informative than Benedict's. The errant pair, it appeared, were on their way to Dover and from there they hoped to take a boat across the Channel and make their way to Paris. Domino was sorry to upset her aunt who had been so kind to her, but the situation in London had become intolerable and she had to escape. Benedict was to escort her on her journey to the French capital so her aunt must not worry!

'Miss Tallis, what are we to do?' Lady Blythe questioned in a broken voice as Christabel finished reading the note. Her hands moved restlessly in her lap. 'I had no idea, no idea.'

'No idea of what, Lady Blythe?'

'That Domino was in love with your brother, of course.'

'She does not say that in her message,' Christabel cautioned.

'Not in so many words, but why else would she have embarked on this scandalous journey with him? I should never have allowed them to ride together with only a groom as chaperon.'

'She says that her life here has become intolerable. Have you any idea what she might mean, ma'am?'

'I can only imagine that she has been carrying on this clandestine relationship for some time and has become frustrated with the secrecy involved. She knows well that her father would never agree to such a match, but if she had only confided in me...' Loretta Blythe blinked back the tears. 'We have all been seventeen and convinced that our romance would last for ever.'

Christabel scrutinised the letter again. It was hardly a message from someone about to elope with the love of her life: no impassioned declarations, no pages blotched by tears. On the other hand, the intolerable situation in London sounded ominous. Could that be, as Lady Blythe surmised, her love for Benedict, which she was unable to acknowledge?

She looked at the older woman, sunk deep in her chair, an expression of quiet despair on her face, the mirror image of her own mother, and cursed Benedict. Someone had to try to put things right, restore their peace of mind and ensure that Richard never discovered this new injury to his name. It would have to be her—there was no one else.

The decision made, she rose briskly from her chair. 'Please don't upset yourself, ma'am, the situation is not irretrievable. We know where they've gone and when they left. It should be possible to catch them before they can board a packet to Calais. Fortunately the weather has turned inclement and sailings are bound to be disrupted. We have a very real chance, you know, of finding them still waiting on the quay side.'

'We? But who can go? My health is not as good as it used to be, my dear. I cannot possibly contemplate such a journey. And Domino's father is thousands of miles across the sea.'

At the thought of Alfredo and what he would say at this latest turn of events, her face lost even the little colour it still possessed and she plunged her head in her hands, weeping copiously.

Christabel thought it prudent to take her leave at this juncture. '*I* will go,' she said quietly. 'I'll be away a day or so, I dare say, but I hope to have good news for you when I return.'

Her companion looked up wonderingly, 'You cannot possibly go yourself! My dear, think of it, you cannot travel alone, without an escort.'

'I'll take my groom. Stebbings has been with our family all my life and is completely trustworthy.'

'A servant?'

Christabel was by now losing patience. 'If you can think of someone else who could undertake this mission, then please tell me. Otherwise I'll do what I'm able.'

The older woman's voice quavered, 'Lord Veryan? I was wondering whether we might venture to call on Lord Veryan's help. What do you think?'

But before her visitor could reply, the slight glimmer of hope had faded from her face. 'But, no, I recollect now, he is on his way to Cornwall, I believe.'

Christabel had reached the door and turned in surprise, 'Surely he would be the last person you would want to know about this escapade,' she murmured as she slipped out of the room, leaving behind her a puzzled woman.

Once back in Mount Street, she hastily threw a few overnight essentials into a small valise and gave orders for the travelling carriage to be brought round to the front of the house as soon as possible. While she waited, tracing and retracing her steps in the hall, her mother emerged unexpectedly from the drawing room. She'd imagined Lady Tallis to be laid down on her bed and had left a brief message of explanation with Mitford. She'd hoped to avoid the confrontation that now looked likely.

'Why are you dressed for travelling, Bel?' was Lady Harriet's immediate question.

She decided to meet trouble head on and said straitly, 'I'm going to Dover. Benedict and Domino are headed to that port, prior to crossing to France. I think if I leave now I may be able to catch them before they embark.'

'To Dover? On your own? You cannot do such a thing!' Her mother's shocked face was testament to the serious impropriety of her plan.

'I'm sorry if it distresses you, Mama, but I can and I must.'

'But why? What good will it do other than besmirch your name even further!'

'The weather has been stormy since they left and it's more than likely they'll be delayed. I'm hopeful that I'll be able to prevent them leaving England.'

'And if you do not, is it your intention to continue this insane pursuit across the Continent?'

She allowed herself a small smile at the image her mother had conjured, but said as soothingly as she could, 'If they've already sailed, then I will return immediately, you have my word.'

Still plainly very agitated, her mother tried another tack. 'But you will never get to Dover and back in a day.'

She indicated the valise at her feet. 'As you see, I'm prepared.'

Lady Harriet's face registered even greater shock at such brazen conduct and her daughter was forced to redouble her persuasion.

'If we must stay the night at Dover, it's surely better

that I accompany Domino.' She looked directly into her mother's troubled eyes. 'As you've already pointed out, Mama, I'm now beyond any consideration of marriage so what better role to assume than that of chaperon.'

'Why are you doing this, Christabel?'

'I've just explained.'

'But not very convincingly. Your chance of success is slight. The packet boats sail in all kinds of atrocious weather, as you must know, and you will be stranded in Dover—a young woman, putting up in an inn alone—and for what precisely?'

'I have at least to try to undo the harm that has been done.' She looked steadily at her mother. 'If Domino continues with this journey, it will be because of my brother's thoughtlessness in aiding her. It will ruin her reputation and make it impossible for her to marry where she wishes.'

'But surely she wishes to marry Benedict?'

'I don't think so. Benedict is her escort. He may be in love with her, although I doubt it, but *she* is in love with Richard Veryan.'

Her mother paused. This certainly accorded with other gossip she had heard. It was more than likely, but why was Bel becoming so involved? Out loud she repeated, 'Richard?'

'I believe they are to make a match of it. No doubt he is waiting until the year's mourning is over before making an official announcement, but I think it clear that they plan to be together. I imagine some silly quarrel must have sprung up between them and would have petered out to nothing if Benedict had not become embroiled.'

Her mother remained silent, still wondering at the intensity of her daughter's concern.

'You must see that I owe it to Richard,' Christabel broke out. 'We have been an unlucky family for him: I broke his first engagement and now Benedict will be responsible for destroying the second. Unless, that is, I do something now and attempt to rescue Domino from her own foolishness.'

'You owe nothing to Richard Veryan, Bel,' her mother said quietly. 'Yes, you broke the engagement and no doubt it was very painful for him, but you have long expiated that sin. And after his behaviour last night, it is he who is in debt to you.'

'That's not so.'

'I think it is. He has cost you your betrothal; more than that, he has made quite sure that you will have little chance of any future marriage. I would say that his flagrant disregard of any acceptable code of conduct has more than balanced the books.'

'I have to help him, Mama.'

'He has ruined you, Bel!'

'I have ruined myself. I tried to follow a path which wasn't mine. For a while I convinced myself that I was doing the right thing, but all the time I was being untrue to the person I really am.'

'You will have plenty of time now to be true to yourself,' her mother remarked tartly, 'and while you're doing that you can enjoy watching your sister snare Sir Julian for herself.'

* * *

It was past one o'clock before the carriage arrived at the front door and Christabel was able to begin the journey to Dover. It would take at least seven hours to reach the town and she made herself as comfortable as she could, nestling into the velvet seat coverings and pulling a cashmere blanket over her legs to shield her from draughts. Outside on the box, his face disapproving, Stebbings set the horses in motion. He had promised Lady Tallis that he would not leave Miss Christabel's side until they were back in Mount Street and this he was grimly determined to do.

They were soon rumbling over Blackfriars Bridge, its elegant Portland stone glinting in the afternoon sunlight. Immediately south of the river paved roads gave way to dirt tracks with cramped and ramshackle buildings huddled on either side. Vast numbers of the poor were crowded into these tenements and everywhere squalor and despair disclosed a very different London to the one Christabel knew. Garbage was strewn at random and open tidal sewers dotted the landscape. She felt a guilty relief once the carriage had left behind these desperate areas and was trundling through the quieter suburbs where market gardening and pasturage for cows still interspersed the dark of London's brick.

It was two hours into their journey before at last they reached the Kent countryside. A panorama of fields and trees passed lazily by and Christabel had ample leisure to think. The more she considered the matter, the more she found it difficult to believe this was an elopement.

Benedict's demeanour had never approached that of a lover and Domino had treated him in the same carefree fashion. It was clear that Domino was the moving force behind this crazy journey. Could she have quarrelled with Richard over some trifle—perchance he'd not been giving her the attention she expected—and decided that running away was a means of teaching him a lesson? She was young enough and foolish enough.

The continual shaking and jolting of the carriage felt to Christabel as though she had been travelling for months rather than hours. After the recent spate of bad weather, the road was potholed and dangerous, with immense muddy banks on either side, and in some places reducing almost to a track. Unable to sleep, she made plans for when they reached Dover.

As long as the delinquents were still in the town, she would find them. She must convince Domino that any fears she had over Richard's indifference were groundless and that if this flight was indeed a stupid gamble to regain his interest, the girl was in grave danger of losing him. He would never allow himself to be mired once again in a scandal not of his making. She would do what she could to bring an end to this reckless journey and protect Richard from any knowledge of it.

This cheerful thought had relaxed her a little and she was at last able to fall into a fitful doze as the coach slowly made its cumbersome way towards the Channel coast. She did not awake fully until she felt the horses moving sharply downhill. Leaning forwards to peer through the window, she could see in the distance a strip of water streaking the horizon. They were descending a steep and winding hill leading to the town and gradually houses began to spring up on either side of the road and the gradient to even out. She would bespeak a room at the Ship Inn, which she knew to be the best hostelry in Dover, her father having stayed there when he made the Grand Tour as a young man. Once settled, Stebbings could make discreet enquiries of the smaller establishments. Hopefully it would not take too long to run them to ground since Dover was not a large town.

The wind had hardly abated from the time they left London, but here on the coast it blew with an added ferocity. As the carriage swung around the last corner and reached the promenade, she got her first clear view of the sea. A sheet of gunmetal water heaved and tossed alarmingly, foaming white flecks of waves splintering the grey. Even from some distance she could hear the thunder of surf crashing against the harbour wall, spray after spray of icy water breaching the top of the wharf ready to drench anyone foolish enough to be walking on this stormy May evening. Her heart warmed; surely no one would put to sea in such weather. She lowered the carriage window and her hat was almost snatched from her head. The titian curls blew wildly in the wind as she attempted to give her groom directions.

'Stebbings,' she had to shout to make herself heard, 'please make for the Ship Inn. I hope to bespeak a room there.'

'That's where I was going,' he replied grimly. 'Nowhere else suitable for you, Miss Christabel, though heaven knows it's a bad day when a young lady has to venture alone to any inn.'

He left her shortly afterwards to find lodgings for himself in the cheaper part of town, but promised that once this was accomplished he would begin immediately to make a round of the smaller hotels and guest houses that lined the promenade and the streets behind. It was probable that if the runaways were still in Dover, they would be discovered in one of these. And so it proved.

Within an hour of arriving in the town, she was entering the tap room of the Pelican and encountering two pairs of startled eyes.

'Miss Tallis!'

Domino had been sitting by the window, gloomily watching the tossing waters, but at Christabel's entrance she sprang from her chair and stood like a statue, a stricken expression on her face. Benedict, too, had jumped to his feet, advancing on his sister impetuously.

'Bel! What on earth are you doing here?'

'Good evening, Benedict. I would think that question better belongs to me.'

She glanced around her at the soiled furnishings of the dismal room, her eyebrows raised and a quizzical look on her face.

'So what *are* you both doing here?'

Domino found her voice. 'I'm on my way to Paris,' she said tremulously, 'and Benedict is escorting me.'

'Escorting you?'

'There was no one else I could ask.' Domino's shoulders drooped in despair guessing that this sudden intrusion by Benedict's sister might mean the end of her plans.

Her escort scowled at her words. 'Thanks,' he said indignantly, 'and after all I've done—planning your escape, paying for the carriage, finding us somewhere to shelter!'

'I don't mean I'm not grateful to you, Benedict, just that you were my last resort.'

'Thanks again.' His face was red with annoyance.

It was evident that both parties to this escapade were so tightly wound that they needed only a small excuse to explode. It would be wise to intervene while she was still likely to get a sensible answer.

'So you're not eloping?'

Both of them looked astounded for an instant and then both burst into laughter. It broke the tension of the moment.

'Miss Tallis, how could you think such a thing?'

'Quite easily. You left a note for your aunt saying that you had to slip away from London because your life had become intolerable and that Benedict was travelling with you. What else was there to think but that you were escaping because you imagined—correctly—that you would both be deemed far too young to marry.'

'Too right,' Benedict exclaimed. 'I'm certainly not in the petticoat stakes and never likely to be. I only came on this stupid journey because she mopped and mowed around me until I was driven frantic. I agreed just to keep her quiet.'

'I did not mop and mow! And you could have refused, but you liked the idea of journeying to France—admit it!'

'Not with you, that's for sure. We've been stuck in this inn nigh on six hours and watched boat after boat set sail. But could I persuade her on to any of them?' he appealed to his sister. 'No, of course not. We have to wait until the sea is dead calm, would you believe.'

'I, for one, am delighted that you decided the weather was too rough to cross the Channel.' She turned towards the young girl, who was now near to tears.

'Domino,' she said gently, 'if it wasn't love for Benedict that drove you out of London, what was it?'

The girl looked frightened and said nothing.

'Come, my dear, there must be a very pressing reason for you to take such drastic action. And your aunt will have to know. So if you don't choose to tell me, at least prepare yourself to confide the whole story to Lady Blythe when we return.'

'Return?! I cannot do that, Miss Tallis.' Domino shrank even further into her chair, her hands twisting the already crumpled muslin of her dress.

'You must. You cannot think to continue your journey now and I am here to take you home.'

'But I must go on. I'm so sorry that you've been put to the trouble of following us and I understand that you will wish to return with Benedict, but *I* must continue.'

Christabel rose and went to the young girl, taking her hands in hers and holding them in a warm clasp.

'I cannot allow you to do so, Domino, your reputation would be ruined. I've found you in time to prevent that disaster. Until we get back to London, I shall act as your chaperon. We can say that we've been travelling together from the outset and that will quash any rumours. I'm sure we can find a distant relative who lives nearby who has suddenly become very sick.'

She began to warm to her invention. 'You promised Lady Blythe that you would pay them a last visit. Yes, that's it. Naturally your aunt's health is not strong enough for such a long journey, so I offered to accompany you. We can forget the part Benedict has played. For the purposes of our story, he never left London.'

'That's fine, write me out of the script,' he complained bitterly.

His sister wheeled on him and said sharply, 'As someone whose conduct has been grossly irresponsible, you should be glad to be written out.'

She turned again to Domino. 'I'm staying at the Ship and have ordered rooms for both of us. You must pack your valise now and return with me there. Benedict can remain at the Pelican and in that way we should be able to counter any possible gossip that might seep out. First thing in the morning Stebbings will bring the carriage round to the Ship and we will all three travel back to London together.'

The girl looked defiant. 'You don't understand. I have to get to Spain. Paris is only the first stage of my journey.'

'You're going to Spain?' Christabel looked astonished.

'I was to visit my relatives in Madrid later this summer, but I intend now to arrive a little earlier.'

'Does Lady Blythe know of this visit?'

'Of course, my father has discussed plans with her.'

'Then surely she is the person to arrange your travel and accompany you on the journey.'

'That's still weeks ahead. I cannot stay in London—I need to leave now.'

'Why is it so important for you to leave town immediately?' Christabel asked wonderingly.

The girl looked scared. 'Tell her,' Benedict advised. 'She knows nearly everything anyway.'

In a small and halting voice Domino made her confession that she was badly indebted to Lord Moncaster and that he was intent on receiving payment in one form or another.

'Threatened her, Bel,' Benedict put in. 'Tried to force her to go to his house on the night of Sophia's ball. That's his notion of her paying the debt.'

The tears began to course down Domino's face as she remembered the terror she had felt at Lord Moncaster's threats. Christabel crossed swiftly to the sobbing girl and put her arms around her.

'He's a scoundrel, my dear, but he has no power over you,' she soothed. 'You're a minor and not responsible for gambling debts. There's nothing he can do to reclaim the money and he knows that well.'

Domino abruptly stopped crying and gaped at her. 'You mean that all this time I was in no danger.'

'None. But you have not acted well.'

The reproof in her voice made the girl wince and she hung her head again. 'I know,' she managed to whisper.

'Lord Veryan would be very disturbed if he knew of your conduct.'

Domino was puzzled at the introduction of Richard's name, but said again, 'I know.'

'We will say nothing to him. He need never know what has occurred, but you must tell your aunt and beg her pardon, not just for such foolish behaviour, but for worrying her so much with this flight of yours.'

'Is Aunt Loretta very angry?' the girl ventured.

'Not angry, just sick with worry. You haven't been thinking very clearly. If you had told Lady Blythe the true situation, she would doubtless have rung a peal over you and been displeased for a while, but she would also have applauded your honesty and forgiven you very quickly. She would have paid Lord Moncaster what he's owed and that would have been an end to it.'

'Told you so, didn't I?' Benedict smirked. 'Now perhaps you'll give me credit for some sense.'

Domino was just about to cross swords again when Christabel decided that she'd had enough. She was very tired from the journey and the thought of having to repeat it on the morrow with two squabbling children in tow was not a happy one. Nor was she anticipating with any pleasure her mother's and Lady Blythe's likely welcome to this wayward little party.

'You will accompany me back to the Ship, Domino,' she said firmly. 'We will order a late supper and you are invited to eat with us, Benedict, if you wish.

'Otherwise, we will see you outside the inn at nine o'clock tomorrow morning. If you're late, you will have to find your own way back to town.'

'No need to get on your high ropes.' He sniffed. He had never before known his elder sister to be so severe.

The image of Richard, never far from her thoughts, fuelled the anger she felt towards her brother and she lashed him with her tongue.

'Your behaviour has been as reprehensible as Domino's—more so, for you are older than she and have been on the town longer. No doubt Mama will have something to say to you when we reach Mount Street.'

He found this to be only too true. Mama had more than something to say and Benedict received the dressing down of his life from his usually mild-mannered parent. He was barely through the front door when his mother pounced, dragging him into the library and subjecting him to a lengthy and irate scolding. Lady Harriet had decided that her son had enjoyed more than sufficient holiday in the capital. He was to start on the long journey back to Cornwall in two days' time and Stebbings would not be driving him. The groom had already been forced to undertake an unnecessary and fatiguing journey beyond his normal duties and Benedict could make his own way to Lamorna Place by stage and then carrier. His mother derived a degree of pleasure in relaying this information; it went some little way to recompensing her for the worry and fright she'd suffered.

Lady Harriet followed him out into the hall where Christabel was waiting, pale but composed, ready to suffer her share of parental wrath. She had directly disobeyed her mother in going alone to Dover, but she could not be sorry for it. Domino was returned safely to Lady Blythe's care and no one else was the wiser. Certainly not Richard. He was at Madron and blissfully unaware of the drama that had been enacted.

Her mother turned back to the library and beckoned her to follow. Although it was early May, a fire burned brightly in the grate in an effort to conquer the wind and rain which battered at the windows. The unseasonable weather matched the gloom of the occasion, but her mother's scolding appeared light.

'I am delighted, Bel, that you are returned safely and that silly young girl is back with her aunt. But I cannot think it right that you involved yourself.'

'I couldn't let her plunge herself into a scandal.' Her voice was as quiet as her mother's and devoid of expression. 'Of all people, I know how dreadful it is to face down gossip and innuendo. And it was Benedict who would have been largely responsible. Surely you would not have had that happen.'

'Benedict is to return to Cornwall,' her mother said, not answering her directly. 'But what of you?'

'What do you mean, Mama?'

'You say that you travelled to Dover to protect the

family's honour and to save Domino from herself—that is understandable, given your own painful experience as a girl—but why else?'

'Isn't that enough?' she challenged, hoping to steer the conversation in another direction.

'For most people, perhaps. But your emotions run deep, Christabel. You told me that you did not wish Richard Veryan to suffer another broken engagement. Why was that so important to you?'

A tell-tale blush suffused Christabel's cheeks and she said hastily, 'I believe him to deserve better. He is an honourable man and capable of true feeling.'

'Ah!' Her mother sighed. 'As I thought. You are in love with him. What a perverse creature you are. Why could you not have loved him when you had the chance?'

The reproach went unanswered and Lady Harriet continued, 'You are in love with him and he is betrothed, you say, to this green girl?'

She shook her head in disbelief, but, seeing her daughter's wounded face, moved swiftly across the room and took her hands in a tender clasp.

'Bel, what have you done? What will become of you?'

'Whatever do you mean, Mama?' The anguish in her mother's voice made her step back in surprise.

'I mean, my dear, that both the men who have figured so large in your life are now promised to others.'

She looked bewildered. 'Both men?'

'Both,' her mother repeated heavily. 'Sir Julian has asked permission to pay his addresses to Sophia.'

Chapter Nine

Richard rode along the headland. On one side of the twisting pathway stretched a patchwork of small fields, ancient granite walls and, in the distance, gently rolling hills. On the other and immediately below him the ocean thundered benignly, the sun glistening on the rocks and the spray thrusting ever higher up the cliff face. It was a glorious morning; for a short while, as he relaxed into the rhythm of the trotting horse, his mind was free of care. It had been an emotional homecoming. He'd arrived amid a torrential downpour but Lady Veryan had come running from the doorway as soon as she heard the noise of wheels on gravel. He'd hardly clambered down the carriage steps before she'd flung her arms around his neck, trembling with a mixture of happiness and sorrow. His father's absence had hovered between them. Until that moment he'd not fully realised how frail she was and how desperate to see him. Guilt at delaying his homecoming had cast a large shadow over his arrival.

But this morning after five days at the Abbey and many hours together, life seemed a good deal brighter. He was home now and home for good. Lady Anne need worry no longer over the upkeep of house and land. Already he'd had several sessions with his father's bailiff and acquainted himself with many of the problems and a few of the pleasures of a landed estate. This was surely one of its most agreeable delights: a solitary ride in the early morning sun, king and master of all he surveyed.

The seclusion was needed. His final farewell to Christabel had been torture. So many things left unsaid between them, so many feelings unexpressed. He'd intended a brief farewell, a mere clasp of the hand and a friendly smile, enough to tell her that she was free of him, free to make the life she wanted with Sir Julian. But all his judicious intentions had vanished like dew in a sunlit haze and the prudent words he'd prepared had died unregretted on his lips. She had looked magnificent, her beautiful form encased in a floating cloud of diaphanous gauze, her every movement sparkling in the light of diamonds. When the musicians had struck up for the waltz, he'd been unable to resist one last dance with her. It hadn't lasted long. Once his arms were round her, he was again a lost man. The intended farewell had been abandoned and in its place that long, lingering kiss. He'd wanted it to go on for ever. Now, looking back, he wondered grimly how he'd ever torn himself away.

But he had and he was home and this morning was a gift from heaven. The physical ache of losing her must one day disappear. He'd lived without her for six years and would do so again. His old defence of suppressing all feeling was now forfeit, but surely he would cease to think of her so often once he knew her to be married.

'Hey, there! Richard? Is that you?'

A faint voice calling in the distance penetrated his thoughts and he turned his head to see another rider beating his way up the headland towards him. The figure was familiar and for a moment his heart skipped a beat. Surely the Tallises had not come home already?

'Ricky, it *is* you. I thought so.' Benedict arrived in a pelter at his side. 'A bang-up morning, hey? Hope you don't mind my trespassing.'

Since the two families had always treated each other's lands as their own, this was by way of being a pleasantry.

'It's good to see you, Benedict, if surprising. Why so far from London?'

'I thought it was time I came home,' Benedict began awkwardly. 'I've been away a fair while and the old man was getting a bit Friday-faced. Started to demand that his son and heir return to the fold.'

'I see. I imagined you were fixed in London for the Season.'

'That was never the plan,' the boy rejoined quickly. 'I was only ever going to stay a few weeks. I'd had enough of town anyway—couldn't wait to get back!'

Richard looked sceptically at his young companion,

but said nothing and they rode on together in silence. Thinking that some further explanation was due, Benedict found himself continuing, 'To tell you the truth, there was a spot of bother and London got too hot for me.' He grinned engagingly.

'That sounds a little more likely.' Richard returned his smile. 'What was it? Boxing the watch, gambling debts, a ladybird?'

Benedict flushed with annoyance. 'She was hardly one of the muslin company, if that's what you mean. Far too respectable, a chit of a girl, and I'm banished to Lamorna because of her.' His earlier carefree air left him as he remembered his grievances against Domino.

'I never thought of you as being in the petticoat line,' Richard remarked smilingly.

'I'm not! Most definitely I'm not. All I did was to try to help someone and look what happened.'

'And dare I ask who it was that you tried to help?'

Benedict flushed again and realised he'd said too much, but it was too late to withdraw. 'Actually you know her pretty well,' he muttered. 'It's Domino de Silva.'

'Domino! What trouble has she got herself in, for heaven's sake? I thought her aunt well able to take care of her.'

'There'd have to be a hundred aunts to keep *her* out of trouble. I can't tell you what bother she was in, but believe me, it was stupid. Still, I'd better keep mum, lady's honour, and all that rot.'

'But why are *you* exiled from the pleasures of London?'

The younger man scowled at the thought of what he was missing. 'The silly chit took it into her head to leave town on the quiet. She wanted an escort and guess who was witless enough to agree.'

Richard's face was inscrutable. 'And where were you to escort her?'

'Supposedly Paris and from there she was going to travel on to Spain, but we never got any further than Dover.'

His companion looked at him enquiringly.

'You wouldn't believe her! Said she couldn't cope with the sea unless it was dead calm. We must have seen half-a-dozen packet boats come and go and she couldn't bring herself to board any of them. I told the silly goose that the weather wasn't likely to improve and if she didn't want to be caught in Dover, she should just close her eyes and walk. But would she listen? Huh!'

'And did you get caught?'

'Oh, yes, and a right shenanigan that was. My sister turned up and gave us a real bear-garden jaw. Then she took Domino back to her aunt and the long and the short of it was that I was ordered to pack my traps and leave London immediately.'

'Sophia?'

'Sophia?'

'Your sister who discovered you in Dover.'

'Of course not Sophia. Can you imagine?'

'Miss Tallis, then?' Richard looked bewildered. 'Why would Miss Tallis come after you?'

'God knows. She's not usually interfering. She seemed very anxious about preventing a scandal.'

'But Miss de Silva is hardly her concern.'

'I suppose she thought *I* was her concern,' he said carelessly, 'although she seemed more worried about your reaction.'

'To Domino's flight?'

'Yes, didn't make much sense to me. I couldn't work out why Bel was so upset. Or why she thought *you'd* be upset if you knew Domino had cut loose. There's been a lot of chatter in the clubs, but I never thought you had any real interest there.'

Benedict looked interrogatively at the rider beside him, but Richard made no answer. His mind was busy reviewing the hints he'd been at pains to drop over the last few weeks. He might not have lied outright, but he had led Christabel to believe that he and Domino might be engaged. She would see Domino's flight as a threat to their betrothal. She had intervened, but was that for the girl's sake or for his? Whatever the case, it was based on a false premise.

'Did your sister travel all the way to Dover just to put an end to this journey?' he continued his train of thought aloud.

'Like I said. Brought Stebbings with her, too. He gave me a jobation as well. That's the trouble with servants who've known you all your life.'

'So Miss Tallis travelled a long distance, alone apart from her groom, to find you both and bring Domino back.'

Richard was slowly trying to make sense of what

had happened. If Christabel *had* braved that journey for him, it meant that she'd wanted to protect him, wanted to save him from the hurt of another betrayal. She must still care for him! Beyond the physical hunger he'd deliberately set out to nurture and with a deep and tender love. He knew himself to be wholly undeserving, but the idea flooded him with its spreading warmth.

Conscious of Benedict eyeing him askance, he blocked these dangerous thoughts and made every effort to continue the conversation.

'I would say you were extremely lucky that your sister intervened when she did. You might well have found yourself in difficulties once you were the other side of the Channel and without friendly help to hand.'

'To tell you the truth, I'm glad to be out of it. I was a bit blue devilled at first, but not any more. I miss the fun of being in London, but not the family's constant carping. And now all this fuss over Sophia's wedding— that's beyond enough. The more I think about it, the better I'm pleased to be at Lamorna.'

Richard stared at him. 'Sophia is getting married? But surely...'

'Turn up for the books, eh? Sir Julian decided that she was a safer bet! He must want his head examined.'

'Are you saying that Christy is no longer to marry him?' He felt the world shifting beneath his feet and inadvertently used his pet name for her.

'That's right. Bethrothal off. Then betrothal on—but different sister.'

Surely Sir Julian could not have taken such serious exception to his fiancée's rescue mission. It had after all been an attempt to avoid scandal in the family. His conduct was inexplicable.

'Do you know why the engagement to Miss Tallis was called off?' he asked cautiously.

'They're puffing it off that they no longer feel suited to one another, whatever that means. Never thought they did suit, if you ask me. But no one ever does—ask me, I mean.'

'It seems to have taken them both some time to come to that conclusion.'

'Between you and me, Rick, and I know you won't spread this around, there's more to it than that. Bel was crazy enough to kiss another man and Julian saw her. That was enough to send him fleeing to the hills. Very straight, very proper, Sir Julian.'

Richard felt an iron bar descend on his chest. Without a doubt he was that other man. Sir Julian Edgerton had seen him kiss Christabel on the balcony and decided that she was not a fit wife for him. The popinjay! The self-righteous popinjay, to reject a woman like Christabel and to turn instead to that screeching harridan of a sister! He was pretty sure that Sophia was responsible in some way for Christabel's downfall; the girl was by nature underhand. Sir Julian would soon realise his ghastly mistake, and there would be no going back on this one. He deserved everything he got, Richard thought bitterly.

They rode on in silence, Benedict aware that somehow he'd upset his companion, but unsure just what he'd said that had been so disturbing. At the old mill post Richard broke the unnatural calm to bid him goodbye.

'I have an appointment with my bailiff, Benedict,' he said with a faint smile, 'and regret I must leave you here. Enjoy the rest of your ride.'

'I will. Perhaps we can ride out tomorrow,' he said eagerly, hoping to put right whatever ill he'd unwittingly committed.

'Perhaps,' Richard said vaguely. 'But there is a great deal of work to be done in the estate office and I can't afford to play truant too often.'

'Surely you can spare an hour or two,' the younger man protested.

'I would hope so, but I fear that my business affairs are likely to take me away again very soon.'

And with that he wheeled his horse around and cantered off towards the Abbey, leaving Benedict puzzled and slightly alarmed at this sudden turn of events.

Richard did not fulfil his promise to go to the estate office, but instead left the stable lad to rub down his sweating horse while he strode towards his study. Flinging his gloves to one side, he wrenched off his boots and sat down in an easy chair to consider what he'd just learned. If Benedict's news was correct, and he could see no reason why the boy would make up such a story, then Christabel was now a free woman. How was she feeling? How deeply would Sir Julian's rejection bite? He'd never been convinced that she loved the man, but in the end he'd accepted that she had the right to find happiness with him if she could. But now? Her whole

life had been overturned and his kiss had been the cata-
lyst. Marriage to Sir Julian was no longer on offer and
as a woman who'd provoked two broken engagements,
she was perilously close to social ruin.

And how must she feel losing the man to that sister
of hers? What was wrong with Edgerton! How could
he prefer Sophia, an ill-dressed, ill-tempered young
woman? Christabel was just too much for him—that
was the truth. She was too beautiful, too intelligent, too
passionate. Edgerton was scared that he would not be
able to live up to her or keep her satisfied. When he'd
seen the way she'd kissed another man, he'd realised the
well of passion within her, a passion that he could not
begin to evoke or fulfil. Sophia was far less daunting
a prospect, Richard could see. But if Sir Julian could
not live up to Christabel, he knew a man who could.
His love for her had made a chaos of his life. It had not
let him go for an instant, even when he was denying its
very existence. It had always been there and now finally
it might have a chance to flourish.

He would post back to London, tell Christy his true
feelings, beg her forgiveness once more and ask her to
marry him. Again. But this time it would work. His
mother would understand his renewed absence when
she knew why he was returning to London. She would
be overjoyed finally to have the daughter-in-law of
whom she'd always dreamed.

In truth, Lady Veryan did not share her son's enthusiasm. She had never wholly forgiven Christabel for
the heartbreak she had caused. The catastrophic events

six years ago had almost wrecked the deep friendship between their two families and here was Richard intending to ask the girl to marry him once more. Even worse, she had received a letter only last week from Harriet Tallis conveying the welcome news that her eldest daughter was to be married at last to a delightful and highly respected man. Anne would love Sir Julian Edgerton on sight, her friend had enthused. And now here was Richard telling her that this very betrothal, only a few weeks old, was ended. It seemed that Christabel was still adept at breaking her word.

She made no attempt, however, to dissuade her son—she could see that he was determined on his course. Six years of fending for himself in pioneer country had turned him into a decisive and forceful man and she recognised that it was useless to try to change his mind.

Happily unaware of his mother's misgivings, Richard made the tedious journey back to the capital in the best of spirits. He'd been foolish ever to imagine that he could excise Christabel from his heart and even more stupid to embark on a campaign to free himself from her powerful enchantment. Now that her betrothal to Sir Julian was at an end, a future together was within their grasp and he was going to make sure that they seized it. Rather than putting up at Brown's again, he decided he would go straight to the family's London home despite its dilapidated state. It was time to open Grosvenor Square after all these years and make it habitable for Christabel. Everything he did from now on would be with her in mind; for the first time in his life he was absolutely sure of what he wanted and what he had to do to get it.

Nevertheless the condition of the house shocked him when he was shown around by a nervous housekeeper. The family had not occupied it since those dreadful events six years ago, his parents having lost any taste for London life. They could not bring themselves to return to a house which had seen such sadness.

'I'm sorry about the state of things, my lord,' Mrs Moffat apologised anxiously as she accompanied him on a dismal tour, 'but there's only me and Mr Moffat here and 'tis a large place to keep perfect.'

Perfect it was not. The furniture was shrouded in holland covers, layers of dust coated every visible surface and in the darkest corners of each room cobwebs hung undisturbed. Richard's spirits sank a little as he contemplated the mournful sight; the contrast with the house's former glory was painful. So, too, were the images from the past which now rushed back at him: Christabel excited and happy, displaying her latest purchases; kicking off her shoes and curling up on the chesterfield ready to chat; descending the staircase on her way to yet another ball, heartbreakingly beautiful. How young they had been then, how untried and untested. He shook his head in an effort to dislodge such memories and strode to the window to pull back the long brocade curtains. Clouds of dust mounted towards the ceiling and the window panes beyond were grimy and streaked. But the sun was high in the sky, its beams catching at the carved architraves and the marble fireplace, and bringing the tired room to life.

He turned to the housekeeper. 'I realise what an impossible task you've had.' Mrs Moffat bobbed a curtsy at this reassurance. 'However,' he went on, 'could you bring the house back to something like its former condition—with extra help, of course?'

'It depends on how much more help there was,' the housekeeper offered cautiously.

'As much as you need. Hire however many people you think necessary. My only stipulation is that the house should be restored within a few days.'

The woman looked stunned at this demand, but the thought of employing an army of helpers to scrub, clean and launder a house that for years she'd watched fall into disrepair infused her with a new energy.

'A few days? At that rate, we'll be working morning and night. If I may ask, my lord, is there a particular reason for the haste?'

'There is. By the end of the week this house must be fit to welcome the most beautiful woman in the world!'

The housekeeper was alight with curiosity but thought better of questioning her master further. Instead she said with renewed determination, 'It will be, sir. I'll get Moffat on to the hiring straight away. Meantime I'll begin in the basement—we'll be using the family kitchen again and it's certain to need a deal of work before it's straight.'

Richard took a last look at the once beautiful salon and smiled easily. He was leaving behind the old tale of misery and betrayal for a new and happier story. Mrs Moffat and her helpers would bring the house back to life and make it a home fit for the woman he loved. In time there would be renovation and refurbishment, but that was for the future. That could await Christabel's choosing—once she became Lady Veryan.

As she came down the stairs at Mount Street, Christabel heard laughter coming from the hall below. Sophia had returned from yet another shopping trip, but this time accompanied by Sir Julian. Her transformation from the sulky and petulant girl of a few weeks ago to the smiling and agreeable young woman of today had been truly astonishing. Christabel rejoiced that both participants to this frankly odd marriage appeared happy. Nevertheless there was a twinge of resentment; it rankled that Sir Julian should have found it quite so easy to transfer his affections. But it proved what she'd always thought—that he was in love with the dream of Christabel and not with the woman herself. He had never truly known her. She smiled wryly—if he had but witnessed half of her shameful conduct while Richard was in town! Those fevered interludes were ample proof that she was an unsuitable bride for such a model of rectitude as Sir Julian. Sophia, for all her moods, was a pattern of conformity and unlikely ever to transgress.

But Christabel had always been what her father called 'hot to handle'. She had slept away these last six years until awoken by Richard's touch. His return had signalled a release of feelings she had denied for so long. From the night he'd danced with her at Almack's, the passionate, unruly girl had risen into being and the cool, clear-headed Christabel gradually sank without trace. She ached for him. If she closed her eyes, she could see him plainly, their bodies a whisper away as he bid her goodbye: his grey eyes silver in the moonlight, the dark hair falling carelessly across his forehead, the feel of him, the smell of him, the sheer physical joy of him.

She had always loved his energy, his sense of adventure, the way he took his pleasures so intensely. In comparison Sir Julian's were muted; the two men she had promised to marry could not be more different. She almost laughed aloud as she remembered that swim long ago in the cove at Lamorna—the scattered clothes, the mad dash to the sea, the cleaving of their bodies together in the cool water. Sir Julian would have been scandalised. Far better then that he'd changed his mind and escaped a life of vexation. Thankfully only a few people had been aware of their betrothal and though there might be a little gossip, Sophia would soon be married. There would always be doubt in the minds of the scandalmongers as to whether there had ever been an engagement between the elder Miss Tallis and Sir Julian Edgerton or whether rumour had simply fixed on the wrong sister.

'Look what we've bought, Bel!'

Her sister's tone was a little defiant, a little smug. Sophia had not yet managed to accustom herself entirely to the change in her circumstances and was unsure that she liked her sister to be so accepting of the new dispensation.

'Good afternoon, Sophia, Sir Julian,' Christabel said in her musical voice. 'I see you've both been very busy. Come into the drawing room and show me what bargains you've managed to secure.'

Sir Julian beamed. Of all of them, he had felt most discomfort with the alterations to his marriage plans. He still could not quite believe how quickly he had changed his mind over such a momentous decision. His sister, Lady Russell, had scolded him roundly and told him he was a fool. If his feelings were so lightweight, she snorted, he should forget the whole business of getting married. But he had not and had daily been surprised at how comfortable Sophia and he were going on together. She was never out of temper these days, he reflected, and she seemed genuinely interested in the details of his charity work. Even her choice of raiment seemed to have undergone modification. Today she was wearing a soft lilac muslin with cream lace, a modest and becoming creation. Christabel, also wearing a simple muslin dress, eclipsed her and always would.

Her ethereal beauty outshone every woman he knew, but ethereal could have its problems, he decided.

And he was not convinced that Richard Veryan had finally disappeared from the scene. Sad to acknowledge, Christabel was just a trifle unsteady. Lady Russell had probably been correct all along. Miss Tallis was not the right bride for him. No further proof was needed than the way she had abandoned all delicacy at her sister's come-out ball, kissing another man in public and in such a fashion. He felt himself grow hot at the thought of it. She was smiling at him now, holding open the door, and he followed her swiftly into the drawing room. On the whole, he thought he preferred her as a sister-in-law.

The front-door knocker sounded loudly just as Sophia had begun to unpack her first parcel. Christabel had little time to consider who could be calling in the middle of the afternoon before a footman was at her side with the message that Lord Veryan wished to speak with her privately.

There was a sudden stunned silence among the little gathering until she recalled herself and said as naturally as possible, 'Please show Lord Veryan into the library, James.'

She turned to her companions with a winning smile, 'I must leave you for a moment but I won't be long,' she promised.

'Well!' breathed Sophia as her sister went out of the door.

'Well indeed!' echoed Sir Julian.

She was astonished by Richard's appearance at Mount Street. She had imagined him well and truly settled at his beloved Madron, acquainting his mother with the news of his betrothal and making preparations for Domino to join him. Why he had returned to town was a complete mystery. His first words did little to enlighten her.

'How can you bear to see that charade?' he flung the question at her, gesturing in the general direction of the drawing room. He'd arrived in a celebratory mood, but the brief glimpse he'd had of Sophia's gloating face had roused him to an angry defence of the woman he loved.

'If you mean my sister and Sir Julian,' Christabel replied coolly, 'I'm delighted they have found happiness with each other.'

'Delighted? Delighted to be rejected for an ill-favoured, ill-tempered vixen?'

She did not reply to the calumny against her sister. His agitation was obvious as he paced up and down the library floor.

'For God's sake, whatever's the matter with the fellow?' he exploded as he came to rest in front of her. The thought was torturing him that he was responsible for the humiliation she must now be suffering.

'As far as I am aware, nothing ails Sir Julian. We simply found that we were not suited to one another,' she replied composedly. 'It was you, after all, who took pleasure in pointing that out.'

'I take no pleasure in what has happened to you,' he growled.

She acknowledged this with a small bow of her head, but then looked directly into his stormy gaze. 'Why are you here, Richard?'

'I met Benedict out riding and he told me the news. I came immediately.'

'But why?' she repeated.

'I have come to ask you to marry me,' he stated baldly.

He'd not meant to make such a stark declaration, but all his rehearsed speeches had simply melted away. She stared at him, dumbstruck.

'Is this your idea of a joke?'

'Hardly.'

'Then you must have run mad. Or—' and she fixed him with a look of contempt '—you are still intent on distressing me and this is part of your plan.'

'Neither. I am sincere.'

'You expect me to believe you?'

'My conduct has been unforgivable, as I've confessed. I set out to destroy whatever happiness you thought to snatch from your liaison with Edgerton and I seem pretty much to have succeeded. You know that I regret the pain I've caused, but I cannot turn the clock back even if I would.'

She remained standing motionless, silent and bewildered.

'And I would not turn the clock back, because now you are free,' he said with something like triumph in his voice. He advanced closer and took both her hands in his. 'We have both made mistakes, Christy—can we not put them behind us?'

'I hope we may,' she replied in a dazed voice, 'but you need feel no obligation towards me.'

'It's not obligation that makes me offer my hand to you in marriage.' He was finding it difficult to contain his frustration. 'Benedict tells me that the engagement was cancelled after that fool in there saw you kissing another man. Who else could that be but me?'

'Benedict is a silly boy. He knows nothing.'

'But he was right.'

'The engagement was already in trouble.' She sighed

wearily. 'The manner in which you chose to say good-bye simply brought it to a swifter conclusion.'

'It was in trouble because of me. Admit it! It was in trouble because of your feelings for me.'

She said nothing, her beautiful face pale and still. The emerald eyes were downcast and she could not answer him truthfully.

'You do have feelings for me, Christy, I know.' He pulled her roughly into his arms, his face buried in the red blaze of her hair.

She pushed him violently away and the green eyes were suddenly shooting fire. 'And what about your feelings for Domino? How dare you ask me to marry you when you are privately betrothed to her! Is there no shame to which you will not stoop?'

'Betrothed to her? Of course I'm not betrothed to her. Whatever makes you think any such thing?'

'You've made it abundantly clear over these past weeks that she will be your bride when the time is right. I believe the clubs have even been running wagers on it.'

'You know as well as I that men will bet on just about anything,' he returned defensively. This was proving more difficult than he'd ever imagined. 'There *is* no betrothal, Christy. I let you believe that I favoured Domino because I wanted to make you jealous.'

'Are you telling me that you have constantly lied about your relationship with Miss de Silva?' she said in a voice tipped with steel.

'I haven't lied. I never told you that I wished to marry her. I just let you think that I was attracted to her.'

'Then you lied by default.'

'You must understand,' he said desperately, 'I thought I'd banished you from my heart, but when I met you again that afternoon in the park, I knew that wasn't true. After all these years, you still took my breath away. You were so beautiful, so desirable. I wanted you for my own and that pompous fool, Edgerton, had you.'

'And that decided you to practise a loathsome deceit?'

'You jumped to the wrong conclusion and, yes, I used it against you. I regret doing so, but there were never any serious feelings on my side. I've never felt anything but friendship for her.'

'And Domino, what of her?' she asked crisply.

For the first time he looked a little shamefaced. 'A mere adolescent fantasy on her part, but it's over now.'

'She is seventeen, Richard, a vulnerable girl, and you took advantage of her to continue a vendetta against me.'

He sighed inwardly; he'd always known that this could be a sticking point. Christabel's strong sense of justice had not diminished over the years.

'She's fine now,' he tried to reply easily. 'There's been no harm done. It was a girlish fancy without substance. I never took advantage of her; I made it clear that I had no interest other than as a friend.'

She was looking shocked and the interview was not going the way he had envisaged.

'A friend? You stand there and tell me that she never

once believed you loved her, that she always knew a serious relationship between you was a mirage!'

It was her turn to stride up and down the library, her mass of auburn curls breaking free from their simple band and tumbling around her face.

'You have not been a friend to her. You have been devious, cunning, even ruthless. Not only have you destroyed my peace of mind, but you have treated her abominably. And you dare to come here and ask me to ally myself with you!'

'I thought, hoped, that you had forgiven the mistakes I've made these past weeks,' he said with quiet dignity. 'When we said goodbye at your sister's ball, it seemed as though the slate had been wiped clean.'

'That was before I knew of this further deception. How can I ever trust you?'

Her anguished tone pierced his heart. Abandoning all pretence of dignity, he pleaded with her in a voice husky with longing, 'Christy, my darling girl, I want you, I need you, please come to me.'

His arms reached out for her, pulling her close, his fingers tracing the delicate white skin of her inner arms until his hands cradled her breasts. She felt herself dissolving slowly, longing for his intimate touch, longing for his mouth to pleasure her again. His lips were caressing her hair now, moving down her neck to her bosom. They were hot and all-consuming. Any moment now she would abandon her paltry resistance. But the image of Domino, happy and innocent, rose before her and she pushed him away with a force that took him by surprise. He staggered back.

'I must ask you to go,' she said with as much composure as she could manage, 'and not return to this house. If by chance we should meet again in the future, I entreat you never to mention this matter.'

'Christabel, wait!'

In response she strode to the library door, her expression unyielding.

'Goodbye, Lord Veryan. James will see you out.'

Christabel was left shaken and trembling. She managed to maintain her self-possession until the front door shut behind him, but it cost her dear. She ought to return to the drawing room and pretend that nothing was amiss, but at this moment she could not face Sir Julian and her sister. Instead she made for her room and cast herself face down on the bed in a paroxysm of sobbing.

It was several minutes before she could regain control of herself and dry her tears. She lay staring blankly into space, engulfed by the jangle of warring emotions: the passion she felt for Richard against his duplicity, the chance of happiness against the likelihood of annihilating failure. Her mind circled ceaselessly. Richard must have returned to London within days of arriving home. When he'd heard of her broken engagement, he'd seen his chance and seized it, retracing the weary miles in order to ask her to marry. It was possible that after all the deceptions he was now sincere in his protestations. But his infamy was even greater than she'd imagined. He'd pretended feelings for Domino to further his own ends. He might have been honest with the young girl, but he'd still exploited her. There had never after all been any understanding between the two of them. The jealousy she'd felt at seeing them together came rushing back as an unstoppable torrent. All for nothing. All that pain for nothing. He'd been trifling with her, playing her like a fish on a line. And Domino, too. She could never trust him again.

Richard made his way back to Grosvenor Square, enraged that she had refused to believe him, enraged that for the second time she was turning him down. But most of all he was angry with himself for making such a mull of things. He'd thought that Christabel was bound to have learned the truth about his friendship with Domino after her rescue mission to Dover. He'd been sure that the enforced intimacy of their journey would have put her in full possession of the facts and she would know that whatever feelings Domino had for him, they were unrequited. Not so, apparently. She had never doubted his pretence and it was only this afternoon that she'd learned his supposed love for the girl was a sham. She was willing to forgive him much, but not this one harmless deception.

But if he were honest, it had been far from harmless. If she truly loved him, his constant intimacy with Domino would have racked her with jealousy. *If* she loved him? But she did, she loved him. When she'd gone to Domino's rescue it had been for his sake as much as for the girl's. She'd thought his reputation would be compromised and she'd not been able to contemplate seeing him hurt and once more the subject of gossip and innuendo. She loved him, he could swear. He hugged the thought to himself, allowing it to flood his body with a powerful energy. He wanted to go back to Mount Street that instant, to hammer on the door, force his way in and simply scoop her up in his arms and tell her that they were wasting time, that they were made for each other and always had been, that he wanted her now and could not wait another minute to claim back his own. In his mind he was with her again, encircling her lithe form in a crushing embrace, imprinting her pale, soft skin with urgent lips, entangling himself in a sheet of fiery curls.

He had reached Grosvenor Square and vaulted lightly up the front stairs to the open doorway. York tan gloves were thrown carelessly on to the battered cherrywood table and a caped greatcoat landed in the arms of the waiting footman. He strode purposefully into his study, calling for coffee to be brought immediately. He had a good deal of thinking to do if he were to win back the woman he loved. He was barred from Mount Street, and trying to thrust his way into the house would do nothing to endear him; he would need to be a great deal more subtle than that. Yet he had to see her, try to make her understand that his dissembling over Domino had been no more serious than the rest of his foolish actions. He must surprise her, create a situation where she was unable easily to escape and compel her to listen to all he wanted to say. He sat down to lay his plans carefully.

Chapter Ten

In the event he could think of nothing else but to intercept her at a time when she was without company and would not be expecting to see him. He knew from the past that she enjoyed riding alone with a single groom whenever she could and he was hopeful that she always hired a hack from the same stables. By dint of a few enquiries he had soon run to ground the mews she patronized, just around the corner from Mount Street. A cheeky stable boy, sufficiently greased in the palm, had let slip the information that a mare had been booked for Miss Tallis the following day. Further largesse elicited the news that the Tallis groom had mentioned his mistress was wishful of enjoying a change of scenery on the morrow and likely to ride in the exclusive but largely unfinished Regent's Park. This had suited Richard's purpose well since there was a good covering of trees running close to the bridle path and he would be able to wait for her unseen by all but the most observant passers-by. The weather had favoured him, too. After recent days of high winds and squally showers, the sun had returned the next morning and he rode out into the balmy air with an excited sense of anticipation.

He arrived at his chosen meeting place close on eleven o'clock. Several groups of people passed by the cluster of trees he sheltered beneath: nursemaids wheeling out their charges to take the morning air, a dowager scolding her companion mercilessly as they made their slow way along the footpath, a lone horseman putting his new mount through its paces. But otherwise the park was remarkably quiet, ideal for the forthcoming encounter. He hadn't long to wait until her trim figure hove into view, the groom keeping a respectful distance behind. She looked sublime in a tight-fitting costume of forest green cloth decorated with golden epaulettes and half-braided sleeves. A tall crowned hat with curled ostrich feathers completed the ensemble. Whatever inner turmoil was ravaging Christabel, the world would see only the fashionable woman they knew well.

As she came abreast of Richard's shelter, he wheeled his mount on to the path in front of her and forced her to come to a sudden halt. The groom moved up anxiously, but she waved him away with her hand. Whatever this ambush was about, she did not want Stebbings to hear.

'A beautiful morning, Miss Tallis.' Richard doffed his curly brimmed beaver, revealing fashionably dishevelled locks. The riding coat he wore was moulded tightly across his powerful shoulders and the palest fawn breeches encased his shapely legs. Gleaming top boots from Hoby and a freshly pressed neckcloth proclaimed him a gentleman of substance. He looked superb and she had to exert every nerve to detach her mind from the impulses of her traitorous body.

The two riders faced each other, their horses gently sidling to and fro until Christabel's mare, growing restive at the lack of action, began pawing irritably at the ground, almost unseating her in its efforts to be gone. Instinctively he grabbed at her bridle and brought their two mounts together. She thought she saw a paleness beneath the lean, tanned cheeks and his grey eyes were crystal clear and piercingly alive. It was as though this was the determining moment of his life.

Attempting to break the tension, she spoke with a boldness she did not feel. 'Good day to you, Lord Veryan. I hope you're enjoying this fine morning. May I ask that you allow me to do so, too?'

Her cold politeness did not daunt him; he retained his hand on her bridle.

'This is crazy. We should not have to meet like this, Christy.'

'The name is Miss Tallis, and you are quite correct, Lord Veryan, we should not. If you would be so good as to release my horse, I will be on my way.'

'Christabel, Miss Tallis, please hear me out. I apologise for accosting you in this fashion, but I've been unable to think of any other way to speak to you. I'll take only a small amount of your time but you must listen to me!'

Stebbings, seated on his mount a few yards distant,

appeared increasingly anxious and she sensed that he was getting ready to intervene. The last thing she wanted was any kind of brawl in a public place. Swiftly she dismounted and threw her reins to the groom.

'I shall be back in ten minutes, Stebbings. Please walk the horses until I return.'

'Yes, ma'am, if you're sure,' he replied uncertainly.

She nodded and strode towards the shelter of the trees. Richard dismounted and followed her.

'What is it you wish to say?' she demanded, turning to face him, her tone uncompromising.

All his prepared speeches were once again forgotten. He could think only of possessing the woman that he loved.

'Simply that we are made to be together. You must know that.'

'I know nothing of the sort.'

'You're not being honest, Christabel, either with yourself or with me. Surely we deserve that of each other.'

'I cannot believe you have the temerity to speak to me of honesty! How much honesty have you shown these past few weeks?'

He made no reply and she continued with barely a pause, 'I will answer for you. None. Since your return to England, you have waged a vendetta against me. You have been ingenious, leaving no avenue unvisited. Not content with destroying my plans to marry, you have shamelessly exploited a young girl's feelings in order to hurt me. I think you will agree that you have been thoroughly *dis*honest and succeeded admirably.'

Her voice was metallic and her eyes pools of emerald ice. She was desperate to harden herself against him, to build a protective shell even at this late hour.

Her clear tones sliced through the air. 'Take pleasure in what you have done, for there is nothing more. You have disrupted my life and made me as deeply unhappy as you could possibly wish.'

His dismay that she could think so badly of him forced him to defend himself. 'You must know that has not been my desire. All I want is to make you happy. I've said I'm truly sorry. I cannot do more.'

She looked stonily into the distance and, exasperated by her obstinacy, he spoke what was uppermost in his mind. 'I accept I've caused suffering, but consider also that I've done some good.'

'What!'

'You say that you and Edgerton found you were not suited. And why is that? Because you discovered that you were suited to another man. If it were not for me, you would be contemplating a very unhappy marriage.'

She looked scornfully at him, but he would not be silenced. 'You may deny it, but you know that it's true. And whatever stupidities we've committed, we belong together.'

'As you belonged together with Miss de Silva?' she asked waspishly.

'I've been honourable and straightforward in my dealings with her. You have to believe me. I would never deliberately set out to harm a young and inexperienced girl.'

The expression on her face told him that she was very far from believing him and he burst out in frustration, 'You know what young girls are like, Christabel, they enmesh themselves in ridiculous dreams which are a million miles away from reality.'

'Yes, I do know what young girls are like. Who better? I was one once, remember, and thanks to another man *my* ridiculous dream almost crushed my heart. I survived—just—and now you've come close to crushing it a second time. But I won't allow you to succeed.'

Her face was pale, and though she remained standing tall and proud before him he knew she was in a state of agitation. Her breath was short and irregular and the smooth curve of her breasts rose and fell with emotion. He longed to reach out to her, pull her close to him and let their bodies end the argument.

'I want to win your heart, not crush it,' he said urgently. 'Despite all that's happened, maybe because of all that's happened, I know I can make you happy. We have tested each other to the limit and we've survived. Our love will be fierce and strong and enduring. Give it a chance, Christabel,' he urged. 'Take a chance.'

'I cannot.' In an instant she seemed visibly to shrink into herself. 'I've already suffered too much and all I want now is to be left in peace. Leave me that at least.'

Her sadness fingered him with its hurt. The fight had gone out of her and he was responsible. He had destroyed the fire and the spirit that he had so loved.

'But—' he tried to rally once more.

'No "but", the game is played out, Richard. This is its end.'

She walked slowly away and he watched immobile as Stebbings helped her remount and together continue along the bridleway. He was as certain as he could be that she still loved him, but in the end he had been powerless to keep her by his side. He knew that nothing he ever said would make any difference. The game between them was indeed played out.

He flung himself into the saddle and struck out across the park, his mind tormented by the destructive passions that had brought him to this pass. It mattered not where he was heading—there was nowhere to go. He had striven to convince Christabel of his love: he'd been so sure that he would be able to win her over. But all his energy and resolution had not been enough. He had thought to free himself of her influence for ever and now when he'd come to realise that to be free of her was the last thing he wanted, it was too late. She would not think of a future with him.

Trotting blindly ahead, it was some while before he heard the voices hailing him. A carriage drew up alongside and he slowly emerged from a brown study.

'Good morning, Lord Veryan, how delightful to see you back in town, and so soon! Has Cornwall already lost its appeal?'

It was Lady Blythe with her friend and neighbour, Miss Anstruther, and sitting squashed between them, Domino, startled by his presence, but smiling shyly.

He made no answer and Lady Blythe went on, 'We

thought we would explore Mr Nash's new project, but there is a sad absence of company in the park.'

'I imagine most of the *ton* will wait until the Regent's vision is more nearly realised,' he replied, trying for an easy tone.

'As we seem to have the place to ourselves, Lord Veryan, I wonder if you would be good enough to walk with us for a while.'

'Of course, Lady Blythe,' he replied gallantly, though wishing himself a million miles away.

He handed the two elder ladies down from the carriage and they began to walk slowly ahead, still animatedly discussing the topic of the empty park. He turned to help Domino, but she had already scrambled down the steps. Offering her his arm, they followed in the footsteps of her aunt and companion. Neither spoke for some while, but when he glanced down at her, he found her eyes anxiously scanning his face.

'I'm surprised to see you here, Richard. I thought you'd left for home and would never return to London.'

'I thought so, too,' he replied evenly, 'but unforeseen circumstances brought me back.'

She did not feel bold enough to enquire what those circumstances might be, but she was struck by the fixed look on his face. She had never before seen him looking so grim or so dispirited.

'Is there something wrong?' she asked at length and when he did not reply, repeated more urgently, 'What is the matter, Richard?'

He had no wish to unburden himself to a girl barely

more than a child, but her sweet face was looking up at him in genuine concern and his heart was sore. He was unable to repress his churning thoughts and found himself describing the recent encounter with Christabel. He was succinct, skimming over his campaign to prove his former sweetheart unworthy and deliberately avoiding any mention of the role Domino had unwittingly played. She must have guessed something of the truth but gave no sign.

'I'm a fool, Domino!' he finished. 'I must not repine. I must learn to accept Miss Tallis's decision.'

She squeezed his arm in sympathy and said impulsively, 'How can you? You love her, Richard. I've always known that. I think that perhaps I knew it before you did. And I'm quite sure that she returns your love. The engagement with Sir Julian never looked likely to stick, or so Aunt Loretta said.'

'Lady Blythe is most perceptive,' he muttered a little sourly. 'But it's clear that Christabel prefers a single life to being with me.'

'I'm sure that isn't so,' she protested. 'Nobody could!' and then blushed bright pink in confusion.

He ignored this telltale comment and said gently, 'Your good wishes do you credit, my dear, but I fear I've made a complete mess of things. There's no chance now that Miss Tallis will change her mind.'

'Then we must make her change her mind,' she said defiantly. He stared at her, his dark brows raised in astonishment.

'*You* must make her change her mind,' she amended quickly.

'I wish that were possible, but it's out of the question.'

An enigmatic 'hmm' was her only response. While they had been deep in conversation, the sky had clouded over and a blustery wind had begun to blow. Loretta Blythe signalled to her groom just as the first drops of rain began to fall. The ladies were swiftly handed into the carriage and Richard bade them a brief farewell. Looking back over her shoulder, Domino saw him riding away in the opposite direction, a solitary figure amid a rain-drenched landscape. She was sorry to leave him so evidently unhappy, but she needed time alone. She needed time to think, to contrive a solution to his difficulties, for she was quite certain there was a way through the maze.

Christabel, too, spent a good deal of time alone in the following days, seeking sanctuary from the prying eyes and listening ears of the household. She wanted more than anything to quit London. The triviality of the Season had never sat well with her and any pleasure she'd had in it was now dust. But she could not go home. Richard was unlikely to stay long at the Grosvenor Square mansion and she could not bear to run the risk of meeting him in Cornwall. She felt listless and unbearably cross. Her mother put it down to Sophia's forthcoming nuptials; the excitement of purchasing bride clothes, planning the ceremony, organising the honeymoon, had taken over Mount Street. It must be a difficult situation for her beautiful elder daughter to bear, even though she had brought this fate on herself.

But Christabel was immune to the upheavals permeating the rest of the household. If pressed, she would have acknowledged a mild happiness that Sophia was no longer proving so intractable, but beyond that she had little interest in the wedding preparations. Instead she was sick to the very heart. Richard had been right when he'd said that she loved him. His physical presence shattered her with an intensity of desire, but this ache, this longing, was more than simple lust. Lust she knew. It was what had destroyed her first betrothal to him. This was love. She loved him, all of him. She loved him but she had no faith in him; that was the nub of it. However much he protested, she could never trust him again, and without trust there could be no lasting bond.

Her mind endlessly played out the conflict, trapping her in a disordered world of her own. It was with only half an ear that she listened to Sir Julian as he detailed his elaborate plans for the family to celebrate his new engagement. This was to include a splendid dinner at his town mansion, followed by an evening at the Drury Lane theatre where he had managed to obtain precious tickets to see Edmund Kean performing in a much-acclaimed *Hamlet*. Sir Julian still felt awkward at the very rapid transfer of his affections and was hoping that a dazzling social occasion would smooth any feathers that were still ruffled. He need not have worried. Christabel felt only gratitude that she'd been spared a loveless marriage and her mother was relieved that one of her daughters at least had found an eligible husband.

The evening's dinner and theatre visit was to be the Season's last social event for the family. In a few days they would leave London for Rosings so that Sophia could be introduced to her new home for the first time. From there they would travel on to Cornwall to make final preparations for the wedding. Unexpectedly her sister had rejected a smart London ceremony in favour of being married from Lamorna and it augured well for her new life, Christabel thought, that the city had lost some of its magic allure.

Sir Julian's town house stood imposingly at the corner of Brook Street and their arrival that night was greeted by liveried footmen at its entrance, holding aloft lighted torches. Once inside two more footmen lined the hall and relieved the ladies of their cloaks, then bowed them into a drawing room glittering in the light of a dozen chandeliers, which ran the length of the ceiling. Heavy velour furnishings in the deepest red, ornamented with gold piping, completed the room's opulence. She felt overpowered by so much luxury, but Sophia, relishing these evident trappings of wealth, did a small dance of congratulation in her head. Sir Julian himself handed round glasses of champagne and made ready for a considered but lengthy toast to his future bride.

The dinner that followed was as lavish as the surroundings, one laden course after another. Tureens of

soup and a series of entrées were removed for platters of baked turbot and salmon, followed in turn by
dishes of roast sirloin and goose with sides of French
beans, peas and asparagus. Once his guests had eaten
their fill of these delights, Sir Julian's well-trained staff
whisked away the starched linen table covering and an
assortment of pastries made their appearance alongside
a chafing dish of pancakes, creams, jellies, ices and
small bowls of preserved fruits.

The room was airless and Christabel ate sparingly
while trying hard to maintain her part in the empty
trivialities of table talk. It was with relief that she heard
the carriage being announced that was to take them to
the main attraction of the evening.

At the theatre Sir Julian had ensured that they had
seats in one of the most comfortable boxes available,
with an excellent view of the stage. Even so she quickly
opted for a chair towards the back, hoping in the darkness to be left to her own thoughts. Until the lights went
down, though, she must force herself to show enjoyment. She looked around the auditorium at the array
of costumes and colours which shimmered beneath the
theatre's blazing lights. The buzz of conversation was
almost deafening, the noise hanging overhead in the
heavy atmosphere. Glancing to her left, she thought she
glimpsed Domino de Silva in an adjoining box and was
about to remark on it to her mother who sat alongside
her when Sir Julian turned to them, holding his finger
to his lips.

'The curtain's going up!'

* * *

Contrary to her expectation, she had rapidly become immersed in the play. Whether it was Kean's electrifying performance or just that her overwrought mind sought some kind of relief she didn't know, but an hour had passed on wings. Before she realised it, an interval was being called.

Their small party filtered slowly out of the box and into the wide carpeted space which encircled the rear of the auditorium. Many other patrons were already taking a turn and attempting to find a little fresh air. It had steadily become more oppressive as the play proceeded, and a thunderstorm appeared likely. She saw Domino out of the corner of her eye walking nearby with Lady Blythe, both women fanning themselves vigorously. Quite how it happened, she was unsure, but in a trice it seemed that her mother was conversing animatedly with Lady Blythe while she found herself walking arm in arm with Domino. After Richard's admission that the girl had been an unwitting pawn, she felt uneasy in her company. Yet she also felt impelled to talk with her; above all she needed to hear that the young woman had not suffered irreparably from his intrigue.

They were walking slowly along the wide corridor, their steps carefully keeping time, when she ventured her first remark.

'This has been a most enjoyable evening. Such a pleasant surprise to see you again, Domino, and this time in more comfortable circumstances.'

'Indeed, yes,' the girl rejoined quietly. 'Our last meeting was not at all a happy one.'

'And how have you been since your return from Dover?' The question was commonplace, but she could not bring herself to hazard more.

'I've been well, thank you, Miss Tallis.'

The uncertain tone did not match her words. She was evidently troubled and the ghost of Richard rose between them. But Christabel was saved from having to probe further when the girl continued, 'I've wanted to thank you properly for rescuing me from my foolishness. I know I should have called on you immediately, but I felt too ashamed after the trouble I caused for Benedict.'

'You need not worry about Benedict. He got himself into trouble and it's far better that he is in Cornwall learning from my father than racketing around town. You've no need either to thank me.'

'Indeed I have, I can't thank you enough; you saved me from scandal when you could have simply turned away.'

They had once more reached Sir Julian's box and Domino paused her steps. Her planned encounter with Christabel had so far gone smoothly, but there was a good deal more to be accomplished before she could walk away. She touched Christabel on the arm in a gently restraining gesture and said slowly, 'I don't fully understand why you came after us, but I think that it was partly for Richard's sake.'

Christabel made no response. It seemed to Domino that now his name was out in the open the beautiful woman beside her had become strangely paralysed. She appeared unable to move or to speak. She was looking blindly ahead at the theatre box, where the door stood ajar, and seemed to want nothing more than to seek refuge in its shadowy depths.

Sensing that her quarry was about to turn tail, Domino said impulsively, 'There was never anything more than friendship between us, you know. I was infatuated, that's all, a naïve romance—nothing more. Poor Richard, he had much to bear with me, but he always behaved impeccably.'

'I'm glad to know that.' Christabel's voice stuttered into life. 'But after all that has happened to you in London, are you truly happy to be here still?'

'Why do you ask, Miss Tallis?'

'Forgive me, but on the few occasions I've glimpsed you lately, you've been looking a little pale, a little anxious. But that's probably my imagination running away with me.'

'No!' Domino said quickly, delighted that her plan was at last unfolding successfully. 'It's not your imagination. I wasn't telling the truth just now when I said I was happy. Things have not been well with me lately, but it has nothing to do with Richard.' She hoped that she was proving to be a convincing liar.

'What then?'

'May I confide in you, Miss Tallis—Christabel?'

Christabel nodded assent but privately took herself to task. She was sure that she did not want to hear this.

'Since I returned from that stupid flight, I've felt trapped.'

Domino was speaking so quietly that she had to bend towards the younger girl to catch her words.

'Aunt Loretta watches me all the time. I know I can't hope to be trusted completely after my flight, but she spies on my every single movement. I have absolutely no freedom.'

Christabel looked shocked. 'Surely you must be mistaken. Lady Blythe has always seemed to be the most indulgent of guardians.'

'She may have been once, but that escapade changed everything. She is nervous of my father, you know, and desperate to make sure that nothing else goes awry during my visit here.'

'But spying?'

'She observes me constantly. *And* she opens all my messages and makes sure that I receive only visitors that she is aware of.'

Glancing across at Lady Blythe still deep in conversation with her mother, Christabel could not help looking sceptical. Desperate to convince her, the girl threw out what she hoped was a clinching line.

'She says she will even accompany me to Spain when I leave in a few weeks' time.'

'But surely that's an excellent idea. You will need a chaperon on your journey and who could be a more comfortable companion than your aunt?'

'Not at all. She will be watching me closely and then will tell tales to my relatives, so that after her return to London they will continue to keep me fast. I will enjoy no liberty whatsoever.'

'But your father, can he not intervene on your behalf?'

'My father is thousands of miles away and the

family has always said that he is far too lenient with me. When my mother died, they pressured him to send me back to Spain to be raised as a "proper" young lady. He resisted and kept me with him. This will be their revenge—they'll keep me locked up, I know,' she finished triumphantly.

'Don't you think you may be exaggerating?' Christabel suggested gently.

'A little, perhaps, but my life in Spain will not be happy. If only I could prevent Aunt Loretta from travelling with me and poisoning minds against me, I might persuade my relatives to believe my story. Maybe then I could enjoy living in Madrid.'

The interval bell rang sharply and it was time to return to their seats. Christabel took the young girl's hands in a farewell clasp, but she felt powerless to help her. The rest of the play seemed to pass in a blur. In some measure she felt responsible for Domino's plight. If she had not intervened in that earlier journey...but she could never have guessed that Loretta Blythe would treat her niece so badly. After their return from Dover, Lady Blythe had certainly scolded Domino soundly, that was to be expected, but she'd seemed too relieved to have her back safely to dwell long on the girl's reckless conduct. It was true that lately Domino was never without her aunt at her side—a proof of their closeness, she'd thought. Surely the situation could not be as bad as the girl had painted.

Yet she had been looking anxious and ailing ever since her return to London and it seemed clear that it was not Richard's perfidy that was troubling her.

She had it on Domino's own authority that he had not deceived her and had always behaved towards her as a gentleman. She felt cheered by this revelation. It meant she could think better of him even if she still could not trust him.

Meanwhile Domino had resumed her seat beside Lady Blythe, well pleased with her evening's work. Her aunt looked questioningly at her, but she simply smiled a sunny response. Better Aunt Loretta knew nothing of her intentions. It was time to proceed to the next stage of her plan; only one or two obstacles to clear and it would be complete. The roll of thunder which just then reverberated through the building was a fitting signal, she thought, for the denouement to come.

A few days later Christabel was sitting alone in the drawing room at Mount Street. Her mother and Sophia were busy paying afternoon calls prior to the family's departure, and she had left her maidservant in the bedroom above, packing up her London wardrobe. Earlier she'd tried to decide on which gowns to take with her to Rosings and which would need to be sent directly to Cornwall, but eventually had left it to Rosa to choose, saying she had a headache. She seemed to be using that excuse frequently of late, but hardly cared if she were believed or not. She wasn't agreeable company for anyone, even herself. Since coming downstairs she'd tried reading one of the marble-backed books from the circulating library, so beloved of Sophia, but its silly plot sickened her. She'd picked up her long-discarded needlework, but it made her eyes ache. She thought she might write to an old friend in Cornwall—she'd been meaning to for an age—but what could she say that would come anywhere near the truth of her life.

For probably the fourth time that hour she wandered over to the drawing-room window, but this time saw with surprise a liveried servant mounting the front steps. In a moment James had knocked and entered the room bearing a crisp, white note on a silver salver. As she took the paper from the tray, she glanced at the signature at its foot; the letter was from Domino de Silva. How strange. With some curiosity she began to read the unexpected message:

Dear Miss Tallis,
I did not want to leave London without saying goodbye or thanking you once more for all your efforts on my behalf. You have been a good friend to me and I hope you will forgive my decision to leave. I find I cannot bear to remain in London a moment longer. My aunt has behaved very properly and on my behalf has settled the debts I incurred. For that I am grateful. But as I told you the other evening she now keeps me so confined that life has become insupportable. I am desperate to travel to Spain on my own for the reasons I mentioned and have decided to set out again for Paris and ask my father's friends for help to finish the journey to Madrid. This time, though, I am determined to leave England on my own. I still feel very badly that I caused so much trouble for your brother. By the time you read

*this, I shall be on my way. Please forgive me for
not coming to see you at this time, but remember
me instead with affection.*
Yours ever, Domino

She stared at the sheet of paper for minutes on end,
hardly able to comprehend the words she'd read. Since
her conversation with Domino at the theatre, a worry
had been niggling at the back of her mind that the girl
might do something foolish, but she'd come to the conclusion that she was fretting unnecessarily. It was more
than likely that Domino had been involved in a minor
altercation with her aunt that evening and was magni-
fying the difficulties between them. But now this! It
hardly seemed credible that the girl had fled again and
this time completely alone. Without even Benedict's
protection, she was exposed to all the hazards facing a
beautiful and wealthy young woman on a long, solitary
journey. She shivered in fear for her.

This time, too, there was no indication of when the
girl had left London or the port she was making for. It
was unlikely that she would choose to travel to Dover
again for fear of being discovered, but there were any
number of small ports dotted along the Channel coast
and searching for her would be near impossible. The
last rescue had been difficult enough when she'd known
where the runaways were headed and when she'd had
the faithful Stebbings to drive her.

It was a desperate situation, yet she could not let the
girl disappear into a world of unknown danger. She
must make some attempt to save her from her own folly.

But she would need help and who could she turn to? Certainly not Lady Blythe. She would be even angrier with her niece than before. No, Domino must be found and brought back before her aunt got wind of her disappearance. Sir Julian would assist if she asked him, but he was caught up in a whirl of wedding preparations and would be shocked to the core by the girl's conduct. The image of Richard swam into her mind and was immediately dismissed. But not for long. His name persisted in her thoughts. He'd said just a few days ago that he had no interest in Domino, but it was undeniable that he'd been close to her, accompanying her on the long journey from Buenos Aires, escorting her about town in her aunt's stead. And Domino trusted him. Even if she were no longer in the first throes of infatuation, she must still count him as a friend. If anyone could run her to ground and influence her to return, it would be him. He would know what to do, what and who to ask, and he would be able to ride to the rescue across country if necessary, travelling far more swiftly than any carriage. She must put aside her own feelings and seek him out immediately.

Casting social propriety adrift, she threw on a silk pelisse, slipped out of the house and walked swiftly to the end of Mount Street. With luck an empty hansom cab was passing the end of the road and she hailed it immediately. She had no idea of the fare, but the jarvey seemed content with the few coins she had in her reticule.

Only thirty minutes had passed from Domino's message being delivered until Christabel stood on the top step of the Grosvenor Square mansion and pulled at the bell.

The footman's stare made her realise how imprudent she was in calling on a single gentleman alone, without even a maidservant as company. Discomforted by his obvious astonishment, she assumed a haughty air and commanded him to find his master immediately. The curt tone had its effect and in a moment he had shown her into the drawing room and disappeared to find Lord Veryan.

She walked nervously up and down the room she knew so well. Signs of neglect were everywhere for the house had remained unloved for too long. The blue brocade curtains had faded in the sun and the deeper-blue velvet chairs exhibited bare patches here and there, but it was sparkling clean and a large Venetian glass vase full of sweet-smelling roses and lilies from the garden gave the room a welcoming fragrance. The minutes ticked by and she began to fear that Richard was not at home, or that he'd decided to punish her further with a protracted wait in a room which held such bad memories. Her face flushed with the shame of remembrance and she was almost ready to flee when his tall, athletic figure strode into the room. His elegance proclaimed him every inch a gentleman, but one who could be trusted to take action.

Warm grey eyes searched hers intently, but his face betrayed none of the surprise he felt.

'Miss Tallis, how kind of you to call,' he said smoothly, as the door shut behind the footman.

Once on their own, he moved swiftly towards her,

taking her hands in his and studying her troubled face with concern.

'Christy, what is it? What's happened?'

Her eyes filled with unbidden tears. Already she had the sense of a burden being lifted from her shoulders in the presence of this strong and capable man—she had been right to come. Mutely she proffered Domino's letter.

He scanned the sheet of paper quickly, but apart from a puzzled expression on his face, there was no other reaction. Doesn't he understand what has happened? she thought; surely he cannot be so unfeeling that he intends to ignore the letter.

'If you have any kindness for the child,' she broke out in an agitated voice, 'please help me to find her and bring her back.'

He read through the missive again, this time more slowly, and the puzzlement was replaced by a wry smile.

'I realise that I should not be here or be asking for your aid after all that has passed between us,' she began again, her voice brittle, 'but will you not help?'

'Why ask *me*, Christabel?' he asked quietly.

'You know Domino well, you have the power to influence her and...' her voice was hardly audible '... you are the only person I can trust in this difficult matter.'

Again he took her hands into his strong clasp and looked intently down at her.

'The word "trust" fills me with hope.'

'Richard!' She snatched away her hands. 'This is

urgent. I don't know when Domino left or which port she's making for. She may have half a day's start.'

He gently stroked her cheek with his hand. 'Stay calm, my darling girl, all is well.'

'I don't understand. And I am *not* your darling girl! You forget yourself.'

'And you forgot yourself in coming here to seek my aid. I imagine that's exactly what Domino hoped would happen.'

She was stunned into silence, thoroughly bewildered by his words.

'Come with me,' he said gently, and she allowed him to lead her by the hand into the adjoining garden room with its tall windows looking out on to a wide expanse of lawn. Beneath the shade of the trees a table was set with a white linen tablecloth and the pretty flowered cups that Christabel remembered well.

Domino and her aunt, looking happy and relaxed, sat chatting and sipping their tea.

She whirled around. 'But I don't understand!' she repeated.

'A hoax, I fear, but one with the very best of intentions.'

'You mean that this letter is false. But why? Why would she wish to upset me so?'

'I'm sure she didn't mean to disturb you this badly. She's very young and not always mindful of the consequences of her actions. But I think I know why she decided on this ruse. After we parted the other day I met her driving in Regent's Park. I was thoroughly downcast and confided to her something of our conversation; I told her that you had lost all faith in me. She must have set out to prove to you that that was untrue, that you still trusted me despite all my attempts at sabotage.'

'But why would she do such a thing?'

'Because she knows how I feel about you. She's always known, even before I realised the truth myself. And she guesses that you feel the same about me. She wants us both to be happy—together.'

She pushed the thought away and instead returned to Domino's deception.

'I really believed she was in danger and was badly frightened for her, quite unnecessarily as it turns out. I don't know what to say.'

'Forgive her, Christy, she's brought us together.' He moved closer to her and she felt his breath on her cheek.

When she remained silent, he said with force, 'Well, hasn't she? My darling, say she has!' And with one swift movement he pulled her into his arms and held her to his heart.

She struggled to disentangle herself. Things were moving far too rapidly. She had to think and her mind was dazed.

'I'm naturally relieved that Domino is safe,' she said carefully, 'though I cannot think her actions anything but thoughtless. Her plan to bring us together was misguided and ill advised.'

'But you're here,' he pointed out, the shadow of a smile flitting across his face.

'I came to seek your help, not to reaffirm my trust in you.'

'But isn't that just what you're doing? Why didn't you go elsewhere, why come to me?'

'Because you are a capable man and you know Domino well,' she answered awkwardly.

'They are superficial reasons. You came to me because you know in the deepest recesses of your heart that I am the one person in the world who is here for you—and always will be.'

He was right. Until her foolish disloyalty had so decisively severed them, he had been her refuge, the rock which had anchored her to the world. But did she still believe that? She wanted to, desperately, but she couldn't be sure.

'And Domino, what of her?' she questioned, eager to change the subject.

'Does she seem to you to have suffered unduly?'

Domino's laugh was ringing out across the lawn. A wasp had evidently interrupted the tea party and she was dancing this way and that to escape its attentions. Richard looked away from this little drama and smiled again.

'Domino and I are the best of friends, but that's all. I hope you can see that.'

Even if she could, Richard remained the cold man who had plotted so adroitly against her. Knowing what he'd done, could she ever really trust him, ever really forgive him?

'Find it in your heart to forgive me,' he pleaded, knowing her thoughts. 'I was shocked when I saw you again, shocked at the way you made me feel. I was wounded and I wanted to escape the hurt which came crashing back at me. I lashed out with this stupid intrigue to prove to myself that you weren't worth the pain.'

But he had failed, she told herself. He might have plotted, but he hadn't been able to go through with it. She thought back to the picnic and the way that he'd looked at her by the lakeside, unable to bear her unhappiness. His campaign had hardly started before he'd abandoned it. Surely it was possible to forgive him.

He was looking fixedly at her, watching her every fleeting expression. Quite suddenly he reached out for her hand.

'Marry me!'

'You don't have to offer me marriage,' she said defiantly. 'I know that you feel you've disgraced me, destroyed my chances. But you haven't. If I stay single, I shall have no regrets.' She almost choked on the brazen lie.

'But *I* shall! Darling Christy, I love you. I've always loved you. I've never stopped loving you. And that love is not going away. And neither am I!'

And once more he seized her in a crushing embrace.

'I don't know what to say,' she repeated stupidly, her mind still blurred, but her body swiftly coming to life.

'Then say nothing.'

He gently nuzzled her face and buried his hands in the disordered mass of red curls.

She began to murmur, but he stifled her protest. 'There *is* nothing more to say. Everything is decided!'

and tipping her face he brought his mouth down hard on hers, urgent and demanding.

A throbbing ache of pleasure shot through her body. Her lips sought his with all the hunger that had built up over days of longing. She was inundated by wave after wave of love, coursing through every small part of her, its power at last sweeping away the iron bonds of fear that had held her captive.

She sighed her surrender. Richard was right, everything *was* decided!

Epilogue

It was a perfect August evening when they met on a headland stippled with flaming yellow furze and strolled lazily down the rocky path towards their cove. The languorous air of what had been a hot summer day bathed them in its warm caress. A gentle breeze was blowing now, signalling the turning of the tide, but it barely lifted the leaves of the tall hedgerows on either side of the lane. The scent of dog roses and meadow-sweet was everywhere, enveloping them in a cloud of heady perfume. In the distance the surf rolled itself lazily against the rocks, the noise echoing back towards them and gradually growing more thunderous as they made their way downhill towards the beach.

'I thought you might not escape this evening.' He smiled down at the carefree girl who meandered beside him.

Christabel wore the lightest of muslin dresses, almost

a shift, her long limbs moving easily in the simple garment. Her hair flowed free, the auburn curls moving in the breeze and flaming in the last rays of the sun. Her smile was luminous. She looked no older than the girl he had fallen in love with so long ago.

'Mama is still fretting.' She grinned. 'She's written and rewritten every one of her lists, but she's convinced herself that something is bound to go awry.'

'So why aren't you there, fanning her fevered brow?'

'I'll have you know that I've worked very hard at being daughterly all day. And don't think I didn't notice your quick exit as soon as the rehearsal was over! When Mama began to wrinkle her brow and tap her pencil again, it was clearly time to slip away.'

'So you're not here for the pleasure of my company after all?' he teased.

'What do you think has kept me going all day?' She reached up and kissed the tanned cheek he bent towards her.

'That's much better, a little appreciation is in order!'

Hand in hand they walked in companionable silence towards the sea and the setting sun. Words were often unnecessary between them.

When he spoke again, his tone was pensive. 'I can hardly believe that tomorrow—finally—we will be man and wife.'

'If we hadn't observed the year's mourning, we would have offended too many people, Richard. And the day *has* come at last.'

'Not soon enough for me,' he protested, hugging her close to him. 'These last twelve months since your sister's strange marriage have seemed interminable.'

'Not so strange after all. By all accounts she and Julian are making a success of married life.'

He shook his head disbelievingly. 'Sophia is the queen of triviality and he's such a...' and he struggled to find a word that would not upset his beloved '...a serious person.'

'Admit it, you were longing to say a stuffed shirt. He's a good man and works very hard for his charitable projects.'

'That's what I meant.' He laughed, unrepentant. 'But how he ever thought you would make him a suitable wife!'

'An illusion, I fear. His relationship with Sophia is far more down to earth and that's why it works so well. He really didn't know me.'

'Just dazzled by the exterior, eh? And what an exterior!' He stroked her arm softly and then slipped his own around her waist, pulling her into him as they walked.

'Richard, be careful, someone may come by.'

'They won't—dusk is falling, and do I care if I'm seen embracing the woman I love? No, I don't think I do.'

'You should. You are the lord of Madron and must set an example to your tenants.'

'I'm setting an example to every red-blooded man, not just in Madron but the whole of Cornwall, by marrying the most beautiful, the most exciting, the most enchanting woman in the world.'

They rounded the last bend in the lane at that moment and the noise of the ocean, which had gradually been growing louder, burst fully on their ears.

Waves crashed headlong into the jutting rocks on either side of the cove but between the two spurs of outlying granite, a crescent of white sand lay virginal and inviting. They ran down the last of the path, holding hands and laughing as they almost lost their footing on the downhill slope. The soft sand swallowed their footsteps and prompted them to kick off their shoes. He watched smilingly as she performed an impromptu pirouette, a homage to the heart-stopping beauty all around them: the green headland and the grey rocks, the indigo sea with its white frills of foam and the evening sky now streaked with pink and purples, a harbinger of good weather.

'It looks as though we will have a beautiful day for our wedding,' she said quietly, intensely aware of the solitary beach and his physical presence so close to her.

'Almost as beautiful as this evening.'

His voice was rough with desire as he ran his hands up the white arms and arrived at her shapely breasts. He pulled the ribbon of her bodice undone and began slowly to roll the dress from her shoulders.

'Richard! This is a public place!'

'Do you see any public here? We are as alone as we possibly could be. You didn't used to be so cautious, Christy.'

She blushed at the memory of their youthful indiscretion, but allowed him to continue undressing her, his gaze filling her with an aching need for his touch.

He had soon divested himself of his own clothes and it was her turn to drink her fill. He was beautifully made and she felt herself grow hot and trembling.

He took her hand then, breaking the spell, and they ran together to the sea's edge. For a moment the water's impact took their breath away, but then they plunged headlong into the surf. Richard struck out immediately, powering through the waves towards the darkening horizon and shouting to her to hurry and join him. The cold fingers of the sea crept insidiously over her body and it was a while before the water began to warm her bare skin and slowly bewitch her with its movement. Richard was already far out and she called to him not to go further. She needed to share her delight.

He turned back instantly and was soon treading water at her side. Both of them were laughing with the sheer joy of the moment. The flaming red tresses of her hair encircled him with their ring of fire, challenging the watery environment and setting him alight. His legs slowly entwined around hers and he held her close to him, supporting her body against his, kissing her face, her arms, her breasts in rapid succession. Then his mouth found hers, his tongue tenderly teasing her lips open. She clung to him, exchanging one rapturous kiss after another, but when he felt her shiver, he released his hold and smiled tenderly down at her.

'We should get out of the water before you catch a bad chill—I'll race you back to the beach!'

'You do realise,' she giggled as they tumbled up the sands to reach their pile of clothes, 'that we haven't a towel between us.'

'Why do you need a towel, when you have me?' The look in his eyes was disturbing and she felt her breath catch.

Before she had time to protest, he had spread his jacket on the sand and pulled her down to join him.

'This should keep you warm,' he said softly and rolled her over to lie beneath him, his body covering hers. His voice was barely audible above the sound of the breaking surf, but its passion was unmistakable.

Slowly and inexorably their bodies melted one into another, and a dull ache of pleasure began to permeate her being. Soon her entire body was infused by a heat which spread in ever fiercer waves. It was dark now but for a handful of stars tossed into the night sky and the light of the moon edging the scene with its silver: the empty beach, the constant surf and two lovers, their bodies entwined, lost to the world.

'Think of all the evenings we have to come,' he whispered.

A river of desire was flowing through her and she sighed with the intensity of its pleasure, arching her body to meet his. His touch intensified and she gave up all pretence of restraint, shamelessly abandoning herself to his lovemaking, her body softening to accommodate the hardness of his form. She wanted nothing more than to give herself without thought or words to this ecstasy. His mouth covered her burning skin with kisses, piling desire upon desire, until she was crying out, swept away by an almost unbearable pleasure.

They lay together, breathless and shaking, Richard's severely crumpled jacket swaddling them in its folds. For long minutes they lay curled in the tightest of embraces while above the black of the distant night sky offered its benign cover. Then he raised himself on one elbow and began to stroke her hair, allowing her tangled curls to flitter lazily through his fingers.

'I can't believe that I've been so lucky, after the mess I've made of my life—and yours,' he murmured.

'We've both been adept at making a mess of life.' She looked up at him tenderly and brushed a lock of hair from his face. 'Do you remember a night like this all those years ago? We came here then to escape mayhem in the house.'

He gave a twisted smile. 'How could I ever forget? It's burned into my memory. If I'd been less of a prig that night, the whole course of our lives would have been different.'

'You were shy,' she excused, 'we both were. We didn't know what to do with such unfamiliar feelings.'

'Not quite so unfamiliar now,' he teased and bent his lips to her breasts to kiss them awake once more.

She sighed her pleasure and scattered butterfly kisses over his body. 'I can't imagine how I ever thought our betrothal meant nothing more to you than a way of bringing our families together.'

He groaned. 'And I can't imagine how I could have been so stupid as to allow you to believe that!'

He tightened his grip, holding her close to his heart.

'What an age it's taken us, Christy, but we've come through.'

Her face was alight with feeling, her eyes an emerald radiance, their lustre warming the moonlit world.

'It was worth the wait.'

'And the pain?' he asked, his voice rough with remorse.

'Love is even sweeter for being so hard-won.'

With one finger she delicately traced the outline of his face, pale and glimmering against the dark of the night, and when she spoke again her voice was not quite steady. 'And it will endure, Richard. For every moment of for ever. Nothing will separate us.'

'Nothing,' he breathed huskily, and took her up into his arms again, covering her face with kisses and meeting her eager lips with his.

* * * * *

Society's Most
Scandalous Rake

ISABELLE GODDARD

Chapter One

Domino de Silva raised her face to the warm sun and
breathed a sigh of contentment. The gentlest of waves
whispered along the pebbles at her feet and the wide
blue dome of the sky spread itself with ease to meet a
distant horizon. She closed her eyes in pleasure. For a
short time at least she was free; all too soon she would
have to return to the house on Marine Parade and her
cousin's inevitable questioning. If only her father would
send Carmela back to Spain, she might truly enjoy this
last summer before the dreary future she was resigned
to. But Papa would not do that. Her stern aunts back in
Madrid had only agreed to her acting as his hostess if
her cousin accompanied her.

'You seem to have dropped this.'

She was startled from her reverie by a warm voice,
disturbing in its intimacy. Shading her eyes against the
sun's strong rays, she detected the outline of a slim but
muscular form. The man appeared to be offering her a
crumpled cambric handkerchief bearing all the marks
of having been trampled in sand and sea.

She shook her head decisively. 'Thank you, but no. The handkerchief is not mine.'

'Are you quite sure?'

'I think I should know my own possessions,' she responded a little tartly.

'Naturally. But you had fallen into such an abstraction, I thought you might not realise if you had dropped something.'

She felt herself becoming ruffled. Whoever the man was, he was intruding on the few moments of solitude that were hers.

'As I said, sir, I fear you are mistaken.'

Her voice was edged with ice, but it seemed not to perturb him for he took the opportunity to move nearer. She became aware of a pair of shapely legs encased in skin-tight fawn pantaloons and a coat of blue superfine perfectly fitted to his powerful shoulders. Hessian boots of dazzling gloss completed an ensemble ill adapted to a provincial beach.

'It would seem I was mistaken,' he admitted, 'but I shan't repine. It's given me the opportunity to speak to a vastly pretty girl.'

She was astonished at his audacity. His voice and dress spoke the gentleman, but no gentleman of her acquaintance would have addressed a lady so.

'I would be glad, sir,' she said in the most frigid of voices, 'if you would leave me in peace to enjoy this wonderful view.'

He let out a low chuckle and for the first time her gaze moved upwards towards his face and she was unnerved by what she saw. She had not realised how young he was or how good looking. His fair hair fell carelessly over his forehead and a pair of golden-brown eyes lingered over her in a way that made her flush with annoyance. A small scar on his left cheek only enhanced his attractiveness.

The gold-flecked eyes considered her with lazy amusement. 'I'm not impervious to your request,' he drawled, 'but it places me in an awkward situation.'

'How is that?'

'My wish to gratify a lady is at odds with my strong sense of duty.'

Her determined silence did not deter him. 'My wish to oblige requires me to walk away this minute and leave you to your solitude.'

'Please do!'

'If only it were that simple,' he exclaimed mournfully, 'but chivalry requires I put my duty first. Since you appear to be entirely without an escort, it clearly behoves me to stay as chaperon.'

'How fortunate then that I can put your mind at rest! Trouble yourself no further. I am used to walking alone and am well able to take care of myself.'

At that moment she was far from feeling so. Her desire to venture out alone had never before exposed her to such persistent harassment. This man would not be shrugged off lightly.

'You're a mere slip of a girl,' he continued blithely, 'and it seems unlikely that you're quite as accomplished as you think in escaping unwanted attentions. Though a most comely slip of a girl, I grant you,' he finished after a slight pause. His eyes, glinting amber in the sunlight, danced with laughter.

There was nothing for it but to turn tail. He was impervious to disapproval and entreaty alike. She turned quickly to make her way back across the beach and her sudden movement impaled the flounce of her dress on a twisted piece of iron, which had detached itself from the groyne. She was well and truly caught.

'Allow me.'

And before she could protest he was down on his knees, carefully unhooking the frill of delicate cream lace from the iron stanchion. She stood rigid with mortification, thankful for the cooling breeze on her heated cheeks. But there was worse to come. Before she could stop him, his hands began to rearrange the crumpled hem of her silk gown and for an instant alighted on her ankle.

'Thank you, sir,' she said in a stifled voice and fled towards the safety of Marine Parade.

'Must you go already?' he called after her. 'I feel we are only just getting acquainted.' He grinned at her departing figure. 'It's not every lady's ankles I get to see before luncheon, you know.'

She hurried away, more shocked than she cared to admit. That would teach her to walk unaccompanied. She must stop breaking the rules; within a year she would be married and there would be no more solitary strolls, no more escapes to the sea. And no chance meetings with impertinent strangers. Relieved, she reached the promenade and looked back to the spot she had just vacated. The man was still there, watching her every step, it seemed. He saw her pause and gave a cheerful wave. Impossible! She turned from the beach abruptly and hurried home.

Joshua Marchmain watched her for some time as she strode rapidly over the wet pebbles and began to climb the worn stone steps to the promenade. He had not meant her to flee quite so precipitately and just as things were getting interesting. He would have liked to spar a little more, for it was an unusual young lady who walked alone and disputed with strangers. And she had cut a most charming figure. The encounter had certainly provided a welcome break from the tedium of ministering to George's whims. How he had become so indispensable to the Regent he hardly knew. For years he had exiled himself from life among the *ton* and it seemed unlikely that on his return he would become a palace favourite. But he had, and quickly. At first it had been amusing to supplant long-serving courtiers in the Prince's favour, but now it was simply a dead bore.

A summer spent at Brighton had promised new interest, but the reality was proving very different. Or at least not different at all, that was the problem. The Prince's life revolved around banquets, gambling, horse racing, music and his love affairs, whether he were in London or Brighton. The sound of the sea was the only novelty. Joshua had spent that morning, as so many others, idling in the hothouse that was the Royal Pavilion but, faced with the six-course luncheon the Regent felt an appropriate midday snack, he had rebelled to play truant in the salt-tanged air.

Almost immediately he had seen her, a small, trim figure in cream silk and lace with a saucy villager bonnet on the back of her head, barely keeping her unruly dark curls under control despite an enormous bow of azure ribbon. Her face, when she'd raised it to look at him, had more than matched the promise of her figure. Her eyes, dark and tragic, set in a heart-shaped countenance, had sent an unaccustomed longing through him. She would never be a diamond of the first water, but her youth and vulnerability spoke to him in a way that perfect beauty no longer did.

The ripple of emotion was over in a trice. Just as well, he thought breezily. Suppressing inconvenient sentiment had made life a good deal simpler over the years. It might have been amusing to dally a while, but in the event the flirtation was over before it had really begun. Regretfully he retraced his steps; it was time to resume his duties before the Regent noticed his absence.

As soon as Marston opened the door to her, Domino knew she was in trouble. Her cousin was in the hall, an apron wrapped around one of the black dresses she habitually wore and a furious expression on her face. The butler made a strategic exit, winking conspiratorially at the young girl as he retired to the servants' quarters.

'And where exactly have you been?' Carmela's tone was as angry as her face.

Domino did not answer immediately. She had meant to provide herself with some excuse for her absence, a frippery purchased from the stalls in Bartholomews, perhaps, but in the flight from the beach she had completely forgotten. In any case her cousin hardly drew breath before the next onslaught.

'You do realise that your father is to host a reception here this very evening and you were supposed to help with the hundred and one things that have to be done.'

She did realise and felt a twinge of guilt. As the new ambassador for Spain, Alfredo de Silva was setting great store by tonight's entertainment. He had only recently presented his credentials at St James's; though the Court had abandoned a hot and dusty capital for the sea, it was vital that he continue his work among those who surrounded the Prince Regent. Only a few days ago he had confided a rumour to her that even George himself might attend this evening's event.

'I'm sorry, Carmela,' she said quietly, trying in vain to mollify the angry woman, 'I felt a little unwell—you know how stuffy this house gets in the hot weather—and I thought it would help if I took a short walk in the fresh air.' Her cousin seemed unable to decide whether to look sceptical or shocked. In the end she managed a mixture of both.

'It's even stuffier outside,' she scolded, 'and how many times have I told you that you must not walk alone? You are imprudent, Domino. Why do you have a personal maid if it is not to accompany you wherever you wish to go? And why go anywhere today?'

'I'm here now, so tell me what I can do to help.'

'Nothing.'

'Nothing?'

'Everything is done. As always, I have worked myself to a standstill.'

It was difficult to see how Carmela had worked so very hard. She herself had planned the event days ago and had left the maids to arrange flowers and set tables. The catering firm and their own kitchen had prepared every morsel of food and drink necessary to entertain the cream of the *ton*. But she said none of this, unwilling to upset her cousin further.

She was sharply aware of the sacrifice Carmela had made. Her cousin was devoted to the family and could even be kind in her own stiff fashion. She had not wanted to come to England, least of all to a scandalous resort known throughout Europe as a den of extravagance, if not downright immorality. But come she had, putting her loyalty to the family before her own comfort and leaving behind the pleasing pieties of her Madrid home. Domino might wish she were alone with her father, but Carmela was part of the bargain, part of the price she had to pay for a few months' freedom.

Hurrying up the stairs to her bedroom, Domino locked the door with relief; she was out of reach here. Marriage, though unwelcome, would at least deliver her from the endless scolding of relatives. Her aunts had already presented her with the names of three suitors they considered eligible and all she had to do, they said, was choose one. Any of the three would make a highly suitable husband, able to oversee and conserve the vast estate she would inherit at twenty-one and certain to be assiduous in keeping the inevitable fortune hunters at bay. It didn't matter who she married. After Richard Veryan, it was utterly unimportant. She had loved and lost, and she knew even at this young age that she would never feel so deeply about any man again. It was enough for her to know that he was happy now with the wife he should always have had, and that she was in some small way responsible for bringing them together. But if only...

She was sunk in the customary forlorn dream when a knock at the door roused her. Fearing a resurgent Carmela, she opened it cautiously, but it was Alfredo de Silva who stood on the threshold, a beaming smile on his face and his arms outstretched in greeting.

'*Querida*, come with me,' he ordered, having hugged

her until her ribs almost buckled under the strain. 'I have a little present for you.'

'I fear that I don't deserve a present, Papa. Ask Carmela.'

'Oh, Carmela—what does she know of deserving? I intend to spoil you to death now that you are with me again. I've missed you more than you will ever know.'

Her father was hustling her along the landing to his own room where the door stood open and a stunning gown of the deepest rose pink tumbled invitingly on the bed. She snatched it up eagerly and held it against her body. A glance at the cheval mirror in the corner of the room reflected back her creamy olive skin and burnished curls, their beauty heightened by the rich rose of the satin-and-gauze gown. Still holding the dress tightly, she waltzed around the bed laughing with pleasure.

'Thank you, thank you so much. It's quite lovely. But far too good for a mere reception, Papa. We should save it for a grand ball at the very least!'

'A ball? No, indeed. You can be sure that when the time comes, I will find something even better,' her father said mysteriously. 'Wear the rose pink tonight and your mother's amethysts. They will be perfect for the dress and perfect for you—you look so like Elena.'

His voice faltered a little and Domino took his hand and squeezed it comfortingly. 'I love being spoiled, but you are much too kind to me.'

'You should know, my dear, that I have an ulterior motive. In that dress you will entrance all my guests and then they will say how lucky Spain is to have such an excellent ambassador!'

She was glad now that she had returned to England

to be with her father, despite Carmela and despite Lady Blythe's warning. Their English cousin had refused to continue as Alfredo's hostess once he left London; Brighton had been a step too far for Lady Loretta Blythe. *Raffish, my dear,* she had warned Domino in a letter to Spain*, please consider carefully whether you will be comfortable entertaining in such a place.* Domino had considered, but the prospect of living with a much-loved parent again, free of her aunts' strictures, had been too appealing.

Returning to her bedroom, she found Flora in a fizz of excitement at the prospect of dressing her mistress for the evening's celebrations. The abigail, the best of a mediocre selection according to Lady Loretta, who had despatched her from London, had never before acted as a lady's maid and this evening would be a test of the skills she had been practising so assiduously. The rose-pink gown with its assorted underpinnings was soon in place, the very slightest brush of rouge applied to both cheeks and a smear of rose salve for the lips. Taming Domino's luxuriant curls into the popular Roman style, though, took a little longer, and it was some considerable time before Flora pronounced herself satisfied with the result. Her mistress's raven locks now cascaded from a carefully arranged topknot to rest lightly in two glistening ringlets on the soft cream of her neck. A careful fastening of the delicate necklace of amethysts around Domino's neck and the placing of matching earrings completed the *toilette*. Both young ladies viewed the finished result in the mirror and smiled with pleasure. Whatever Domino might lack in willowy elegance, she made up for in sheer prettiness.

'I'm determined to enjoy this evening, Flora,' she pronounced, her dark eyes sparkling with anticipation. She had begun to feel the old excitement returning even though she was once more about to enter the lion's den.

'Of course you are, miss, why ever wouldn't you?' her maid asked innocently.

'When I agreed to come to Brighton in Lady Blythe's place, the prospect of helping my father entertain seemed nicely distant. But now!'

'You'll be fine, Miss Domino, you always know exactly the right thing to say and do,' Flora soothed.

'My aunts have schooled me well, it's true, but this is the very first *ton* party I have ever hosted.'

And it had arrived rather too quickly, she thought. It seemed as though they had hardly settled themselves in the elegant town house on Marine Parade before Alfredo announced that he wished to give a reception. But it was more than that. Her last foray into the social life of England's top one-hundred families had ended in disaster. She saw the young girl she had been, so open to all the pleasures of that first London Season: balls, picnics, exhibitions, ridottos, Venetian breakfasts. How young and foolish! She had fallen in love with the wrong man and fallen foul of one who meant her nothing but dishonour.

'It's time you went downstairs, miss. I've just heard Miss Carmela's door close.'

The maid fussed around her, adjusting a tendril here, a fold of the dress there. Domino bestowed a warm smile on her. 'Thank you so much, Flora. You've had magic in your fingers this evening. I hope I shall live up to your handiwork.'

'You will, Miss Domino, for sure. You look fair

'ansome.' Flora grinned, betraying her rural heritage and forgetting for the moment the town bronze she was painfully acquiring.

The hall had been sumptuously decorated with tall vases of early summer lilac and as Domino walked slowly down the marble staircase, their perfume rose in a sensual spiral to meet her. The main doors were open and in the still evening air she could hear the rhythmic beating of waves against stone parapet. Her father and Carmela were already waiting by the front entrance to receive the first of their guests, her cousin having forsaken her usual black gown for a slightly less funereal mauve. They looked up at her approach and Alfredo glowed with pride; even Carmela gave her a tight smile of approval. So far, so good, but her nerves were taut. Would her planning stand up to the *ton*'s stringent demands? Could she perform the role of hostess with aplomb? She had not long to find out.

Lord Albermarle was the first to arrive and his bluff good nature put Domino immediately at ease. Most of their guests that evening would be men—an inevitable imbalance in a diplomatic reception—and she had not been certain whether to feel this as an advantage or not. But Lord Albermarle's gentle compliments and genial smile decided her. Far better to make her début without female whispers to disparage her efforts. Soon the ground floor of Marine Parade was throbbing with life. Most of the guests were involved in some way with the Court or with Parliament, but there were a few without any diplomatic or political interest who came simply to look over the new ambassador and his household. They appeared to like what they saw.

Sir Henry Bridlington spoke for many when he observed, 'Señor de Silva seems a very good sort and his daughter is bound to make a stir in Brighton this season.' He took a long pinch of snuff. 'The girl has looks, breeding and she's no fool. Refreshing to meet a woman with opinions!'

'It depends on the opinions, I imagine.' The man who spoke was flaxen haired and his tawny eyes glittered with amusement.

'Nothing outlandish, I swear,' Bridlington responded. 'In fact, I thought she spoke most sensibly. And a very attractive face and figure, don't you know.'

'Ah, now you're talking sense. A woman's opinions are as changeable as the sea. But her looks! That's a different matter entirely. I must ensure I make the acquaintance of this nonpareil.'

So it was that Domino, busily circulating among her guests, came face to face with her tormentor of the morning.

He smiled lazily down at her while a flush gradually suffused her entire body as she realised who was barring her way. He had looked complete to a shade during this morning's encounter. Now he looked simply splendid. He was dressed in the satin knee breeches and black long-tailed coat befitting a gentleman attending an evening party, but the way he wore them singled him out from every other man in the room. His clothes fitted him impeccably—the work, she surmised, of a master tailor—and clearly suggested the perfect male body beneath. A dandyish silk waistcoat of maroon-and-grey stripes was countered by the restraint of a crisp white neckcloth, tied in an elegant *trône d'amour* and fastened by a single diamond stud. Her gaze travelled slowly over him, but always came back to those amber eyes, sensual and appraising.

'Miss de Silva, I imagine? Joshua Marchmain, at your service.' He bowed with a languid grace.

She bobbed a bare curtsy and inclined her head very slightly. His smile deepened at her evident reluctance to recognise him.

'Forgive my somewhat unorthodox approach. I lack a sponsor to introduce me at the very moment I need one.'

She remained tense and unsmiling, but he affected not to notice.

'I am forced therefore to introduce myself,' he continued. 'I would not wish to leave this delightful party before thanking my hostess—that would be grossly discourteous.'

'Discourtesy should not concern you, sir. You seem to have a fine stock of it.'

Her high colour was fading fast and she felt control returning. She was not to be overpowered by this arrogant man; she would make him acknowledge his earlier impertinence.

'How is that?' He was looking genuinely puzzled and she was reduced to saying weakly.

'I think you know very well.'

'But then I would not have been so discourteous as to mention our delightful…' he paused for a moment '…rendezvous.'

'It was not a rendezvous,' she remonstrated, 'it was

harassment and you were abominably rude. How dared you accost a lady in that fashion?'

'But, Miss de Silva, consider for one moment, how was I to know that I was accosting a lady? No lady of my acquaintance would ever walk alone.'

'So you feel you have *carte blanche* with any woman you don't consider a lady?'

'Let us say that solitary females are not usually averse to my company.'

Domino seethed at his arrogance; he was truly an insufferable man. 'You deliberately trespassed on my seclusion,' she said wrathfully. 'Despite my pleas, you refused to leave me alone.'

The golden eyes darkened and not with amusement this time. 'But naturally,' he said in a voice of the softest velvet. 'How could I? You were far too tempting.'

She felt the tell-tale flush beginning again and longed to flee. But her training stood her in good stead and she drew herself up into as statuesque a figure as she could manage and said in an even tone, 'I believe, Mr Marchmain, that we have finished our conversation.'

He bent his head to hers and said softly, 'Surely not, Miss de Silva; I have a feeling that it's only just beginning.'

In an arctic voice she made a last attempt to put him out of countenance.

'I don't recall my father mentioning your name in connection with his work. Do tell me what your interest in this evening's event might be.'

He moved away from her slightly, but his manner remained as relaxed as ever.

'Which is a polite way of saying, what am I doing

here without an invitation? You're quite right, I have no invitation. However, I believe the Prince Regent's presence was expected and I am here as his humble representative.'

'Then he's not coming this evening?' She felt a keen disappointment and, despite her dislike of Joshua Marchmain, found herself wanting to ask more.

'Did you expect him to?'

'My father was told that he might attend.'

'Then I'm sorry to disappoint you.' He smiled that lazy smile again. 'George is a somewhat indolent prince, I fear, and only rouses himself to action when he anticipates some pleasure from it.'

She was taken aback by his irreverence. 'You are a member of the Prince's household?'

'For my sins and at the moment, yes.'

'Then how can you speak so of a royal prince?'

'Believe me, it's quite easy. If one knows the prince.'

'It would seem that you hold the Regent in some aversion. If that's so, why do you stay?' she enquired with refreshing candour.

'That is a question I ask myself most days. So far I haven't found an answer. Perhaps you might provide me with one.'

She looked puzzled. 'I cannot see how.'

'One never can at the time,' he replied cryptically.

Domino was rapidly tiring of the continual fencing that Mr Marchmain appeared to find essential to conversation, but was too eager to learn of life in the Pavilion to walk away. 'Is the palace very grand inside?' she asked impulsively and then wished she hadn't. She had no wish to betray her gaucheness in front of this indolently assured man.

He smiled indulgently, seeming to find her innocence enchanting.

'Yes, I suppose you could call it grand; although I
would rather say that it is eccentric. But surely you will
see the Pavilion for yourself very soon and will be able
to make up your own mind.'

'Perhaps. My father has not yet told me of his plans.'

'It is to be hoped they will include a visit to the
palace. If so, allow me to offer my services as your
guide.'

Domino had no intention of ever seeking his company, but she made the expected polite response. At
least for the moment he was conducting himself unex-
ceptionally. Then out of nowhere he disconcerted her
once more with a passing remark.

'I understand that you have been living in Madrid.'

'How did you know that?' she demanded.

'I ask questions and get a few answers,' he murmured enigmatically. 'There's a wonderful art gallery
in Madrid, the Prado. Do you know it?'

'My home in Madrid is close by.'

'Then you are most fortunate. To be able to look on
the genius of Velázquez any day you choose.'

She stared at him in astonishment. 'You are interested in art?'

'A little. I collect when I can. I have recently acquired
a small da Vinci—a very small one—so at the moment I
am quite puffed with pride. When you visit the Pavilion,
I would like to show you the studio I have set up.'

'You are an artist yourself?'

'I am a dauber, no more, but painting is a solace.'

If she wondered why a man such as Joshua Marchmain should need solace, she had little time to ponder.

Carmela had arrived at her elbow and was hissing urgently in her ear that they were running out of champagne and would she like to come up with a solution. The party had been more successful than they had hoped and people had stopped for longer to drink, eat and gossip.

Domino excused herself and Joshua swept them both a deep bow. Carmela glared at him fiercely before following in her cousin's wake. She must warn Domino to keep her distance from that man. She knew nothing of him, but every instinct told her he was not to be trusted and her young relative had spent far too long talking to him. At the best of times it would look particular, but with this man it was likely to begin gossip they could ill afford. Domino was to be married next year and it was Carmela's job to guard her well until such time as the wedding ring was on her finger.

Joshua watched them out of sight, smiling wryly to himself. He knew Carmela's type well. How many such duennas had he taken on and vanquished in the course of an inglorious career? But Domino appeared to have a mind of her own. That and her youthful charm made her a prize worth pursuing; the next few weeks might prove more interesting than he had expected. He weaved his way through the chattering guests to receive his hat from a stray footman before sauntering through the front door of Number Eight Marine Parade, his step a little livelier than when he had entered.

The next morning was overcast. The sun hid behind clouds and the sea looked a dull grey. The prospect of a walk was uninviting, but it was Sunday and attendance at the Chapel Royal was essential for the ambassador and his daughter. Carmela had refused point blank to accompany them; nothing would induce her to attend a Protestant church, she said. She would stay at home and follow her own private devotions. If Domino and her father felt a little jaded from the previous evening's exertions, a vigorous walk along the promenade soon blew away any megrims. Tired they might be, but they were also in good spirits. The reception had gone without a hitch and Alfredo was feeling increasingly optimistic for the success of his mission. Domino, too, was cheerful, seeing her father so buoyant. To be sure, entertaining the *ton* had been a little daunting, but she had come through her first test with flying colours. Apart from the impossible Mr Marchmain, nothing had occurred to spoil her pleasure. And even he had intrigued her. He was an enigma, a man of contradictions. She had thought him nothing more than a highly attractive predator, but then he had announced himself a lover of great art. He was sufficiently wealthy to laze the summer away in the Prince Regent's very expensive retinue, but seemed to lack the responsibilities that accompanied such wealth. And far from enjoying his exalted social position, it appeared to give him little pleasure.

A wind had sprung up by this time, blowing from the west, and Domino was forced to pay attention to her attire, hanging on with one hand to the Angoulême bonnet with its fetching decoration of golden acorns, while with the other she strove to keep under control the delicate confection of peach sarsenet and creamy tulle that billowed around her legs. They walked briskly, her father enumerating his plans for the week while she listened, but all the time her mind was busy elsewhere.

'Papa,' she said suddenly, when he fell silent for a moment, 'what do you know of Mr Marchmain?'

'Only a very little. He is one of the Regent's court, I understand, so no doubt expensive, idle, possibly dissolute.'

She felt dismay at her father's description. Marchmain was certainly persistent in his unwanted attentions, but dissolute!

'Do not concern yourself, my dear.' Her father patted her hand. 'Members of the Prince Regent's entourage are a law unto themselves. We will have dealings with them only when we must.'

She tried another tack. 'How is it that Joshua Marchmain is only a plain mister? Surely if he belongs to the Regent's company, he should have a title.'

'I believe the young man is related in one way or another to any number of the nobility and has inherited a wealthy estate, which he will certainly need if he keeps company with the Regent for long. But why this interest, *querida*?'

'No real interest, Papa,' she said stoutly. 'He just seemed an odd person to be attending the reception, a fish out of water.'

'I think we can say that Mr Marchmain's appearance at our small entertainment was the Regent's overture to Spain. We must accept the overture politely, but still maintain a distance.'

He took her arm firmly in his. 'Come, we should step out smartly if we are not to be shamed by our lateness at church.'

They walked quickly on, the summer wind skirling

around their feet and sending up dust and abandoned news sheets into a choking cloud. Brighton was a fashionable resort—almost too fashionable, she reflected—and Marine Parade was a less-than-ideal residence. It was too near the centre of town and attracted promenading society far too readily. She had quickly realised that lodgings close to the Pavilion were in general reserved for young bucks, looking forward to a lively few months by the sea, and for the sprinkling of dandies with their pencilled eyebrows and curled mustachios who were always ready to ogle any stray female who crossed their path. She had come to wish that her father had chosen a house on the outskirts of town but, this morning, proximity meant they had only a short way to travel before they arrived at the church a few minutes before the last bell ceased tolling.

The Chapel Royal was a square building in the classical style with rounded sash windows and a row of Doric columns flanking the main door. It was the custom for visitors without their own pew to be charged an entrance fee and Domino and her father obediently joined a straggling line of people, all waiting to pay their shilling. The queue was moving slowly and they waited for some while to disburse their fee, but as they neared the imposing front door of the church, there was a sudden commotion behind them, a servant pushing his way forwards to clear a pathway for his employer. She turned to discover who this grand personage might be and received a terrible shock; she found herself staring into the eyes of the man she had come to loathe when last she was in England.

Leo Moncaster smiled grimly at her. 'Miss de Silva?

Imagine that. And there was I thinking never to see you again.'

Her father had turned around and was looking with surprise at the sneering stranger. 'Is this gentleman annoying you, Domino?' he asked her quietly. She was quick to reassure him and he turned back to pay their shillings.

'I see you have brought reinforcements with you this time.' The sneer became even more pronounced. 'And is your aunt here also, ready to come to your defence at any moment?'

'Lady Blythe remains in London, sir, although I see no reason why that should interest you.'

'On the contrary, Miss de Silva, everything to do with you interests me. I have a long memory, even if you do not.'

And with that he pushed past beneath the pediment displaying the Prince Regent's coat of arms and into the church. She was left trembling from the encounter, but anxious that her father should not suspect anything amiss. She linked arms with him and smiled as bravely as she could.

'Shall we go in?'

Seeing Leo Moncaster had been a crippling blow. When she had agreed to play hostess for her father, she had never for a moment imagined that she would meet the man who had done her so much harm. If she had been thinking sensibly, she might have known he could well be here and living at the Pavilion. Moncaster was an inveterate gambler and it was said that fortunes were won and lost on a nightly basis at the Regent's tables. Where better for such a man to spend his summer? It was clear that his malevolence was unabated despite

Lady Blythe having paid her niece's gambling debt in full. Of course, he had not wanted the money. It was herself, or rather her body, that he had wanted. That was the prize of which he'd been cheated. But how could she ever have thought him attractive? A shudder ran through her as though she were tiptoeing over a grave, fearful of disturbing dark layers of memory. Her only comfort was her father's assertion that they need have little to do with the Prince Regent or any of his cronies.

Certainly the Prince would not be in evidence this morning. Although he had laid the church's foundation stone some twenty-five years ago, he had stopped worshipping at the Chapel Royal when a sermon on immorality had offended him. But there was some compensation to be had. An enormous man with creaking corsets was heaving himself into the pews reserved for the Royal Family a few rows in front of her: the Regent's brother, the Duke of York. He kept up a constant muttering, hardly audible, but nevertheless highly embarrassing to his companions. Their attempts to stifle him made her smile; for the moment she forgot the dreadful meeting she had just endured and was emboldened to look about her. The galleried church was filled with decoration, its supporting columns and pulpit highly embellished, while a large organ in burnished copper thundered from above the altar. It was a rich man's building.

She looked sideways across the aisle, scanning a busy canvas of faces, hoping to keep out of Moncaster's sight. Immediately beneath one of the galleries a countenance she was beginning to know well swam into view. Joshua's gaze was on her, sporting an appreciative smile as he took in her situation just behind the noisy Duke. She noticed that he was dressed more soberly this morning, but the familiar lock of fair hair trailed over his brow and his sprawling figure exuded his customary confidence. Her glance moved on to the woman who sat next to him; there was something proprietorial in her posture. She was richly dressed in an ensemble of emerald-green Venetian silk and her hair was covered with a headpiece of ostrich feathers. The feathers swayed slightly in the current of air and their height ensured that those who sat immediately behind could see little of the service at the altar.

Domino did not profit from the parson's homily that morning. She was too conscious of both the men she wished to avoid and was relieved when the final hymn reverberated through the rafters and she was able to walk from the church into a burst of sunshine. The rector was at the door to greet his parishioners and once again they were forced to wait patiently in line before they could pass through the narrow entrance.

'Pious as well as pretty,' a voice said softly in her ear. 'It gets better all the time.'

She turned to face him, grateful that her father was engaged in talking to a fellow communicant.

'Still accosting unwilling women, Mr Marchmain?' she snapped back.

'Never unwilling, Miss de Silva.'

Her face flushed scarlet as she took in the implication of his remark. She was just about to retort angrily when another voice cut across their interchange.

'Joshua, why don't you introduce me to your delightful new friend?'

It was the richly dressed woman she had seen sitting next to him in the pew.

A look of irritation flitted across his face, but was gone in a moment.

'But of course. Miss de Silva, may I present the Duchess of Severn. Charlotte, Miss de Silva—the daughter of our new ambassador from Spain.'

'How delightful to have you in Brighton, my dear.'

Domino wasn't sure she liked the woman. She seemed to purr when she spoke and the glances she cast towards the waiting Joshua verged on the covetous. But she curtsied decorously and made her father known to the duchess.

'You must both come to one of my small soirées as soon as possible,' Charlotte Severn said smoothly. 'I will send an invitation this very week. I am sure Joshua will know your direction.'

Domino sensed a hidden meaning, but managed to smile politely and hope that her father would conjure some excuse for their not attending.

'She is a very fine lady, is she not, Papa?' she remarked as they made their way back along the promenade.

'Who?'

'The Duchess of Severn.'

'Finely dressed at least.'

'You don't sound as though you like her.'

'I don't know her, Domino, but I do not like the set she moves in. I would prefer you to have as little to do with her as possible.'

'Mr Marchmain seems to know her well,' she ventured.

'Indeed he does,' her father said grimly, then abruptly changed the subject.

She was left to puzzle over just what had vexed him so badly.

Chapter Two

Joshua turned abruptly on his heels and headed back towards the Pavilion, his temper frayed. He needed to be alone and Charlotte Severn could easily be left to the escort of Moncaster, whom he had noticed in the distance. He was angry with her for intervening in his conversation with Domino and even more annoyed that she had promised an invitation to one of her celebrated soirées. He didn't know why, but he wanted to keep Domino to himself, or at the very least not expose her to the intimacies of the Severn household.

He had no intention of seducing the young girl, that was not his style, but neither did he want her knowing a woman such as Charlotte. That lady might be the wife of one of the premier dukes of the land, but she had the soul of a courtesan. The role suited her well and she should stick to it, he thought, rather than attempting to befriend the young and inexperienced. The Royal Pavilion was a suitable milieu for her. Every kind of dubious pleasure was available there and she had a husband happy to look away while she played. His Grace was content in his declining years to puff off his wife's beauty and retire to the lure of the gaming table. He was one of the Regent's most assiduous companions, not least because he was so wealthy that it mattered little to him how much money he lost.

Charlotte had access to wealth untold—but that was not enough, Joshua reflected wryly. It hardly compensated for a dull and ageing husband. He remembered when he had first seen her two years ago—Wiesbaden, it was, at the town's most opulent casino, and seated at the hazard table. She had looked across at him, her eyes staring straight into his, their porcelain blue still and expressionless, but nevertheless saying all they needed to say. That very night they had become lovers and from time to time continued to meet. But for long stretches of the year the duchess could not shrug off the duties incumbent on her position and that suited him well. There were always others happy to keep him company and lengthy periods of absence had until recently staved off the inevitable ennui which acquaintance with any woman produced. Or any woman since that first disastrous love affair.

But things were changing. He didn't know if it was the sea air stirring his blood and making him restless, but something had altered in him. Charlotte Severn no longer beguiled him and his frustration at being part of the Regent's sycophantic court was beginning to acquire a sharper edge. And the girl—she had something to do with it, too. It wasn't just that he wanted to bed her; that was as certain as it was unlikely. It was, he thought, that he had enjoyed their encounters, enjoyed her vitality, her verve, the zest with which she resisted his raillery. He had met her on three occasions and each time behind his gentle mockery he had wanted to explore, to discover more, to begin to know her. Today she had looked enchanting in peaches and cream and yet another rakish bonnet, those dark tragic eyes looking out at him so scornfully from beneath its brim. They could be made to wear another expression, he was sure. If ever he felt mad enough to risk exile again, he would savour the challenge. Charlotte's companionship had never seemed more irksome; she had stepped between them, muddying the waters, placing her footprint where only his had previously been.

The duchess was waiting for him in the outer vestibule of the Pavilion. If his temper had improved with the circuitous route he had taken, hers certainly had not. He barely had a foot through the door when she addressed him in a voice crisp with indignation.

'There you are, Mr Marchmain. I had begun to think I had lost you.'

'Why is that, Your Grace?' He would be as formal as she.

'Not unnaturally, I awaited your escort from the Chapel Royal. But when I turned to call on your services, you had gone.'

'Forgive me. I felt in need of a slightly longer walk and I am aware that it is not a pastime you favour.'

'A walk with you is always a pleasure, Joshua,' she replied in a more conciliatory tone.

'Then forgive me once more. Had I known, I would certainly have requested your company,' he lied.

She fixed him with a cold, enquiring eye. 'How is it that you know the ambassador's daughter?'

'I was representing the Regent last night, if you

remember,' he said indifferently. 'We met at her father's diplomatic reception.'

'You seem already to be on good terms with her.'

'Why should I not be? I understand the need for England to maintain a good relationship with Spain.'

'Ah, so that's what it is.'

Leo Moncaster strode into the Octagon Hall as they talked and viewed the two tense figures with satirical amusement.

'Quite a breeze blowing out there,' he offered with an assumed bonhomie. 'That's the problem with being beside the sea, never without a wind. Still hopefully Prinny will soon get bored with coastal delights and leave for Carlton House within the month.'

His audience remained resolutely silent and his eyebrows rose enquiringly.

'Have I been guilty of interrupting a private conversation? If so, my profuse apologies.'

'Apologies are unnecessary. Your manners are never anything but perfect, Moncaster,' Joshua remarked acidly, unable to conceal his dislike. 'Her Grace and I were just about to part.' And with that he strode off to his rooms, leaving Leo Moncaster looking quizzically at the duchess.

'I realise I am hardly a favourite of Marchmain's, but, beyond my unwelcome presence, what ails him?'

'I imagine no more than a tedious sermon and a cold walk from the Chapel Royal.'

'He seemed ruffled—uncharacteristically so.'

'I may have annoyed him,' the duchess admitted, her voice carefully neutral.

'How so?'

'I invited a young woman who appears to have

become his protégée to one of my soirées. That apparently is not something to be done.'

'And why not exactly?'

'Possibly he thinks I may corrupt her innocence,' Charlotte said with a knowing little smile. 'Would you be so good, Leo, as to escort me back to Steine House? A trifling distance, I know, but I prefer to have a reliable man by my side.'

Lord Moncaster offered his arm and they sailed past the waiting footman. He was not to be put off the scent, however, and as they walked through the Pavilion Gardens enquired, 'And what innocence would that be, if she knows Joshua Marchmain well?'

'Don't be so crude, Leo. Joshua is a gentleman.'

'You think so? Never trust a man not to sully innocence.'

'I suppose you should know,' she answered in a bored voice, 'your reputation precedes you.'

'At least I make no pretence to be other than I am,' he responded harshly. 'Marchmain is as much a rake; his pretence is to be something else.'

'Joshua is a man of the world, but he is not a rake. He has discrimination.'

'In seeking you out, dear lady?'

'In seeking out a woman who is mature and experienced and with whom he can enjoy life to the full.'

'As opposed to a girl who is young and naïve, yet sends his heartstrings singing.'

She bit her lip viciously, Moncaster observed with a sly glance. 'Don't say, my dear, that you've fallen in love with him. Not a good policy, not at all.'

'Joshua and I understand each other very well.'

'I wonder.'

'What do you mean by that?'

'I wonder how well. After all, you knew nothing of this girl.'

'That is because he made her acquaintance only yesterday.'

'And who is this paragon of unsullied innocence?'

'Her name is Domino de Silva. Domino, what a ridiculous name! Why, what's the matter?' The man beside her had stiffened imperceptibly.

'De Silva, you say?'

'Yes, do you know her?'

'Shall we say I have had dealings with her.' It was Lord Moncaster's turn to look grim.

'It sounds as though they were not entirely to your liking.'

'They were not. I have a score to settle.'

'I see.' Charlotte Severn glanced covertly at the polished man accompanying her. He took his time before he spoke again.

'Are you interested, perhaps? We might work well together.'

'We might,' she replied consideringly, 'but for the moment I prefer to see what I can accomplish alone.'

'Then let me give you a hint. Gaming.'

'Gaming? In what way?'

'A small chink in the armour. It is so fatally easy, is it not, when one is young and inexperienced, to find oneself adrift in a world one does not understand? Fatally easy to lose money, for instance, that one does not have. Then think of the shame, the scandal that would necessitate instant withdrawal from society.'

'You are a wicked man, Leo.'

'A practical man, my dear. And practical is what

you should be. Marchmain may be the gentleman you profess, but he is a man, and a very attractive one, too. Think of that.'

The duchess did think of it. She hurried away to her chambers, a frown on her otherwise unblemished forehead, and immediately called for paper and pen.

Domino thought little more of Charlotte Severn. If her invitation ever materialised, she was sure she could depend on her father to rescue her. Alfredo was busier than ever and it seemed to Domino that whole days passed when she barely saw him. Looking for occupation, she decided to seek out one of the many art galleries that had sprung up in and around Brighton under the Regent's patronage. Prince George loved art and so, by default, did his courtiers—or, at least, they maintained the pretence that they did. But rather than attend the Picture Gallery on Grand Parade, which boasted an unrivalled collection of Italian and French art, she chose a newer and much quieter gallery situated to the north of the town. It was an unfashionable area and little visited by the nobility, but Domino had recently seen a flyer advertising the Grove Gallery's latest exhibition and had been intrigued by the more experimental art it was offering for sale. Mindful of Carmela's repeated injunctions, she took Flora with her.

It was a beautiful early July morning when they struck inland towards New England farm and the scattering of modern houses that had been built nearby. A delighted Flora chattered incessantly as they walked, for accompanying her mistress was a rare treat and she was determined to provide amusement on the arduous walk uphill. Listening to the unending flow with only one ear, Domino hoped fervently that her maid would run out of words well before they reached their destination.

Thirty minutes walking had brought them to the top of the Dyke Road, the main thoroughfare north out of Brighton, and Flora was still talking. They found the gallery easily enough, the only building apart from a scattering of new villas, set amongst fields where cows were placidly grazing amid the shadows. Not even Carmela could find dangers lurking in such a tranquil setting, Domino thought, and felt justified in asking the garrulous Flora to await for her outside. Gratefully she trod over the threshold and felt the silence fall like a gentle cloak on her shoulders. The interior was bright and airy, a large rectangular space, its walls hung with green baize and its floor covered by a rough drugget. The paintings were displayed seemingly at random, but the brilliant light emanating high up from latticed casements that encircled the entire top of the rectangle illuminated them perfectly. She looked about her with pleasure and began to relax.

The paintings were certainly unusual. She wasn't at all sure she liked them, though they were for the most part ingeniously executed. But there was one landscape that caught her eye and slowed her steps: the Downs on a tempestuous day, the grass, the bushes, the trees, all bending seawards in the westerly wind, seeming to tumble unstoppably towards the troubled and racing waters in the distance. A glorious sense of freedom, brought to life so strongly in the painting, swept through her. She wanted to awake every morning to that wild landscape, feel its energy and be invigorated. But the price tag was far beyond her means. Perhaps, she thought wistfully, she could return next year when she had inherited the very large fortune that awaited her—but then someone else would hold the purse strings. Perhaps that someone else would have a love of art too, would see how very special this picture was. But no, that was too fanciful. If he took any pleasure in painting, it would not be an English landscape that would hang in his bedroom. Our bedroom, she thought, and quaked at the thought of the intimacies that must be shared with a virtual stranger.

'Are you going to buy it?'

Joshua Marchmain! The man seemed forever destined to disturb her peace. He had expressed a strong interest in art, but why had he chosen to visit this morning, and this gallery? The latter was soon explained.

'You would be doing a friend of mine a favour if you did—buy it, I mean.'

His voice was light and amused. She looked at him smiling lazily down at her, a shaft of sunlight pouring through the glass atrium above and reflecting pinpoints of light in the gold of his hair. As always he was immaculately dressed: a perfectly cut coat of dark blue superfine, an embroidered waistcoat of paler blue and close-fitting cream pantaloons. Despite the fashionable dress, he was no dandy. Domino was acutely aware of his body so close, so taut and hard, a body a woman could easily melt against. A wave of desire suddenly knotted her stomach and began its destructive trail through every fibre. She was genuinely shocked at her response and there was an uncomfortable pause before she was able to gather her wits together and wish him a prim good morning.

'I take it that your friend is the painter and this is his exhibition.'

'It is, and he is doing the painterly thing and starving in a garret.'

'Then, surely, you should be helping him.'

'I am very willing, but he won't hear of it. He maintains that he must live by his brush and his brush alone, and there are only so many paintings one individual can buy. So you see how important it is that you purchase his most treasured work. It's a splendid scene, is it not?'

He wondered if she would listen to the alarm bells clanging in her head, murmur something innocuous and move on, but her reply was one of genuine warmth.

'I think it wonderful—so wild and natural, so full of energy and joy.'

'Now I wonder why those qualities should appeal to you.'

The familiar flush flamed her cheeks and, seeing it, he made a vow to tread more carefully. He was intrigued by this delightful girl and, if he wanted to know her better, he would have to be sure to confine his remarks to the unexceptional. He offered her his arm.

'Since we are both here, Miss de Silva, do allow me to escort you around the rest of the exhibition.'

She hesitated for a fraction and he was relieved when good manners triumphed over churlishness. A lace-mittened hand was placed lightly on his arm and they began a stately progress around the gallery. He was hopeful that she would share his enthusiasm for the art and delighted when she willingly joined him in appraising the pictures they viewed, her dark eyes glowing with pleasure.

She was simply dressed in sprig muslin, but its soft folds and pleats revealed an exquisite young figure. From time to time her warm limbs touched his as they walked slowly side by side around the vast space and he felt his body stiffen in response. He wondered what those delightful curves would feel like beneath his hands and how soft that full mouth would be in meeting his.

'How have you become so knowledgeable, Mr Marchmain?'

Her words cut through this delightful fantasy and he was forced to administer a sharp mental shake before he could reply calmly, 'I think you might find the experts would quarrel with your use of the word *knowledgeable*. But I have travelled widely in Europe and have always made a point of seeking out the very best art each city could offer.'

'And have you kept travelling?' she asked wonderingly.

His voice when he answered was unusually sombre. 'There were a few years when I stayed put, years when I rented rooms in a Venetian palazzo. I found that an ideal location for painting.'

'It must have been. I've only ever seen pictures of Venice and I long to visit myself.'

'Then you must and as soon as possible. I would say that you were made for that city.'

And his gaze swept lingeringly over her: creamy olive skin, upturned nose and sorrowful dark eyes did not make a classical beauty, but something infinitely more charming. She blushed again and he silently chided himself. She was bewitching, that was the problem. She was so serious and yet so full of youthful energy that he wanted to open up the world for her and watch her smile. He was surprised by the force of his feelings.

'Do you still stay in Venice?'

'No longer, I fear. I inherited a property in England and it became necessary to return and become a responsible proprietor.'

'And where is your home now?'

'I would hardly call it home, but the house is known as Castle March. It's in Norfolk. Do you know it?' She shook her head. 'It is a large estate and needs managing. I ought to spend more time there, but ruralising in the depths of the English countryside is not exactly my forte.'

'I am sure that country living must have its own attractions.'

'Possibly—but only, I imagine, if you have someone to share them with.' Instantly he wished he had remained silent. That was the kind of remark that sent her into retreat. 'It can be pretty bleak in the fens for much of the year, so company is always welcome,' he offered, trying to retrieve the situation.

But she had taken alarm and detached herself from his arm. She adjusted the ribbons of her bonnet and thanked him prettily but firmly for his escort. In a moment she had disappeared out of the door and he was left to fume at his clumsiness. For a man of his address, he was managing extremely poorly, he thought. What was it about her that made him as maladroit as some untried adolescent? It could only be the enchantment of youth. For years he had strictly confined his most intimate attentions to experienced women; he had forgotten how utterly disarming innocent beauty could be.

* * *

The minute Domino stepped through the front door she saw the letter lying menacingly on the hall table and knew immediately from whom it came. The envelope was of thick cream vellum and bore a ducal crest. Charlotte Severn's invitation had arrived. The duchess's words uttered in the heat of the moment had been made good, but Domino had no wish to open the letter. She had taken the woman in dislike; why exactly she was unsure, but her father's condemnation had served only to underline the distaste she felt.

It was clear that the duchess was a close friend of Joshua Marchmain and he was certain to attend her social events. For that reason alone she would be reluctant to go. She had spent an engaging hour with him this afternoon, but he was a man she needed to avoid. He was dangerous to her peace of mind; the laughing eyes flecked with gold, the languorous gaze, had made her whole body burn in shameful response and promised the kind of pleasure she dared not think of. He was most definitely not a gentleman. He might dress as one and mix with ease in *ton* society, but he was rash and reckless and constantly put her out of countenance. How very unlike Richard, who was just as handsome but mindful of the proprieties and careful never to overstep the line. Joshua would not even recognise the existence of a line. He was undoubtedly a rake—a charming one, but someone with whom she should have no further commerce.

Her assumption that her father would prevent her attending the entertainment at Steine House proved false. When he walked into the dining room that evening, he was waving the duchess's card in his hand.

'The Duchess of Severn.' Then, seeing his daughter's long face, he said firmly, 'I think we must attend, Domino.'

'Could you not go alone, Papa?'

'I would prefer to, certainly. I am not at all keen that you further your acquaintance with the lady. But I fear we would give grave offence if you were to refuse.'

'But I am of no importance,' she persuaded eagerly. 'It is your position as ambassador that has prompted her to write.'

'I think not. The invitation was issued directly to you at the Chapel Royal. And my position, as you put it, means that I dare not offend anyone as influential as the Severns. The duke belongs to the Regent's inner circle.'

Domino made no reply, but sat erect, hands in her lap, and looked blankly ahead.

'Will it be such a trial, *querida*? We will stay no more than a couple of hours, I promise. And you will have me by your side the whole time.'

'I'm sorry, Papa, I'm being a goose.' Domino leaned across the table and gave him a loving hug. 'I had hoped the duchess had forgotten me.'

'Unfortunately not. I only hope her remembrance does not signify that she wishes "to take you up", as they say here. Your standing would not be enhanced by her favour.' Alfredo sighed deeply. 'Negotiating our way successfully through the English Court was never going to be easy, but I may have underestimated the difficulties.'

A thought struck him and he brightened. 'Carmela

can attend with us, then your being singled out for an invitation will not look so particular.'

Carmela, who had retired from the table and was sitting on the cushioned window seat reading an improving work, put her book down with a sharp slap. Her face glowered.

'I mean no disrespect to you, cousin, but nothing on earth would induce me to attend that woman's party.'

'Carmela, how is this? She may not be precisely to our taste, but she is a great noblewoman,' Alfredo chided her.

'Is that what you call it? We have a different word for it in Spain.'

He looked warningly at her and then back to Domino.

'What is that, Carmela?' Domino asked innocently.

Her cousin compressed her lips. 'Suffice to say that she is a married woman, but does not behave as one. She would not be welcome at any house belonging to our family.'

Domino looked shocked. 'You mean she has lovers?'

Carmela appeared to struggle with herself for a moment, but then decided where her duty lay.

'I do not generally indulge in idle gossip, as I hope you know,' she said repressively, 'but I think it right that you should be on your guard. In the few weeks we have been in Brighton I have heard disquieting things about the Duchess of Severn. I believe that her current lover has followed her here and is even now residing at the Pavilion.'

Domino glanced at her father, urgently seeking his reassurance, but no denial was forthcoming. His face was set and he refused to meet her eyes. Suddenly she understood. Joshua Marchmain was that lover. That was why he had been so irritated at the Chapel Royal. He had not wanted her to make the duchess's acquaintance, had not wanted her to know the truth of their supposed friendship. She felt herself flushing hotly, embarrassed at having been so naïve. Flushing, too, with a kind of pain. But why on earth did she feel that? Had she been stupid enough to think there was any kind of connection between them?

It was true that he had singled her out at her father's reception and engaged her in lengthy conversation. He had even talked sensibly and interestingly about art. But that was misleading. She should remember her first encounter with him as she walked by the sea; his conduct had been predatory, light-hearted and amusing, it was true, but nevertheless predatory. Even outside the church on Sunday he had not been able to resist throwing out lures to her. He was a womaniser for whom every female was fair game, even as his mistress was living a mere stone's throw away. The thought of visiting Steine House was loathsome.

A few days later, an unwelcome message arrived at Marine Parade. Señor de Silva was required to return to London immediately. News had arrived from Spain too confidential to be entrusted to a messenger and it was necessary for the ambassador to post up to Manchester House. He would spend only one night away, but it looked unlikely that he would return to Brighton in time for Charlotte Severn's soirée.

Alfredo was faced with a quandary. He had no wish to expose his daughter to the malign influence of Steine House without his protection but, at the same time, he knew that it was essential he was represented at what would be a prestigious affair. He would let Domino herself decide.

'I hardly like to ask this of you, my dear,' he began tentatively, 'but would you be willing to go to the duchess's concert by yourself for a short while? I could no doubt arrange for an older lady to take you under her wing until I return. Once I am back in Brighton, I will make haste to join you at Steine House. Or perhaps Carmela could swallow her misgivings? If she would agree to attend, it would make things a great deal more comfortable.'

The women's despondent expressions hardly promised comfort. Attending the event without the support of Señor de Silva was the last thing either of them wished to contemplate. But they both found themselves agreeing to his suggestion, Domino because she loved her father dearly and knew that he would not ask this of her unless it was necessary and Carmela because the family's honour was at stake and that was sufficient to call forth her loyalty.

So it was that at six o'clock on a balmy Friday evening the two of them set off in a hired carriage for Steine House. It had an infamous reputation, for it was the home the Regent had purchased for his long-standing mistress and unofficial wife, Maria Fitzherbert. She still resided there and was hardly ever seen beyond its walls, though the Prince was said even now to visit her frequently, despite a legal marriage and many subsequent lovers. Rumour insisted that a tunnel ran via the adjoining Marlborough House to the basement of the royal palace. The Duke of Severn was an old friend of Mrs Fitzherbert and he and his wife were always made welcome in her home when they visited the town. The duke in particular could not bear to live permanently in the overheated Pavilion and always availed himself of this hospitality.

The whispers that swirled around Steine House could only sharpen the aversion both Domino and her cousin felt at having to enter its portals. But when their carriage stopped outside, they saw only a graceful white stucco building with an Italian-style façade and a trellised verandah and balcony. A balustrade of carved ironwork led up a single flight of steps to a heavily ornamented glass door. Domino pinned on what she hoped was a polite smile and made ready to greet her hosts. She received a courteous welcome, the duke seeming to her young eyes horribly withered and old. No wonder the duchess looked elsewhere, she found herself musing, then promptly castigated herself for such an appalling thought. Steine House was already having a noxious effect. Once inside the main door, they were directed up a bamboo and iron staircase to a salon from which the strains of music could already be heard.

'This is the staircase Lord Barrymore once rode his horse up for a bet,' Carmela hissed in her ear.

Domino paused on the staircase, startled for a moment by her staid cousin's incongruous knowledge of *ton* gossip. Where on earth did she hear such stories? As she stood balanced on one foot, she caught sight of her reflection in the long pier glass at the top of the stairs. She was pleased with what she saw. The apricot silk she had chosen, trimmed with gold edging and worn with an overdress of cream-coloured gauze, set off the creamy olive of her complexion perfectly. Her glossy ebony curls hung naturally to her neck in ringlets this evening and her eyes were sparkling, if only in apprehension. Carmela leaned forwards and tapped her wrist sharply with her fan, a painful reminder that in her cousin's book any sign of vanity was sinful.

In a few moments they were in the large salon, a huge scarlet cavern of a room hung with red satin curtains and upholstered in red plush velvet. A uniformed footman ushered them to one of the rows of little gold chairs that had been arranged in the shape of a wide semi-circle. Domino sat down gingerly on one of the tiny chairs.

'Be careful, Carmela,' she warned, 'these chair legs are so thin that one false fidget and the sound of matchwood will drown out the string quartet.'

Carmela permitted herself a slight smile and looked searchingly around the room. 'I see nobody who came to our reception,' she remarked disappointedly. 'How strange when a most famous soprano is to sing.'

'Evidently they have decided to miss the delights on offer.' Including Joshua Marchmain, she noted wryly.

She told herself she was glad that at least this evening she would not have to face him. Yet, unaccountably, she felt a pang of disappointment. She had enjoyed her tour of the Grove Gallery. True, she had been put out of countenance once or twice by his infelicitous remarks, but she had spent nigh on an hour in his company discussing nothing more incendiary than art and European travel. He was interesting and intelligent, and though he had visited places she could only dream of, he had not made her feel the gauche girl she knew herself to be.

But rumour had named him the lover of any number

of married women, including Charlotte Severn. Could rumour have possibly lied? In her heart she knew it could not. Mr Marchmain was a thorough-going rake and, if the sensations of her own unruly body were anything to judge by, he did not have to work too hard for his success. The shaft of intense desire that had pierced her so suddenly and so unexpectedly signalled clearly that she was in danger of being drawn into a whirlpool of feeling, with him at its centre. It was well for her that he was not here this evening.

'My lords, ladies and gentlemen, I give you the illustrious soprano, Bianca Bonelli.'

The duke led the famous singer, who had journeyed from Milan at his request, to a raised platform, kissing her hand enthusiastically while the string quartet began to play the opening piece of music. Domino set herself to listen with what she hoped was a thoughtful expression.

A late-arriving Joshua, hovering in the doorway, spotted her immediately and almost laughed aloud at her face, screwed up in concentration—or was that pain? If it was, it was a pain he shared. He made a swift escape to the library, where he would not be disturbed, but from where he could still hear the concert's end.

And end it did, with a great deal of relief on Domino's part. Carmela wore her usual severe expression but her spontaneous applause made clear her enjoyment. Hardly surprising, Domino thought, for the music had evinced a moral seriousness sufficient even for her cousin. The latter seemed eager to meet the musicians personally and, when the duchess suddenly appeared at their side, Carmela was whisked away for introductions and Domino found herself led by Charlotte into an adjoining salon where liveried footmen were circulating with drinks and canapés.

Her Grace deftly lifted two large flutes of champagne from a passing tray and said with an enticing smile, 'I am so pleased you were able to come, Miss de Silva, as I collect your father has been forced to post back to London on urgent business.'

'Indeed, Your Grace. He sends his most sincere apologies and will make every effort to join us this evening.'

'I understand,' she cooed, 'and really it matters not. You are my prize, after all. I was entranced when we met at the Chapel Royal on Sunday and have spent all week wishing to know more of you.'

Domino doubted that very much. The woman's insincerity was blatant, but she managed a gentle smile in response.

'Tell me, do,' the duchess continued, 'how long are we to have the pleasure of your company in Brighton?'

'For the Season, ma'am. I have undertaken to stay with my father while the Court is absent from London.'

For a moment the expression on her hostess's face suggested she was not best pleased by this news, but she rallied immediately.

'How delightful, for we are also destined to be here until the Prince returns to Carlton House. Let us toast our new acquaintanceship, Miss de Silva. I am sure we will be the best of friends.'

Domino could not think so, but politely raised her glass. Champagne bubbles shot up her nose and she had difficulty in preventing herself sneezing.

'You see,' Charlotte continued, 'one meets so few

new people in Brighton, the same dreary crowd year after year. So when a bright new star appears, one is drawn immediately towards them.'

Domino concluded that she must be the bright star, but was at a loss how to answer. She need not have worried, for the duchess was now in full flow.

'You are so beautiful, my dear, and have such charming manners, that I prophesy prodigious success for you—you will be the toast of the town.'

This was so patently absurd that Domino was hard put not to laugh aloud. She knew herself to be well enough but, against the duchess's blonde perfection, she was nothing. And she certainly had no ambition to take Brighton by storm. Quite the opposite—she anticipated several agreeable months by the sea, close to her father, before she returned to Spain to make the decision of her life.

The duchess continued to talk while she sipped her champagne. The drink was gradually becoming more acceptable, and when her companion substituted her empty glass for another fizzing to the brim, she hardly noticed. When the older woman took her by the hand, she allowed herself to be expertly steered through the crowd towards a smaller chamber at the far end of the salon.

'In proof of my friendship, Miss de Silva—but may I call you Domino? Such a sweet and unusual name—I would very much like you to meet some particular friends of mine. Just a few congenial spirits whom I know you will esteem.'

Her head had begun to spin a little, but she retained enough caution to remind her hostess that Carmela should be with them.

'But naturally, my dear. I shall introduce you to a few dear companions and then collect your cousin and bring her instantly to you.'

They were through the door before Domino could protest further. The room they entered, though smaller than the salon, was still a substantial size, thickly carpeted and curtained, deadening all sound and cutting the space adrift from the outside world. A number of people were gathered around three large tables set at different angles in the room; even in her befuddled state, she knew instantly that this was a gaming room. She pulled back sharply.

'I am honoured, Your Grace, that you should wish to introduce me to your friends,' she stumbled, 'but I do not play cards or any other game of chance.'

'Allow me to advise you, my dear, since you are still so very young.' The duchess's voice was honey. 'You have undertaken to play the role of hostess for your father. In England, you know, polite society expects always to have the opportunity to indulge in games of chance and a hostess must be as well versed in them as her guests.'

'I thank you again, Your Grace, but I do not gamble.'

'Who said anything about gambling? Just a few friendly games, my dear.'

Domino felt deeply uncomfortable. She was finding it very difficult to continue refusing her hostess, but games of chance, whether money passed hands or not, were something she had sworn never again to engage in. She had learned her lesson all too well the last time she was in England. Gambling had a fatal attraction for her and she could not risk getting involved. But she could hardly say this to someone she barely knew, to a woman who occupied such an exalted position. Her head was definitely swimming now and her legs feeling decidedly unsafe. She felt the duchess's hand on her shoulder and began to sink downwards to the waiting chair. The faces around the table looked up at her expectantly. In the distance other faces at other tables blurred into a misty vision. She longed to get away but she could not, in politeness, leave. Surely just one hand of cards would not matter. She would satisfy the demands of hospitality and then depart straight away. She took hold of the arms of the chair, making ready to sit down, and the support made her feel slightly less shaky. She smiled hazily at the assembled company and then, out of the blur, a face swam into her vision. A dark, wolfish, horribly familiar face. Leo Moncaster!

Chapter Three

She gave a sudden choke, shaken by an irrational panic, and would have collapsed but for a supportive hand at her elbow.

'Miss de Silva? How nice to see you here,' Joshua Marchmain was saying smoothly. 'I hope you found the music to your taste.'

'Yes, indeed, thank you,' she stuttered.

He was holding his arm out to her and she took it. Nervously she glanced at the woman who stood at her left side. Charlotte Severn's eyes were narrowed, but there was no mistaking the daggers she was sending forth.

'The concert was delightful, was it not? And such a privilege to hear Signora Bonelli. I believe she is judged one of the finest sopranos of our day.' His voice was unruffled, but even while he spoke he was skilfully extricating the apricot silk from the entanglements of chair and table.

By now the duchess had regained her composure

and, in a gesture of seeming warmth, clasped hold of Domino's other arm.

'But must you go already?' she addressed the girl directly, excluding Joshua from the conversation. 'I am delighted that you enjoyed our small concert, but do stay for the rest of the evening's entertainments.'

Her head still whirling, Domino was caught between the two and had no idea how to cope with the dreadful situation. It was one scenario that the etiquette books failed to mention.

Joshua locked glances with the duchess. His voice was imperturbable as ever, but there was an edging of steel that Domino had never heard before.

'It does not seem, Your Grace, that card playing holds much attraction for Miss de Silva, so I will engage to reunite her with her cousin.'

Leaving their hostess stranded with outstretched hand, he propelled Domino firmly towards the door and whisked her through it. Once on the other side he cut a swathe through the milling crowd to arrive unerringly at Carmela's side. Her cousin wore a worried expression, which rapidly turned to exasperation once she saw Domino safe and well. She nodded curtly to Joshua and grabbed Domino by the arm. Social politeness was brushed aside and, without waiting to bid their hosts goodbye, Carmela made for the bamboo staircase. The carriage had been ordered and was already waiting outside.

Catching her breath at the head of the stairs, Domino had only time to glance briefly over her shoulder. Joshua Marchmain had not spoken a word as they'd threaded their way through the crowded room, but now she saw him in conversation with the duchess, their heads close and talking animatedly together. Her heart lurched as she took in the intimacy of the little tableau. But why did the image cause her such distress? All the while Carmela was bundling her down the stairs and into the coach, she struggled to find an answer. Why on earth should Joshua's relationship with the duchess matter? She knew them to be lovers—naturally they would have much to say to each other. He would be keen to explain his absence from the concert and to excuse his intervention with Domino, even keener no doubt to make an assignation with his mistress for later that evening. It all made perfect sense, but it only served to intensify her misery.

Unknown to Domino, her departure left the two locked in a furious exchange.

'What exactly were you thinking of?' Cold anger permeated Joshua's voice.

'I don't pretend to understand you.'

'I think you understand me perfectly. Miss de Silva is still a minor and yet you were encouraging her to break the law by gambling.'

'Don't be ridiculous.' The duchess fairly spat the words. 'I merely suggested to her that she might like to join a select gathering and play a few rounds of loo.'

'A select gathering—is that what you call it?' He snorted derisively.

'I take it that you finally decided to put in an appearance this evening for reasons other than to be unpleasant.'

'It's as well I did. It was clear that the girl did not want to stay and just as clear that you were intent on forcing her.'

'What rubbish. How could I ever force her to do anything she did not wish? If you had not interrupted us in that nonsensical manner, she would be happily playing cards this very moment.'

'Playing cards, I am sure, but happily I don't believe.'

'I say again, how could I make her play cards if she did not wish it?' The duchess's expression was scornful.

'I imagine a few judicious glasses of champagne might help to do the trick, together with pressure from her hostess which she would find difficult to resist.'

'You talk as though she were an innocent. It won't have been the first time that she has supped champagne, I'm sure, and from what I hear she has been more than happy in the past to engage in games of chance—even, dare I say, to accrue considerable debts.'

'How can that be?'

For an instant Joshua appeared less composed and the duchess watched him with a gloating expression. 'Why don't you ask her? The two of you seem remarkably thick with each other. And why are you so late? The concert is long finished.'

'I am devastated to have missed it,' he said with barely concealed irony, 'and naturally I apologise. I was visiting—an artist friend—and was unexpectedly detained.'

'That must have been important,' came the brittle rejoinder, and she walked away to mingle with her guests in the inner sanctum. Leo Moncaster was waiting for her.

'I can see why you wanted to handle the matter yourself.' His smile was sardonic.

'I was wrong. She was far more stubborn than I gave her credit for. But I think I would have succeeded in the end if Marchmain had not turned up at that moment and spoiled the game.'

'And you still feel that she is of no interest to him?'

She did not answer him directly, but said slowly and deliberately, 'I need to get rid of her.'

There was a slight pause before Moncaster said in a heartening voice, 'Don't be too discouraged, Charlotte. It would have been difficult to coax her to stay once she saw my face. There must be more subtle ways to catch our little bird.'

'You have some ideas?'

'I have some ideas. Shall we now work together?'

Charlotte Severn's nod was almost imperceptible but Lord Moncaster retired that night a contented man.

Domino slept fitfully and woke unrefreshed to a new day. The events at Steine House still crowded her mind, filling it with jangled impressions only half-understood, but all of them contributing to her despondency. How was she to make sense of such a dreadful evening? The concert had evoked stifled yawns, but at least it had been innocuous. It was the Duchess of Severn herself who had seemed far from innocent. She had appeared to be so friendly, so keen to make Domino's acquaintance that she should have felt flattered. Despite her dubious reputation, Charlotte Severn was enormously influential and her notice of a mere ambassador's daughter would for most be a cause of pleasure and gratitude. But Domino had felt neither pleased nor grateful. Instead she had felt manipulated, even coerced. She had not wanted to abandon Carmela, but the Duchess had been insistent. She had not wanted to enter the inner room, yet had found herself propelled through its doors unable to protest. And once there her fears had multiplied. Seeing Leo Moncaster had been the final straw. His malevolent face still lowered in her dreams. Three years ago he had been her undoing and here he was once more, ready to do her harm if he possibly could.

Rescue had come, but at what cost? Just when she'd decided that on no account must she have further dealings with Joshua Marchmain, he had made her beholden. How shameful to be dependent on a rake for rescue! He had said not a word as he'd walked her towards her cousin and sanctuary, but he must have thought her a silly and naïve girl, out of her depth and drowning. It was evident that he had been angry with the duchess—at one point Domino had felt literally pulled between the two of them—and she might have found comfort in that, but for the last glimpse she'd had of the pair.

They had stood as though closeted, their heads so close that his cheek was almost grazing the woman's hair. Any animosity had vanished. They had been talking easily together and she had a sinking feeling that she had been the main subject of their conversation. Her face burned; they would decide that she was a foolish young girl who had become hysterical when invited to partake in a game of chance. Then a worse thought struck, making her face burn even brighter. What if she really had been that foolish, foolish enough to imagine the whole thing and misinterpret the duchess's conduct? This high-born lady had gone out of her way to be friendly and her seeming coercion might simply be a desire to encourage a reluctant young guest to enjoy herself. The duchess would not know her unfortunate history with Lord Moncaster; she would be ignorant of the dread he evoked. And how had Domino responded to Charlotte's overtures? Blind, inexplicable panic and a dreadful lapse of good manners. She and Carmela had left the party without a word of thanks or indeed a word of farewell. It was appalling.

She told herself that she must not dwell on such harrowing thoughts, but dwell on them she did. The evening's events continued to revolve in her mind until they began to assume hideous proportions. She wished that her mother was by her side to guide her. She knew that she could have told Mama everything— well, nearly everything, she amended inwardly. Her feelings towards Joshua would have remained under wraps. She did not even understand them herself. How could she feel this strong attraction to him when Richard had been the only man she had ever loved?

Remember him, remember him, she told herself fiercely. Richard, the new Lord Veryan, and she a whirling figure in pale blue, dancing with him at Almack's for the very first time. How wonderful that had been. She hugged the memory, warmed by its still-powerful glow, chasing Joshua and her confusion away. But then another image emerged: Richard dancing that very same night with Christabel, the woman he contended he despised, the woman who had so cruelly jilted him, but the woman he still loved. Domino had known even then, deep in her innermost self, that his feelings for the flame-haired beauty had not died and that he was deceiving himself in thinking he was free of her power. But how resolute she herself had been in refusing to see the truth of the situation, wishing, hoping that he would turn his head and see the girl who was so often by his side through those long summer months, the girl who idolised him. But all he saw was a scrubby schoolgirl, without guile or wisdom, too spontaneous for her own good. Was that what Joshua saw? Was this another situation in which she was blind to the truth?

For much of the day she stayed cloistered in her room, venturing downstairs only at mealtimes, though in truth she had little appetite. At the table Carmela made no mention of yesterday's tribulations and Domino could only assume that her cousin had vowed herself to silence. Señor de Silva seemed to have taken the same vow. He had arrived from London in the early hours of the morning and Domino had expected to find him eager to hear details of their visit to Steine House. But not one question did he ask. Perhaps Carmela had alerted him to the wretchedness of the evening. Domino had committed a serious impropriety in disappearing for some considerable time without a chaperon, but neither her father nor her cousin appeared to blame her.

Indeed, they both treated her with unaccustomed gentleness and, during the days that followed, were careful never to comment on her fondness for her room and her refusal to venture out for even a short walk.

It was Alfredo who finally broke the impasse on a morning that sparkled with light.

'The weather is so fine, *querida*,' he said heartily, embracing her in one of his bear hugs. 'Why don't we walk on the Downs, perhaps even take a picnic?'

Carmela nodded silent approval and he continued persuasively, 'The breeze will keep us cool and we should easily find sufficient shade to enjoy our meal.'

She said nothing, but her expression was downcast. Her father, though, was not to be defeated. 'Just you and I,' he coaxed.

She did not wish to disappoint him, but shrank at the idea of walking on the Downs, or indeed anywhere in the vicinity. What she wanted most was to hide away—from the duchess, from Moncaster and particularly from Joshua Marchmain. Every time she stepped outside the door, she risked meeting with one or other of them. Brighton was not a large town.

'If that is too far for you, we could take a short walk through the Lanes.' Alfredo would not be dissuaded, and she saw how concerned he was. 'It's not good, Domino, to be confined in these four walls for too long.'

She knew he was right. Eventually she would have to emerge from her refuge and face whatever or whoever came her way. She was compounding her folly at Steine House with even greater folly. And showing a drastic lack of spirit too, she castigated herself. She needed to regain her usual vitality and show the world that she was ashamed of nothing. She could do that, must do that. If she met Charlotte Severn, she would smile and curtsy and leave it to the other woman to set the tone. If she met Lord Moncaster, her father would be there to defend her. And if she met Joshua—but she would not, she was sure. She had been shut away in Marine Parade for nearly a week and had heard nothing of him. He had his own tight little circle and would not have noticed her absence from the social scene.

'I need to change my books at the library, Papa,' she offered, 'and if you are agreeable we could walk there.'

The library she patronised, one of the many that

were dotted across Brighton, was in the west of the town and would furnish a satisfying stroll. On the way, there was the distraction of any number of tempting shop windows filled with exquisite silks and laces, almost certainly smuggled from France. She chose her dress with care, searching for as plain a gown as possible, and ended by donning a simple but stylish jaconet muslin. Once out of the house, she kept her eyes lowered beneath the deep brim of her straw bonnet, but she need not have worried, for the *ton* were out of town that day it seemed, enjoying themselves elsewhere. They walked through near-deserted streets while her father told her of his trip to London and the worrying news from Spain.

'A change of government usually means a change of everything else,' he confided to her. 'I am no longer certain of my position. It could be that I am recalled to Madrid very soon and perhaps reassigned elsewhere. I am sorry, if that happens, *querida*. Your holiday by the sea will come to an abrupt end.'

She squeezed his arm reassuringly, but felt a tremor of foreboding. Leaving Brighton would mean separation from her father when they had so recently been reunited. It would mean an inevitable return to Spain and the future that awaited her. The life she had agreed upon just a few weeks ago seemed increasingly dreary. Nothing had changed and yet everything seemed different. She was still pondering this paradox when they arrived at the fashionable new subscription library, which fronted the western end of the promenade.

Usually its coffee rooms and lounges were filled with residents and fashionable visitors but, as with the rest of the town today, it was nearly empty. A few ladies were browsing the bookshelves and a small card game was in play at one end of the smallest saloon. Another gentleman was busy sifting through music sheets, evidently keen to find something new for the musical evening he was planning.

'All at the Race Ground,' he explained succinctly when Alfredo mentioned the scarcity of people. 'The Regent's Cup today, y' know. Big prize money.'

'I wish we had known...' her father turned to Domino '...you would have enjoyed the meeting. That's what comes of staying too close to home.'

She could only feel gratitude that her father had not heard the news. At the race course she would have been sure to see everyone that she most wished to avoid.

Thirty minutes of browsing the floor-to-ceiling bookshelves secured a neat pile of small volumes and they made ready to leave. They were almost out of the door when her father spied a tattered poster taped insecurely to the wall.

'Look, Domino, Henry Angelo has set up a new fencing academy here in Brighton. I was tempted in London to try a lesson or two with him.'

She could not help but smile. Her father's physique in middle age was hardly conducive to fencing.

'Why do you smile, little one? You think I couldn't do it?'

'No, Papa, I am sure you could, but wouldn't you prefer to watch rather than participate?'

'Perhaps you are right, though in my youth I was a match for anyone.'

'Yes?'

'I actually beat the legendary Don Roderiguez.'

She looked questioningly.

'You wouldn't know of him. It was well before you were born, but he was worshipped in Madrid for his skill. I took him on as a wager and nobody expected me to win, but I did.'

'And Don Roderiguez?'

'I have to admit that he was probably not quite himself. I managed to fight him after a particularly boisterous party.'

They both laughed and she said wistfully, 'Gentlemen are so lucky; they have many channels for their energy. All we have is embroidery or the pianoforte.'

'I don't notice either of those featuring heavily in your life, my dear.'

'Exactly, Papa, that is just what I mean. Fencing would be far more enjoyable.'

And it would get rid of some of my restlessness, she thought, even perhaps beat the blue-devils that have been plaguing me. Yes, men were lucky. A woman had simply to sit, to watch and to wait.

Unbeknown to her, Alfredo had taken note of his daughter's interest and promptly committed to memory the address of the new fencing school. He would arrange a small treat for her. Lately she had seemed unusually dejected. He knew the evening at Steine House had not gone to plan, but he was in the dark about his daughter's true state of mind. Anything that would distract her could only be good.

So it was that Henry Angelo had an early morning visitor the next day. The request was unusual and certainly unconventional, but he had a business to establish and an ambassador was too important a personage to offend in these early days. His school had already attracted the attention of those members of the *ton* spending the summer in Brighton, but Señor de Silva could prove useful in bringing new clients from the diplomatic circles in which he moved.

Summoned to an early breakfast, Domino found her father already at the table, seething with barely suppressed excitement.

'What have you been doing, Papa?' she asked guardedly. 'You look like a naughty schoolboy.'

'This morning I have important papers to clear, but this afternoon, Domino, we are to play truant together!'

'And Carmela?' Her cousin had not yet put in an appearance.

'Carmela and playing truant are not compatible, I think.' Señor de Silva smiled happily. 'This is just for you and me.'

'Not a picnic on the Downs?' she asked in some alarm. Despite her resolve to be brave, she still feared places where she risked meeting the world and his wife.

'No, no picnic. The wind today is far too strong even for the English to eat outdoors.'

Through the windows she saw the grey surf breaking harshly on the sea wall and spilling through the iron railings that defended the promenade. A few hardy souls, determined to complete their daily constitutional, were making their slow progress along the seafront. They were bent nearly double as they headed into the fierce wind, clutching wildly at flying garments.

'Then indoors somewhere?'

'Indeed. But you must probe no further. It is to be a great surprise!'

* * *

She had hoped to spend the day curled on the sofa reading some of the library's offerings, but it was evident that Alfredo had made special plans and she was sufficiently intrigued to hurry upstairs after a modest nuncheon and change her dress. Choosing suitable raiment proved difficult, for she had no idea where she was going. Eventually she settled on a primrose sarsenet flounced with French trimmings: modest enough for an informal outing, yet not too plain. She quickly threaded a matching primrose ribbon through a tangle of black curls and joined her father in the hall.

'We will go by carriage,' he announced as Marston battled to hold the front door ajar. 'The weather is far too rough to walk.'

Soon they were bowling past fishermen painting boats that had been pulled high on to the beach, past their women tending the nets and then past Mahomed's much-patronised Vapour Baths, until they reached the end of East Cliff. The imposing mansions that lined the road gradually became far less in number as they travelled eastwards, but just before they reached open countryside the carriage pulled up at a small establishment tucked between two much larger white-washed dwellings. An arched wooden door painted in luminescent green beckoned a greeting and, even before they had taken a step out of the vehicle, a sprightly, dark-haired man bounded out to greet them.

'Welcome, welcome,' he enthused, executing a deep bow. 'I am most honoured by your visit.' Domino supposed him to be the proprietor of whatever establishment they had come to.

'Follow me, please, come this way.' The man ushered

them into the house, fairly dancing down a narrow passageway to a small but comfortable sitting room. All the time he kept up a stream of lively chatter.

Looking around her she saw a pair of highly polished rapiers crossed above the fireplace and all four plastered walls closely hung with prints of sword fighting. Her father had brought her to none other than the fencing academy they had seen advertised! It was hardly the outing she would have chosen, but she owed it to him to look pleased. For days he had good humouredly tolerated the Friday face she had been wearing and must have gone to some trouble to arrange what he clearly thought an interesting diversion.

Henry Angelo proved an attentive host. She had to suppress a smile; this most Italian of men was intent on solemnly observing the rituals of an English tea. He did it with aplomb, pouring the steaming liquid himself and handing around the Crown Derby teacups with a splendid flourish. Small delicate scones with a selection of jams were offered, followed by pastries and fruit cake. The whole time Signor Angelo bubbled along with his tea.

'My father moved from Paris, you know, forty years ago to set up a fencing school in London. It was a gamble, but he has been very successful!'

'So I understand,' Alfredo acknowledged, 'and you are continuing the family tradition, I see.'

'I hope so. These new premises in Brighton are a venture, but I am gradually becoming known. And it helps that my father has many powerful friends. He knows the great boxer, Gentleman Jackson.'

'Really?' Alfredo appeared genuinely interested.

'Yes, indeed. He numbers Mr Jackson among his

closest friends. Years ago he helped him establish a boxing club next door to our Fencing Academy in Bond Street.'

Reminiscences of the Gentleman's many successful prize fights, and a listing of all the great and the good that had frequented both establishments, followed at breakneck speed.

'The Regent himself honoured us with a visit to Bond Street,' the younger Henry announced breathlessly. 'We hosted an exhibition of fencing just for him, you know, and he asked for a set of foils used by the master fencer of the day. Masks and gloves, too!' he concluded triumphantly.

The heat of the small sitting room, combined with the unbroken flow of small talk, was making Domino's head swim. She was heartily glad when their host danced once more to his feet and made ready to show them around the Academy of which he was inordinately proud.

Once in the school proper, there was far more space and air and she breathed more freely. Signor Angelo led them from one practice room to another. The building was far larger than it appeared from outside, stretching back seawards a considerable distance. Each room was flooded with natural light, the ceiling consisting almost entirely of glass panels open to the sky. Collections of foils, their guards decorated with a variety of acanthus leaves, anchors, cherubs and serpents, filled the corners of each room. Still voluble, their host was explaining at length the distinctive style of French epées, Italian rapiers and English swords. From a large oak cupboard in one room face masks and padded bibs spilled out on to the floor.

'*Señor*, please, try one of these,' he invited Alfredo, holding up a stiff white corset. 'It is the very latest in design.'

The body padding was a cause of some humour since Señor de Silva's rotund figure defeated all attempts to accommodate it. Alfredo smiled ruefully.

'My dream of fencing is again dashed!'

They had passed through a series of such rooms when their host suggested that they might like to see a demonstration.

'I have just now one of my best instructors engaged in a training bout with a most proficient amateur. They are upstairs in an arena I keep for more serious competition.'

Alfredo looked a little uncertain, but Domino smiled easily and they mounted the steps to a large room that filled the whole of the first floor of the building. Signor Angelo waved them to the chairs situated at the very edge of the room. The two combatants were at some distance, but immediately she became aware of the sheer volume of energy crackling in the air. Their white-clothed figures circled each other, lunging, parrying, occasionally retreating to recover position. It was impossible to tell who was the instructor and who the pupil, since the opponents were so well matched and first one man, then the other, gained the advantage.

She found herself being pulled into the drama of the fight. It was a practice session only and the buttons were firmly secured to the top of the men's foils, yet there was a sense of restrained danger. Both men were at the prime of their fitness: one small and angular, buzzing forwards and backwards like an angry bee, the other slim but muscular, agile and menacing in his weavings. She watched his body tauten and slacken in response to the other's constant teasing, his muscles hardened and contouring his body. He had such natural grace and such power in his limbs that she was mesmerised into following his every movement, imbibing his male strength almost like a drug. She would have liked to reach out and touch him, stroke the line of his rippling arm, his slim waist, his powerful thigh. For a moment she found herself breathless, liquid with desire.

Then she shook herself awake. She had not felt such a powerful emotion since Richard had smiled at her and turned her body to water. With a shock, she realised she had not thought of Richard once during the past few days. Somehow he had begun to drift into the distance, remote from the pressing concerns of her life. And thinking of him now no longer evoked the same eager yearning that it had always done. What could that mean? That she was ready to give herself to another, ready perhaps for the husband who was even now awaiting her return to Spain? Would he evoke the same intense desire that had just shaken her? It seemed unlikely.

The bout was over and the opponents shaking hands. Signor Angelo rushed forwards and congratulated his pupil.

'That was *magnifico, signor.* You get better all the time.'

The man addressed laid down his foil and raised his mask. Of course, it could only be him, she thought.

Joshua Marchmain smiled across the length of the room and walked slowly towards her. She drank in his shapely form. Really, fencing clothes left little to the imagination. He wiped the beads of sweat from his forehead and smiled that leonine smile.

'If I'd known I had such an audience, I would have finished off Guido in double-quick time!' He bowed courteously and raised her hand to his lips, just grazing the surface.

She found herself unable to speak. His touch had reignited the earlier fire and she was helpless to dampen its ravages. It was left to her father to fill the silence that spread between them.

'Thank you for a splendid display, sir. I have not seen such skill for many years.'

'You fence yourself?'

'I used to.' Alfredo smiled wryly. 'But tell me, was that the Italian style?'

'Always the Italian style,' Henry Angelo put in. 'Mr Marchmain fences like a professional.'

'I had to wait until I reached Italy before I learned the true art of fencing,' Joshua said in explanation.

'But now you don't have to do it for real, eh?' Henry interrupted. 'English husbands are more complacent.' And he waved his hand at the scar that Joshua bore on his cheek.

The barely disguised reminder that this man was an out-and-out rake brought Domino back to her senses. In seconds she had recovered her poise.

'How often do you fence, Mr Marchmain?' she asked in a neutral voice.

Still flushed with annoyance at Angelo's intervention, Joshua turned to her, suddenly smiling so sweetly that hammer blows again began to afflict her heart.

'As often as I can, Miss de Silva. Are you interested in the sport?'

'I have never seen it until today, but I can understand why men find it so exciting.'

'But not women,' he mocked.

'I am sure if we were allowed the necessary freedom, sir, we too might find it exciting.'

'Any time you wish to strike for freedom and would like a lesson, Miss de Silva, I am at your service.'

The golden eyes darkened and she felt his voice caressing her with a warmth akin to velvet. She was quite certain that it wasn't only fencing he had in mind.

Her father was frowning, looking from one to the other, and when he spoke his tone was brisk. 'I am sure it is an excellent way of keeping fit, but my daughter enjoys riding. In Argentina she was constantly in the saddle.'

'And do you still ride in England?'

'A little. The fresh air is beneficial, but trotting tamely on Rotten Row is hardly exacting.'

'Then perhaps you should try something else.'

'What would you suggest?' she challenged, hardly daring to imagine what form of exercise he had in mind.

'For something a little more demanding, why don't you try sea bathing?' His voice was bland, but she felt sure he was laughing just below the surface.

'I hardly think that would be suitable,' her father interrupted.

'I assure you it is all the fashion. The ladies have their own part of the beach, you know, and are well looked after by the "dippers"—the bathing attendants.'

'But still, it would not do. Your aunts…' Alfredo left the sentence unfinished.

'They would certainly not contemplate sea bathing.'

Domino's face lit with amusement at what those very proper ladies would make of such a suggestion.

'But should you not enjoy all that Brighton has to offer before you return to London?'

'My daughter will not be returning to London,' Alfredo said decisively.

Joshua did not look at him, but instead fixed Domino with an intense gaze. 'You will not be staying in town this autumn?'

'I will be returning to Spain,' she said quietly.

'That is sad news.' His voice held genuine regret. 'But before you go, you can surely spare us a few weeks in the capital?'

Her father once more intervened. 'I regret not. My daughter has a very important date to keep and must leave for Spain immediately when the Brighton season ends.'

Joshua looked at her enquiringly.

'I am to be married, Mr Marchmain, and must return to Spain to meet my bridegroom.' She touched her father's arm and, with a brief bow in Joshua's direction, they were gone.

For a moment he stood motionless, hardly able to believe her words. Then he wheeled around abruptly and made for the changing room, his mind buzzing noisily. Married? But to whom? She had said that she was going to Spain to meet her bridegroom, which meant, dear God, that she did not yet know the man. She did not know the man with whom she was destined to spend the rest of her life. An arranged marriage! Fury welled up in him and he slashed blindly at the walls as he strode along the passageway. Whatever Charlotte had intimated, the girl was an innocent. How

could her father dream of sacrificing her in such a way;
how could she think of agreeing to give herself to a
stranger? The idea that any young woman might offer
herself to a man she did not know sat uneasily with
him, but this was Domino. Domino! A girl so enchanting, so full of youthful joy, that he could have wept iron
tears. He dressed quickly and every layer of clothing
was donned in rage. He did not understand the fury
that was shaking him, but he could not remember ever
feeling so angry.

He had to get himself under control. He hardly
knew the girl—it was madness to react so strongly
to an arranged marriage. In his world they were frequent; indeed, his personal world was built on them,
he thought cynically. Loveless partnerships were the
hunting ground for any self-respecting rake. And that
was what he was—an ugly label, but one that suited
him. A rake never pondered the past, for he had no past.
He suffered no confusion, for he knew exactly who he
was and so did the women who chose to tangle with
him. And what he also knew was that innocent buds
such as Domino were best avoided. That particular
lesson had been seared early on this rake's soul. He
should need no reminding.

Seated beside her father as they rattled their way
home, Domino was gratified that she had startled
Joshua from his customary calm. He had looked genuinely shocked when she had announced she was to be
married. Could it be that he cared for her, or was it
simply that he found appalling the idea of an arranged
marriage? Hardly. Over the years he must have benefit-
ed from any number, the comforter of wives who had

no love for their husbands. Yet his face had shadowed with the news, as though he would wish to save her from that fate. Or preserve her for his own dishonourable intentions—that was more likely. He could not have developed a *tendre* for her, she reasoned. Rakes didn't do that; it was more than their career was worth to care for the women they made their lovers.

Her father's words had brought home to her how swiftly the weeks were passing. Marriage was ceasing to be an abstract notion and rapidly becoming reality. Once Richard had disappeared from her life, she had not cared who she wed. She would endure the intimacies of married life, impassive and acquiescent. But the events of this morning suggested otherwise. Joshua Marchmain's face and body were his stock in trade but, even knowing that, her response had been intense. Hungry, even. She had loved Richard passionately, but she had never experienced the sheer elemental need that just a short while ago had swept through her. And it was not the first time that she had been in danger of succumbing to this magnetic attraction. Every time Joshua arrived on the scene she had to exercise the tightest control over her emotions. Today she had lost that control. Surely she could not be seriously attracted to such an arrogant user of women. Yet those golden eyes had only to settle on her, that lazy smile flicker her way, that hard muscular body move close to her, and she became someone she hardly recognised.

Her restlessness reached a new peak in the days that followed. She needed to be constantly on the move and forgot her earlier reluctance to be seen abroad. Every morning she set off with her maid in tow to explore an unknown part of the Sussex landscape, winding through the town and up the hills to a viewpoint far above the sea, or along the shoreline itself, or following the pathways that circled the foot of the Downs. Poor Flora was hard put to keep up with her mistress. On one of their walks along the seafront, they came to the ladies' beach that Joshua had spoken of.

'Look, Flora.' She drew her maid's attention to the horse-drawn bathing machines carrying the swimmers into shallow waters. From there the professional dippers helped their female customers into the sea.

Her maid shuddered. 'It's not proper, miss.'

'The women change in the carriages and then just slip into the sea. It seems quite modest,' Domino said thoughtfully.

Flora sniffed, unconvinced. 'Mebbe, but I don't reckon Señor de Silva would be too keen, nor Miss Carmela neither.'

'But if so many women take part, it must be acceptable,' Domino pursued, her interest now thoroughly aroused.

'You're never thinking of joining them, Miss Domino.' Flora's tone was scandalised. 'And think how dangerous it must be.'

A number of apprehensive women, clad in flannel gowns and caps, emerged from the carriages and cautiously dipped their bare toes in the water. Courage gained, they were soon venturing further out and in no time at all a flurry of bonneted heads were bobbing up and down in the waves.

'I don't think so,' Domino reasoned. 'The water is shallow close to the shore and the dippers are there to provide security. Once the women are used to the sea, they're all right. Just look at them.'

She had a sudden longing to be there with them, to ride the waves thundering into the distance, to cleave her way through the surf out to the far horizon, to swim to an escape.

But seeing Flora's concerned expression, she only laughed and said reassuringly, 'Don't fret, it's merely a silly fancy.'

The next day she excused herself from accompanying Carmela to a lunchtime recital at St Nicholas's Church. Her father, too, was engaged, dealing with the daily round of official business, and she was able to slip out of the house unseen. Flora had been given the afternoon off and was already deep in the excitements of the stalls at Bartholomews. A ten-minute walk brought Domino to the ladies' bathing beach and another five saw her slipping into the flannel bathing costume provided by the attendant. She gave a little gasp as she glimpsed her bare arms and legs but, peering out of the carriage doorway, she saw other women happily disporting themselves, seemingly without anxiety for their unclad state. It was female territory after all, she comforted herself, and the water looked delightful.

It was. Soon she was luxuriating in the feel of the flowing tide, her body tingling to its touch. At first she bobbed up and down amid the waves, allowing the foam to swirl and curl around her toes. But then, more daringly, she began to cut a path through the undulating waves, feeling the sun warm on her bare face and arms. She was lighter than air, her body and mind at one in a weightless existence, all her troubles and confusions suspended. She swam effortlessly, on and on as though she would reach the horizon. But there was a strict time limit imposed on the bathers and all too soon she was forced to begin the return.

The horse-drawn carriages once more loomed into close view, lined up on the shore like so many sentries watching over precious treasure. Reaching the shallows, she found her feet and picked her way carefully over the pebbled seabed. The wet costume clung tenaciously to her body and a thrill of womanly pleasure passed through her at the sensuous form it revealed. Tearing the cap from her head, she waded the last few yards ashore, black curls streaming wildly down her back. For an instant before she reached the shelter of the bathing machine she looked towards the promenade and turned scarlet with vexation. Joshua Marchmain again! How dare he! This was an area reserved only for ladies and all men were banned. Of course, he would not care for that. He cared for no convention. He would embarrass anyone he wished for his own pleasure. He had suggested to her that she should try sea bathing; it was clear now why. Not from any wish to afford her enjoyment, but so that he could view her better and nearly naked. Her anger turned to chagrin. How could she have imagined that he might harbour any genuine feeling? He was a rake through and through.

Chapter Four

She had looked like a water sprite from the deep and Joshua, watching her voluptuous progress ashore, had to restrain himself from wading out into the shallows and catching her in his arms. He had barely seen her since that evening at Steine House, just those few moments at Angelo's when he had reacted so angrily to news of her future marriage. He had known then that he should put all thought of her out of his mind and had tried very hard to do so. Nevertheless he'd found himself looking for her at every gathering and her unexplained absence had only increased his interest. His desire for her was becoming insistent. All too familiar, but this time complicated by something else, something deeper and unfathomable. Desire he knew, but not this nagging need to take her in his arms, to protect her from harm, to kiss her tenderly awake to the passion he was sure lay dormant within. Caught by her magic, transfixed by her fluid movement up the beach, he had remained in full view long enough for her to see him.

* * *

He was still there, an appreciative smile on his face, when she emerged fully dressed from the land side of the bathing machine. She did not speak and made to walk past him with a bare nod of acknowledgement, but he was too quick for her and barred the way.

'Did sea bathing live up to its promise, Miss de Silva?' he enquired laughingly.

She turned abruptly and her voice sliced the air. 'Did ogling female bathers live up to yours, Mr Marchmain?'

He looked taken aback by her words and the fury in her voice, but in a moment had recovered his poise. 'One bather did!'

'You are insufferable!'

'Because I appreciate female beauty? That is hardly fair.'

'Because you seem intent on pressing your attentions on unwilling women.'

'As I've mentioned before, they are not always unwilling,' he said drily.

'Let us be clear, sir. Whatever your customary experience, I find your attentions wholly distasteful.'

'And what attentions would they be? All I have done is stand on this small spot of promenade and enjoy the pleasurable sight of women, for once free of the shackles imposed on them.'

Since she was so much in tune with this sentiment, she found it difficult for the moment to continue the quarrel. But not for long.

'The only reason you told me of the sea bathing was to enable you to spy on me.'

'An over-dramatic interpretation, I think. I am no spy.' His voice was no longer amused.

'Call it what you will. I have no intention of being ogled by men, and particularly not by a man with your reputation.'

'And what reputation would that be?' he said dangerously.

'I have no wish to continue this conversation. Please allow me to pass.'

He made no move, but instead looked her fully in the face grimly.

'You are a delightful girl, Domino, but young and naïve. You know nothing of me or my life, so take care in passing judgement.'

'I am not so naïve that I cannot recognise a rake when I see one.'

There, she had said the shocking word, and to his face. She waited for the explosion, but none came. Instead he was smiling down at her with a condescending expression on his face.

'A rake, am I?' he drawled. 'And all because I dared to see one second of your beautiful body in a bathing costume—and not a particularly revealing one.'

She flushed scarlet. 'You have done nothing but distress me since our paths first crossed.'

'A somewhat overwrought statement, wouldn't you say? I have simply been going about my usual business. It is you who appears so eager to suffer distress.'

'Are you suggesting that I have no cause for complaint?' she fumed.

'I am suggesting that you may be a little too prone to exaggerate my interest in you. Forgive me, but encouraging such fancies cannot be healthy.'

She longed to hit him very hard, but by a supreme force of will managed to stay her hand. Instead she took a cold, calm breath and launched the most wounding insult she could think of.

'You claim to be a gentleman. If you are indeed such, then you will leave me alone, now and in the future.'

She saw him stiffen. It was one thing to fling at him the insult of rake but the insinuation that he was not a gentleman would cause the deepest rancour.

'I regret, Miss de Silva,' he said in a newly aloof manner, 'that you have found meeting me so distasteful.'

'I have.'

'Then I will no longer discommode you with my presence. As far as I am able, I will stay out of your sight.'

'Please do.'

'Dare I enquire,' he asked, his tone now heavy with irony, 'if you intend to be at the Lewes race meeting tomorrow?'

'I believe my father has reserved places for us.'

'In that case you can be certain that I will spend the day a hundred miles from Lewes.'

'I am delighted to hear it,' she flung at him and stormed past, her cheeks still flaming and her head held high.

A blind rage had sustained her on the short walk back to Marine Parade, and it was only when she was in sight of the house that she began to question why Joshua Marchmain's conduct had so infuriated her. His blatant voyeurism was, after all, only what she would have predicted. Why, then, was she so out of temper?

Or was it that she had expected better of him? Somehow she must have held a secret hope that the stories about him were exaggerated, that gossip had distorted his true nature. In short, she had wanted to believe he was the kind of man she could trust. How very stupid! He was right, she was naïve. He was and always would be an inveterate rake, for, even though she might acquit him of deliberately luring her to the bathing station, he had still gazed his fill. An honourable man would have turned away; an honourable man would not even have been there! She wondered wearily how many disappointments she must endure before she finally accepted that she was a very poor judge of men. Once back in Spain, she would trust her aunts to choose a husband. They could do no worse than she.

Deep in these unpleasant thoughts, she walked through the door of Number Eight to hear her father's voice raised in protest.

'It is simply a day out, Carmela, a social occasion, nothing more.'

'Naturally I realise that in this society a day at the races is just one more entertainment…' Carmela shuddered '…but you cannot deny that a racecourse is a place of sin.'

'Come, I know that you have—definite views.' Her father phrased his words carefully. 'But in this instance, are you not being just a little severe?'

'I think not. Gambling wherever it occurs is sinful.'

'Domino will not be gambling and neither will I. We will enjoy a day in the fresh air and the excitement of seeing horses compete.'

'But you will be surrounded by every kind of vice!' Fired by moral zeal, her cousin was not giving up easily.

'We should be doing all we can to protect Domino from the work of the Devil, not exposing an innocent girl to temptation.'

'Enough!' Alfredo held up his hand. 'I am taking my daughter on an outing of pleasure whether you approve or not. And I will personally guarantee that she returns as innocent as she went.'

He strode along the hallway to his office, his shoulders stiff with annoyance, and closed the door rather too noisily. Carmela sniffed just as noisily and hastened back to the purity of her own room. Even after they had both disappeared, the atmosphere crackled with irritation and Domino was left thinking that for all kinds of reasons it might be a good idea to return to Spain sooner than she had hoped.

However, the next morning she had changed her mind. A perfect English summer day greeted her, cotton-wool clouds drifting lazily across an azure sky, and the green perfection of ancient downland rolling out its smooth carpet to welcome them as they drove the few miles inland to Lewes. The racecourse, some five hundred feet above sea level, was idyllic on a tranquil day such as this. Shaped like an elongated horseshoe, it ran along the crest of a valley and then downwards towards the sea, its natural undulations making it a test of stamina and tactics for both horses and riders.

A decidedly mixed crowd had already gathered by the side of the track and Alfredo silently wondered if he had dismissed Carmela's qualms too readily. Every type of person, it seemed, had come to the Lewes races that day: prosperous farmers and their wives; rural workers in smocks and gaiters; smartly dressed professional men and their clients; sellers of every kind of food and drink vociferously shouting their wares and any number of ragged urchins. As their hired vehicle drove on to the course, he saw with relief that the cream of society had decided on keeping a comfortable distance from this ragbag of humanity. A large white-painted grandstand was alive with the colourful swathe of silk gowns and feathered hats. It seemed that the Regent and his party were already ensconced in commodious chairs with an unparalleled view of the entire course.

As the races began, Alfredo felt even greater relief. The gambling that Carmela had so feared was modest and conducted with decorum, so much so that, towards the end of the programme, he was encouraged to place a wager on a likely looking horse. The result of the race was in doubt right up to the finishing point and Domino, immersed in the spectacle, cheered on her horse with such verve that her father was delighted they had come. For some weeks, he fancied, she had not been herself. In his presence she tried to be bright and talkative, but whenever she thought herself unobserved, she fell back into a preoccupation that he could not fathom. Now the glorious weather and glorious land-scape, the sheer excitement of the chase, had prompted her to throw herself into the moment as only she could. Her arms waved wildly in the air as their horse breasted the finishing post first. With difficulty she restrained herself from jumping up and down.

'I see you have been a clever girl and backed the winner. I fear that my luck is completely out today.'

Domino looked round at the woman who had spoken and her heart sank. She had been relieved to find that Joshua had kept his word and stayed away. Now her father had chosen the worst moment to collect his winnings, leaving her to face the duchess alone. This was the first time she had met Charlotte Severn since that dreadful evening at Steine House. But the older woman, resplendent in sapphire satin, was smiling invitingly at her and patting her hand in what Domino supposed to be a motherly fashion.

'Such energy needs sustenance.' The duchess's voice had taken on the cloying tone that was so discomfiting.

'Do accompany me to the marquee,' she persuaded, 'we must take tea together.'

The girl began to demur, but Charlotte immediately linked arms with her and urged her forwards. 'Don't worry about your papa. When he returns he will be sure to know where you have gone and will come to collect you.'

Very quickly Domino found herself seated at one of the small ironwork tables that dotted the interior of the marquee, a waiter pouring the pale straw of China tea into delicate white porcelain.

The duchess fixed her with eyes that smiled through a pool of ice.

'I am so pleased to see you again, Domino,' she was saying sweetly. 'I do hope I may call you by your first name.'

Domino was hypnotised into assent.

'I was most upset by the way that we parted at Steine House. Such a dreadful misunderstanding on my part. I had no idea that you were so averse to cards—though obviously not to gambling in general.' Her voice momentarily lost its honey as she nodded pointedly towards the races still taking place.

Her victim squirmed, remembering her gauche

behaviour that evening. And to be discovered now in the very pastime she had rejected so publicly!

But Her Grace was continuing smoothly, preparing her ground with the girl she was seeking to undo. 'I am so very sorry,' she trilled, 'if anything I did or said at the time upset you.'

Domino could hardly reject the older woman's plea after this show of contrition. The duchess's deep blue eyes held hers in a seemingly sincere appeal and she found herself softening towards their owner.

Her natural good nature won over whatever reservations she still harboured and in a small voice she confessed, 'I am sorry, too—my conduct must have seemed a little strange.'

'No, my dear, absolutely not.' Charlotte Severn was determined on complete abasement. 'The fault was entirely mine. But I hope we can mend our fences. I so much wish us to be friends.'

Domino would have liked to believe her, but could not. An older female friend—someone she could confide in, someone with the maturity and experience to guide her through the pitfalls of English society—was a luxury she must do without. She had lost the person who might have filled the role admirably; Christabel was long married and living many miles away.

'It is as I told you, my dear,' the duchess was saying pleasantly, 'there are very few new people in Brighton. An old hand like myself can become seriously blasé, not to say boring, if we are not kept on our toes. I adore young people and you are so bright and lovely.'

Charlotte was having an effect. Today she appeared more genuine and more approachable. 'You know, if Mr Marchmain had not interrupted us that evening, I am sure we would have quickly resolved our differences. But Joshua is always so hot-headed.' She gave a soft sigh of pain. 'Have you not found that also?'

'I hardly know Mr Marchmain.' Domino stammered.

'Really? I understood that you were a good friend of his.'

'Indeed, no, ma'am,' she replied indignantly.

'I hope you are not too cross with him. I know he can be a little unconventional.'

'As I said, I hardly know him.'

The girl's flushed face warned Charlotte not to pursue her line of questioning and she changed tack.

'Tell me what you have been doing since we last met,' she invited.

Relieved at the turn of conversation, Domino gladly searched her mind for something to report. 'Nothing very noteworthy, I'm afraid—reading, walking—and I did try sea bathing,' she ventured.

'You are so brave, my dear. I would be utterly scared of immersing myself in water.'

'I learned to swim as a child—we lived by the sea in Buenos Aires.'

The duchess looked questioningly at her, hoping to probe a little more deeply.

'In Argentina,' Domino said helpfully.

'Yes,' the duchess responded a trifle waspishly. 'I am aware of that city's location.' Then, quickly recovering, she cooed, 'I have the greatest admiration for ladies who can boast such sporting prowess. As for myself, all I can claim is to ride well and I do pride myself on that.'

'I adore riding, too. Papa put me on my first horse

when I was three. But riding in Argentina is very different,' Domino confided wistfully.

The duchess scented an opportunity. 'How is that?'

'Once out of the city you can gallop forever—the pampas stretches for miles. And on a proper saddle, too, just like the gentlemen use here.'

Charlotte repressed a shudder and murmured encouragingly, 'How wonderful.'

'Here—' Domino warmed to her theme '—one feels so constrained. Always having to ride sidesaddle and so tamely. Ladies are not permitted to gallop and certainly not to race.'

'If it were possible, would you do so?' the duchess asked cannily.

'It would certainly be fun!' and Domino threw back her head and laughed aloud.

Seeing the girl's dark eyes alight with merriment and her shining curls dancing in pleasure, the older woman felt a surge of envy.

'Of course one would not race openly, but maybe a race in a more secluded place?' she suggested, apparently absorbed in stirring her tea.

'Wherever would that be, ma'am?' Domino's voice conveyed interest and the duchess moved in for the final scene of the little drama she had been busy staging.

'Have you heard of Prince George's famous wager?'

The girl shook her head.

'He bet that he could drive a coach and four down Keere Street, just a short way from here. It is the steepest and narrowest of roads in Lewes. And do you know, he won that wager!'

'He must be very expert.'

'Yes,' her companion said judiciously, 'but I have it in mind that we women could undertake something even more masterly.'

'How could we do that?'

'Why, by racing our horses down Keere Street,' the duchess produced triumphantly.

Her companion at first looked nonplussed, then her face fell into a frown. 'But surely that would be dangerous.'

'Skilful, shall we say?' Charlotte said in her smoothest voice. 'We would not be hurtling down the road pell mell. It would take considerable expertise to negotiate the steep gradient and find a clear way over stones and cobbles. A very considerable feat!'

'It would certainly be a test of horsemanship.'

'So what do you think?'

'You mean that we should race?'

'Why not?' The duchess smiled as warmly as she could. 'I am longing to do something a little more daring than attending routs and receptions; it seems that you feel similarly. You said a moment ago that you have been in the saddle since you were three years old, so now is the chance to prove it.'

'I would love to, Your Grace, but I doubt that my father would allow me to undertake such a race.'

'Charlotte, my dear, call me Charlotte. It's really quite simple. Say nothing to your father and I will tell no one either. It will be our little secret.'

'But how could we prevent people knowing?'

The duchess's patience was wearing thin, but she made one last effort. 'We ride over the Downs to Lewes very early in the morning before anyone stirs. It is a shame that we will never be able to boast of our exploit, but we will have the satisfaction of knowing just how clever we have been.'

Domino was seized with a sudden panic. 'Are you quite sure that it's possible to ride down that road?'

'I would not have suggested it if I had thought otherwise, but if you are fearful then, of course, you must not attempt it, my dear.'

Annoyance rippled through Domino as her courage was subtly brought into question.

'And we will not tell anyone?' she asked, seeking more reassurance.

'Not a soul. No one will ever know—just we two.'

'When shall we hold the race?'

A silent joy engulfed the duchess. She had caught her fish at last. 'What about the day after tomorrow? That will give us the opportunity to choose suitable horses.'

'And when shall we meet?'

'Just after dawn I think, around five o' clock. The Downs will be wonderful at that time.'

'And we will both come alone?'

'Completely alone,' Charlotte reassured her. 'We will meet at the crossroads that lead into the town and then ride the few paces to Keere Street together.'

She paused for a moment and then said musingly, 'I think I shall make a laurel crown for the victor— though whoever wins will have to keep it hidden!'

Domino laughed brightly, but her determination to win the laurel crown was strong. She had agreed to the duchess's wild suggestion because she had not wanted to appear cowardly, but she was filled also with a fierce desire to beat the woman. A sharp *frisson* of pleasure had shot through her at the idea that in this one respect she might vanquish the duchess, even though she could not rival her in love. It was not a thought she intended to examine too closely.

Her father was walking towards them and bowing courteously. 'Your Grace. The races are nearly over, *querida*. Shall we go?'

'You are not cross, Papa?' she enquired, as he led her back to their place in the grandstand.

'No, my dear, I am not cross, but don't make a habit of spending time with that lady.'

Domino said nothing but consoled herself with the thought that she would be spending only an hour or two with the duchess and that, in any case, no one would ever know.

As the last folds of Domino's jonquil gauze cleared the tent flaps, Leo Moncaster appeared from the shadows and took her vacated chair.

'Well?'

'It's fixed, I have caught her. The day after tomorrow.'

'So I can spread the good news?'

'As quickly as you can, Leo. Make sure one of your cronies opens a book and encourage all your acquaintance to wager on the result. When the scandal breaks, I want it to be as big as possible. But don't let the news get to her father.'

'Isn't she likely to mention it?'

The duchess smiled wryly. 'How little you know! Girls never divulge their misdemeanours to their papas. In any case it's to be "our little secret".' She screwed up her face in distaste. 'The sooner I rid the town of the *señorita*, the better!'

'To have men betting heavily on the race will destroy her reputation completely,' Moncaster muttered grimly. 'She will be the only topic of gossip for months ahead.'

The duchess's smile creased her face until her companion continued, 'But what about you? You will be subject to the same gossip.'

She looked at him stonily. 'I think, Leo, that my credit will stand me in better stead than our young friend's.' Then, shrugging her shoulders, 'There is no way I will ride that road. It's a death trap.'

'So you won't turn up?'

'I shall meet her as planned, but only to lead her straight to the audience waiting at Keere Street. You must invite the most inveterate gossips you can find as witnesses. I will be the good friend who is trying to protect her from scandal. I shall be outraged that she should have considered such an exploit!'

Leo looked doubtful. 'That's all very well, but she is bound to expose your part in setting up the race.'

'She may try, but nobody will believe her. I shall say that she was intent on persuading me to race. I tried to deter her but without success. I have come now only to make one last effort to save her.'

'I like it,' Leo mused, rubbing his chin thoughtfully. 'You will be seen as a saintly Samaritan and she a reckless girl who cares nothing for her reputation and is happy to outrage the *ton* for some shocking spree.'

'Exactly. When she sees that everyone is against her, she will flee English society. I warrant she will be on the next boat to Europe.'

'Very neat, Charlotte. It will destroy her utterly, but leave you glowing with virtue.'

'Admit it, I am as good a conspirator as you!' the duchess blazed with pride.

'Don't forget that I was the one who revealed her weakness to you.'

'And how has that helped today?'

'Simple. With her predilection for gambling, it was always probable that she would be seduced by a likely wager.'

The duchess was in benevolent mood. 'Let us call it a draw. If all goes the way I have planned, we will both end content.'

Domino started to entertain doubts even before she regained Marine Parade. This mad adventure offered her a last exhilarating grasp at freedom, but it began to strike her as being a little too mad. Still, it had been Charlotte Severn who suggested this daring exploit and, though her father did not approve of the duchess, she was a great lady and moved in the very best circles. Nothing she did could ever be truly wrong, or rather, Domino corrected herself, ever be truly challenged. And the race would wrongfoot Joshua. While she was revelling in the company of his mistress, he would still be abed and unknowing. For once she would be free of his interference.

Nevertheless, the more she considered the matter, the less sure she felt. She could not tell her father what was afoot, certainly not Carmela, and it would be wrong to involve Flora. It was a secret she must keep alone. She hugged the knowledge to herself, gradually building the pleasures of the race in her mind. She was an accomplished horsewoman and there was a good chance she would beat the duchess. Charlotte Severn would make a satisfying adversary; to defeat her would be worth every one of Domino's present anxieties. She could not warm to the woman and the spectre of her liaison with Joshua was never far from mind. Even if she were to lose, forbidden pleasures were in store: to ride at full stretch for the first time since she had left Argentina, to feel the wind in her hair and herself lone mistress of the Downs.

And so it proved. She had taken the precaution of ordering a horse from stables some way from Marine Parade. They were situated at the very beginning of Juggs Way, the winding path used by Brighton fish-wives on their way to sell their menfolk's catches to the good citizens of Lewes and surrounding villages. It was a lengthy walk from the seafront and meant Domino had to rise very early. The sun was only just emerging from a dawn mist when she swung herself up into the saddle and coaxed the neat bay she had hired over the courtyard cobbles on to the Downs. She had been assured that the pretty mare was the swiftest in the stables.

It was a glorious morning, the air still and trans-lucent, with the sun's emerging rays only just begin-ning to warm her face as she headed eastwards. Small hedges fenced the lower slopes of the Downs and were filled with the scent of honeysuckle and the sound of birdsong. Once clear of them, she allowed the horse to stride into a canter over the close-cropped grass and rolling folds of the hills. She wanted the mare to be fresh for the race, but not too fresh.

The miles had melted as though by magic and within half an hour she could see the roofs of Lewes beginning to appear. She wondered if the duchess was already at the crossroads.

A figure appeared just breasting the misty line of the horizon; it must be Charlotte come to meet her. That was unexpected, but it would be companionable to ride into the town together. As the form drew nearer, though, she could see the figure was not that of a woman and began to feel uneasy. She was still a long way from any dwelling and there was no other soul in sight. The man was cloaked against the morning chill, but bareheaded; in the shaft of sunlight that flooded suddenly over the hills, she could see the colour of gold. It could not be. It was.

'Good morning, Miss de Silva,' the figure hailed her.

She found herself clenching her fists until her fingernails drew blood. Was she never to be free of his intrusions? As he drew closer, she saw his face. It was unsmiling and his bow was brusque.

'Forgive my trespass, ma'am. I have been at pains to absent myself, but find that today I must break my own rules.'

She recovered from the shock of seeing him sufficiently to execute a minimal bow. By now they had both come to a halt, their horses beginning to sidle against each other.

'And why have you found it necessary to encroach yet once more, Mr Marchmain?' she enquired in a freezing voice.

'I understand that you have engaged yourself in a contest. I've come to warn you that you should not take part.'

Her eyebrows lifted. 'I was not aware that I had appointed you the arbiter of my conduct.'

'It will not be I who judges your conduct,' he said grimly. 'Although it will be judged—and harshly.'

'And why is that, pray?' Her anger was tangible and filled the space between them.

He allowed himself a slight smile. 'Ladies do not engage in races, nor do they risk breaking their necks as you assuredly will.'

'What makes you so certain?' His smile was infuriating her. 'Your arrogance is breathtaking. You should know that I am accounted an excellent horsewoman.'

He did not respond directly, but instead said bluntly, 'Have you seen Keere Street?'

'No.'

'Then you should before you accuse me of arrogance. To race a horse there would place you in certain peril—and not just you, but that delightful mare you are riding.'

'I understand that it has been done before,' she retorted.

'You refer to Prinny's little escapade, I collect. That nearly ended in disaster and he had a coach behind him to act as a brake. He is also a prince of the realm and princes tend to be forgiven their foibles.'

'Are you saying it would not be seemly for me to follow his lead?'

'Not just unseemly, but quite shocking. If you value your reputation and that of your father, you should abandon this race. I cannot imagine how you ever agreed to such a foolhardy exploit.'

'I agreed because the proposal came from a person

I thought trustworthy—someone you introduced me to,' she said bitingly.

'That does not absolve you from making sensible decisions. I reiterate, give up this race immediately!'

She bristled with annoyance at his words, but his tone was urgent and carried conviction. Astride a powerful black stallion, he looked magnificent. He also looked serious. She had never previously encountered him in such a severe mood and, though still smarting from his unwelcome interference, she was beginning to take notice of what he said. But how on earth had he come upon her here, miles from anywhere? And how did he know about the race?

'This morning's arrangements were secret,' she protested, 'and I cannot understand how you knew of them.'

'All of Brighton knows of them. The whole town is buzzing with the scandal. There is even a book being run.'

He saw her puzzlement. 'Wagers, Miss de Silva, bets on who will win. Regretfully I have to report that you are seen as an unlikely victor.'

His light tone did not disguise the gravity of his news and she was appalled by the turn of events.

'I don't understand how this is,' she faltered. 'How could the race have become common knowledge?'

His gaze swept over her, at first sardonic and then with something approaching sympathy. 'No, I imagine you don't.'

'We had an agreement,' she stammered. 'It was to be just between the two of us.'

He was silent, but his face made plain that he knew everything.

'And the duchess—surely she would not be a part of anything openly scandalous?' Domino was still groping her way through the dark, trying to make sense of the morning's bewildering events.

'I doubt that she would,' he replied tight-lipped.

'But she is meeting me.'

'Yes?' He smiled derisively, his gold-flecked eyes glittering in the sunlight now flooding over the downland.

'I have an appointment with her at the crossroads in just a few minutes.'

'Then allow me to keep it for you.'

She gasped. 'But—'

'My advice,' he interrupted roughly, 'is to turn around and ride back to Brighton immediately. Return to Marine Parade as fast as you can and say nothing to anyone about this day's doings. To the world, you never left your father's house.'

'But nobody will believe that, especially not the people who have placed bets.' Her voice wavered.

He looked at the long dark lashes downcast over soft cheeks, the full lips trembling despite all her efforts at control, and had a strong desire to punch someone.

'It was a joke, was it not?' he suggested encouragingly. 'A joke got up between you and the duchess. You never meant it seriously. Why would you willingly risk your life in such a foolhardy escapade?'

'And the duchess?'

'She will tell her own tale, no doubt.'

'But she will still be waiting for me.'

'I will undertake to put her mind at rest,' he said caustically. 'I will ride to the crossroads this instant and tell her that you have reconsidered the propriety of taking part in such a race.'

'I see you have it all pat.' Her fear and frustration came tumbling out.

'Don't be angry, Domino.' His voice softened and she felt herself once more caressed by velvet. 'You have been misled, but the situation is not irreparable. Allow me to be of some small service.'

His sincerity was evident and, battered by what she had just learned, she could only acquiesce. 'I thank you, sir,' she responded in a small voice.

She had no wish to be further indebted to Joshua Marchmain, yet he was offering her a way out of the morass into which she had plunged. How could she have been so stupid as to involve herself in something so evidently scandalous? How could the whole town have known of her intentions? Joshua had lodged no accusation, but it was clear that he believed Charlotte Severn to be the malign influence behind her troubles. If so, his intimacy with the woman made him the very man to deal with the problem.

She turned the horse to retrace her steps, all pleasure in the lovely morning gone. She had been foolish enough to believe Charlotte's repeated assurances that their race would remain secret and in her innocence had trusted the older woman to be sincere. She had been betrayed, but, if she were honest, she herself had contributed richly to that betrayal. She had been so intent on beating Charlotte, on avenging her humiliation at Steine House, her humiliation over Joshua, that she had lost all sense of perspective. She must never again make such a mistake. In the meantime all she could do was to rely on Joshua to stifle the gossip that must already be circulating.

As soon as he reached the crossroads, he saw Charlotte pacing irritably up and down, her horse grazing by the roadside. At the sound of his approach she wheeled around, her face startled at the sight of this unexpected visitor.

Joshua reined in beside her. 'Your Grace, how charming to see you out and about on such a fine morning. I trust you are enjoying your ride.' His voice was calm and gave no hint of his feelings.

The duchess's eyes narrowed. 'And why are you riding so early, Joshua? That is most unusual.'

'I can rise with the best of people if I have a reason.' His smile was ominous.

'And what would that be?' she enquired sweetly.

'Let us say, a little pre-emptive action.'

'I see. And since when have you played the shining knight?'

'Since I found myself wading through the festering garbage of a corrupt Court.' His eyes glittered.

She turned white and raised her whip hand in fury as though to strike.

Unperturbed, he continued, 'But don't let me detain you. For myself, I have friends to meet—I believe our rendezvous is Keere Street, somewhat singular, but one can never account for the whims of one's friends.'

And with that he rode off into Lewes, leaving the duchess furiously snatching at her horse's bridle.

A crowd of young bucks had already gathered at Keere Street and there were even a few grey heads among the crowd, Joshua noted. What people would do for a titbit of scandal in the hothouse environment the Regent created around him!

'Good morning, gentlemen,' he hailed them, relaxed as ever.

'Morning, Marchmain, come to see the fun?' asked one budding young dandy, almost muffled by a shirt collar whose starched points reached to his cheek bones.

'I fear not.'

'Why ever not?'

Joshua looked with distaste at the coarse-looking man who had spoken. His high colour signalled his partiality for claret. 'That Spanish filly—they say she's an out and outer on a horse, but I'm still backing the duchess. Tactics will win the day!' he rumbled floridly.

'Quite possibly, but not this day. Neither lady will be coming.'

'How can that be?' A sporting gentleman in a high-crowned beaver hat and a driving coat of many capes was indignant.

'It was all a joke, my dear fellows.' Joshua was at his negligent best. 'You cannot seriously imagine that two ladies of such impeccable virtue would engage in horse racing!'

'You mean the whole thing is a hum,' the dandy said disconsolately.

'The joke is on us, I am afraid. The ladies have proved that men will place a wager on just about anything.'

There were some disgruntled mutterings among the group, but Joshua cut it short by suggesting that one of the present company might like to pick up the gauntlet themselves. As one they peered down the steep hill, watching it bump and curl on its way, finally to vanish in a dark pit of shadow.

Lord Wivenhoe summed up what they were all thinking.

'We'd have to be mad! Let's get a heavy wet—the Lewes Arms should be open by now.'

Chapter Five

Joshua rode slowly towards Brighton, well pleased with his morning's work. He was confident that he had managed to quash the torrent of gossip that might have poured unhindered if Domino had made an appearance at Keere Street. Now he'd had time to think, he could see Charlotte's strategy clearly. She would have delivered the girl into the lion's den, then stood back and protested her own innocence while the lions devoured the lamb. He smiled wryly. Domino was hardly a lamb. She had provoked him at every opportunity and by rights he should have left her to fend for herself; she had made no secret of the fact that she despised him, had even called him a rake to his face. So why put himself out? She was charming, but he had known far more beautiful women. She was interesting and intelligent, but she was also young and untried. So what was it? She was a challenge, perhaps, no simpering miss certainly. And though her impulsiveness led her into danger, it sprang from a fresh, unconstrained spirit. She still possessed a joy in life which he had long ago lost—whether she was dreaming by a quiet sea or walking windblown on the downs or taking up this ridiculous wager, fearing it, no doubt, but ready to brave her fortune. How long would that free spirit survive the bludgeoning of an arranged marriage?

She had begun to penetrate his heart, he realised, and that was troubling. When she was close he found himself captivated, unable to think or act the man he had been for so many years. He looked deep into those expressive eyes and wanted them to speak only to him, longed for them to sparkle with mischief just for him, to cloud with passion just for him. He must put an end to such feelings and make sure that she made no further inroads into his life. He had no wish to be drawn into the kind of intimacy that for years he'd been at pains to shun. It could only lead to disaster, and all-embracing disaster at that. Once upon a time he had been overpowered by youthful passion, had convinced himself that love had finally bloomed in a hitherto barren life. He had been heedless, inviting the spread of vicious scandal, piling further hurt on his despairing family and sacrificing the one friendship he had learned to treasure. That first and last wretched experience of love must surely be a lesson for life: never tangle with innocence. He was fairly sure that he need not fear Domino's attachment; this morning's events would have done nothing to change her attitude. He would still be a rake to her, a man to avoid.

Charlotte Severn would also avoid him. Their liaison had grown stale and unsavoury months ago, and this recent encounter was as good a way as any to draw a final line beneath it. He had suspected Charlotte to be venal, but had not realised before the depths to which she would stoop. He had mistrusted her intentions towards Domino since that evening of the soirée. Recently she and that cur, Moncaster, had had their heads together a little too often and when news of the race reached him, he had guessed that the two of them were involved. But why Charlotte should wish to destroy the young girl mystified him. Even less understandable was why Moncaster should be privy to the plot. He wondered if either of them would be waiting for him at the Pavilion—that would be an interesting conversation!

The duchess, though, had ridden straight to Steine House and found Leo Moncaster pacing up and down the pavement, his face wolfishly eager. She swept past him and up the steps to the open front door. They walked together into the drawing room and for the first time he had a clear view of her face and knew that something had gone badly amiss.

'She never came,' she said baldly. 'Marchmain must have intercepted her and persuaded her to return home.'

'And you let him!'

'What else could I do? She was already riding back when he met me at the crossroads. It was clear that he would expose my part in the plan if I did not also return to Brighton immediately.'

'And…?'

'And he must have ridden on to Keere Street and told the men there some tale to account for both our absences,' she concluded wearily.

Moncaster began his pacing once more, this time up and down the pale grey drawing-room carpet, leaving a dark tread in his wake. His face was thunderous and he bit his lip constantly, his agitation finally spilling over into words.

'It is hard to see how you could have managed this more badly,' he exploded.

'What do you mean?'

'You were the one who insisted that this would work. You would humiliate the girl, you said. Now look—she has humiliated you!'

'She has not. And let me remind you that you agreed to the plan; in fact, I recall that at the racecourse when we spoke of it you expressed complete confidence.'

'Clearly I was wrong to rely on your ability to bring this tiresome girl to account. From now onwards, I will be the one making decisions.'

'As you wish. I have no further interest in the matter.'

'You had sufficient interest until today.'

'It is unlikely that after this morning's events I will enjoy any kind of friendship with Joshua,' she said dully, 'and since that is so, I no longer care what happens to the girl.'

Moncaster moved towards her and took her hands. 'Do you not think, Your Grace,' he said courteously, his tone markedly different, 'that Mr Marchmain might still be persuaded back into the fold if this wretched girl were no longer around?'

The duchess remained silent, but broke free from his hold and walked towards the door.

'In any case, don't you want revenge?' he called after her retreating figure.

Charlotte stopped mid-room. Deep in thought, she beat a tattoo with her riding crop against the blue velvet of her modish ensemble.

'Can you deliver me revenge, Leo?' she asked slowly.

'I can. We have been too complicated. It needs something simple, something obvious.'

'You have an idea?'

'I have. Will you trust me with it?'

'As you have been at pains to point out,' she responded tartly, 'my plan has failed dismally, so what have I to lose?'

Domino was lucky to regain Marine Parade before any member of the household became aware of her absence, for it had taken time to return her horse to the stables and walk back to the seafront. Slipping into the house through the rear entrance, she heard muted sounds coming from the kitchen, but no servant appeared to embarrass her. She was still unhooking the last gold fastenings of her riding dress, when Flora knocked on the door with her morning chocolate. Seeing her maid's perplexed face, she gestured to the heavy gown she had just removed.

'I have changed my mind about riding this morning, Flora. I feel too tired to go far today.'

The girl looked concerned, but hung up the riding dress without comment and very soon left Domino to her thoughts.

Few of them were pleasant. The irony of the situation was crushing: she was relying on a man of dubious reputation to save her own. Joshua would save her, but why? She had not endeared herself to him. She had rejected all his advances and made clear that she found his presence odious. She need feel no guilt at the harsh treatment she'd meted out, for his behaviour had been intolerable. But not this morning. This morning his face had been grave, his tone abrupt and his words a million miles from seductive. There had been no trace of the reckless rake. Instead he had been stern and insistent; his rebuke over her conduct could have come from Richard himself. She thought she had discerned some sympathy in those gold-flecked eyes as he'd turned to go—maybe even a little tenderness. It seemed unlikely, but the thought made her feel slightly giddy. In her mind's eye she saw him again, handsome and unyielding. Seated on that large black horse, his caped greatcoat flung carelessly over his shoulders, he had looked superb, a master of the landscape. He had also looked like a man on whom she could depend, and so she had consigned her fate to his hands—or, rather, to his silver tongue. She could not imagine the tale he would tell those eager scandalmongers waiting at Keere Street, but she knew without doubt that he would make her safe.

It was to be some days before she set eyes on him again. For a while she had been watchful, keeping close to home, a little afraid of the gossip that might still be bandied around the town. But no startling news had reached her and she felt sure that if her name had become common currency, her father would have known of it. She had felt reassured, but strangely dull. Joshua's continued absence from her daily round was naturally to be welcomed. It could do her no good to be in the company of a known womaniser, but if she were honest, life without him was a little tedious.

Then the summons had come. Piqued by the success of the duchess's evening, the Prince Regent had been persuaded to hold a soirée of his own. He was well known as a devotee of music and was intent on outdoing Charlotte Severn's offering. Not just one Italian soprano, but three had been invited to perform on the following Saturday. Leo Moncaster's suggestion that the same audience be invited that had flocked to Steine House had appealed to George's vanity and his desire to stage a superior triumph.

Despite reservations over the Regent's lifestyle, the household at Marine Parade had been greatly excited at the prospect of an evening at the Pavilion. Even Carmela had taken to perusing fashion plates, a few years out of date to be sure, but with a view to having a new gown made swiftly for this very special event. On the Friday morning a large parcel bearing Domino's name arrived at the door—the eagerly awaited dress, promised by her father on the night of their own reception. She peeled back the layers of rustling tissue and pulled from the parcel an exquisite white-satin underdress and an overskirt of the palest pink gauze, together with new pink kid slippers and a fillet of tiny pink blossoms to be woven though her curls. Flora was entranced—such possibilities for dressing her lady!

Saturday came and Domino felt nervous. She doubted she would see Joshua at the Pavilion. If he knew that she had been invited, he would stay away. He seemed intent on keeping his promise not to importune her. Really, it was most disconcerting, but more worrisome was the strong possibility that one or both of her tormentors would be present at the Regent's entertainment. She made up her mind that she would not give them the satisfaction of knowing how much they had unnerved her. She would face them down. The prospect

of exploring the unknown splendours within the palace
was an incentive to bravery.

Punctually at eight o' clock the de Silva party drove
through the Pavilion gardens and alighted from their
carriage in the shelter of an illuminated portico, its
design modelled on an Indian temple. Domino had
often walked around the perimeter of the palace, looking with wonder at its oriental façade, and she could
scarcely believe that she was now about to penetrate its
mysteries. An impassive footman ushered them through
the octagonal vestibule into the entrance hall, a square
apartment lit by a Chinese lantern suspended from a
tented roof.

'Papa,' she whispered amazed, 'those statues are
wearing real robes!' She pointed to the life-size Chinese mandarin figures, which stood in each corner of
the room.

Carmela took in this abomination and pronounced
her verdict, 'Ridiculous! And it is so very hot in here,'
she grumbled. Despite it being July, a roaring fire filled
the marble fireplace.

From the Inner Hall they made their way into the
Long Gallery, which linked all the state rooms arranged
along the east front of the building. There three further
fireplaces threw out yet more heat and the atmosphere
was already sultry. Domino was relieved that her dress
was of the most delicate material and that both she and
her cousin carried fans.

'Let us wait by the glass doors,' Alfredo advised.
'That should be the coolest spot in the room.'

They made their way towards the long windows,
which looked out over lawns, still dappled by sunshine even at this late hour, and waited for their turn

to be presented to the Regent. Domino looked around her in awe. The Gallery walls were covered with painted canvas, a peach-blossom background with rocks, trees, shrubs, birds and flowers pencilled in pale blue. The room was divided into five different sections and the Regent stood in its centre in order to welcome his guests. He caught Domino's eyes immediately, for he was dressed in the greatest of finery, but with little consideration for his bulk. She had leisure to study him and saw the lines of dissipation etched on his face, a testimony to his selfishness and excess. But when she advanced to meet him to make a nervous curtsy, she was disarmed by the kindness he showed in seeking to put her at her ease.

The hum of conversation was gradually abating and people began to move towards the vast mirrored doors at one end of the Gallery.

'Everyone is making for the Music Room,' her father said quietly. 'We should do the same.'

A blaze of red and gold oriental splendour made Domino gasp. If the Long Gallery had been superb, the Music Room was overwhelming. The ceiling was gilded, supported by pillars covered in gold leaf and decorated with carved dragons and serpents. A lamp made to resemble a huge water lily and coloured crimson, gold and white hung from the centre with gilded dragons clinging to its underside. More dragons embellished the crimson canopies of the four doorways leading out of the room and still more writhed above the blue-and-crimson window curtains. Large ottomans decorated with fluted silk and covered in enormous satin bolsters lined all the walls and an Axminster carpet of spectacular design flooded the floor: a riot of golden suns, stars, serpents and dragons on a pale blue ground.

'Utterly vulgar,' Carmela pronounced sharply, causing Alfredo to glance anxiously around in case his forthright relative had been overheard. But Carmela was unrepentant.

'To think of all the money wasted on such immoral foppery!' she exclaimed.

The ambassador made haste to usher her to one of the yellow satin covered seats that had been set out for the audience.

'I think we should have a good view of the musicians from here,' he said soothingly.

She made no reply, but noisily unfurled the fan she carried. The heat was even more oppressive than in the Gallery and many of the ladies were already cooling themselves vigorously.

The Prince's own private band of wind and string instruments, formed from the cream of Europe's musical talent, accompanied each of the three fabled sopranos. Domino once more set herself to sit stoically through the entertainment. She hoped her reward might be to explore further this strange and exotic building. Throughout the recital, the Regent, who had learned to play the violincello in his youth, beat time with his foot. When the last note had faded, an army of footmen whisked away the audience's small chairs and yet another army carried in tray after tray of refreshments. Domino, her cousin and her father began to walk around the room, taking in the expensive array of Chinese vases, pots, glasses and pot-pourris that decorated every available surface.

They had stopped in front of a particularly ugly

ceramic jar when a modestly dressed, grey-haired man came to her father's side and whispered a message in his ear. Alfredo looked surprised, but immediately touched Domino on the arm and signalled that they should go with the retainer. Equally surprised, she followed and found herself confronting the Regent himself. The Prince, large and perfumed, smiled graciously down at her, seeming pleased with what he saw.

'Señor de Silva, lend me your daughter for a few minutes.' The Prince's languid tone did not disguise that this was a command rather than a request.

Alfredo was uncertain, particularly as a faint aroma of chartreuse hung in the air, mixed imperceptibly with the heady scent the Prince affected. The Regent seemed unimpaired, however, and the ambassador, mindful of his position, felt unable to quibble.

'I was wishful of speaking to you at greater length, my dear.' The Prince smiled archly down at her and offered his arm. She found herself returning his smile.

'I love to welcome foreigners to my modest little abode and I am most interested in how you are enjoying your stay in Brighton.'

'Very much, sir,' she responded politely. 'I love living by the sea, for in Madrid we are landlocked.'

George looked gratified. 'I remember when I first came to Brighthelmstone—that was Brighton's original name, you know. It was a small fishing village then, but I was captivated. I simply had to build myself a little folly by the sea!'

She smiled again. 'It is very beautiful,' she concurred dutifully, though not at all sure that it was.

'Come, let me show you,' and Domino found herself once more walking around the Music Room while he described in detail every one of his purchases. She knew she should feel flattered, but the heat of the room, the proximity of the rotund prince and a slight, inexplicable feeling of panic made her wish that he would not be quite so gracious.

He steered her expertly into the Long Gallery, still talking smoothly about his possessions.

'This vase, you see, came from a most remote province of China. I had my envoy negotiate for months for it. Do you think it worth the effort?'

'Indeed, it is most striking, your Highness.'

He looked satisfied. 'How delightful to find a young woman of such discernment! So different from some of your countrymen…' The sentence drifted away. 'But I have heard only the very best things said of you and you have more than proved them right.'

She was left little time to wonder what exactly he had heard and who could have spoken of her. They had left the Gallery by this time and traversed the library without stopping. They were now in a room even hotter than anything she had so far experienced.

'The Yellow Drawing Room,' George announced. 'We can be private here.'

'Your Highness, should I not call my cousin?' She was fearful of offending such an important person, but becoming more anxious by the minute.

'Your cousin is occupied,' the Prince returned cheerfully, 'and you have only to say that you were with me for there to be no trouble.'

She felt doubtful on this point, but found it difficult to rebuff a man who was old enough to be her father and a royal prince to boot.

'These are my private rooms,' George repeated, 'and

so much more pleasant than the public areas, do you not think? So much more tranquil.'

She had unfortunately to agree. As she looked around, there was not another person in sight. By now she had become accustomed to the assault on her senses and she took in the room's array of mirrors, Chinese pictures, flying dragons and white and gold pillars wreathed by serpents without a flicker of surprise. What was more disturbing was the sight of an open doorway leading to another room beyond. This was clearly the Prince's personal chamber; she was horrified by a glimpse of a huge bed in the far reaches of the room, massive and mahogany-panelled with at least five mattresses and crowded with satin bolsters and pillows.

The gnawing panic, which had been growing ever stronger, overcame her; but when she should have fled, she found herself transfixed. The light from a hundred candles bounced from mirror to mirror, reflection after reflection, disorientating her further and making her dizzyingly weak.

'I see you admiring yourself,' the Prince joked heavily as she turned this way and that to avoid the piercing light. 'And so you should. You are a taking little puss—my spies have not lied.'

Now thoroughly alarmed, she tried to extricate herself as diplomatically as she could, but the Prince was before her.

'I have brought you here to see some very special treasures,' he whispered hotly in her ear.

Her mind went into a tailspin at the thought of what treasures he meant. How was it that she seemed destined to fall from one scrape into another? She had little time to consider, for he was pulling out a series of drawers from a small chest that sat on the nearby table. The drawers contained the most brilliant collection of jewellery she had ever seen.

'What do you think?' he asked grandly.

Shaken, all she could utter was, 'Magnificent!'

'Which of these gems would you choose above all others?'

'It would be impossible to make such a choice. Every piece is exquisite.'

'Try,' he pressed.

To hasten her departure, she pointed to a small butterfly brooch studded in diamonds. 'This is very elegant, I think.'

He frowned; it was obviously the wrong choice. 'I agree, most elegant,' he said a little too heartily. 'But have you seen the other butterfly brooch? This one here.' He pointed to an item at the back of the drawer. 'Filigree, of course—not as expensive—but I would say far more fitting for a young girl.'

The Prince lifted the filigree butterfly from its bed of satin. 'Here, my dear. Take this as a small token of my friendship.'

Domino had thought it could not get any worse, and yet it had. 'I am most grateful for your kindness,' she stuttered, 'but I cannot accept, your Highness.'

'Cannot?'

His frown deepened and his eyebrows rose haughtily. He looked an entirely different prince.

She was forced to reconsider. 'It is most kind of you,' she said faintly.

He beamed again. 'I am well known for my generosity, but you must think nothing of it. You are a delightful child and deserve to have pretty things. Now how about a little thanks?'

'Indeed, yes, I thank you very much,' she stammered, unsure of just how effusive she had to be.

'You can do better than that, surely!'

And with those words he lunged towards her, wrapping his arms around her in a bear-like clasp and pushing her towards the open door and the bed that lay beyond. The feel of his breath on her cheek and the overwhelming scent he wore repulsed her. She tried to struggle free, but the Regent was no lightweight and she was inexorably propelled towards danger.

'I like a little resistance, my dear. That is all to the good. But not too much, you know, not too much,' he was saying.

She felt herself reeling and tried desperately hard not to faint. That was the last thing she must do; she had to keep control, but she was losing the struggle.

Then a toneless voice spoke from the door. 'Excuse me, sir, Signora Martinelli is about to leave and I know that you will want to thank her personally.'

Joshua Marchmain was dressed in the conventional dark coat, embroidered waistcoat and light-coloured satin breeches of a gentleman's evening attire, but to Domino he wore angels' wings.

The Regent stopped pawing at her and was annoyed, but soon recovered his composure and waved away the intruder.

'No, no, Marchmain, you must thank her for me. I am sure you will find just the right words. As you see, I am a little busy,' he finished irritably.

'I should mention perhaps, sir, that Miss de Silva's father is also waiting—he wishes to see his daughter.'

The Regent turned an angry red and finally released his captive.

'We will speak later, Marchmain,' he barked. 'Leave me now.'

'Certainly, sir,' Joshua said smoothly. 'Miss de Silva?' and he ushered her out of the room and towards the library. As the door closed behind them, she heard the Regent mutter quite distinctly, 'Drat Moncaster, telling me the chit was a likely romp.'

At the sound of that name, she stumbled and Joshua had to step quickly forwards to offer a supporting arm. She was shaking uncontrollably now. All the time she had been in the Regent's apartment she had managed to keep her nerve, but once rescue came, reaction set in.

For a moment she clung to his arm, then, drawing herself up straight, she said decisively, 'I cannot go back to the Gallery just now, Mr Marchmain, I need a few minutes alone.'

His gold-flecked eyes surprised her with their concern and when he spoke his voice lacked its usual mocking note. 'Will you allow me to escort you to my studio?' he asked gently. 'It is close by and I can promise solitude. You may be alone there for as long as you wish.'

She nodded agreement and he led her towards the western side of the Pavilion. It was not so lavishly furnished as the rooms she had previously seen but a great deal cooler. At the entrance to his studio, he paused and waved her through the doorway, motioning her to take a seat. She noticed that he kept the door ajar.

'I will leave you to your thoughts. But before I do, tell me about Moncaster.'

The request came out of the blue and she looked at him, startled.

'It's evident that he was behind that little unpleasantness just now. I heard the Regent's words as well as you.'

Her face was bright red, but she remained silent.

'Domino, answer me,' he said a little less gently. 'Why has Leo Moncaster been hawking you to the Prince as a likely lady-bird?'

She still said nothing.

'He was also behind the Keere Street race,' he continued inexorably. 'He seems to be trying to ruin you. Why?'

She supposed he deserved to know the truth since he had rescued her more than once from Moncaster's evil. But it was still painful to talk.

'I crossed him in the past and he is seeking revenge.'

'In what way did you cross him?'

'I met Lord Moncaster three years ago,' she began falteringly. 'It was when I came to England to stay with my aunt, Lady Blythe.'

'Yes,' he encouraged.

'I stupidly lost money to him at faro, money I couldn't repay. He took my handkerchief as a token of payment. I didn't realise that it was a scandalous thing to do and when I tried to get it back, he blackmailed me.'

'That sounds like the man. But could you not have confessed your troubles to your aunt and asked her to pay the debt?'

'He would not take money,' she said without elaborating further.

Joshua looked grim. She imagined that he must

know Moncaster well enough to guess the depths of his villainy.

Aloud he said, 'Would it be indelicate to enquire how you resolved your difficulties?'

'I eloped.'

'What!'

'Not exactly eloped,' she clarified. 'A friend helped me escape from England. The plan was to go to my father's friends in Paris and then on to Spain, but we only got as far as Dover.'

He seemed to smile at the innocence of this recital. 'What happened at Dover?' he prompted.

'Benedict's sister arrived and made us return to London.'

'Benedict?' A frown passed swiftly across his face.

'Yes, Benedict Tallis. Do you know him?'

'I have heard of him,' he said shortly.

'He got into immense trouble because of me and was sent back to Cornwall. But at least there was no scandal. And it turned out that as I was under age, Lord Moncaster could not insist on the debt and had no hold over me. My aunt paid him anyway.'

'You seem to have a lively ability to get into scrapes, Señorita de Silva.'

'I do, don't I?' And she looked so comically concerned that he burst out laughing.

'A girl after my own heart! Come, let us forget Prinny and his dastardly ways. Will you let me show you around my workroom or would you prefer to remain alone?'

'I would enjoy seeing your workroom,' she said a little shyly.

Though small by palace standards, the room was

bright and airy. The last rays of the evening sun flooded through open doors, which led to the gardens beyond, and a breeze gently lifted delicate voile curtains hanging either side of the long windows. She breathed in the fresh air with relief, then walked slowly around the room, looking with interest at the pictures hung four deep on the walls and the several piles of canvases stacked against a large chest. A battered paint-splashed smock was thrown carelessly over an easel and to one side a tray held paint tubes of every conceivable hue.

'What do you think?'

'It is a genuine artist's studio,' she responded warmly.

'A studio at least—and I keep plenty of "genuine" art as a reminder of what I should be aiming for.'

She saw at a glance that the walls were hung with a plentiful display of works by the painter she had admired at the Grove Gallery. He was certainly a fine artist. She felt Joshua watching her as she wandered the room, every now and then pausing to look at a particular painting, viewing it from different angles until she was satisfied. He made no attempt to follow, but when she began to browse the canvases stacked against the corner chest, he moved swiftly towards her and placed a restraining hand on her wrist. In the companionable silence, she had regained much of her composure and his sudden prohibition jarred.

'They are mere daubings,' he explained smoothly, 'without interest and not good enough to frame.'

'This looks a little more than daubing...' she gestured to the canvas that fronted the stack '...it catches the light and the Sussex coast perfectly.'

'You are generous, but the rest are much the same

and hardly worth your attention.' His tone admitted no disagreement. 'Can I get you some refreshment before we return to the Gallery?'

'A glass of wine would be welcome.'

She sounded politely neutral, but felt irritated that he had changed the subject so determinedly. It was strange that he was opposed to her viewing the remaining works. It was probably just vanity; no doubt the pictures deteriorated in quality the further you explored. But when he left her for a moment to pour the wine, she was sufficiently intrigued to defy his wishes and surreptitiously began to flick through them. He had been right about the similarity of the paintings; they were virtually all seascapes, the light clear, the atmosphere still and the meeting of sea and sky a hardly perceptible line. As she skimmed each canvas it seemed that their horizons grew more and more distant, attempting almost to span infinity. Something about them called to her, their sense of freedom perhaps, their suggestion of escape.

More and more seascapes, but then in the middle of the stack, a lone portrait. It was the image of a young girl. Dark eyes looked searchingly out at her, glossy raven curls tumbled on to soft shoulders and the creamy skin of arms and breast gleamed translucent in the dying light of the day. She gasped: she was looking at herself.

He turned at the sound, a glass in his hand, and stood motionless as her eyes travelled from the painting to his face.

'This is me!'

'I am glad that it is recognisable, at least.' The joke felt a little flat.

'But why have you painted me?'

'I take my inspiration where I find it.' His tone was negligent. 'Your face intrigued me—it's not an English face and I wanted to try to capture it.'

'It's very good,' she said slowly and looked back at the portrait.

The face was a study in radiance, the eyes sparkling with vitality, the curls glistening and tumbling with hidden life. Every line of the painting spoke feeling and she felt dazed at the thoughts that came unbidden to her mind. Was it possible that she stirred such emotions in him?

He cut her reverie short with a brusque enquiry. 'Your father mentioned that you would shortly be travelling to Spain. How long exactly are you fixed in Brighton?'

She ceased dreaming immediately. The return to her aunts had been temporarily forgotten, lost in more pressing concerns, but recurred now with unwelcome clarity.

'I'm not sure. For as long as my father thinks it worthwhile. I imagine that Papa will return to London when the Regent travels back to Carlton House.'

'And you will leave for Spain?' She found his questioning unsettling, but nodded a silent assent.

'Then be on your guard during the weeks you remain here. You have attracted the enmity of people in high places, the Duchess of Severn as well as Moncaster.'

'I cannot understand why I should have done so. Until I came to Brighton, I had never met the lady.'

'Charlotte Severn is a jealous woman,' he said obliquely.

She sipped at her wine, unsure of his meaning. Joshua enlightened her.

'It seems that Her Grace feels my interest in you is too great, hence her rather clumsy attempts at your social humiliation.'

A ready blush flew to her cheeks and she dared not look at him.

'She is mistaken, however. You are a piece of perfection, but I'm not in the market for *ingénues*. I leave that to the connoisseurs of Spain.'

His words were unexpectedly biting; he appeared to blame her for a future over which she had little control.

'I am sure the duchess will be delighted to hear the news,' she said witheringly. 'Perhaps you should tell her yourself and quickly. Then I might be spared any further "unpleasantness".'

Her indignation found vent in a swift walk up and down the room, her skirts swishing in noisy displeasure as she passed close to him.

'What the duchess knows or doesn't know is of no concern to me,' he said, equally withering. 'I am insulted that you believe me willing to consort with a woman capable of such base trickery.'

'Your friendship is at an end?' She could hardly believe her ears.

'It has been at an end for some time.'

'I did not know that.'

'Of course you did not,' he responded acidly. 'After all, I am the lowest form of masculine life, am I not?'

Her heart did a strange little dance. Whatever had tied him to the duchess, the knot was well and truly broken. It was time to call a truce.

'You have been good enough to rescue me,' she began with difficulty.

'On a number of occasions.'

'On a number of occasions,' she agreed. 'It would be unbecoming in me not to acknowledge that.'

'It would—and so…?'

'And so I should apologise for calling you a rake.'

'You should not,' he said unexpectedly, 'for that is what I am.'

She let out a long breath. Really he was impossible.

'But,' he continued hurriedly, 'I give you my word that you will never find me other than an honourable man.'

A deeper flush spread across her soft cheeks, beckoning him closer. He resisted the invitation.

'Why do you always paint the sea?' she asked suddenly.

'I hardly know. Perhaps because the sea is ever changing and I am equally restless.'

She considered this for a moment, but before she could reply, he went on, 'Perhaps because the sea offers a constant promise.'

'And what does it promise?'

'Liberty, movement, transformation—all of these and more.'

She was intrigued. 'Why would you wish for such things?'

'Why not?'

'I can think of a dozen reasons. You already have the liberty to be or do what you wish. You are wealthy, popular with those you live among, a favourite with the Regent. Why would you want to transform?'

His laugh rang hollow. 'Nothing in your list persuades me. The palace is a web of lies and popularity at Court is as transient as the gossip that it feeds upon. As for wealth, it's certainly better to have money than not, but that is the sum of its importance.'

For a moment she was taken aback until she recalled his words the very first day they'd met. She had wondered then why such an obviously successful man needed the solace of painting.

'It is always possible to change one's life,' she said tentatively, 'for a man, if not for a woman.'

'You think so? That is the innocence of youth talking. Once one's feet are set upon a path, Domino, they are generally doomed to tread it forever more.'

She was disconcerted by the weariness in his voice, but then he seemed to shrug off his depression and was studying her intently. 'Why do you think a woman is not able to change her world, if she has enough spirit? I cannot believe you to be wholly powerless in deciding the course of your life, for example.'

She flushed. 'There are circumstances,' she murmured faintly. 'It is not that easy.'

'Really? And what are those circumstances?'

She did not answer his challenge directly. She had no answer. Instead she took refuge in a timeworn phrase. 'I suppose that change may not necessarily be for the better.'

'Ah, yes, the old cliché. The trouble with truisms is that they are so often true. You're right, change isn't always good, the sea doesn't always deliver its promises.'

For a second only she glimpsed the deep well of disillusion beneath the surface calm.

'Does not your home in Norfolk hold any promise?'

she said quickly. 'It would seem an ideal place in which to set up a permanent studio.'

'I have little interest in the house.' He had swiftly regained his nonchalance. 'I inherited Castle March from an uncle a few years back. It was not where I grew up; I hardly know the area.'

'Where did you grow up?'

'Oxfordshire.'

'Do you ever visit the county?' she was emboldened to ask.

'No. I no longer have ties there, or indeed anywhere.'

'But your family?'

'Yes?' The monosyllable should have warned her that she was approaching dangerous ground, but she pressed on. She wanted to know as much as she could about him.

'Your family is still in Oxfordshire?'

'I have a brother living there.' His voice lacked emotion. 'I hardly know him—he is ten years older than I. My parents have been dead these five years.'

'I am very sorry.' She felt bad now at having obliged him to offer information he evidently wished to keep to himself, but he seemed unperturbed.

'Don't be. We were not a close family.'

'They did not share your interest in art?'

'They did not share my interest in anything.' His laugh was laconic. 'I must confess to being an embarrassment to my family from the moment I was born. My parents were more than contented with one child and my arrival was inconvenient to say the least. And then I managed to continue the good work by being a permanent black sheep. Naturally my brother was the model son. I spent my youth breaking every known prohibition, so it's hardly surprising I was expelled from the family seat at an early age. Hence my wanderings.'

She looked stricken and he said in a rousing voice, 'There's no need for tears. I hated my home, whereas the time I spent travelling in Europe gave me lasting pleasure.'

'But you must have been very young when they sent you abroad,' she said sadly.

'Young enough, but I survived. Families have to be negotiated, do they not?' he asked slyly. 'Yours, for instance, seems intent on marrying you to a man you do not even know.'

'They are not forcing me,' she protested. 'I have agreed.'

'But why would you do so?' He sounded genuinely perplexed.

'I have to marry.'

'Then choose someone you love.'

'As you have?' she retorted.

'Learn from my mistakes. Life without love is hardly worth living.'

'I have loved,' she returned with dignity, 'but it was not sufficient.'

For the first time she found that she could openly acknowledge the hurt she had suffered; somehow the memory of Richard no longer felt so distressing.

'He must have been blind, deaf and insane to boot,' he said roughly, hearing the past pain in her words. Then, catching her hands in his, he demanded, 'Tell me his name and I will personally knock some sense into him!'

She smiled up at him, warmed by the sincerity of his voice and the glow from those leonine eyes.

'I fear you are too late', and she allowed herself a small gurgle of laughter. 'He has already made his decision and married another.'

'Then he deserves even more of a kicking.'

He let go of her hands to reach out for a stray tendril of hair and then curled it around his finger. Slowly he brought the curl to his lips. She stood motionless as his fingers moved from her hair to her face, lightly touching her cheek and then softly brushing her neck to come to rest on her bare shoulders. A breathless, slow heat began to uncurl within her. He was looking hungrily down at her, his eyes a molten brown flecked with that golden intensity. She felt herself mesmerised, falling into a vortex that was drawing her inexorably to his very centre; hardly knowing what she was doing, she brushed a flaxen strand of hair from his forehead and allowed it to drift through her fingers. The gesture seemed to unleash in him the passion he had so far restrained and he lowered his head and brought his mouth down on hers in a kiss of such aching pleasure that all rational thought vanished. She could think of nothing but the feel of him, the scent of him, the taste of him. He kissed her once more slowly and tenderly and then again, exploring, savouring and finally allowing the full force of his desire to wash over her. She was reduced to trembling sensation. When he lifted his lips it was to trail kisses down her neck, her shoulders and to settle whisperingly against the creamy swell of her bosom. A throbbing arrow of heat pierced her and she found her body arching, cleaving desperately to him. Somewhere in the distance she heard herself moan softly.

The sound seemed to bring him to his senses; in

a moment he had stepped back from her, breathing heavily and looking considerably less polished. It was a while before he spoke and when he did his voice was still ragged with passion.

'You should keep your distance from me; I will only bring you distress.' Then, in a quieter tone, he continued, 'Forgive me, Domino. You are a beautiful girl in all senses of the word, but that does not excuse my breaking the promise I made—and so quickly.'

Still in a daze of desire, she managed to stammer a disclaimer. Neither felt able to say more and the silence between them was filled with unexpressed feeling until Joshua, in an attempt to make light of the situation, joked, 'As an experienced rake, I should advise you that now would be a good time to return to your family!'

As he spoke, he proffered his arm and she took it with as much dignity as she could muster, her head held high. Retracing their steps across the library and down the corridor, she saw them reflected in the many mirrors lining the walls. He may be dangerous, but what a comely couple we make, she thought. Almost respectable! She could have laughed aloud but for the mantra beating inside her head: she must never allow herself to lose control like that again. Her father must never know what had just occurred. He must never guess at the force of her desire. Nor Carmela and her aunts—certainly not—and as for the unknown Spanish husband, he must stay forever ignorant of such unmaidenly passion. And there was no reason that any of them should ever know. At least rakes did not kiss and tell or they would hardly be so successful.

Joshua caught sight of their reflection at the same time as she and smiled back at her. The scar on his cheek was hardly noticeable, but it gave him distinction, she thought softly. Not that he needed it, he was so beautifully made. Guiltily she caught herself up; from now on, such thoughts were taboo. She must focus on a very different future.

Once in the Long Gallery amid the noisy buzz of chatter, he stopped and turned to her, a serious expression on his face.

'Remember my warning. There are those close by who wish you ill. If you need me, I am here.'

She saw her father rapidly approaching, a worried look on his face, and had no time to reply.

'We have been looking for you everywhere,' Alfredo fussed. 'Carmela is even now questioning every footman in the building.'

She was startled. 'Please stop her, Papa. As you see, I am well. Mr Marchmain was kind enough to offer me his escort from the Prince's apartments.'

It was Alfredo's turn to look startled. 'The Prince's apartments?'

'His drawing room, sir,' Joshua said soothingly. 'He wished to show Miss de Silva his magnificent collection of brooches.'

Her father's expression remained uneasy. 'I am sure his Highness was most gracious, but the time has come to leave.'

His tone was severe, and in a short while they had collected Carmela and were bowling down the driveway towards Marine Parade.

Joshua was left looking after the carriage, a prey to uncertainty. Domino was to be sacrificed on the altar of family duty—indeed, she was willing to be sacrificed—and there was little he could do. He was a disreputable man and could have no voice in her future. That kiss—those kisses, he corrected himself reminiscently—could only ever be an interlude, but what an interlude! It was ridiculous that his heart still sang. How many kisses had he known in his lifetime? Not like this, a small voice within him argued, not like this. She had been a revelation, all her youth and vitality poured into those moments of pleasure. He had known instinctively that she was a girl of strong emotion, that beneath her modest exterior lay a sleeping passion waiting to be roused, and he had been right. He had wanted to kiss her until she begged him never to stop, and she had wanted him to. She desired him as much as he desired her. Another conquest to add to the many, he thought acidly. All the more reason, then, to keep his distance. Otherwise he would hurt her, and hurt her badly. It was inevitable—for didn't he damage everything that became dear to him?

An unbearable restlessness seized him and he knew he had to get away from the chattering foolishness all around. He turned on his heel and strode back the way he had come. Once in his studio, he threw off his black evening jacket and shrugged himself into the spattered smock. A blank canvas was before him and he picked up his brush. In his mind's eye he saw her as she had stood just minutes before. His painting would capture that moment, would capture her lovely young face as he kissed her into mutual submission. It was as close as he would ever get to possessing her and with that he must be content. For her sake his heart must remain well defended: she was too young, too trusting, too innocent. For his own sake, too. The life he had fallen into was predictable, often unlovely, but always free from the pain of feeling; it was a life he intended to keep.

Chapter Six

It was a long time before Domino fell asleep that night. The visit to the Pavilion had proved a kaleidoscope of sights, sounds, happenings, that tossed and tumbled through her mind without settling. The strange architecture, the exotic furnishings, the overpowering heat, had all contributed to a strong sense of disorientation even before she had been assailed by the Regent's clumsy advances. For a while she had truly feared for her virtue; then came the sweet relief of rescue. It seemed it was her destiny to be saved from disaster by the one man who should have spelt the greatest danger to her.

Yet it was some time since Joshua had played the rake, if indeed he ever had. When she thought back to their first meeting on the beach, she had to acknowledge that it was her peace of mind that he'd threatened rather than her person. In fact, she had never felt seriously threatened in his company. Ruffled, irritated, occasionally shocked by his unconventionality, but never genuinely alarmed. He was simply adept at provoking her. But this evening he hadn't provoked; he had seemed almost a different person. From the outset hints had surfaced that more lay beneath the devil-may-care exterior than he cared to admit; but seeing him in his studio tonight, so much a part of his setting and among the things he valued, a serious and interesting man had assumed control. She'd felt a powerful connection to the paintings he loved and a powerful connection to him.

In her imagination she returned to his studio. She was flicking through the stack of canvases once more, then stopping abruptly. That picture of her! She saw it clearly in her mind's eye and pondered long over what it meant. He had said it was her foreignness that captured his interest, but the intimacy of the painting seemed to say far more. And the kisses that followed—what had they meant to him? They had certainly turned *her* life upside down. She had melted under their onslaught, every worldly consideration banished; all she had felt or known in those moments was him. She had never before experienced such emotion: her heart, her body, her whole being had shaken with the pulse of feeling.

Richard had never kissed her; if he had, she suspected that any kiss would have been but a poor reflection of what she had felt tonight. In retrospect her sentiments for Richard had been just what he had always said they were, a schoolgirl crush, painful and deep, but a mere rehearsal for the real thing. Was tonight the real thing? The thought scared her mightily, for if so it blew to pieces the future she had ordained for herself. She had left the Pavilion vowing never again to lose control, never again to succumb to her desires so shamelessly. She would block the moment from her mind as if it hadn't happened. Yet here she was thinking of it again and again, endlessly repeating those kisses, endlessly drowning in their delight.

After a restless night, she dragged herself from bed the next morning, feeling tired and dispirited. Doubts crowded out the euphoria of last night's lovemaking. She no longer knew what to think or how to behave. When she could label Joshua a rake, it had been easy to ignore the promptings of her heart. She could ignore them no longer and her heart lay exposed, raw and vulnerable. She tried to give it covering by dwelling on his past iniquities and telling herself how foolish it was to believe in his caresses, but the attempt was flimsy.

Without doubt he was a sexual buccaneer. It was not just his past relationship with the duchess: mistresses were a fact of life in the *ton*, never openly acknowledged, but discreetly tolerated. No, not just the duchess. His name had been linked to half a dozen others currently residing in Brighton; though she did not know the truth of these insinuations, the old adage of no smoke without fire came to mind. In short, he was a wholly unsuitable person to consort with. And how she had consorted! She had been utterly brazen.

With her mind torn this way and that, she was undecided whether to hide herself at home or fight the blue devils that threatened by venturing into town. Carmela made the decision for her. Her cousin was in a particularly disagreeable mood and it looked likely to last for hours.

'I do not understand why you felt it necessary to disappear last night,' she greeted Domino crossly as the latter took her seat at the breakfast table.

'The Regent wished to show me his collection of jewellery,' she replied in a tired voice. 'Papa knew where I was.'

'He did not, or else why would he have been looking for you everywhere?'

'But he took me himself to meet the Regent.'

'In the Music Room, Domino. You were to stay in the Music Room and not wander off to goodness knows where without a word.'

'The Prince wished to escort me to his drawing room. I could hardly refuse and there was no chance to let you know where I was going.' She thought it wise not to disclose that the Regent had resisted her plea to send for her cousin.

But Carmela had not yet finished her scolding. 'Your lack of thought caused both your father and I much worry and also a great deal of talk. What must people have thought when you left the room with the Regent and without a chaperon?'

'I imagine my absence would have gone unnoticed if you had not taken it upon yourself to alert every footman in the palace.' Domino's response was tart.

Her cousin bit back a retort, appearing to concede silently that she had been at fault in broadcasting Domino's truancy. But it was clear that she blamed her charge for the evening's troubles and for falling into one mischief after another. Doubtless she was counting the days until the family could leave Brighton and all its shocking attractions.

Domino left the breakfast table before her cousin could continue the harangue, but her father, encountered in the hall, proved no more benign. He was making his way to his office and the daily round of papers and, though he greeted her courteously enough, it was evident from his distant manner that he was far from happy. Her relatives appeared suspicious that she had conducted herself ill last night, but their suspicion fell squarely on the Regent. What would they think if they knew about Joshua?

The cloud that hung over Marine Parade spurred her to leave the house as soon as possible. In an effort to brighten a day which had started so badly, she slipped into the white figured muslin newly arrived from the dressmaker, and chose a charming gypsy straw bonnet, embellished with cherries and trailing matching ribbons. Flora, who was assisting her to dress, was delighted to learn that she was to accompany her mistress.

'It will be good to be on one of our adventures again, miss,' she squeaked excitedly.

Not much of an adventure, Domino reflected; a walk to the Level and back would have to suffice, but at least she would be in the fresh air and safe from any further recriminations. And there would be plenty to see, for the Level was a popular leisure area, frequented by local people as much as by the members of visiting London society. It was spacious and grassed, with a variety of attractions, even a cricket ground that had been laid out years before for the Regent when he was still Prince of Wales. The broad avenue of elms, their branches almost interlocking overhead, made a soothing walk and she could imagine herself in the country while the town thronged busily around her.

Today they had hardly reached the beginning of the walk when music came drifting to them on the breeze.

'Oh, Miss Domino, do let's go and look.' Flora was

jigging up and down in her eagerness. 'It's the military, I'm sure. I can hear the drums.'

The Prince's own regiment, the 10th Light Dragoons, was based at the Church Street barracks and, in the absence of another French invasion, spent their time mounting guard on the Prince's estate and occasionally taking part in parades, grand reviews and mock battles as part of the town's seasonal entertainments.

Domino felt a surge of interest. Italian opera might leave her cold, but a military parade was another matter.

'I'm sure you're right, Flora,' she said happily. 'The soldiers must be practising for the Regent's birthday—it can only be days away now.'

'What do you think they're planning to do?' The maid screwed up her face in concentration, as though by sheer force of will she could conjure up the mystery entertainment.

'My father said there was to be the usual parade, but he thought something quite special too, possibly a re-enactment of the Battle of Waterloo.'

At this intelligence Flora could contain herself no longer and began tugging at her mistress's arm in a fashion which Carmela would instantly have decreed unseemly.

'Quick, miss, let's go and see!'

They hurried along the wide avenue until it suddenly opened on to a large clearing. Here a dazzling display of deep blue and gold met their eyes. The soldiers were a moving panorama, the brilliant gold braiding of their tight fitting jackets glowing in the morning sun and their ebony shakos sitting proudly atop their heads. Raised in the air, a cluster of curved swords gleamed wickedly. A band played nearby, the drum they had heard earlier beating out an insistent time as the soldiers moved smartly first one way, then another, wheeling and spinning in such orderly fashion that to the dazed spectator they seemed not five hundred single men, but one dashing entity.

'Ain't that just a sight, Miss Domino,' Flora breathed, forgetting her acquired polish in a moment of wonder.

'It certainly is,' said an amused voice a short distance away. 'Flora, isn't it?' and a smiling man doffed his high-crowned beaver hat in her direction.

'Yes, sir.' She bobbed a nervous curtsy.

Joshua must have been at the far end of the parade ground where officials from the Prince's household were gathered and she had not noticed him until he was nearly upon them. As always the deep blue coat he wore was moulded like a second skin to his powerful shoulders. Beneath she glimpsed a paler blue, ornamented Venetian waistcoat and the palest and most close fitting of fawn pantaloons. On his feet were glossy black Hessians with little gold tassels, which swung jauntily as he came towards them. Her eyes drank him in: he was a pleasure to behold.

'And Miss de Silva,' he said, his voice coolly welcoming. 'How delightful to see you here.'

She took her cue from him. They were to meet as acquaintances, nothing more. Was this for Flora's benefit or was he refusing to acknowledge the kisses of a few hours ago?

'So what is to be—soldiers or sopranos?' His golden eyes, now laughing, smiled down at her.

'Soldiers, I fear.' Flora looked perplexed but Domino glowed inwardly. The mutual joke brought them closer.

'Why fear? They are a splendid sight, are they not? And so much easier on the ear!'

Laughter bubbled up. 'I doubt the *ton* would agree.'

'They would not, or at least they wouldn't admit to it. A preference for low pursuits denotes an instant loss of face. I seem to recall that when the circus visited town, opinions were most scathing!'

'When was that?' Her face lit up at the mention of a circus.

'It was a while before you arrived in Brighton, but I would place a heavy wager that if they were to return, you would be first in the queue.'

She was the most enchanting child, he thought, all youthful eagerness despite the womanly curves, which even now filled the figured muslin so becomingly.

'I would! I visited Astley's when I was in London a few years ago and saw an equestrian ballet,' she added guilelessly.

'And you enjoyed it?'

'Immensely. It was an amazing spectacle.'

'I imagine it would be. I have never managed to visit Astley's myself, but I've heard legendary tales of their performances.'

Her cheeks flushed with remembered excitement. 'I think it was the very best event I ever attended.'

She was adorable, but he must keep a sharp watch on himself. He had painted through the night and emerged serene; all he need do now was to keep his distance.

'Did Lady Blythe take you?' he asked, disconcerting her for a minute. 'I would not have thought it to her taste.'

'Do you know my aunt?'

'Only very slightly,' he said smoothly. 'So who was brave enough to escort you?'

'Just a friend.'

Her tone was awkward and she seemed keen to change the subject. He wondered if it was the same friend who had spurned her youthful love and married elsewhere. She was a girl of great spirit, but also intensely vulnerable; he must tread very carefully.

'Flora and I were speculating', and she gestured towards the soldiers who had now come to a standstill and were awaiting commands from a scarlet-sashed officer. 'We thought the soldiers must be practising for the Regent's birthday celebrations. Do you know what they intend to present?'

'There will be the usual parade, of course, but I am not allowed to discuss the *pièce de résistance*—it's a state secret!'

She laughed out at him, her dark eyes alive with mischief, and he gazed back at her for as long as he dared; then, seeing Flora's enquiring expression, looked quickly away.

'Have you had a hand in this great surprise, Mr Marchmain?'

'I was dragged into the early planning and I am supposed to oversee rehearsals, but other than that I cannot claim to have taken a very active role. I enjoy the dash and colour of the military and that's about it. I am looking forward to seeing the final performance, though. It will mark a splendid end to the summer season.'

She looked at him questioningly and, when he responded, his voice was stripped of expression. 'Prinny is planning to leave Brighton the week after his birthday, you know. I am due to accompany him back to Carlton House and from there travel on to Norfolk.'

He saw the shadow skim her face and there was a part of him that rejoiced. 'You will be leaving for Spain at the same time, I imagine.'

'I will.'

Silence fell. They stood side by side, looking blankly into the distance, hearing their own words, but not quite able to accept them.

'Our stay has passed very swiftly.' Her tone was wistful and her high colour betrayed her feelings. He pretended not to notice, and almost immediately she continued in a much brighter voice, 'I am surprised that you intend to visit Castle March so soon. I thought you would make a stay in London.'

'It's time I returned. I've been away too long, though I doubt I will be there many weeks. Just long enough to hang my da Vinci before the Norfolk weather drives me to warmer climes.'

'That is sad. Houses need to be loved, I think. But if you dislike the place so very much, why don't you sell and buy an estate you find more congenial?'

'It's true that I have little love for the house but, in gratitude to my great-uncle, I feel bound to keep it.'

'Because he made you his heir?'

'Because he left me Castle March at the right time.'

'And when was that?'

'When I'd grown tired of being a vagabond. And a country seat is not to be sniffed at—a gentleman with a large estate always commands respect!'

While they were talking, Flora had sauntered away to mingle a little timidly with the soldiers who were now relaxing at the side of the parade ground. With her maid out of earshot, Domino seemed emboldened to ask a question he had no wish to answer.

'Could you not have found a home with your brother?'

His face assumed a darker expression and with a jagged motion he pushed back a strand of bright hair from his forehead.

'My brother and I have nothing in common,' he said, his tone verging on the curt. 'In any case, he has a family of his own to concern him and I can only ever be a discomfort.'

'But why?'

'He is convention made flesh. I was a constant thorn in his flesh while I was growing up, and once I hit town my conduct was unspeakable!'

'Whatever you did to make your family disown you is long past.'

Her sweet concern touched him, but the truth was brutal and he had no wish to hide behind pretence. 'For him, Domino, the scandal lives on. Believe me, it is for everybody's good that I keep away.'

'What did you do, exactly?' she asked shyly.

'I badly failed two people who were dear to me and who deserved better.'

She looked dismayed and he said tersely, 'It isn't a pretty tale and my parents were justified in packing me off to Europe as soon as they could. But I won't have you think me the victim. The family made sure I had a decent enough allowance.'

'But still…' Dismay had turned to bewilderment.

'My parents are dead, and I have regained a little respectability by inheriting Castle March. Life is easy for me; my brother can be forgiven for wishing to keep a hundred miles between us.'

He watched her closely to see the effect of his words. He had not wanted to have this conversation but, since they had, he hoped it would serve to push her away. She was already too close for his comfort. Last night had been a very bad mistake; he was damaged goods and his was a solitary future.

Despite that, he could not stop himself wanting, intensely, to see her again—and again and again. He found himself saying, 'What is this I hear about the Cunninghams' extravaganza on Thursday evening? Something quite out of the ordinary, I believe. Are you invited?'

Lady Cunningham was generally despised as an empty-headed woman who greedily extracted gifts from the Regent and flaunted them in public. But because of her influence over George and because of the opulent nature of the hospitality she provided, her parties were never short of guests. Domino had not liked Lady Cunningham when she met her, nor had she wished to be involved in her lavish preparations; the idea that ladies might perform on stage for their peers seemed of dubious propriety. But a combination of Carmela's horrified response to the invitation and her father's reassurance that these days the most respectable of ladies took part in such informal entertainments had persuaded her to accept.

Alfredo had convinced her that he knew the perfect role she could play. He had preserved a single dress of her mother's, a dress Elena had worn when she was not much older than her daughter, and Domino could appear in tableau as a grand Spanish lady. When she saw the dress for the first time, she had gasped. It was a dress as red as passion; a dress for flamenco. As soon as she'd put it on, she had felt its power. It had needed no alteration, fitting her curves to perfection, and no addition other than a scarlet flower for her hair and a pair of high-heeled black shoes. She had been feeling somewhat disquieted about wearing such a revealing costume, but the thought of Joshua being there made her face flame.

'Yes,' she assented as unconcernedly as possible, 'my father wishes us to attend.'

He chose to ignore the deep blush and replied easily, 'Then I shall see you there. Meanwhile I must report to the palace on the progress of the birthday plans', and, lifting his hat once more in salutation, he turned and walked away.

She was left prey to conflicting sensations: about him, about the party. His confession of wrongdoing had upset her. But so, too, had learning of his family's conduct towards him and his brother's determination to remain estranged. Whatever Joshua had done in his youth, the two were still flesh and blood. After all these years he must surely have expiated his crime. Was this brother so pure that he had done nothing wrong in his life? Joshua had failed those he loved, had not treated them as they deserved, but wasn't that true of many others? And she doubted that the case was as black and white as he'd made out. He'd declared his misdeed baldly and for a moment she'd felt dismay, but not for long. She was herself guilty of sufficiently bad things not to judge him: gambling illicitly, falling into debt, falsely eloping with Benedict when they were both minors—the list was worryingly long.

And now the Cunningham party was looming and bringing a new set of anxieties. The dress was magnificent and, wearing it, she was a warrior queen. But how warlike would she feel with Joshua in the audience? And Charlotte Severn and Moncaster, too? Their threat was always present to her, thrumming in the background. Joshua had warned her to be on her guard against them; if she drew attention to herself, what wickedness might that encourage? But unless she told her father of their continued persecution, she could not refuse to perform her part in the evening's entertainment. And to tell him would be to reveal the whole sorry business of her previous stay in England.

Her father had reassured her that all she would have to do was to walk across a small stage, a painted Spanish fan in one hand and a pair of castanets in the other. In general, he said, English people were woefully ignorant of other nations and even a simple appearance in traditional dress was sure to be greeted with interest.

But when the time came to leave on Thursday evening, she had worked herself up into a ball of terror. Reading the dread in her mistress's face, Flora ushered her quickly to the corner of the room and angled the cheval mirror.

'You should take a look, Miss Domino,' she said gently. 'Everyone will say you're all the crack!'

Her maid's attempt at *ton* slang made Domino smile faintly and she plucked up sufficient courage to look at herself properly in the mirror for the first time. The red taffeta of the dress fell in ruffled tiers to the floor. Each tier was ornamented with sparkling crystals and the final layer trailed alluringly behind her. The bodice was plain and modestly covered her bosom, but her arms were bare, framed by more ornamented frills. The dress moulded her figure so closely that every undulation, every softness, was accentuated. She caught her breath when she saw the stranger looking back at her. Could she really be this tantalising, sensual creature? She drew herself up to her full height, made prouder by the heeled shoes, and tossed the frilled skirt this way and that in sweeping gestures. Her dark eyes began to glow with anticipation, and when Flora placed a scarlet blossom in the ebony curls, now free from restraint and flowing to her shoulders, she smiled back at her reflection, captivated by the image she saw there. At her right hand, Flora gave a sigh of pure ecstasy.

'You don't look like yourself, miss. You look like...' and she struggled to put her feelings into words '...like a Spanish princess.'

'Dear Flora.' Domino hugged her. 'I fear that a genuine Spanish princess would be far too scandalised to wear such a gown!'

She ought to be scandalised as well, she thought, as the dress nipped at her curves and caressed the flowing lines of her young body. But she wasn't; instead, a strange exultation was rippling through her. She practised a few turns, swishing the deep frills of the gown from one side to another. Then holding the castanets aloft, she began to experiment with dance steps, gradually recalling the flamenco lessons she had taken without her aunts' knowledge. Another transgression! But it might serve her well this night. She wanted to perform splendidly and she knew why. She wanted to leave Joshua with a memory that he would never forget. She was not destined to be a part of his future, but she was determined to be a part of his history. All she needed was the courage to carry it through.

* * *

Once at the Cunninghams, Domino and her father were soon parted. He was ushered into a large salon, decorated in overpowering crimson, and filled with rows of delicate gilt chairs set out in a semi-circle. The first part of the evening's entertainment was to be the tableaux and mimes got up by the young ladies Sophia Cunningham had importuned. Later there would be an informal dance to the strains of a professional quartet. Before selecting his seat, Alfredo handed the musicians the gypsy music that would accompany his daughter across the stage. He felt relaxed. Knowing that the Regent had declined the Cunninghams' invitation, his fears were allayed that the Prince's recent conduct at the Pavilion might be repeated. There would be no danger from that quarter and taking part in something a little out of the ordinary would keep Domino busy and out of trouble.

Meanwhile she had been whisked to an adjoining room, already awash with nervous young ladies and their personal maids making last minute adjustments to what appeared to be highly elaborate ensembles. Domino herself had little to do but remove the black velvet cloak that covered her flamenco gown. She glanced around at the whirl of activity and was comforted by the sight of costumes a great deal more revealing than her own.

It seemed to be taking an inordinate amount of time for the gaggle of nervous girls to make ready, but at last they were being shepherded towards the rear part of the drawing room which had been curtained off to form the wings of an improvised stage. In no time what had initially appeared a large expanse had been flooded with a bevy of eager girls: Greek goddesses, Virgin Queens, Cinderellas, even Boadicea. Fussing and mingling around her, some of the groups looked askance at Domino's unfamiliar costume. That only made her hold her head a little higher.

As they waited for their turn to come, the girls could clearly hear from behind the curtain the ripples of polite applause that greeted most of the participants as they made their stately way across the stage, posing a while to enable the audience to absorb fully their finery, some of them embellishing their walk with a twirl, a curtsy or, even more daring, blowing a kiss to the audience. One Cinderella, clad in stylish rags and dolefully sweeping the floor with her birch broom, received a particularly rousing reception. Three girls dressed as Greek goddesses floated on to the stage and formed a small circle. For some minutes they danced fragrantly with each other, weaving a fragile pattern with their gauze robes. At their appearance a murmur of surprise, not all of it appreciative, had travelled around the room. One of the goddesses had been ill advised to wear a damped and transparent petticoat beneath her gauze and the more august members of the audience showed their disapproval of such flagrant exposure.

But it was Domino, far more robustly clad, who burst upon the audience with a thunderclap. She crossed the stage in one fluid movement, her heels already beginning to click and rap to the strong beat, her arms gesturing in dramatic flight and the castanets enforcing a compelling rhythm. The beat sounded at first slowly, then more rapidly, first quietly, then more loudly, alternating in tempo, but always there, throbbing, insistent. The musicians accompanying her threw themselves into the moment and music and dancer became one. Gradually the more forceful beat began to dominate, working its way to a crescendo while the dancer's feet stamped and twirled a mesmerising motif across the floor. Domino's supple, young body flexed and swayed in one direction while the red taffeta frills swished and coiled in another. The audience were silent, hardly daring to breathe. She had them wholly in her power, thrilled by the mastery of her dancing. At first the dance had appeared so daringly sensual that they could not believe they were watching it in a lady's drawing room, even Lady Cunningham's. But as the black heels weaved their sinuous pattern across the stage and the lithe scarlet form twined and turned in sympathy with the music's yearning, they forgot where they were and gave themselves up to the fantasy.

Standing at the back of the room, Joshua forgot calm detachment. He was caught in the music's powerful rhythms, caught by the sensuous ebb and flow of Domino's body, so that he felt he was with her, moving with her, away from her, against her. He wanted to be there, he belonged there, but just when he felt he could not remain apart from her a second longer, the music reached its crescendo and with a last stamp of her heels, a last flourish of castanets, she was still. The applause was tumultuous. Emerging from her trance, Domino realised it was for her and smiled shyly back. Then, as quickly as she could, she left the stage.

After her performance there was little appetite for further tableaux and with one accord the guests began to move towards the dining room where a substantial buffet had been arranged. She felt unable to face her fellow guests immediately, but instead took shelter in a secluded corner of the salon. She had seen Joshua at the back of the room and she had danced for him. He had warned her away and she knew well that the kisses they'd shared would be the only kisses. They were treading separate paths; very soon they would say farewell for good. His future would be a procession of women, one after another, passing in and out of his life. He was sure to forget her, but she wanted so badly for him to remember. If they were destined never to meet again, she wanted him to hold this memory of her. She had danced to stun him, to leave him dumbfounded and dazed. Her cheeks flamed as she thought of the invitation she had offered, but she could not be sorry.

Almost as she thought of him, he was at her side. 'I won't ask you where you learned to dance like that,' he murmured slyly. 'I imagine your father knew nothing of your talent.'

She looked towards the doorway at Alfredo, still wearing a dazed expression, and inundated with extravagant compliments on his daughter's performance.

'Papa insisted I wore a flamenco costume,' she excused herself feebly.

'Then Papa got what he deserved!'

'I should not have danced,' she conceded shamefacedly. 'I was supposed only to walk across the stage. The dress was my mother's, you see, and Papa wanted to see it come alive again.'

'He certainly had his wish granted.' A wry smile lit Joshua's face.

'Yes, I fear he did,' she said quietly and then more

emphatically, 'I really never meant to dance, but the music...'

'You have dance in your soul, Domino. You should not be sorry; you were magnificent!'

She peeped up at him. 'I *was* good, wasn't I?'

He laughed aloud. 'You *were* good, my little one. By God, you were good!'

Hearing his laugh as she entered the dining room, the Duchess of Severn glared in his direction.

'That chit seems to go from strength to strength,' she remarked acidly to Lord Moncaster, a few steps behind. 'She leads a charmed life.'

Leo handed his companion a glass of wine and said thoughtfully, 'She's a deal too close to Marchmain for her father's liking. Watch his face.'

They both glanced across at Señor de Silva. He was looking with some alarm at his daughter smiling softly at the exquisite figure beside her.

'Can we do nothing?' The duchess's voice was sharply edged, her frustration spilling out despite her best efforts at control. 'I despair of ever confounding the girl.'

'I understand she is to be married off to some Spanish grandee in the very near future. Marchmain will be history.'

'Before that happens it would be pleasant to torture her a little. I feel I deserve some small satisfaction.' The duchess's mouth twisted into an unpleasant grimace, surprising Moncaster by its ugliness.

'Hell hath no fury?'

'Not just for a woman scorned, Leo, but a man baulked of his prey,' she reminded him.

'It's true that I have not yet settled my score with the little upstart. But I have been giving it some thought.'

'Dare I say, it's about time? Since that débâcle with Prinny, you have been remarkably silent.'

'Marchmain skewed our pitch in that instance,' Moncaster began.

'Not just in that instance,' she interrupted bitterly.

'The joy of this plan, however, is that Marchmain cannot ride to the rescue. Indeed, he will be the very problem—we can use his name against her.'

The duchess looked sceptical and, stung by her lack of enthusiasm, he put down his glass on a side table and drew closer to his companion, almost whispering into her ear.

'I have a little knowledge of the señorita's past history that might serve our purpose.'

'Such as? I hesitate to remind you, Leo, but we have already employed your knowledge of her past and failed miserably.'

'We won't this time. She does not yet know the truth about our friend Marchmain. When she does, I am sure it will give her great pain. Her father, too—he will be most anxious to return her to Spain where she belongs.'

'Tell me!'

Moncaster readily obliged and the duchess's face was wreathed in an unholy smile.

'Excellent. But why now? We could have used this ammunition weeks ago.'

He gave an impatient shrug. 'Now that Marchmain has well and truly caught her, it will be so much more effective. Always keep your powder dry until you really need to use it, my dear.'

The duchess said nothing, but her smile broadened.

* * *

By this time a number of couples had been encouraged back into the salon where the chairs had been cleared and a small dance floor established. The musicians were striking up for a cotillion and Joshua, still by Domino's side, immediately offered his arm.

'Will you join us mere mortals?'

'Are you asking me to dance with you?'

'Yes, Domino, I'm asking you.'

The look in his gold-flecked eyes made her body turn to water. She stood gazing wonderingly up at him until light pressure on her arm encouraged her forwards and they joined the lively procession of couples already assembled. Her first dance with Joshua would forever stay in her memory. It was as though she moved through it in slow motion, every moment etched indelibly into her soul. The feel of solid muscle beneath her hand, the musky male scent filling her breath and the heat of his body as he drew close to her, their figures touching and parting in the graceful movements of the cotillion.

The dance meant they were separated for long periods, but always eventually they came together, their limbs warm and eager, their hands caressing fleetingly. For Joshua it was torment. Each time they were forced apart by the pattern of the dance, a voice screamed through his head that this was the stupidest thing he had ever done, but then—the wonderful moments when they came together again, the voice obliterated and his body touching hers, lightly, gently, promising delights he must not think of.

Eventually the music stopped and partners were bowing graciously to each other, but they stood motionless and silent, in thrall to the spell that encircled them. It was Joshua who gathered his wandering wits and realised the spectacle they were creating. Hastily he ushered Domino from the dance floor. By now, the room was very hot; he led her towards one of the curtained windows overlooking the wide spaces of the Steine. Its bay formed a small enclave and, as they entered, the crimson and velvet curtains closed behind them, cutting them off from the rest of the room.

'The temperature must rival that of the Pavilion,' he managed to joke, pushing the casement doors wide open so they were able to walk out on to the small ironwork balcony.

She smiled a little shakily. After the intimacy of their dance, her knees felt ready to buckle. He was feet away, though, and seemed intent on keeping a distance between them.

'Domino,' he began and then he was beside her and she had walked into his arms. His lips were on her hair, brushing the stray tendrils aside and then gently trailing kisses down the line of her cheek until his mouth found hers. As though in a dream she reached up and buried her hands in his hair, destroying its modish style in an instant, pulling him ever closer. Her eyes darkened with pleasure and her lips parted invitingly. Again and again his mouth found hers, kissing her long and hard, his tongue gently exploring at first, then growing more urgent, until she tasted him to the full. He undid the small crystal fastenings of her bodice, slowly and carefully, and his lips on her bare skin flickered fire through every nerve, every fibre. His hands cradled the gentle swell of her bosom and then his tongue was there, teasing the dress aside, closing over her breasts, bringing her aching flesh to an ecstatic hardness. She closed her eyes and gave herself up to rapture.

Once again, he was the first to come to his senses. What madness! In the middle of the Cunninghams' drawing room with a hundred people just a curtain's thickness away. And after he had sworn never to touch her again! Her dancing had aroused an elemental passion in him and, once they were close and alone, he had felt himself powerless: powerless to stop his arms from enfolding her, powerless to keep his lips from her mouth and from her body. It was ridiculous. A man of his experience, to be overwhelmed by emotions he could not control. He had to fight this insane desire or he would wreck her on the rock of scandal. For himself, the gossip mattered not a jot. The whole world knew him for a rake; people would simply shake their heads and say what else could you expect? For Domino, though, it could mean utter ruin.

But the more he saw her, the more he wanted her, and this after years of indifference, years of ensuring that he felt nothing. With every encounter his emotions deepened and he knew, even if she did not, where it would inevitably lead. He must stop. While she remained in Brighton, he must remain her friend, and nothing more. Yet he had never before felt such raw hunger as when she'd pressed her slender body into his and offered herself to him. Blame the dress for that, he muttered silently to himself, but he knew it to be a poor excuse.

He led her back into the drawing room as discreetly as he could and went to procure drinks, but her father was before him. Alfredo had been unnerved by the sensuality of his daughter's dancing; watching her disappear into the window embrasure with Joshua Marchmain, he became thoroughly fearful. He had been on the point of following the couple when they emerged from their shelter. He noted the tell-tale flush on Domino's face and Joshua's dishevelled hair, and suspected the worst. He must remove her from Brighton immediately. First that unpleasantness with the Prince Regent and now this man—less exalted, perhaps—but still of questionable morals. He knew enough of Marchmain to fear for his daughter's reputation. The aunts had been right. He had been too indulgent. Carmela had been right. She had been warning him of just such a disaster for weeks, but he had refused to believe her. Now he had seen the truth with his own eyes. Domino must leave for Spain immediately.

Joshua, returning with glasses of fruit punch, was in time only to receive a hurried curtsy from Domino and a curt nod from her father. In a moment they had bid Lady Cunningham goodbye and were on their way home.

The thunderous look on Señor de Silva's face meant only one thing, Joshua decided. Domino would be shipped back to Spain before she had time even to pack her wardrobe. In a day she could be gone and he would never see her again. He quickly downed the punch and as swiftly bid his hosts a gracious farewell. In a moment he was in the Steine and strolling towards the sea. He wanted fresh air and he wanted space. The evening was closing in, but the heat of the day had not yet disappeared. Lightly clad couples were hastening to and from the different entertainments on offer and the town had a subdued hum.

He needed to think. He had to see Domino again

before she left, had to tell her…what, exactly? He hardly knew. Only that her kisses had marked him enduringly, that their lovemaking had mattered to him. He stood stock still, an arrested expression on his face, neither seeing nor hearing the constant murmur of water as it greeted the pebbled shore. It *had* mattered, truly mattered!

He'd been charmed from the start by her youthful beauty and intrigued by her boldness of spirit. She was fascinating but nothing more than a passing whim, he'd thought, and he had known plenty of those. He had sparred with her, flirted with her, but always made sure to keep his distance. Until that moment in the studio. Afterwards he'd convinced himself that their kisses had simply been a reaction to the drama with Prinny, a fragile moment to treasure, which would soon be forgotten. But tonight? How was he to explain that?

Was it possible that he was falling in love with her? He hardly dared think it; he could not, must not, lose his heart. He had loved before, just once, and the affair had ended in catastrophe. She, too, had been young and passionate and given herself willingly. Together they had broken every rule in the book and made themselves pariahs, cut dead in the street by friends and enemies alike. They had lost reputation, lost the world they knew, and broken their parents' hearts. And for what? A few months of madness, for he had not the guts to see it through. He had betrayed his best friend, provoked social mayhem, but finally lacked courage; he had left his lover to face the music alone. After that, how could he live with himself? The answer, of course, was that he could not. He had become a different person and lived with him instead. And now, after he'd deliberately suppressed every painful memory of that time, had thought himself forever incapable of tenderness, indeed hoped that it was so, he found himself in danger of loving this enchanting child.

It was foolish to imagine that allowing his feelings the licence they craved would change his world in any way. His reckless, empty life would continue; Domino's youthful innocence was not his to spoil. She would never be a mistress and he would never be a husband. The man she married should be as carefree and innocent as she. He knew himself well enough to recognise that he would not stop wanting other women once Domino was no longer with him. He thought cynically of all the females who had literally passed through his hands. No, his life would continue along the self-same path. But he would never again feel untrammelled pleasure, for Domino's sweet face would always be before him and her firm, young body always entwined with his.

Dusk had fallen and the lights of the small boats anchored just offshore winked out at him. The gentlest of breezes had whispered itself to a stop. But he made no attempt to move. Instead his hands began to drum against the promenade railings in an impatient tattoo as his mind beat in unison. Whatever she might feel for him, she was still willing to return to Spain to marry a man she did not know. He would not try to persuade her otherwise, for he could offer her nothing but the shell of the man he had once been. They were destined to play roles already determined for them and there was to be no deviating from the script. Nevertheless, he had to see her again, if only to bid her a final farewell.

Chapter Seven

Domino cast a concerned look at her father as the carriage rolled its way homewards to Marine Parade. His face was impassive. She wished he would say something, anything, but he remained mute. It was clear that he judged her conduct unbecoming, but his refusal to discuss her crime meant she could not defend herself against the charge he was silently bringing. He might not say anything, but she was sure that he would act: her return to Spain appeared imminent.

And what exactly was her crime? The answer was simple: she had fallen in love with a rake. She was in love with Joshua and that was improper. Stupid, too. It didn't feel so—it felt warm and wonderful. Naturally it would, she counselled herself. Rakes don't become rakes by not giving pleasure. They don't become rakes by not being able to kiss. And he could certainly kiss. Moments ago she had burnt in a firestorm of passion and she had wanted more, much more. She had wanted to throw reputation to the winds and satisfy that fierce consuming desire. And she still did. She could no longer marry the nameless husband; she could no longer marry anyone.

Hunger for Joshua must remain unfulfilled, but anything less was now unbearable. In retrospect the love she'd had for Richard had been mere baby steps on the pathway to maturity. This was what it felt like to belong to a man, body and soul. Joshua would not change. He would remain the restless, untamed creature he had always been. He would never wish to marry, but that made little difference. She could not wed another. On the morrow she would go to her father and tell him she would not be returning to Madrid to choose a bridegroom.

When the morning arrived, however, it brought two surprises. A letter had been delivered the previous evening and sat waiting for her on the hall table. Neither she nor her father had noticed the envelope on their return from the Pavilion, for they had been too absorbed in their own thoughts. But this morning it was the subject of animated discussion between Flora and the upper housemaid. Such personal missives were rare in what was an official residence. Flora placed the letter carefully on a tray alongside her mistress's hot chocolate and made haste to the bedroom, eager to hear its contents. But Domino was not in a confiding mood. She thanked her maid prettily and, ignoring Flora's evident disappointment, told her she might go.

Once alone she examined the envelope with curiosity. The handwriting was vaguely familiar, but it was not until she had extracted the two sheets of stiff paper and spread them flat on her lap that she realised the identity of her correspondent. The charming note had travelled the long distance from Cornwall and brought unexpected news of Lady Christabel Veryan. Since Christabel's marriage to Richard, Domino had communicated with her from time to time, although never easily. Three years ago she had been the one to bring the couple together; she had known even before Richard himself that his happiness lay with Christabel and she had wanted him to be happy. But her own rejection at his hands had remained raw and she had resolutely refused all invitations to Madron Abbey, contenting herself with the occasional letter addressed to Christabel alone.

Now all sense of strain had miraculously disappeared. Her feelings for Richard had faded into insignificance and she re-read the letter with genuine pleasure. Lady Veryan, it seemed, was in an interesting condition and her husband and family were most anxious for her to consult a doctor in London's Harley Street. Her father would accompany her to Brighton, she wrote, and she hoped that her dear friend, Domino, would lend her support for the short journey up to the capital. Before that it would be a great treat to spend a few days in the Regent's seaside paradise.

For the first time in their acquaintance, Domino felt that she could meet Lady Veryan without pretence and make a true friend of her. She badly needed to confide in someone and Christabel, a seasoned married woman, would be the very best confidante. She wanted to tell her about Joshua.

When, later, she knocked at the door to her father's office, it was not to tell him that she no longer wished to marry a man of her aunts' choosing, but to request that she entertain a friend she had made during her previous stay in England. For a brief moment her father looked nonplussed. Overnight he had perfected a plan to despatch his daughter immediately to Spain and had been on the point of sending a courier to warn the aunts of her arrival. But he could not be inhospitable. It was an annoying hiccup, but when he thought more about it, he could see advantages to the visit. Lady Veryan was a mature and experienced woman, and a pregnant one at that. She was likely to offer sensible advice to her younger friend and their time together would be spent largely within the confines of Marine Parade and not on the dangerous territory beyond its doors.

It would be beneficial for his daughter to enjoy new company: Carmela was hardly the most joyous presence, nor was a middle-aged parent who had too much work. The lack of suitable companionship, he reflected, might be one of the reasons that Domino had gone a little astray. A woman nearer her own age, but sensibly married, might be just what was needed. Lady Veryan could help prepare the girl for the wifely role that lay in front of her. If she were able to bring Domino to a more rational frame of mind, he might never have to raise the distasteful subject of her conduct last night. He would infinitely prefer to forget the whole disturbing series of events that had culminated in their tense ride home together.

Feeling happier than he had for days, he made his way to Raggett's, the town's most prestigious gentleman's club, and a useful place for garnering the latest political gossip. Equally happy, Domino returned to her bedroom to reply to Christabel's letter. How fortunate that Carmela was laid up with a chill and that the invitation could be issued and accepted before she was up and about again. She would almost certainly object to any unknown guest.

Domino had just laid down her pen when the second surprise of the morning arrived. A scratch at her door revealed Marston, looking perplexed.

'A caller is below, Miss Domino.'

'A caller?'

'He asked particularly for you, miss.' She noted the reproachful expression that the butler could not quite conceal.

'And does this caller have a name?'

'He is Mr Joshua Marchmain.' The voice was expressionless, but she knew that very little went unnoticed by Marston; he would be well aware that Joshua was not a welcome visitor.

Without wasting further words, she slipped past the butler and tripped lightly down the stairs, her heart beating a little too loudly. But when she reached the hall, it was empty. The front door was open to the sound of a booming sea and she crossed quickly to the doorway and looked along Marine Parade. Sure enough, there he was at the corner of Chapel Street and about to retrace his steps. He was leading two horses, walking them up and down to prevent them taking cold, for the day was sunless and there was a chill in the air.

In that instant he saw her and waved cheerfully. 'I'm glad to find you at home. I took a chance in hiring a horse for you. See, it's the pretty mare that you rode before.'

She blushed slightly at his reference to the ill-fated race, but there were more important concerns. She was bemused by his presence and needed some answers.

'What are you doing here? And with horses?'

'Riding! I thought you might appreciate a morning on the Downs. It should blow the cobwebs away.'

'But I'm not dressed for it,' she said weakly, indicating the simple dress of jaconet muslin that she had donned in anticipation of a day at home.

'I will walk the horses for ten minutes—I'm sure you and Flora can work wonders in that time.'

Aware of a disapproving Marston in the shadows, she ignored this sally and sought a further pretext. 'My father is away from home and I should not leave the house without his knowledge.' It was convenient to forget all the times she had done just that.

'We won't be gone long,' he said encouragingly. 'And no one will be around to tell tales—it's too early for most people. We might even manage a gallop!' She wavered. After her father's severity last night, it would be prudent to ask his permission, but he was not in the house and Joshua was on the front steps. He saw her hesitation and pressed home his case.

'It's a morning for being out of town, Domino, and I wish very much to talk to you. Where could be better?'

The prospect of a private conversation was too tempting to refuse and she flew up to her room, calling to Flora on the way. Together they managed the change into riding dress in record time. Domino's costume of pomona-green velvet ornamented with gold epaulettes was tailored to mould itself to her lithe young form. She watched Joshua's eyes warm with appreciation as she came down the steps to meet him, but she was glad that he offered her no compliments. She could pretend that the ride was simply a meeting between old friends and that the absence of a chaperon was unimportant.

The chill in the air had turned the sky slate grey and made the promise of an energetic gallop even more enticing. They soon left the town behind, riding single file along one of the narrow chalk paths that led upwards to the smooth contours of downland. The wind was in abeyance and the white gulls dipping and calling seemed almost to hang in the air. Once they reached the expanse of open grass, their genteel trot was abandoned for a headlong gallop. Both riders launched themselves forwards and sprinted in harmony across the turf, Domino's ringlets loosening from their hold and streaming behind her like a soft, waving banner. On and on for miles until, exhausted, the horses came to a halt at the top of a particularly steep rise in the ground. Below, the town of Brighton stretched itself lazily towards a dreaming sea, not a breath of wind ruckling the water's surface.

They sat for a moment, taking in the sweep of grey stone and white cliffs while they regained their breath. Then Joshua slid easily from the saddle and secured his reins on the branch of a solitary tree. As he did so, a shaft of sunlight broke through the leaden sky, catching them in an illuminated circle. She smiled down at him, her face radiant with pleasure and her unforced joy in the ride evoking an answering smile. Before she could join him, he had turned aside and picked a small bouquet of wild daisies and cowslips and presented them to her with a courtly bow.

'Does Spain have its own language of flowers? Here the daisy means innocence and the cowslip winning grace—what could be more apt?'

She blushed at the extravagant compliment, but said

lightly, 'I think the language of flowers is universal, is it not?'

He reached up to help her dismount. 'Shall we rest the horses and walk a little?'

She nodded agreement and took his proffered arm. They strolled in companionable silence over the springy turf, wending their way along the ridge of the hill. When he spoke at last, there was some hesitation in his voice.

'I was hoping you would accept my invitation this morning. I wanted to apologise for ending your evening so badly.'

When she looked bemused, he added, 'I imagine your ride home wasn't the most pleasant you've ever taken.'

She coloured. 'There's no need for you to apologise. I was as much to blame for...' she was looking straight ahead, her cheeks now bright red '...for the incident.' Despite her embarrassment, she wasn't quite able to repress the smallest of giggles. 'You should know that my scandalous conduct went unremarked!'

'I am relieved to hear it. I was worried that you might already be on your way back to Spain. But your father seems a most level-headed gentleman. You are fortunate: families are not always so sensible.'

'You are thinking of your own?'

When he didn't respond, she said gently, 'I can understand why you should. They appear to have been very quick to judge you.'

'They had past history on their side.'

'Then you must have been in some very bad scrapes while you were growing up.'

His smile did not quite reach his mouth. 'I was.'

'But why?'

'Why? That's a strange question.'

'Not really. Boys are naturally a little wild, but why were you so very wild?'

They continued to walk in a leisurely fashion along the narrow chalk path, but she felt his figure tense beside her.

At length, he said, 'Perhaps because no one was paying me too much attention. I wasn't much use, you see. My parents already had a perfectly satisfactory heir—indeed, a paragon of an heir. And then ten years later another son came along at a time when I imagine they must have thought themselves clear of child rearing.'

He had never before revealed so much of what was evidently still hurtful. She unlinked her arm from his and took his hand in a warm clasp. 'You're saying that you were unwanted.'

'I'm saying there was no point to me,' he said in a deliberately light tone. 'It didn't seem to matter what I did. So I suppose that goaded me into exploits that became more and more outrageous.'

'Including breaking faith with those dear to you?' She knew she was venturing into dangerous territory, but it seemed important to know all there was to know.

'That was the final icing on the cake.' The light tone had vanished and his voice was riven with bitterness. 'My perfidy ensured my parents disowned me. My brother, too—the scandal I caused jeopardised his betrothal to an earl's daughter.'

'But the marriage went ahead?'

'Yes, he married. But the bride's family made it clear

that the wedding would only happen if I disappeared for good.'

'And so you went abroad.'

'And so I was sent abroad. It was the perfect solution. I'd ruined my parents—I was responsible for their early demise, or so my brother always maintained. I'd badly injured my sibling, my best friend and my first love. Going to Europe and staying there was the best thing I could do.'

The atmosphere had become heavy with the bleakness of the memory and, in an attempt to break through the grey cloud, he said in a falsely cheerful voice, 'I imagine it won't be long before you'll be on *your* way to Europe, too.'

She said nothing, but her silence told him he was right. 'Before you leave, Domino, there's something I need to say.'

She felt apprehensive, but also strangely excited. After last night's heated encounter she had come to see the impossibility of following her family's wishes, but she had also been forced to swallow the bitter knowledge that a solitary life awaited her. The only man she could ever marry was walking here by her side and there was to be no future with Joshua. He was not looking for a wife; she doubted if he was looking for a permanent liaison of any kind. Yet this morning he had sought her out and brought her to this deserted spot in order to have private conversation. Could it be that he cared enough to prevent her return to Spain? Was the bleak future she had envisaged about to vanish? She hardly dared think it. That was just as well, since the very faint hope was instantly extinguished.

'I respect your decision to return to Madrid and to

your aunts' protection,' he was saying, 'even though I may not agree with it.'

He put up his hand as she tried to interrupt and repeated quietly, 'I respect your decision, Domino. But before you leave I need you to know one thing.'

'Yes?'

'I need you to know that I meant every one of those kisses last night.'

She felt baffled. What was he saying? That he was happy to see her go as long as she realised that his feelings had been honourable? Her silence seemed to urge him to another attempt.

'I have not led the most creditable of lives, but in all my dealings with you, I have been honest—unusually so. I realise that it makes little difference to either of our futures, but it matters very much to me that you know my lovemaking has been sincere.'

She was still uncertain whether her heart should be leaping skywards or plummeting to earth. To gain time she repeated, 'Sincere?'

'Genuine. A difficult word for me—I am a rake, after all!' His tone was jesting, but when he spoke again, there was a new heat to it. 'I *meant* those kisses.'

And then swiftly, before she could respond, 'You must not worry. I won't disturb your life further, but I could not allow you to leave England without confessing what knowing you has meant to me.'

She turned to face him, grasping his hands in an impulsive movement.

'You may disturb my life as much as you wish, Joshua. Should I return to Spain, it will not be to live with my aunts.'

It was his turn to look baffled. 'When did you make *that* decision?'

'Last night,' she murmured shyly.

She could not bring herself to confess the whole truth of her feelings. Some small vestige of doubt held her back. The memory of Richard's rejection still played through her mind and she did not know if she could bear the far worse pain of Joshua's dismissal.

'Why have you decided this?' he was asking.

She prevaricated. 'My aunts are insistent that I wed a man of their choosing, but I can no longer contemplate an arranged marriage.'

'And why is that?' His amber eyes seemed to probe deep into her heart.

'There are reasons.'

He was looking at her in a way that made her stomach tie itself into the severest of knots, but some distant warning voice kept her from saying more.

'And I am not to know those reasons?' he asked softly.

'They are not important.' She must continue to hide her secret. Joshua would not want to hear words of love, words he could not reciprocate. But though she could not speak the truth, her body was pushing her to be honest. She reached up to touch his face and her finger lovingly traced the scar on his cheek.

He stood stock still for a moment, hardly believing the touch of her hand; then, in a sudden movement, he pulled her roughly into his arms, showering her hair and face with a torrent of kisses, until they were both breathless and forced to stop. For a moment they stood immobile, holding hands and laughing foolishly at each other. Then he wrapped his arms around her once more and kissed her again, this time slowly, tenderly, savouring every touch and taste of her. She breathed in his familiar scent and closed her eyes. The memory of last night's kisses still lingered on her body and she wanted his lips back where they belonged. Soon she had her wish. His mouth began to trail slow kisses down her neck. Then, expertly unbuttoning her riding dress, he raised the satin skin of her breasts to his lips. She gasped with pleasure and fell back against the tree they had stopped beneath. He teased her with his tongue and she pressed into him, moulding herself like a second skin, her soft warmth cleaving to his hardness. They paused for a moment, shaken by the intensity of their feelings, but an irresistible force made them greedy for more.

He picked her up in his arms and laid her down on the soft turf, then he was beside her, drawing her towards him, fitting his body to hers. Whirls of shocked pleasure eddied through her. The gold-flecked eyes were dark as he hungrily sought her lips once more, bruising them in his need. She reached out and unbuttoned his shirt, imprinting her kiss on his chest and burying her face against his muscular frame. With a tender delicacy he began to undress her and her bare skin flamed with desire. Each item of clothing was hastily discarded, each part of her body caressed, gently at first and then more and more urgently. There was a burning coal in her stomach and its fire was spreading outwards and outwards until the very tips of her body were consumed by its heat. She tugged urgently at his shirt; she had to feel his naked skin on hers and in response he threw shirt and breeches roughly to one side. His fingers were thrilling her in ways she could not have imagined and when she felt she could bear it no longer, his mouth followed where his hands had led, melting her into an ecstasy that had to be fulfilled. In one swift movement he pulled her beneath him, covering her with his body. She felt him moving slowly against her, hard and ready.

'Love me,' she whispered.

But suddenly he was disengaging himself, setting their dress to rights, pulling them both to their feet. He met her bewildered gaze directly, but when he spoke it was as though the words were being dragged from him.

'I must not. We must not...' His voice trailed away.

She looked at him uncomprehendingly. Was this the cruellest twist of all, was this the way rakes disencumbered themselves from the women they no longer wanted? By bringing them to a frenzy of desire and then walking away? A minute ago, a second ago, she had shown him as plainly as any woman could that she needed his love in all its fullness. As any immodest woman could, she corrected herself flinching. She felt humiliated and desperate.

He turned away and gazed blindly into the distance. She heard his breath coming short and harsh. Then he swung round to face her, grabbing her hands and pulling her towards their waiting horses. Without a word he tossed her into the saddle and turned his mount towards the town. They rode in silence until they were once more outside the house in Marine Parade. He dismounted swiftly, springing up the front steps to summon Marston to the door. Ashen faced, Domino slid from her saddle and brushed past him into the open hallway. With a brief bow, he turned and led both horses away.

* * *

Once in the privacy of her bedroom, she allowed the tears to flow. How could this happen? Walking together this morning, she had felt closer to Joshua than ever before. He had never hidden his dislike of his family, but today she had realised for the first time the powerful hold the past still had on him. He had let down his guard and confided in her. She'd felt sad and distressed at the story. Angry, too, at his parents, at his brother, even at the friends he'd betrayed. None of them, it seemed, had really loved him, not enough to save him from himself. She had even begun to understand why, after that last catastrophic event, he had fallen into a rakish life. He must have thought himself permanently tainted, a danger, a bad omen for anyone unwise enough to get too close. But after all these years, he *had* allowed himself to get close—to her.

He'd sworn that the kisses they'd exchanged meant more to him than simple physical pleasure and she had gloried in the feeling of being wanted by the man she loved, even though their futures would remain separate and unchanged. She had given herself up to his lovemaking with such joy, such abandon—only to be made a fool of. How could he take her so far, only to spurn her? It could only be that he was playing with her. His fine words had been meaningless, spoken only to lure her into believing that she mattered to him, a notion destroyed forever by his rejection at the very moment they were to seal their love. It was a brutal but effective ploy. Their passionate encounters must have scared him. He had needed to rid himself of a clinging woman, make sure she would not importune him in future. Well, she too would do some ridding. She would smother her feelings; more, she would destroy them utterly, cut them off at their very roots and never ever let them bloom again.

Joshua slammed the door of his studio shut. He had no intention of painting, but he had to be alone, and this was the only room in the palace in which he could be sure of privacy. He had to be alone, he had to try to make sense of the morning's events. Methodically he began to sort through a stack of old canvases which he intended to reuse; the tedium of the task allowed his mind to wander. The news that Domino did not intend to return to her aunts' chaperonage had fallen on him like a lightning bolt. He was still trying to absorb its import when she was in his arms and asking to be loved. She was not going ahead with the arranged marriage because she could no longer wed a man for whom she had no feeling. That meant only one thing: she loved elsewhere. He'd known that he was the man she loved; it could not have been plainer. He had been carried away by the sheer physical delight of wanting her, but when she had breathed that command, when she had asked him to love her totally, the reality of the situation had hit him and hit him hard. He had paused long enough to realise that what they were doing was madness. She was in love with him and she was willing to give herself, without thought for the future, but he could not let her. It was too great a sacrifice; no longer a virgin, she would be consigned forever to spinsterhood—and, even worse, she would be cast out from society. He had pulled back instantly. He cared too much for her.

But now in the quiet of his room, with time to

think and think deeply, he grew certain that in pulling back from the path on which they'd embarked, he was already too late: she had already sacrificed herself. He knew little of Spanish society, but enough to realise that in its eyes she had committed a grave sin. Whether she were a virgin or not was doubtless irrelevant; she had lain naked with a man and that in itself would place her beyond the pale. She would no longer be considered a suitable wife for any decent man. He could not believe he had done this to her. How could he have been so stupid as not to realise the true import of his actions? She had not realised either, he was sure, but she was young, trusting, blinded by love. It had been his responsibility to keep her safe and he had failed miserably. She would say that she did not care, that she had no wish to marry any man, but he knew from long experience of women that such vows rarely held. There would come a time when she did want to marry and she would have to confess to her intended husband something at least of her past. He was quite certain that, however mild the confession, it would damn her irrevocably. He had quite simply ruined her young life and could offer her no recompense.

Swept with remorse, he angrily tossed the pictures aside and walked to the open windows. An unkempt profusion of honeysuckle and dogwood looked back at him. How could he ever make it up to her? It was impossible, except...

The mad notion of asking her to be his wife flitted through his mind and was immediately dismissed. He spelt disaster for anyone who came too close. He could not possibly ask her to marry him. The old Joshua would have plunged in fearlessly, but not this one, not the man he had become. As long as he remained at a distance, he could not be responsible for another's suffering. It was the only way to get through life. He could never return to the old Joshua.

Or could he? He paced up and down the floor, wooden boards creaking and cracking as he went. Dared he embrace a different kind of life, a life where he was no longer in control, one which held unknown pitfalls and sorrows? To live as he had these last six years was undemanding and free of pain. But she was in trouble. She needed him. Was he such a coward he could not step up to that challenge? Because of him, she had turned away from the future she'd envisaged—and to what? A wasteland. There was no longer any future for her. He might have burned his fingers, but he had burned hers, too. He had to put it right. He had to step right into the fire, there was no other way. He had to marry her.

Domino's resolve to obliterate Joshua Marchmain from her world was put to the test almost immediately. She had slept little and was making her way bleary-eyed to the breakfast table the next morning when a disapproving Marston put a small posy of wild flowers into her hand: blue bellflowers and pink eglantine roses interweaved with strands of ivy. She carried them into her small downstairs parlour and sat staring at them for what seemed an age. There was no note, but she knew from whom they came. Reluctantly, she took down the dictionary of flowers from its resting place and flicked through the pages. Here they all were: bellflowers for thinking of you, the roses for a wound to heal and the ivy for friendship. And this was his response to her complete humiliation! She threw the book on to the table and strode into the hall, grabbing the posy on the way. One of the undermaids was busy dusting a console table and bobbed a small curtsy as she saw Domino approach.

'Lizzie, isn't it?' The maid nodded nervously, wondering if her dusting was at fault. It was usually Miss Carmela who took her to task.

'I'd like you to have these, Lizzie. They will cheer your bedroom.'

The maid gaped and Domino said in a voice that brooked no argument, 'You will need to put them in water—now.'

The hall clock was striking eleven as the maid scurried away and Domino, still trembling slightly, walked back into the parlour. Almost immediately she spied his figure through the small square panes of its window; in the distance Joshua walking slowly back and forth along the promenade. He was waiting for her, she knew. Her anger had begun to cool and in its place the impulse to run to him was gathering strength. Determinedly she beat it back, but it cost her dear and she thought it wise to retreat to her bedroom, which faced the opposite direction. An hour later, she returned to the parlour and saw that he was gone. She felt empty and aching but knew that she had done the right thing. Twenty-four hours dragged by and brought with them another bouquet. This time Marston could hardly bring himself to hand the posy to his mistress. She ignored the servant's deep frown and took them in silence. But her anger was reignited and she stomped through to the back kitchen and plunged the flowers unceremoniously into the rubbish bin. She had no idea what Joshua's intentions were, but if he thought that two bunches of wild flowers would erase the pain he had caused, then he was more arrogant than she had ever believed. She felt proud that she had ignored his siren call and marvelled at her resolve, but a small, hard nut of anguish had settled itself firmly within her and she knew it would be her companion for years to come.

For three days she dared not venture beyond the front door for fear of being waylaid, but when no further offerings arrived and Joshua's figure no longer strolled the seafront, she thought it safe to leave the house. A travelling fair had come to Bartholomews and Flora was mad to attend. The fair's unsophisticated pleasures were unlikely to soothe Domino's anguish, but she knew that she could not stay indoors forever. After the ravages of recent days, modish clothes had ceased to be important and she donned an inexpensive sprig muslin and a plain straw bonnet for the outing. With Flora chattering by her side, they began the walk along Marine Parade towards the Steine. They had barely walked fifty paces when, at the corner of Chapel Street, an immaculately attired Joshua stepped across their path and forced them to a halt.

He could not have known we would be walking here today, Domino thought. He must have been waiting nearby for days. He bowed deeply and she nodded briefly in response, edging around him in an effort to continue her journey. Already she could feel her traitorous body working against her.

'Would you do me the honour of allowing me to escort you this morning, Miss de Silva?' he enquired formally.

'Thank you, Mr Marchmain, but as you see I have my maid with me and she is all the protection I need,' she was glad to be able to reply with equal formality.

He bowed again and she could see him looking searchingly at her face. She hoped he would not remark her pallor and the dark circles beneath her eyes. The longer he stood there, the harder it was to avert her gaze from his beautiful person. And she needed to.

'We are a trifle short of time this morning, sir. If you would excuse us...' and she edged even further ahead.

'So short of time that you cannot spare five minutes?'

There was something in his voice that made Domino pause. He was dressed in his usual elegant fashion, his skin lightly tanned and his hair glinting gold in the late summer sun; as ever he looked the perfect man. Yet there was something different, she felt. Could it be that he was nervous? Surely not!

During their interchange Flora had been looking from one to the other, her mouth opening and closing like a fish searching for water. She was evidently confused and now the flush on her cheeks signalled her annoyance at the unwanted intrusion on her mistress. She looked likely to find her tongue at any moment.

Domino made a swift decision. 'Go ahead, Flora, I will catch you up.'

'But will you be all right, Miss Domino?'

'Perfectly. I shall be with you in an instant.'

They watched the maid walk unwillingly towards the town before Joshua spoke.

'I sent you flowers.'

She said nothing.

'I hoped you would understand their message.'

'I understood.'

'Then why did you not respond?'

She would have liked to harangue him with her opinion of his message, but instead she settled for scorn. 'Since when have I had to account to you for my actions?' Her voice trembled only slightly.

He wasn't deterred. 'I wanted to speak to you, Domino—badly.'

She raised her eyebrows and he continued hurriedly, 'I've been a fool. I was a fool on our ride. Not because I escorted you home—that was the right thing to do—but because I should have told you...' he paused uncertainly '...told you what I am about to say.'

Her eyebrows climbed higher. She had no idea what he was about. All she knew was that she must not look at him, but concentrate very hard on what he was saying.

'You are no longer willing to accept an arranged marriage?'

She nodded mutely, wondering where this was leading.

'So you are free to make your own choice of husband?' he was saying. Then the bombshell. 'I think your choice should be me.'

'What!' She was stunned.

'I think you should marry me.'

'Is this some kind of perverted joke?'

'I can't blame you for judging me harshly. But it's no joke, though it may seem so. In truth, marriage to a rake is unlikely to advance your social standing.'

She was incensed and hurt in equal measure. His false proposal was yet another dagger to her heart.

'I do not deserve your mocking, sir. If this is no joke,

then it is a Banbury story. If I were foolish enough to accept your offer—which, rest assured, I am not—you would be sure to decide that your proposal was after all an unfortunate mistake.'

'However much to the contrary it may appear, I was sincere in our lovemaking, Domino, and I am sincere now.'

She was still recovering from the first shock of his announcement and could hardly take in what he was saying. Bewilderment made her cutting. 'You would not know the meaning of the word.'

'Please believe that I have always had your best interests at heart.'

'And now you have my best interests at heart by asking me to marry you? Forgive me if I am very slightly sceptical.'

'Your feelings are understandable. But I have done a good deal of thinking over these last few days and I know this is right.'

'And when did this improbable revelation visit you exactly?'

'I've made you angry. I'm sorry for that. You see, I never wished to disrupt your life and I didn't think I was the one to make you happy: I carry too much of the past with me. I should have kept away, but somehow I couldn't, and now that you've given up all idea of marrying to please your family, I'm asking you to marry to please me.'

Seeing her desperately trying to make sense of his words, he pressed home his case. 'Please believe me when I say that I don't ask you this lightly. I know that I want to live with you, to make a home with you—if you will have me.'

She was weakening. He sounded so earnest, but this change of fortunes was too much to swallow. 'It's not possible. Joshua, you cannot want to marry!'

He looked at her so fiercely that she was almost afraid. 'But I do.' Then, in a weak attempt to return to the Joshua she knew, 'If we marry, I may even allow you to hang my precious da Vinci!'

The quip faded and his expression took on a rare seriousness, 'You should know, Domino, that if you take me as a husband, you will do yourself little good socially and are sure to upset a great many people. Marriage to me may be a step too far.'

'It is a step I never thought to take,' she said slowly, but her face had gained colour, the olive skin of her cheeks lit by a slowly spreading inner glow. This morning has brought a miracle, she told herself, and like any miracle it had to be believed rather than reasoned. She could not understand how he had come to this decision, but it was clear that he meant every word he spoke. This was no cruel jest, no mocking overture. He had asked her to marry and all she had to do was say yes.

'You have turned my life upside down—but you are the only man I could ever wed.'

'And…?'

'And if you are truly honest, you have my answer!'

He held out his arms and she walked into his embrace. For long minutes they remained nestled in each other's arms while the waves lapped gently in the distance. But then the unwelcome thoughts began arriving.

'What about my father?'

'You haven't told him that you are not returning to your aunts?

'No, not yet. That would have been difficult enough, but now this!'

He stroked her arm to still her agitation. 'It's easy—we'll see him together and tell him that we are wishful of marrying.'

'If only it were that simple.' She hesitated, unsure of how to phrase the unpalatable. 'Papa is aware of Court gossip. He holds some strong opinions.'

'Don't let's sham it. He knows me for a rake and will be horrified that his beloved daughter has chosen to throw her lot in with such a loose fish.'

'So…'

'So I will have to prove him wrong, prove that my inglorious career belongs to the past—that you are now my future.'

'That could take some time.'

He pulled her towards him again, burying his hands in the tangle of silken curls and lifting her face to his.

'Another year is neither here nor there, my darling.'

'A year!'

'Have patience. Before the time is out my charm offensive will have him begging me to marry you.'

She smiled a little wanly, a furrow still creasing her brow. 'There are my aunts, too—they will be completely opposed.'

'Aunts are no problem. I can deal with any number of aunts,' he said easily.

'You will be very busy, then.' A smile flitted across her face at the thought of Joshua 'dealing' with those fearsome matriarchs. 'They will do anything to protect my fortune.'

'I have a fortune, too,' he pointed out. 'Not, I imagine, of the same magnitude, but still a cool ten thousand a year. Who could want more? You can sign your inheritance over to the aunts and never have a thing to do with it.'

'That still won't make them happy with the match; I fear they will make sure my father refuses his consent.'

'But if we wait until you are twenty-one, you can marry where you wish.'

'I don't want to upset Papa,' she said miserably.

He hugged her even more tightly, 'Don't despair, darling Domino. Let me talk to him, get to know him. Make him see I will look after his little girl.'

She looked dubious, but Joshua was encouraging. 'I will invite him to dinner and then the theatre—just the three of us, if you can bear to leave your duenna behind—so that we can at least break the ice.'

'However will you get him to agree?'

She doubted if anyone could persuade her father to spend an evening with Joshua Marchmain, let alone include his daughter in the arrangement. Yet persuade him Joshua did.

The following Thursday on the stroke of eight, he arrived at Marine Parade in a carriage hired for the evening. As always he looked complete to a shade, satin knee breeches and black tailcoat throwing into relief the dazzling snow of ruffled shirt and cravat, the latter arranged in precise and intricate folds. A silk-lined cloak completed a picture of refinement. But Domino's choice of dress more than matched his style. A cloud of jonquil gauze over a white satin robe furnished a perfect foil for the ebony curls that framed her lovely young face.

Her father greeted his host with a stiff little bow,

but she curtsied shyly to her lover, giving him her hand with the most mischievous of smiles.

They were to dine at the Old Ship, the oldest hostelry in Brighton, and one that frequently accommodated the Regent's guests. Domino had attended a ball at the Ship's magnificent assembly rooms the previous month and marvelled at the ninety-foot-long ballroom with its spectators' and musicians' galleries. But tonight Joshua had bespoken a private parlour, equally luxurious, but a good deal more intimate. He had obviously gone to a great deal of trouble, Domino thought, in planning this evening. Not only was the room he had chosen a perfect backdrop for a congenial dinner, but the meal itself had been carefully ordered to appeal to the tastes of a middle-aged Latin gentleman.

A modest but delicious repast ensued, beginning with a turtle soup served alongside a series of entrées including the omelettes her father loved. He ate well, but remained chilly and aloof. For a while the talk was general: the beauty of the Sussex landscape, the benefits of sea air, the numbers of dandies parading Brighton's seafront with their ridiculously padded shoulders and collars so high they were unable to turn their heads. It was not until the serving of a second course of goose, lobster and a braised ham alongside chafing dishes of French beans, peas and asparagus that Señor de Silva made mention of his unexpected invitation.

He lay back against his chair, sipping a second glass of wine with undoubted pleasure. 'I must thank you, Mr Marchmain, for a superlative dinner.'

'I am very glad the meal has met with your approval, sir,' Joshua responded politely. 'It is always hazardous to order for another at whose tastes you can only guess.'

'Indeed. Would it be discourteous of me to ask why my particular tastes interest you? Why, in fact, you have invited me to accompany you this evening?'

'Not discourteous at all. On the contrary, I find it understandable and very simple to explain. I wish to marry your daughter.'

The announcement, quiet and measured as it was, did not prevent Alfredo choking violently on his wine. When he recovered sufficiently to speak, his voice seemed not to belong to him.

'You wish to marry Miss de Silva?'

'I do. I am hopeful of winning your consent and thought it right that we should further our acquaintance as soon as possible.'

'Marry!' her father repeated. Then, turning to Domino, he said in a voice barely above a whisper, 'Can this be right, my child?'

'Yes, Papa. I love Joshua. He is the only man who will make me happy.'

'But—'

'I am aware of the misgivings you must have,' Joshua interrupted smoothly, 'and naturally I am happy to give, in private, whatever reassurances you need, but Domino and I are quite resolved. We will marry— whether it's next month or next year.'

Her father drew himself up proudly, looking every inch the Spanish noble.

'You may not realise it, Mr Marchmain,' he pronounced haughtily, 'but my daughter's choice of husband is of the greatest significance. Through her mother's family, she will inherit a very large estate when she reaches the age of twenty-one. That may influence your decision.'

'I cannot see how.'

'You would not, I am sure, wish to be seen as a fortune hunter.'

'Papa!'

'You are right, Señor de Silva. I would not. But since Domino's fortune is neither here nor there, I think it unlikely. I have a considerable inheritance of my own and am more than happy to share it.'

His cheerful insouciance stung Alfredo. 'When I said a very large fortune, I doubt you have any idea of its size.'

'Papa, don't you see?' Domino felt incensed by her father's wilful lack of understanding. 'Neither of us is concerned with my inheritance. Joshua has a splendid country estate of his own and enough money to keep us both in comfort.'

'Not concerned with a massive fortune? What nonsense is this?' her father spluttered.

She leaned towards him, her tone placating. 'Could not my aunts devise a new plan for how best to use the money? I know them to be involved in any number of charitable causes and my fortune would be well spent.'

Alfredo struggled to digest this heresy and there was an uncomfortable silence.

'Papa, dear Papa', and Domino reached across the table and took his hand in hers. 'I love Joshua. That is surely what is most important.'

'And I will look after her, you can be sure,' Joshua put in. 'Who better, after all, than a reformed rake?'

Domino gave him a sharp glance, feeling that her lover's intervention was hardly helpful. But Joshua's words had set Alfredo thinking. This match was the very last thing he desired for his daughter; his instinct had been to grab her by the hand and incarcerate her immediately within the confines of Marine Parade until arrangements could be made for her travel to Spain. Lady Veryan, when she arrived, would have to get on as best she could without her young friend. But what Marchmain said made a kind of sense. Who better to look after a young and naïve girl than a man who was thoroughly experienced in the wiles of the world? If she was compelled to marry a man she did not love—not that he would insist on such a thing, but the aunts could be very forceful when they chose—well, what kind of trouble might result? He had seen, with his own eyes, the power of his daughter's budding sexuality. He shuddered to think of the likely outcome of an unsuccessful marriage. And as for the fortune she would inherit, Marchmain seemed genuinely unmindful; no doubt the marriage settlements could ensure the rightful disposition of such a large estate.

The third course of creams, jellies and a basket of pastries had been virtually untouched, but the mood was mellow as they made their way to the Theatre Royal where Charles Kemble was once more the star of the stage. Fifteen years ago the actor had launched the new theatre with a stunning performance of *Hamlet*, but this evening he was playing comedy at which, it was universally agreed, he excelled. The box Joshua had reserved ensured them an extensive view of the auditorium. Domino surveyed the gold and glitter of the fabulous building with pleasure, its elaborate decoration scintillating in the sparkle of newly installed gas light. An ocean of faces and a thrum of excited chatter filled the entire space, from the Royal Box, housing members of the palace household, to the cheapest seats in the furthest recesses of the theatre. She had never before attended a performance at the Theatre Royal, since Carmela naturally dismissed acting as a pretext for sin. To do so this evening, and beside the man she loved, was a double enchantment.

The squabbles of Beatrice and Benedick were soon filling the auditorium as *Much Ado about Nothing* unfolded the foolishness of its hero and heroine. Sitting close by on a matching gilt chair, Joshua stole glances at his betrothed whenever he thought himself unobserved. The perfectly sculpted cheeks, petal soft, beckoned him to touch, but the presence of her father forced him to observe the proprieties. She was enthralled by the play, face alight and hands clasped together in excited pleasure. *She has forgotten that I exist*, he thought wryly. Then she took her eyes from the stage and looked across at him with a smile so radiant that his heart almost stopped. The doubts that had plagued him momentarily disappeared. He had done the right thing. He smiled back at her and a wave of emotion rippled towards him.

As if sensing a disturbance in the air, her father shifted his position, rearranging the red velvet cushions better to support his back, for this latter part of the evening was proving something of a trial and he was barely managing to keep his eyes open. When the curtain came down for a short interval he was more than willing to stretch his legs alongside his host in the galleries behind the auditorium. Domino declined the offer to accompany them, realising her lover intended to use the opportunity to advance his acquaintance with the man he hoped to make his father-in-law. Instead she set herself to study her theatre programme.

She was not long to be left in peace. Almost as soon as the door closed behind Joshua, it opened again to reveal a female figure rustling forwards in stiff taffetas and emanating a powerful, musky perfume. Domino looked up in surprise.

'My dear,' the duchess cooed, 'forgive me for disturbing you, but I was sure you would not mind. It's high time we renewed our acquaintance.'

With Joshua's warning ringing in her ears, Domino smiled politely, but said nothing. She would like to believe Charlotte innocent of plotting against her, but common sense told her otherwise. Joshua had made clear to this woman that he wanted nothing more to do with her. At the same time he had also made clear that he wanted a great deal to do with Domino. That was hardly conducive to friendship.

'I haven't spoken to you for such a long time,' the older woman mouthed, echoing the girl's thoughts. 'We seem to have become almost estranged, but that is certainly not my wish.'

She slid smoothly into one of the vacated chairs and continued to flatter.

'You look so beautiful tonight, my dear, so young and vital, it makes me feel almost sad.'

Domino closed her ears. Did the duchess really think her compliments would renew trust?

'It is such a shame.'

This time the words penetrated and the young woman became alert.

'A shame?'

'Yes, my dear, a dreadful shame. That's why I am here, you see.'

'I am afraid I don't, Your Grace.' She felt a gnawing anxiety begin to take hold.

'Charlotte, my dear, do call me Charlotte. We know each other better than to stand on ceremony, I hope.'

Domino was silent. Whatever Charlotte had to say, she was not going to help her.

'Yes, a shame,' the duchess repeated meditatively, 'but you are still very young and I am certain that you will rise above these problems.'

Domino could not stop her brow furrowing. The cat-and-mouse game the duchess was playing was beginning to find its mark.

'If I did not think you would recover easily,' the woman continued silkily, 'I would say nothing, even though I feel you are entitled to know what might be vital for your future happiness.'

The duchess's voice had assumed the cloying sweetness that always made Domino feel slightly sick. She sat mute, perched rigidly on her chair, and waited for whatever blow might fall.

'Of course, it may not *be* a problem,' the older woman was saying. 'The man may mean nothing to you. But I cannot take that chance. You are too precious!'

If only Joshua and her father would open the door this moment and put an end to this dreadful interview.

'If you care nothing for him, then all will be well, but otherwise…' The duchess allowed her voice to fall away in mock concern.

'Who are we talking about?' Domino managed, barely above a whisper. As if she did not know.

'Who? Why, Mr Marchmain, naturally.'

'And why should that interest me?'

'Would it be foolish to point out that you are here this evening with him?' Charlotte queried archly.

'I am here with my father. We are both Mr Marchmain's guests.'

'How very civilised. I should not disturb what is so obviously a delightful evening.' And she got up to leave, her skirts rustling noisily behind her.

Domino wanted to scream, *What is it? What do you know that is so bad?*, but she managed to maintain a posture of indifference. The duchess's hand was on the door handle when she turned back to face her quarry.

'I understand that you have a dear friend who now lives in Cornwall—or perhaps we should say a *former* dear friend.'

Christabel? What on earth did Christabel have to do with anything? Her mind was skittering in confusion, but she willed herself to maintain an impassive face.

'Her name is Christabel Tallis, although she is now a Veryan. But of course, you know her name,' Charlotte purred, 'after all, how many dear friends would you have in Cornwall?'

'What of Lady Veryan?'

'An extraordinarily beautiful woman, I believe, and one with an unusual past. A little colourful, shall we say?'

'I fail to see what such tittle-tattle has to do with me.' Domino's voice was glacial. Whatever this woman was engaged in, it was tawdry.

'Let us see, shall we?' Charlotte Severn let go of the door handle and walked back a few paces into the room. She looked Domino in the eyes and a derisive smile lit her face.

'When Christabel Tallis was engaged to the man who is now her husband, she allowed herself to go just a little astray.' And the duchess drew out the 'little' in a mocking fashion. 'And who could blame her, faced with so particularly charming a temptation? Thank goodness it ended well. But the man who enticed the ravishing Christabel from her fiancé and who—I blush to mention this in a young girl's hearing—who seduced her and then left her amid a mountain of scandal, was the man you have made your particular friend. In fact, *our* particular friend: Mr Joshua Marchmain.'

It seemed that the theatre walls were closing in on Domino; the ceiling hovered lower, its beams heavy and threatening; crystal chandeliers rocked and the wall sconces with their bright, bright gas jets ripped themselves adrift from their moorings and crashed down on her. A huge weight seemed to be breaking her body in two. Yet she knew she must respond to this wicked woman. After what seemed an age she managed to speak, although how she never knew. She kept her face blank and her voice steady by sheer overpowering force of will.

'You are misinformed, Your Grace. Mr Marchmain is not a particular friend of mine. The tale you tell is indeed sad, but is of no interest to me.'

'I am delighted to hear it,' the duchess returned and, with one last false smile of condolence, whisked herself through the door.

Domino hardly realised her visitor had left. She was staring into an abyss, a black nothingness. She felt herself hardly able to breathe. She had to get away. She had to get out of this place. She jumped to her feet, upsetting the delicate gold chair, and stumbled out into the gallery. Her father and Joshua were making their way back to the box, ready to resume their seats. She saw, but didn't see their startled expressions; she was looking through them, falling down into a dark and endless void. She had to get away, get away, get away.

'Domino?' Her father approached her uncertainly.

But she rushed past him along the gallery, down the sweeping staircase and out of the front door. Carriages had not yet been called for and New Road lay peaceful in its solitude. A moon rode high in the sky, only occasionally obscured by tattered fragments of cloud. She looked on the scene blindly; the world no longer existed. In the ghostly silver light she ran for shelter like a frightened mouse. Marine Parade was reached in minutes and a surprised Marston summoned to the door. Not a word did he get from his young mistress. At the sounds of arrival, Carmela appeared from the drawing room, her embroidery still in her hand. She called something to Domino, but Domino neither saw nor heard. Up the stairs, past a dozing Flora on the landing, and finally to sanctuary. Only now could she rest, here at the bottom of this dark, dark pit that had swallowed her whole.

She fell on the bed, dry eyed, too stricken to cry.

How long she lay there she had no idea, minutes perhaps, hours even, before Alfredo's anxious face appeared in the doorway.

'*Querida*, what on earth is the matter?'

'I am sorry, Papa,' she whispered hoarsely, 'I felt most unwell and had to get home.'

'But why did you not tell us? Mr Marchmain would have ordered the carriage immediately. He is most worried about you.'

She could no longer bear even to hear his name.

'Papa, you will forgive me, but I feel too ill to talk this evening.'

Her father looked stern. 'How can this be? We left you perfectly well and out of nowhere you become so ill that you behave with the utmost discourtesy. I demand to know what has happened, Domino.'

'Nothing has happened, Papa. I am simply unwell,' she repeated in a failing voice.

'But to rush off like that—what will Mr Marchmain think?'

'I no longer care what Mr Marchmain thinks,' she said in a much stronger voice.

Alfredo's face expressed surprise, but he did not press the matter.

'At least allow Flora to help you undress.'

She agreed, hoping that, in doing so, she would be left alone. But the misery of the evening was not yet finished, for her father was the bearer of more unwelcome news.

'Did Carmela tell you that while we were at dinner, Lady Veryan arrived?'

'Lady Veryan?' Her voice shook.

'The friend you very much wished to see.' Her father's tone was unusually tart.

'But she is not due for another day.'

'That, too, was my understanding. It seems she decided not to stay in Winchester overnight, but continued instead to Brighton. Her father is already on his return to Cornwall; he did not wish to be long away, I believe.'

'Christabel is here!' and her voice broke with wretchedness.

'She is, my dear, so whatever ails you, it would be wise to find a swift cure. Carmela reports that Lady Veryan was tired from the journey and decided on an early bedtime. But she is looking forward to seeing you on the morrow, for she has a good deal to tell you and is sure that you will have much to tell her.'

And with that, her father called Flora into the room with instructions to help her young mistress into bed immediately. Domino was hardly aware of the maid's presence and mechanically permitted herself to be undressed and slipped between the covers. Left alone, she lay prone, her newly brushed hair streaming wildly across the pillow and her eyes staring blankly ahead. Where once there had been colour and light and the sounds of pleasure, now there was nothing. She felt nothing, her whole body had retreated into a pitiless limbo. She pinched herself and it did not hurt. That should scare her, but it didn't. Nothing scared her, nothing touched her, nothing ever could touch her again. Three years ago she had lost the man she loved to Christabel. It did not matter that Richard had never returned her love, did not matter that her love now seemed juvenile. It had hurt so badly then, cut her into little tiny ribbons until she had thought she would never be whole again. But over the years she had remade herself. And finally she had found the man she thought would fill the rest of her life. Now he was gone also: another love lost, but this so much greater than the first. This time she would not be able to stick the pieces together again. And how had she lost this man, this man who was to crown her life with romance and adventure and love and joy? Why, she had lost him to the very same woman, indirectly perhaps, but indisputably she had lost her love to Christabel once more. Such bitter irony!

Chapter Eight

Flora brought her the message while she was still abed. Her chocolate had grown cold on the bedside chest and the hot water for bathing had cooled in its basin. But she had not stirred. She had no wish ever to leave this room, no wish ever to move again.

'I think you should read it, Miss Domino,' the maid dared to suggest, aware that something dreadful had happened, but able only to guess at what the cause might be. It was a man, she reasoned, no doubt the same man that had been sniffing around her mistress for weeks. The one who had stopped them in their tracks just a few days ago, then come to the house very early this morning and personally handed her an envelope with strict instructions to place it only in her mistress's hands. She tried again, this time folding the envelope into Domino's listless grasp. Then she withdrew, sighing heavily to herself.

Left alone, Domino glanced indifferently at the message. She knew its author and she knew that she did not want to read it. But something still impelled her to rip the seal open and scan the few words within.

It was brief and to the point.

Whatever has gone wrong, I need to know, he wrote. *I hope you will feel able to tell me in person. I shall be by the groyne directly opposite your house at noon today. Please meet me there.*

It was signed simply *Joshua*.

He had named the very place they had first met all those months ago. Two months ago, to be precise—was it only that long? She felt that she had lived a lifetime since then. She recalled her feelings at their very first meeting. There had been an undercurrent of excitement, but also a distinct unease. He had been mockingly persistent, caring little for her discomfort. Surely that had been an omen for the future. He'd behaved in much the same fashion more than once. But deceiving her so wretchedly about his past was of a different order; he had destroyed her trust, her belief in herself, and left her vulnerable to the cruelties of a woman like Charlotte Severn.

But it made no sense. Hadn't Joshua also rescued her from the same woman's clutches, protecting her, defeating attempts to wound her, not just once, but again and again? He'd warned her to be on her guard against the duchess and Moncaster. So why, last night, had she not been? Why had she chosen to believe Charlotte? The frailest whisper of hope began to bloom. The duchess had lied before and proved unscrupulous, even malicious. The tale she'd told at the theatre could be another attempt to destroy, a fabrication concocted out of desperation when every other of her despicable plans had failed. The more Domino thought of it, the more likely it seemed. It was such a far-fetched story.

True, Joshua had lived a rakish existence—she was well aware of that—and she knew that as a young man he'd failed his friends badly and been exiled for his wrongdoing. But it would have to be the most diabolical coincidence that the friends were Christabel and Richard. Why had she been so willing to believe the worst? Was it that her earlier unease had never quite disappeared, that she'd never quite believed the rake had reformed? Or, more honestly, that she'd been the woman who could reform him? When he'd asked her to marry him, she had thought at first it was a cruel joke, then she'd settled on it being a miracle. She had not believed she was that special. After all, Richard had rejected her—why should this man, with even more worldly experience, choose to change his life completely because of her?

She had been foolish! Joshua's feelings were genuine; he loved her. Of all the women he'd known, he had asked *her* to marry him. She *was* special! And what had been his reward? To have his chosen bride believe a scurrilous story from a corrupt woman.

She started out of bed. She could see now that she had behaved very stupidly. She must go to him and make an immediate apology. Their meeting would give him the chance to deny the duchess's evil words; his answer to a simple question would set everything to rights. She pulled the first gown she could find from the wardrobe and dressed quickly, her face a pale oval against the gown's drab olive.

Slipping unseen from the house, she made her way swiftly towards the groyne. The sky was overcast, all trace of summer having for the moment disappeared, but only a light breeze blew and the water was unnaturally calm. She clambered down the sea-stained steps to the lower promenade. Then she saw him. Suddenly, out of nowhere, the night's harrowing events were back and landing with a sickening thud. Her stomach was aflutter, but she continued to pick her way stone by stone across the beach until she stood only a few feet from him.

'I cannot stay long.' It was nerves that made her brusque. The certainty she'd felt minutes ago in her bedroom was deserting her.

'Then I must be grateful for the few minutes you can vouchsafe me.' He spoke lightly, but his eyes wore a puzzled expression.

It was better to ask the dreadful question at once, she decided; then they could clear the air and be comfortable together once more. But her voice when she spoke was hesitant. 'Please accept my apologies for the way I behaved last night. I heard a disturbing story and it upset me greatly.'

He was still looking baffled. 'Last night, Domino, we were at the play and enjoying ourselves, as I thought. What could possibly have disturbed you?'

'The Duchess of Severn,' she said baldly. 'She visited in the interval.'

'Dear Charlotte—and what now have I to thank her for?'

His tone was so much one of levity that Domino was convinced in that instant that the duchess's spiteful story had been a complete falsehood. There was not the smallest shadow of guilt in Joshua's face. Instead he was smiling gently at her, waiting it seemed for her to come to her senses.

In the face of his good nature, she was finding it difficult to continue and her words came haltingly. 'The tale she told was most dreadful—and it concerned you.'

His look was still one of bland enquiry. She tried again, her words so quiet they were hardly audible against the soft swell of the tide. 'Some years ago, she said, you seduced a young woman on the eve of her wedding; you were the bridegroom's best friend.'

She was watching him closely as she spoke and saw his eyes narrow. A terrible premonition began to burn through her that he knew the rest of the story and she turned as white as the chalk cliffs that rose in the distance.

'Say something, Joshua,' she pleaded. 'Say that it is not true—surely it is not true.'

'Alas, my dear, for once the duchess is telling the truth. But it is an old story and I wonder how she came by it. No doubt Moncaster could tell us.'

She was speechless. Her rekindled trust in his innocence shattered in one savage stab. She had mentioned no names, but still she knew that her worst fears were confirmed. He had confessed, yet he was shaking it off as if it meant nothing. The vision she held of him crumbled into dust. He was no longer the man she had thought him. A different person stood in his place, a person that she could neither trust nor revere. She felt the dark abyss opening again beneath her feet, but this time she did not turn tail and run.

Gathering every ounce of resolution she possessed, and with a voice hardly wavering, she said, 'Mr Marchmain, I regret that I cannot marry you.'

'What! What are you saying?

'I cannot marry you,' she repeated dully.

'This is a nonsense, Domino. Last night we were to wed. Last night you were eager to persuade your father that I would make an excellent husband!'

'Last night I also learned of your past. And it is a past I cannot forgive.'

His head was shaking in disbelief and he began to stride back and forth, crunching the pebbles beneath his boots. After some moments he came to a halt in front of her, his gold-flecked eyes keen and lacking any trace of his usual lazy amusement.

'My dear', and he made to move towards her, but she stepped nimbly to one side, evading his touch.

His expression clouded, but he continued calmly, 'My dear, you knew of my past, if not its details. I am too old and have wandered the world too long not to have a history. But that's all done with. You are my only concern now, the only woman I have need or desire for.'

'This has not to do with *your* desires, but everything to do with mine. I cannot marry a man for whom I feel contempt.'

It was a most terrible thing to say. Had she meant it? She must have done, since the blurted words had come instinctively, involuntarily. They had their effect. Joshua appeared thoroughly shaken. His face darkened into a scowl and when he spoke his voice was edged with anger.

'I am not proud of my past. But, tell me, what exactly has earned your contempt?'

'The people you hurt were dear friends of mine, and you hurt them not by accident, but purely to pursue your own pleasure. Her name was Christabel Tallis and the man she was to marry was…was Richard Veryan.' Her face coloured with a suddenness that caught his attention.

'Christabel and Richard Veryan!' His brow furrowed for a moment, then she saw a dawning comprehension. 'And was Richard the man you loved so hopelessly?'

He was mocking her, but she ignored the provocation. 'It matters not. He was your friend and you betrayed him. Then you betrayed Christabel.'

'I repeat, I am not proud of my actions. But it happened a long time ago when I was a shallow youth. You said yourself that I should be forgiven for crimes committed as a stripling. I distinctly remember that you were unhappy with my brother for the very conduct you now seem intent on emulating.'

'That was before I knew what you had done.'

'You knew what I had done. I told you the day we met on the Level.'

His jaw jutted pugnaciously; he was damned if he would let her rewrite their conversation to suit her own quixotic ends.

She was beginning to unravel, but she pulled her defences together and fought back. 'You told me that you had failed friends. I did not know then the manner of that failure, or that it was my own very dear friends that you had treated so wickedly.'

'So your moral code is relative, is it? My actions are forgivable, but only if the wounded parties are people for whom you have no care.'

She realised he was right and that her stance was illogical. But it did not change the way she felt. She had known too well the damage done to Richard, known how helpless she had felt to comfort him.

Her long silence seemed to encourage him and he softened his voice in persuasion. 'Christabel and Richard are happy now, are they not? Isn't that what is important? It was a bad deed, but good eventually came of it.'

She had no intention of disclosing that Christabel was staying just a few yards away and that a great deal of good had eventually come of it. But only eventually; so much unhappiness and suffering had gone before.

'If they are happy, can we not be happy, too?' he was asking.

That was simple to answer. 'I can never be happy with a man who would deliberately cause such heartache.'

'You refine too much on what is long past.'

'How can you dismiss your wrongdoing so casually?'

'I don't. I am well aware of my sin. But I was a stupid boy—and now I have grown up. My life is different.'

'Precisely how different?'

She was regaining courage. If he had shown true remorse, pleaded with her, asked for forgiveness, she might have found it impossible to resist. But he had done none of those things. Instead he continued to be at his most mocking and combative.

'Have we returned to my improper life and my fearsome reputation? Now let me see… You haven't exactly baulked at consorting with a rake these past weeks. And, if I were being ungallant, I might say more than consorting.'

'How dare you!'

'And nor did Christabel mind,' he continued inexorably. 'Don't forget it takes two. What happened was not my fault alone.'

'You should have known better and acted better.'

'I agree, but then so should she. It was she, after all, who was betrothed.'

Domino made to turn, hitching the skirts of her gown clear of the uneven strand. 'I have no wish to continue arguing.' And in the quietest voice yet, she added, 'It is too painful.'

He seized on that one small phrase. 'That would suggest that you still care for me.'

She said nothing and he pressed her, 'If that is indeed so, why are you doing this?'

'I have told you.'

Exasperated, he burst out, 'Are you sure it's not because you still love Richard Veryan and wish to punish me for the fact that he married elsewhere?'

It was an unkind stab. She turned back to him and, in a voice that wobbled only slightly, made her final adieu. 'I have nothing more to say, Mr Marchmain. This is goodbye. Please do not attempt to contact me again.'

And with that she was gone.

Left alone, Joshua stared sightlessly out to sea. He had wanted to make amends to Domino for disrupting her life so badly and had offered her his hand in the best of faith. It had not been easy to breach the detachment that had protected him for so long, but he had done it. Only for her to walk away on a whim; it could only be a whim. It was absurd, he thought. He was no angel. He had behaved badly, once very badly, but that had been years ago, years when he'd been barely more than a fledgling and had understood nothing, neither who he was nor what he wanted. Surely youth offered some mitigation. They had been years of heady excitement, of feeling that every day as he ventured forth he could renew his world. He had certainly done so when he met Christabel. Renewed her world and Richard Veryan's, too.

Fresh faced and inexperienced, he and Richard had launched themselves on the town in the very same month and become firm friends. Then one summer Richard had left for his home in Cornwall and returned with Christabel on his arm. A single look and he'd fallen immediately under her spell. She had been so alluring and so eager to seize life, so tempting and so easily tempted. He had cast caution to the winds, ignoring every demand of friendship. There had been nothing deliberate about the passion that had flamed between them; it had simply been too wild to control. That was no excuse, but why couldn't Domino forgive such an old tragedy?

He guessed at the answer and his rancour began slowly to subside, dissolving into the sea air and on the cry of the gulls. He had destroyed her belief in him. Only very slowly had she grown to trust. At the outset she had been mightily suspicious, writing him down as a dangerous individual and one to avoid. But she'd been unable to avoid him. He had rescued her from her follies, one after another, and gradually she had begun to see him for the man he was, to see beyond the label society bestowed. And it turned out that the man she saw fitted her so perfectly that she had tumbled into love with him. Now the image she held had been shattered by a moment of careless talk.

But how careless? he wondered savagely. It had all the marks of spite, the marks of the vendetta waged by Charlotte Severn since first she became aware of the girl as a rival. The woman was stupid as well as vindictive. How could she not realise that the affair between them had ended months ago, that the plots she had been busily engineering against Domino were pointless? He would never return to her.

But she had wreaked all the damage she could possibly desire. It mattered not to Domino that Christabel and Richard were content. He had caused them pain, and there could be no defence for that. But if they had suffered, so, by God, had he. For years he had wandered Europe, seeking the most sublime art it could offer. He had taken solace in the beauty he'd found and tried to blot out the ugliness he'd known. Women had come and gone, his physical needs satisfied, but always there was beauty to strive for, a beauty just beyond his reach. He had begun to paint in the hope that here at least he would find what he so desperately desired. The seascapes he painted, one after another, the endless seascapes with their limitless horizons, spoke of escape from the unlovely life he led and the person he had become. But there could be no escape. For a brief moment, rescuing Domino from her plight had offered the prospect of a new wholeness, but that too had turned to ashes. He was not made for beauty. His decision to marry had been foolish, a transgression duly punished. The doubts that had bombarded him ever since he'd proposed were justified. He took a deep breath and began the climb to the promenade. He would live as he'd always done, he thought grimly, and go to hell in his own way. For years he had been doing just that and with some success.

'Mr Marchmain and I have bid each other farewell, Papa.'

Domino stood just inside Señor de Silva's office, ready to flee the room as soon as she was able. She was humiliated by this confession, for she was telling her father that she no longer wished to marry the man she had been mad to have only a matter of hours ago. This was an interview she wanted to be over before it had begun.

'Farewell? What do you mean, *querida*?'

'We have decided that, after all, we do not suit,' she said as composedly as she could, silently praying that there would be no questions.

'And are you quite sure of this, my dear?'

'Yes, quite sure.' But her heart was breaking. Surely any moment her father must hear the pieces falling to the ground.

'You do not wish to marry him?' Alfredo repeated, almost to himself.

He felt suddenly a good deal lighter. Domino's determination to wed a man he considered grossly unsuitable had shocked him. It had been a struggle to appear complaisant, not wanting to be alienated from his only child. But now it looked as though her plans had come to nought. He would not have to suffer Joshua Marchmain as a son-in-law.

'No, Papa, I no longer wish to marry him.' *Please*, she begged inwardly, *please don't ask me why*. Then thinking she should offer a little more to her long-suffering parent, she added, 'I am sorry to have caused confusion.'

'No confusion, my dear. You are right to draw back if you have doubts. And it seems that you do.'

She nodded miserably. Her father put his arms around her and gave her a comforting hug.

'You have made a sensible decision,' he said consolingly. 'And now you must put it out of your mind and think what is to be done. Have you had a chance to consider?'

She had no idea what her life was to be. How very different to just a day ago! But she must not upset her father and, freeing herself from his arms, she fixed him with what she hoped was an unwavering look.

'Lady Veryan will soon be travelling to London to consult a practitioner in Harley Street. She is wishful that I accompany her before I return to Spain.' She congratulated herself that she spoke with hardly a tremor.

'As her friend, that would naturally be a kind thought.'

'Then I will do so, but she is to know nothing of this, Papa', and she gestured vaguely in the air. 'I mean nothing about Mr Marchmain. It cannot interest her and may cause her distress if she feels that I am upset.'

'I will say nothing, you have my word. And Carmela knows nothing, so your friend will stay in ignorance of these doings. But *are* you upset, *querida*? You seem very calm.'

'I know that I am doing the right thing, Papa,' she answered obliquely. He must never know that her heart was crushed.

Her stay with Christabel in London would be brief. Beyond that, she hardly dared to think. Once her father was back in the capital, he would no longer need her services, for Lady Blythe would once more act his hostess while he remained in London. And Domino had no desire to linger in a place where at any moment she might come upon the man she most wished to avoid. She supposed that she would return to Spain—where else could she go?—but it would not be to marry as her aunts wished. Of that she was sure. After Richard she had been indifferent, ready to marry whatever husband they chose. But that was no longer possible. The sorrows of youthful infatuation had given way to an all-consuming passion, but for a man she could not wed. And if she could not wed him, she would wed no other. Always in the deepest recesses of her heart there would be this pain: sharp, nagging, insistent. A pain with Joshua's name written on it.

Her father was speaking again. 'I shall not be far behind you in leaving Brighton, my dear. But there is an important event to consider before we are finished here—the Regent's birthday celebrations. I am sure you won't have forgotten that the palace is throwing a grand dinner and ball in the Prince's honour.'

The gentle reminder left her dazed. Her mind shrank from the idea of ever setting foot in the Pavilion again.

'Friday's celebrations are to be the most sumptuous occasion, I believe, and we have been greatly honoured by an invitation. It is fortunate that you will not have left for London by then.'

Surely she might be spared this further anguish. But, no, her father clearly expected her to accompany him. And she owed him that at least, for she had caused him nothing but trouble this summer. If he had an inkling of her true feelings, he would not wish her to go within a mile of the palace. But he saw a composed face and heard a calm voice and suspected nothing.

'I shall be pleased to attend, Papa.' Her voice seemed to her to travel from a great distance.

'Then it is settled. After the ball you and Carmela will accompany Lady Veryan to London. From there, you can journey with your cousin on to Spain. I shall make sure that I am back in town in time to see you both safely on your way.'

Her father began idly to leaf through the sheaf of messages on his desk and she judged it time to go. The interview was thankfully at an end, but she still had to face the forthcoming encounter with Christabel. That would be far more difficult to negotiate, for women had much sharper antennae. She must prevent her friend from tuning into any hint of the distress that was tearing at her soul.

She was to be allowed a few more hours of grace. Christabel had endured a disturbed night and did not appear in the drawing room until almost noon, and, when she did, Carmela was in attendance. From the moment Lady Veryan had arrived at Marine Parade, Carmela had taken the expectant mother under her wing. Delighted to have a charge to coddle, she was busy now fussing over the likely need for shawls or slippers or footstools. She seemed intent on wrapping their guest in thick coils of cotton wool.

'You will never go to the parade, Lady Veryan,' she said in a shocked tone when Christabel mentioned that she was looking forward to visiting the Level that afternoon to view the Regent's birthday parade.

'I don't see why not.' Christabel's musical voice held

a note of amusement. 'I cannot sit indoors forever and I'm quite sure that my young friend will be looking forward to the spectacle as much as I.'

Her young friend, coming into the drawing room at that moment, felt herself grow heavy with despair. She had counted on hiding herself away until Friday when she must endure the Regent's party before a final escape to obscurity. It was not to be.

'You would like to go, Domino, wouldn't you?' Christabel asked coaxingly.

'Naturally we must not miss such a display,' she returned bravely. 'We can stroll to the Level after luncheon. I believe the ceremonial marching is to begin around two o' clock.'

They arrived well before that hour, hoping to secure a good vantage point. Alarmed at Lady Veryan's imprudence, Carmela had insisted on accompanying them. The dowdiness of her dress contrasted almost jestingly with the flamboyant colour that was every-where around. Her severe distaste for ostentation was well known and Domino watched in surprise at her cousin's interest in the preparations that signalled a beginning to the military display.

The square on which the soldiers were to parade was the Regent's old cricket ground, now transformed by a hard covering underfoot and decorated with fluttering flags and bunting of every shape and hue. Crowds were gathered along the intersecting pathways leading to the marching square and a tiered stand had been built at one end for the more genteel visitors. The little party made their way to seats on the front row from where they would enjoy an uninterrupted view. The chattering throng and a military band already playing with gusto added to the sense of anticipation. The sun was bright for a late August afternoon, but a cooling breeze blew inland from the sea and the striped canvas awnings, which had been erected over the stand, stood ready to protect delicate complexions.

Christabel looked around her in appreciation. She had been living retired from *ton* society so long that she had forgotten the exciting hum of people intent on pleasure. Glancing right and left at the fashionable silks and satins, the poke bonnets, the little pieces of gauze and tinsel masquerading as hats, she began to feel a complete dowd. Life in the countryside was wonderful but it had its drawbacks, particularly for one who had long been considered a diamond of the first water. She must make sure that she returned from London with new gowns as well as medical advice. She need not have worried. Whatever she wore, she was instantly the centre of attention. Her flame-haired beauty ensured that. A number of people recognised her and she nodded in response. A woman three rows back craned her neck to see who accompanied Domino de Silva.

The music made it impossible for anyone to be heard and nobody sitting nearby attempted to strike up a conversation. Domino was thankful since she had lost all desire to socialise. Her anxious scan of the stand revealed no sign of Joshua and she could only hope that his role in planning the event would remain backstage. He must have deliberately absented himself, guessing that she would attend. He would not know of Christabel's presence, of course. And it must stay that way. The thought of a meeting between the two was unbearable.

'Isn't that the Dragoons?'

Christabel leant forwards in eagerness as the band struck up an altogether more martial note. The Light Dragoons had arrived, decked in their resplendent ceremonial uniform. They marched proudly towards the square, a thousand limbs moving as one. A drum major strode at their head, beating time with his golden mace. Their show of military prowess began with a display of intricate marching patterns, dizzying in their complexity and breath taking in their co-ordination. There followed individual feats of daring and skill until finally the stupendous conclusion of a mock battle complete with enemy infantry and a troop of cavalry.

An hour had slipped easily by before the last hurrahs of the crowd were sounding and they made ready to leave.

'Domino, my dear. How agreeable!' A perfumed figure crossed their path. 'I forgot to ask when we last met if you intended to come to the parade, but somehow I knew the uniforms would bring you!'

Carmela glared at the newcomer and Domino bowed stiffly. 'As you see, Your Grace, we have been enjoying the display.'

Slightly in the rear of the group, Christabel caught up with them at that moment. She smiled shyly at the duchess and Domino had no alternative but to introduce her.

'Your Grace, this is Lady Veryan.'

'Veryan?' the duchess queried faintly.

'That's right,' Christabel said warmly, 'Christabel

Veryan. How do you do? Was that not a most magnificent spectacle?'

Bewilderment, mortification, naked fury flitted across the duchess's face in rapid succession. But her rigid training stood her in good stead and a mask of indifference slipped into place as she responded levelly, 'The Dragoons can always be relied on for a superb exhibition. The dear Prince dotes on them, you know.'

Christabel marked the condescension but as the woman appeared to be a friend of Domino's, she felt it incumbent to be courteous. Her two companions seemed to have been struck temporarily dumb. She waded gallantly into a smooth stream of small talk. The duchess ably played her part in the charade, automatic responses issuing with ease from her practised lips, while all the time questions laid siege to her mind. Why was Lady Veryan here? Surely after what she had divulged to Domino de Silva, this woman should not be her friend! Something had gone badly wrong. She broke off what she was saying and looked wildly around. She needed to see Leo Moncaster urgently.

Christabel was nonplussed by the older woman's evident disquiet but hoping the duchess would soon recover her composure, she persevered. 'I spend my life in the depths of the Cornish countryside, so you see today has been a most wonderful treat.'

Charlotte Severn pulled herself together with enormous effort. 'And what brings you to Brighton at this time, Lady Veryan?'

A last hope had flashed into her mind and she was clinging to it. Christabel had come to Brighton to commiserate with Domino, to reiterate that she too had suffered from Joshua Marchmain's iniquity. She had come to tell her that the man was bad through and through and that Domino was right to separate from him forever.

'I'm on my way to London,' Christabel said happily. 'My husband insists that I see someone in Harley Street, though goodness knows why. Everything…' and she patted her expanding stomach lovingly '…seems to be progressing just as it should.'

The duchess's hope flickered and died. 'And will you also be travelling to town, Domino?'

Desperate to appear unperturbed, Domino found her voice at last. 'I will, Your Grace. Lady Veryan's arrival is timely. We can enjoy at least a sennight together in London before she returns to Cornwall.'

The duchess digested this. 'Then you are staying in England?

'I imagine so,' she lied.

'And not returning to Spain?'

'Not for the moment. My father has need of me still. And I am enjoying my stay greatly and would be loth to cut it short.'

She had the satisfaction of seeing the duchess blanch. Let her think that she and Joshua were still together, that the return to London signalled a deepening of their relationship. This spiteful woman had recounted her poisonous news for one reason only. She had wanted to ensure their separation. She had succeeded but Domino would never give her the pleasure of knowing it. Let her feel chagrin that her plan had not worked, let her feel anguish that Joshua would never return to her. In time of course he would. That was inevitable but every moment of pain inflicted on this malevolent creature was worthwhile. The strength of her own venom shocked her. If she could have heard the duchess's embittered conversation just a few hours later, she would have prized the small triumph.

'It hasn't worked!'

Leo Moncaster looked ruminatively at the furious woman opposite him.

'Why is that, my sweet one?' he asked drily.

'Do not call me that.'

'I cannot think why I did.' He glanced at the sour expression distorting her face. 'Anything less sweet would be hard to imagine.'

'It hasn't worked,' she spelt out angrily. 'Christabel Veryan is here in Brighton and quite clearly friends with that chit. The girl has no shame. Wasn't she supposed to be desperately in love with Richard Veryan? Yet she is happy to consort with the woman who broke his heart and unconcerned that Joshua was the willing accomplice. She is shallow beyond belief.'

Moncaster raised his eyebrows and seemed about to comment, but evidently decided otherwise.

'I know what you are about to say. Don't! I may be shallow, but at least I am consistent. The girl is happy to entertain Lady Veryan in her own home; more than that, she's happy to accompany her to London in a few days' time. What would you wager on her being equally happy to see Marchmain there, whatever ill she knows of him?'

'Let it go, Charlotte,' he advised her roughly. 'I would like to punish the girl as much as you, but we have failed at every attempt and done nothing but make ourselves look foolish. It might be as well simply to let her disappear to Spain.'

'That's because you haven't heard the best of it. The chit is staying in England!'

Moncaster's brows knit together in annoyance, but he spoke calmly. 'So what do you want to do?' His equanimity infuriated the duchess.

'Do! Do! I want to get rid of the girl forever. You know what I want to do.'

'Then we must hazard a final throw of the dice, my dear. No hesitation this time. No misgivings.'

'You are right. I have been too kind to her.'

Lord Moncaster grimaced, but the duchess went on. 'Far too kind. I have allowed her to flourish instead of nipping the life out of her from the very outset. We will do what we've had in mind for weeks. Are you ready?'

'I can be ready at any time, dear lady.'

'Good. Then the Regent's ball, the day after tomorrow?'

He took her hand and slowly brought it to his lips. 'A perfect occasion, I feel. It will prove a splendid finale to an overlong drama.'

Chapter Nine

By the time they wended their way back to Marine Parade, Christabel was feeling very tired. It had been an entertaining afternoon, but a long walk and prolonged sitting had taken their toll. Once in Domino's own small parlour, she cast off her bonnet and sank gratefully into a comfortable chair.

'You should rest in bed, Lady Veryan,' Carmela scolded. 'It cannot be good for the baby to be forever on your feet.'

'Thank you for your concern,' she replied sweetly, 'but I can rest here.' She reached for a cup from the tray the housekeeper had just brought in. 'The tea is sure to restore my energy.'

'But, Lady Veryan…'

'I will stay.' Her voice was firm. 'Such a delightful room—it must catch every glimmer of sunlight and its view of the sea is unmatched. I can understand why you chose this for your own, Domino. And it's perfect for a comfortable coze.'

The last thing Domino wanted was a comfortable

coze. She hoped that Carmela would remain and put paid to any chance of intimate talk, but her cousin rose almost immediately and announced that in that case she had many things to do, and all of them urgent.

'This afternoon has been wonderful,' Christabel began gently as the door shut, 'and thank you for taking me. It felt strange to be among a fashionable crowd again, but thoroughly enjoyable. Not that I would ever forsake Cornwall!'

'I don't imagine you would. Tell me about life at the Abbey.'

If Domino had hoped to deflect her friend from the personal, she hoped in vain.

'The best thing about this afternoon was sharing it with you. I've been waiting a long time for you to come to Madron and discover the house for yourself.'

'The moment never seemed right,' her young companion hedged. 'My aunts would not have taken kindly to my travelling abroad again. They only permitted my return to England because Papa needed help.' A small white lie would not hurt, she thought.

'Perhaps once the baby is born you will feel able to make the journey to Cornwall.'

Domino smiled non-commitally. By then she would be back in Madrid and there would be little opportunity to venture far.

'We never had time to know each other really well,' Christabel was musing. 'But I'm sure if we had, we would have become the best of friends. One thing of which I *am* very sure—I have you to thank for my happiness.'

Her friend flushed and made haste to disclaim any such thing.

'My dear, yes. If it had not been for you, I might never have felt able to trust Richard. And with what result! We could not be happier together and this child will only bring us closer.'

Domino felt genuine pleasure. A few months ago, a few weeks ago even, her enjoyment would have been compromised by regret but that had melted like summer snow. She had a new and far heavier burden to bear.

'It's wonderful to see you so happy,' and she pressed Christabel's hand, 'but my role was very small—a silly letter only. You were always destined to be with Richard.'

'You made me see that and I cannot thank you enough. I did some foolish things but you made me realise that I could have a different future.'

The young girl swallowed hard, but said nothing.

'It seems that no matter how badly one has behaved,' Christabel continued thoughtfully, '—and I did behave badly—past events don't have to ruin the rest of one's life.'

There was again no response from her companion and Christabel paused and looked intently at the girl seated beside her. 'I hope you'll forgive me for saying this, my dear, but you have not been looking quite as carefree as I remember. I wonder—is there anything wrong?'

Danger leaped out in mile high letters. Domino knew that she must drive the conversation away from this treacherous ground.

'There's nothing wrong, I assure you. I'm just a little tired. Brighton is a town made for leisure and that can be hard work! This summer has been very busy.'

'I can imagine,' her friend said sympathetically.

'Wherever the Regent is in residence, there's unlikely to be a deal of tranquillity.'

She paused again, as if wondering whether or not she should say more. 'But *should* anything be causing you unease, Domino, my best advice would be to meet it bravely and then not look back.'

'There is nothing.'

'I'm glad to hear it. No doubt you are far too young to fall into anxiety.' She leaned back in her chair and gazed through the bow windows at the ruffled sea beyond. 'But, truth to tell, I was only your age when I managed to fall into a maelstrom of trouble that took years to resolve.'

Domino could hardly speak. If Christabel intended to confess her youthful folly, she did not want to hear. Or did she? There was a part of her that needed to know why this woman had abandoned an honourable man like Richard—the same part, perhaps, that needed to excuse her own all too easy fall into the arms of the same philanderer.

'How many years?' she heard herself ask in a constricted voice, though she knew the answer well.

'Six wasted years. I thought I could never forgive myself for what I'd done, nor forgive the man involved. But I was wrong.'

'How did you forgive?' Domino's throat was dry.

'I was foolishly naïve, on the town for the first time in my life. And so was he. We were both too young and heedless to bear the responsibility of our actions.'

Her words were almost an echo of those Domino had heard from Joshua himself.

'And you didn't blame the man?' she ventured. 'Should he not have taken responsibility?'

'But why? We were both to blame. In fact, I can thank him now. Until I met him I had taken Richard for granted. I was sleepwalking into marriage. A short-lived affair, for that was all it was, may have destroyed my betrothal but it made me realise that I had forsaken a deep, abiding love for a momentary passion, one that had no substance to it, no depth. If I were ever to meet that man again, I would shake him by the hand and thank him truly.'

Domino was shocked. How could Christabel speak so lightly of an event that had almost ruined her life and, even worse, almost ruined Richard's? Six wasted years, she'd said. But here she was exculpating Joshua and willing to share blame for the catastrophe, even grateful to him for showing her the true nature of her feelings!

Christabel put her teacup gently down on the table and rose to leave. 'Carmela may have been right,' she said softly, sensing that her words had in some way hit home. 'A rest in my room before dinner will refresh me. I will see you later, my dear', and she bent her graceful form towards her young friend and lightly kissed the top of her head.

Left alone, Domino wrestled with the conversation that had passed between them. A blissfully happy Christabel could afford to forgive the past, she thought churlishly. But it is *her* past to forgive, a small voice murmured, not yours. What have you to forgive? This sorry story took place when you were not much more than a child. Christabel is happy, Richard is happy. Why can't you be? But she knew she was confusing the symptom for the cause. And the real cause of her unhappiness was the fear that Joshua Marchmain was the rake everyone said he was, and that she could never trust him to be otherwise. For a moment she had believed him capable of changing. But how short that moment had been! Knowledge of the wicked path he had trodden six years ago had brought home to her the magnitude of his offences—his flagrant immorality, his uncaring selfishness—and had damned him in her eyes forever. Joshua had not changed, would never change, and if she gave herself to him, she would live a lifetime of heartache.

Fortune favoured her the next day when Carmela decided to forsake her household duties. It was her cousin who escorted Christabel on a shopping expedition to Bartholomews market and her cousin who sat with their visitor sewing and reading in the small parlour. Domino was able to disappear for long stretches of the day, citing the necessity of helping Flora to pack her wardrobe. It was a job that appeared to take an inordinate time but while she sorted muslins and silks she tried to keep her mind a determined blank. The grand dinner and ball at the Pavilion was one more trial to face, the final trial, and she needed to keep at bay the thoughts that constantly harried her.

When she met her friend later in the day, she greeted Christabel with guilty warmth, infusing her voice with as much geniality as she could muster.

'It's a great shame that you cannot come to the ball. Papa would have been happy to obtain a ticket for the dance, if not to the dinner.'

Her visitor gave a rueful grin. 'My dear, look at me, I am in no case for dancing. Carmela and I will go on very well at home, don't fret. But if I can be of any help in getting you ready for the grand event, send your maid to me. I shall not be sleeping—merely waiting in readiness for the call!'

Domino was not to need her friend's expertise. Since coming to Brighton Flora had improved as a lady's maid by leaps and bounds and tonight's grand occasion was to be the fitting climax of her apprenticeship.

When her mistress presented herself in the drawing room a few hours later, conversation stopped and her audience gazed wonderingly at her.

'Dear Domino, you look gorgeous!' Christabel was lavish in her praise.

Her father nodded, his chest seeming visibly to expand with pride. Even Carmela gave her a brisk smile of approval.

'You are sure that you're happy to stay home?'

Domino wanted only one answer to her question. If Christabel remained at Marine Parade there would be no chance of her meeting her former lover.

'I am very happy to. Carmela and I have planned a light supper together and then we intend to do a little sorting of baby clothes before an early bedtime. In my present condition, it makes for a perfect evening.'

'Far better than junketing with the most undesirable people,' Carmela could not resist saying.

'Unfortunately, cousin, we are forced to partake of a little junketing, but I promise I shall have Domino home well before midnight.' Alfredo's voice was cold and crisp as though he, too, wished to get the evening over as swiftly as possible.

Domino had not wanted to dress finely, but Flora had been adamant. This was to be the last grand event of the Brighton summer. In her maid's opinion it was the time to shine, the time to leave a splendid final impression. When she looked at her mistress that evening, Flora knew Domino would do just that. The gown of orange blossom crepe worn beneath a tunic of bespangled gossamer clung lovingly to the curves of her lissom young figure. A shawl of spider gauze covered her bare arms and on her feet she wore cream satin slippers ornamented with cream roses. A circlet of orange blossom was threaded through the glossy curls that cascaded gently around her face. She looked every inch a young princess on her way to a magnificent evening of pleasure. Only the pale face gave a glimpse of her true feelings.

As before, they approached the Pavilion through newly planted gardens and alighted from their carriage in the shelter of the portico. As before, a footman escorted them to the Long Gallery, low-ceilinged, but as opulent as the rest of the palace. Here the guests who had been invited to dinner waited to be summoned to the table. In a swift glance Domino established that Joshua was not among them. Dinner was always served promptly at six in the evening and there were already upwards of thirty people in the gallery. She knew that many more would arrive for the ball, but first a copious meal, an essential part of the Regent's evening entertainment, had to be endured.

'This is extraordinary, Papa,' she whispered as they were ushered into the Banqueting Hall.

It easily rivalled the Music Room for drama. From the central dome hung the biggest chandelier she had ever seen, held in the claws of an enormous dragon.

A host of smaller chandeliers shimmered light around the room, reflecting back and forth the sweeping decorations of silver gilt until the great space resembled nothing more than a huge treasure casket.

'Extraordinary!' her father whispered back, beginning a search for their place names.

Everything in the room was designed to overwhelm, from the painted canopies with their intricate patterns of moons and stars to the spectacular ormolu candelabra positioned in the centre of a dining table which stretched as far as she could see.

Almost immediately the first serving of food was brought to the table by a dozen uniformed footmen. Elaborate soups were followed by a choice of fish, then patés and meats, followed in turn by a dozen different entrées of meat and game. Should any of the guests feel the need for additional nourishment, seven rosewood sideboards positioned at intervals around the room groaned with platters of cold beef, venison, game and pies.

She cast a worried glance at her father. 'How on earth am I to eat even a fraction of this?' she asked in a low voice.

'Do your best,' was all he could offer in reply.

She picked her way delicately through the dishes offered, taking a very small helping of a very few of them. After nearly an hour she had done her best and was beginning to relax, when worryingly a second serving of food began to arrive. Four different roasts with their accompaniments and a multitude of sweet and savoury side dishes were scattered across the massive table. Her spirits sank as she encountered myriad jellies, tarts, ices, meringues and cream puddings. But by dint of engaging her neighbours in animated conversation, she managed to talk more than she ate.

Although many of her fellow guests seemed similarly disconcerted by the sheer volume of food, the Regent himself ate happily and solidly for the two hours apportioned to dinner. She was grateful to have been seated alongside her father at the lower end of the table and therefore unlikely to catch George's eye. After her last encounter with him, she was determined to remain unnoticed. There would be no Joshua Marchmain to rescue her from the Prince's clutches this time. He was still nowhere to be seen but she remarked the duchess and her husband occupying a prominent place to the left of the Prince. And when she heard a sniggering laugh ring out in a sudden interval of silence, it was clear that Moncaster, too, was in attendance. Only a few more hours to survive this monstrous evening, she shuddered, taking her father's arm on the walk to the ballroom.

'Thank heaven someone has had the presence of mind to open the windows,' Alfredo commented as the late August breeze, tangy with salt, wafted through the long glass doors of the ballroom. An ornamental front garden lay beyond, cool and green, a welcome foil to the overpowering heat within.

The orchestra, auditioned personally by the Prince, was already striking up for a country dance and dance pairs were being formed. Domino looked around the room and felt grateful that she hardly knew a person there. She could sit decorously with her father and watch from the fringes the revelling that Carmela so despised. But out of nowhere, it seemed, a string of young men materialised at her side. The enchanting

young girl, barely known to them, had piqued their
interest and become a prize to win. With one accord
they rushed to claim her as a partner. In a moment
almost every dance on her card had a name beside it.
Almost—not even an indulgent father would oppose
her aunts' dictate that on no account must she ever
allow herself to waltz. Over the next hour she danced
with one young man after another, all of them person-
able, all of them eager to please: they found a safe place
for her gauze wrapper, fetched her lemonade, sat out
a country dance with her as she cooled by the open
window. Obliging young men, delightful young men.

But she could not dance away the heartache. She
must go through the motions, smile prettily, dance
daintily, and hope for the hour to come very soon
when Alfredo would consider that sufficient respect
had been paid to the Prince Regent and they could
retire. It was during a lively quadrille that she saw
with a jolt that Joshua had joined the throng in the
ballroom. His elegant figure marked him out from the
crowd, his light-coloured satin breeches and dark coat
fitting him where they touched. An embroidered waistcoat and lace cravat with one single winking diamond
completed the modish ensemble. He was soon dancing. With the duchess, naturally. Who else? She could
see he was eager to talk with her whenever the dance
brought them together. He would have a good deal to
say, she thought bitterly, after wasting so much time
on a new and unsuccessful dalliance. Charlotte Severn
would forgive him. She was hardly a stranger to dalliance herself. In no time they would be together again,
the lovers they had always been. As the dancers traced

the figures of the quadrille, the duchess's flushed face seemed to leer out at her. This was her victory.

Domino looked quickly away and bent an attentive ear to her partner. The social mask must never be allowed to slip, though her life was in ruins and the ashes of its destruction all around. She stumbled slightly and her partner steadied her.

'I am so sorry,' she apologised, 'I wasn't paying sufficient attention to my feet.'

'You are a most accomplished dancer, Miss de Silva.' The willowy young man guiding her round the floor was nothing if not gallant.

She began to watch her steps fiercely. She must try to concentrate even though her mind was determined to stray. Knowing him to be so very close, Joshua consumed every thought. So close and yet as distant from her as the jungles of Africa. Her body moved mechanically in time to the orchestra's tune, but another refrain played through her mind: the past need not determine the future. Christabel had followed that advice and freed herself of the past. *Unlike me*, Domino thought. For three long years she had allowed herself to be governed by a pointless infatuation with Richard. And the moment she had freed herself from that shadow, another had arrived to manipulate her life, only this time more painfully than she could ever have imagined. It was history repeating itself a hundredfold. The anguish she had felt in saying goodbye to Richard was in retrospect a mere pinprick. It was Joshua who had taught her real suffering.

The quadrille had come to an end and her partner departed on a mission to find refreshments. She sat down on one of the ebony chairs dotting the edges of the room. How could she ever follow Christabel's advice? She had learned to trust Joshua, to discount the label of rake that hung so easily on him. He had taught her to love. Then came the devastating details of his history. How could she put such knowledge behind her, forget it existed? It was impossible. In her heart she had made the image of a man she could venerate and he was no longer that man.

Refreshments arrived and she sipped at her second glass of lemonade. All too soon she must return to the dance floor and time passing ever more slowly. She danced on, partner after partner, her feet nimbly performing the correct steps, her face smiling just enough.

The evening was half gone when the orchestra struck up a waltz. This was the moment she'd hoped her father might deem it fitting to leave. But out of the corner of her eye she saw he was engaged in a deep discussion with some of the Court's political men. He must think she was enjoying the ball and had decided to delay their departure. She allowed herself to slip wearily towards a seat once more and hoped his conversation would soon flag.

At first she didn't notice the figure. He must have walked towards her in a wide arc and only when he was bowing courteously over her hand did she realise that Joshua stood before her.

'I hope you will do me the honour, Miss de Silva,' he began formally.

His beautiful gold-flecked eyes were as warm as ever but his gaze was challenging. She was utterly disconcerted. That he should dare to approach her this evening and then behave as though they had never endured a harrowing goodbye!

'Thank you, sir, you are most kind, but I do not waltz,' she managed at last, in a voice which hardly seemed to belong to her.

'I thought that possible,' he conceded, 'but I was hoping you might make an exception.'

Whatever possessed him to think that she would dance any dance with him, let alone a waltz? The answer to her question arrived swiftly.

'We have never danced the waltz together, much to my regret, and I imagine that this will be our only chance to do so.'

His voice was as smooth as crushed velvet and his bright hair glinted in the light of a thousand candles. His glance sought hers and she could not drag her eyes away. *Concentrate*, she scolded herself. *Keep your mind focused. Get him to leave.*

'I do not waltz, sir,' she repeated dully.

'But for old times' sake?'

He was refusing to take her refusal. He was incorrigible. He was also magnificent. Unwillingly she registered the power of his body, the satin breeches clinging in all the right places.

'There are no old times,' she snapped. 'And if you had an ounce of propriety you would not address me in this manner.'

'That's better, Domino!' he cheered. 'For a moment I was a little worried that you might have gone into a decline. But I see you are as spirited as ever. Come, my dear, a few minutes only.'

He was holding out his hand and several people near them had begun to look in their direction, sensing an unfolding drama. She must get away, leave immediately. But where was her father? She could have stamped with vexation when she saw that he and his companions were now nowhere to be seen.

'Domino?' Joshua's voice caressed her. The strains of the music had begun to thread their magic through her veins and she no longer seemed to own her limbs. His warm eyes glinted gold at her and her body softened dangerously. Why did her father not come?

Joshua was still holding out his hand, beckoning her to him. The people on either side were looking even more interested. She felt herself take a step forwards and then she was in his arms.

'I will dance,' she said angrily, 'but only because I do not wish to be the centre of a scene.'

'Naturally, why else would you dance with me?' he mocked. 'It was such a long time ago, was it not, that you were happy to do a great deal more than dance.'

'You are insufferable. Why can you not leave me alone?'

'One final dance and I promise all the solitude you could wish.'

She kept a resolute silence and in response his arms tightened and he swept her into the middle of the floor, manoeuvring her dexterously between couples and clasping her firmly against his chest. She tried very hard to hold herself at a distance, but her body was soft beneath his touch and growing softer with every minute. He smiled down at her, his honey-glow eyes bewitching in the subdued candlelight.

'You waltz well. That's a surprise. I had supposed you would not have been allowed to learn the dance.'

'You supposed correctly,' she found herself saying,

the corners of her mouth crooking themselves into a small smile despite her best efforts.

'You never disappoint me!'

She was beginning to slide under his spell and she must resist at all costs. She saw Charlotte Severn standing at the side of the room in a small knot of people. The woman shot her a look of hatred.

'Do you not think, Mr Marchmain, that you would be wise to forgo this dance and ask another to partner you?' she asked in a voice that was deceptively steady.

He followed her gaze. 'I think not, Miss de Silva. I had my fill of that particular pleasure many months ago.'

'I find that difficult to believe, so enthused were you in each other's company earlier this evening.'

'Enthused, no, irritated, yes.' And his arms tightened even more firmly around her.

'Why irritated?' she found herself asking.

'It is taking Her Grace longer than I had hoped to understand my changed feelings,' he said diplomatically. 'She did not take kindly to my reminding her.'

Domino said nothing. So they were not together again. Why did a sharp arrow of delight fly straight to her heart? It should not matter to her, must not matter. And yet it did, crushed as she was to his chest, moving with him to the enticing rhythms of the waltz. Their limbs shadowed each other, touching, separating and touching again. She felt his warmth through the light clothes he wore and savoured the indefinable musky smell of him. His lips brushed the top of her hair, coming to rest just behind her left ear. Slowly, delicately, she felt the tip of his tongue taste her skin. She was melting, melting, diffusing into liquid pleasure.

His arm slowly slid down her back and pulled her body even closer until she felt his answering hardness. His mouth trailed kisses down her neck. He was seducing her, here on the dance floor and in full view of a hundred pairs of eyes. And she was letting him! She could not bear it. She broke from him abruptly and fled, leaving him alone in the middle of the ballroom floor.

Incensed by her abandonment and caring little for the tittle-tattle that would ensue, Joshua made to follow but, as he drew near, a servant in the Prince's livery approached her with a message and he stopped in his tracks. He turned away, ignoring the interested stares from around the room. She had deliberately exposed him to ridicule!

But it was his own fault. He should have accepted her refusal to dance and walked away. He should never even have asked her. But an angry frustration was driving him: he had foolishly broken the unspoken law by which he lived. For longer than he could remember, he had avoided intimacy. The scourging he'd received from the Tallis affair had left him wanting no more such hazards. He might flirt with young women and acquire the reputation of a dangerous man, he might enjoy the challenge of confounding their duennas, but he was always careful never to step across the line. Discreet, and sometimes not so discreet, liaisons with well-born ladies bored with their husbands served his physical needs. Such relationships were often tedious, occasionally joyless and always sterile, but they caused him not one jot of discomfort.

His life had flowed smooth and unruffled—and then he'd met Domino. He had been resolute in his refusal to fall in love, but that hadn't prevented him being constantly by her side. Her youthful spirit had enchanted him, holding as it did the promise of beauty he had so long sought. He had been beguiled even into offering his hand. But the summer had proved a mere dream and after their last tempestuous encounter, he had vowed to put her from his mind. The fantasy was over and his old life awaited him.

But tonight, seeing her once more in all her loveliness, a slender flower of a girl, the craziest desire had overpowered him and all he'd known was that he had to be close to her again. One more time, one final time. And look where that had led. He would be the object of derision in the Court for days, but it didn't matter. Nothing mattered.

Domino rushed from the dance floor, her cheeks aflame and her heart hammering. She must find her father immediately, she had to leave this place and never return. But a footman in knee breeches and starched shirt was barring her way.

'Yes, what is it?' she asked impatiently, her breath still uneven.

'A message, Miss de Silva, from your father.'

'My father? Where is he?'

'He awaits you at the eastern exit of the palace. A coach will be ready to take you home.'

It seemed strange that her father should disappear without a word and send a servant to fetch her.

'Why has he not come himself?'

'I am to tell you that he has gone ahead to summon the carriage so that you will not catch cold awaiting its arrival.'

How very like Papa, she thought with sudden warmth, forgiving him his earlier desertion.

'But my shawl and reticule? I must find those first.' She smiled at the retainer. 'They cannot be too far away.'

'Señor de Silva has them already, I believe. They await you in the carriage.'

Her father had been unusually busy. She was surprised for she had thought him far too engaged with his political friends.

'Then I have nothing to do but find him,' she replied almost gaily in her relief that she was at last on her way home.

She made her way out of the ballroom and along the passage indicated by the footman. There was nobody to be seen, yet she had a nagging feeling that she was being watched. How very stupid. The alarms she had suffered that evening were making her overly sensitive to the atmosphere. The corridor itself was narrow and bare and meagrely lit by a few branches of candles at irregular intervals along its walls. It was an odd whim of her father's to have his daughter traverse the length of the Pavilion to the little used eastern exit. But he was there waiting to take her home. All would be well.

The colonnade which gave on to the gardens was smaller here and far more enclosed than the portico at which they had arrived. Tall trees shaded the building at this point and the covering of gravel was a mere path rather than a carriageway. Her father was nowhere to be seen, but in the dusk ahead she could make out the silhouette of a coach, and she made her way gladly towards it.

She walked swiftly through the small porch and out

of the palace. Her footsteps sounded unnaturally loud in the silence which seemed to fill the air like a palpable presence. A few steps forwards and then two figures came looming from the darkness on either side of her. She started back but before she could regain the shelter of the Pavilion, they had grabbed her arms and pinioned her between them. Their clothes were unwashed and they smelt strongly of liquor. Terrified, she imagined she had been attacked by thieves but she had little on her person worth stealing. Their rough hands dug into her flesh as they jostled her forwards. Then she realised—they were dragging her towards the waiting coach. This was not a robbery, but an abduction! In a moment they had wrenched open the carriage door and made ready to bundle her inside. She struggled furiously, but she was no match for two hulking men and found herself being thrust into the coach. Then a loud shout sounded nearby. The hands loosened their grip and she was dumped, spread-eagled across the rear seat of the carriage.

She scrambled to her feet and down the coach steps. The dusk was dense, almost impenetrable, the moon shining only fitfully from between lowering clouds, and she could hardly see a foot in front of her. She could hear, though. There was a crack as two skulls were smashed expertly together.

'Run—back to the Pavilion and find your father.'

It was Joshua. As she turned to flee, she saw that her assailants had recovered their footing only to be floored again, one after another with several punishing left hooks.

'Run!' he repeated.

She needed no second urging and rushed towards the

Pavilion entrance, desperate to find help. Both attackers lay on the floor, prone and unmoving. Joshua, his cravat askew, stood back ready for a further onslaught. But their loud groans were heartfelt and they seemed unlikely to give more trouble. She was back in the Pavilion now and about to retrace her steps along the passageway when a sudden noise from outside made her turn again. Surely those villains could not have recovered so quickly.

But it was Leo Moncaster who stood to one side of the carriage, brandishing a sword.

'Get up, blockheads,' he swore at the men, 'and find the girl. Else what use are you to me?'

One of the men made a feeble attempt to stagger to his feet but then crumpled to the ground again. The other managed to crawl to the colonnade and haul himself upright on its wooden pillars. Domino felt him grab her skirt as she tried to whisk herself from sight. She had not run, could not run with Joshua in such danger.

Moncaster gave a growl of annoyance and turned to the cause. 'When will you learn, Marchmain, not to interfere? I draw comfort from the fact that this is the very last time.' He slashed at the air with his sword, its evilly sharp point threatening the unarmed man.

'You are a cur, Moncaster. I don't fight with dogs.'

'Who said anything about a fight, dear friend? You will not have the chance. Regretfully I cannot allow you to regain the palace and tell your story. It would be too degrading.'

'What then do you intend, or need I ask?'

'I imagine not. Sadly, you will be found a victim of robbery. Such dubious creatures hang around the Pavilion these days, it will occasion few questions.'

'And Miss de Silva?'

'My plans for her must change. Your intervention has done her little favour. Instead of a few days' incarceration, she must now be lost for months. She may be allowed to surface in Spain eventually if she proves a sensible girl. By then no one will believe a word of any story she chooses to tell.'

The moon suddenly swam free of its cloudy cover and a shaft of silver illuminated the scene. It flooded everything in its path, glinting along the horses' glossy coats, embellishing the scratched panels of the coach and flashing its light on to a lone strip of glittering steel. In a second Joshua had seized the dagger from its resting place in the lining of the carriage door and made ready to defend himself.

'You will hardly inflict damage with that poor object,' his adversary mocked.

'We shall see. Any blade is gold if it destroys a mongrel such as you.'

The fight was ugly. No graceful swordplay, but a tense game of cat and mouse. They circled each other warily, each waiting for the other's move. Then Moncaster's sword was swinging through the air and Joshua nimbly retreating out of reach. Moncaster tried again, but with the same result. Again and again he struck and each blow Domino expected to be final. Both men were tiring in this inelegant ballet, but only when Joshua was sure that his opponent was sufficiently winded did he begin to advance. Then it was a swift run beneath Moncaster's sword blade and a desperate attempt to wound at close quarters. His enemy was too quick and retreated out of harm's way. The man who held Domino was gradually loosening his grip on her as he watched the fight, enthralled by its savagery. She thought she might manage to pull herself free but knew she could not leave. She was watching Joshua as though her life depended on it as much as his. She had to be there, stay with him, whatever their mutual fate.

Moncaster was growing ever more furious and began to slash wildly, circling the sword over his head, hurling its blade from right to left. But still Joshua evaded him. Years of practice with the most exigent of fencing masters had taught him skills of defence as much as offence. And he needed them. He could fight only at close quarters and the sword had a very long reach. Moncaster, tiring faster than his younger and fitter opponent, determined to make an end to his adversary. He saw his chance when Joshua for an instant came to a standstill. He lunged forwards to catch the younger man off guard. In the blink of an eye Joshua saw his danger and dipped beneath the oncoming sword so low that he almost knelt on the gravel. Then in a swooping movement from the ground he raised the dagger upwards and into the man's right arm. He pinked it neatly and Moncaster's sword clattered to the ground.

'Still so disdainful of a humble dagger?' Joshua's face was pale, but in the moonlight his eyes glittered with an unholy joy.

Leo Moncaster roared in pain and struggled blindly to free himself from Joshua's iron hold. But footsteps were running towards them from the passageway behind. The ruffian holding Domino suddenly let her go and loped off into the darkness, the summer growth of bushes shielding him from view.

She was free and her father was by her side. Two of the Prince's guards had pinned Moncaster between them and were forcing him back into the palace. Joshua, his beautiful coat rent with sword slashes and his golden hair sadly dishevelled, faced her father.

'Take her home,' he said hoarsely. 'I believe she has had sufficient excitement for one evening.'

Alfredo nodded grimly and placed the spangled shawl around his daughter's shoulders. Together they stumbled through the back corridors of the palace to find again the familiar entrance. Domino sat back in the carriage, pale and exhausted. Only then did the tears begin to roll slowly down her cheeks.

Chapter Ten

She slept late the next morning. When she opened her eyes, Flora was bending over her, a look of concern on her face. Domino smiled and Flora smiled back.

'It's so good to see you awake, Miss Domino. You gave us such a fright last night.'

'I did?' She struggled to sit up, blinking at the brilliant light that was streaming into the room from chinks in the drawn curtains.

'It was as though you were sleepwalking, dazed like. You didn't seem to recognise any of us, nor your own room. I put you to bed and you slept straight away, real deep, too, and you've been sleeping like that ever since and it's past noon.'

'You sat with me all night, Flora?' Domino propped herself up on one elbow and pressed her maid's hand affectionately.

'What else would I do, miss? We were so worried.'

'And my father?'

Flora piled the soft white pillows as high as she

could and her mistress collapsed back on them with a sigh.

'My father?' she prompted.

'He's at the palace. He's gone to enquire of Mr Marchmain. Seemingly he did you a great service last night.'

'He did.' Her voice was barely above a whisper and the tears again began to flow. Her maid's face puckered in fright.

'Whatever is it, miss? You're safe and Mr Marchmain has come off with barely a scratch, or so I believe. That villain, they say, has packed up and gone back to London. He should be in prison, but Quality never goes to prison.' She sounded bitter.

Domino rallied herself and said in a far stronger voice, 'Are you saying that Lord Moncaster has left Brighton?'

'So Cook says. Her sister works in the Pavilion kitchens and such a to-do. The Regent himself was involved. After your father brought you home, *Lord* Moncaster—' and she emphasised the title with considerable scorn '—was taken to the Prince by the guards and had to confess what he'd been up to. Cook's sister says that Moncaster has been told he ain't welcome any more at the Pavilion, nor at Carlton House neither.'

Flora's acquired gentility was rapidly vanishing in the face of her honest indignation.

'Where has he gone, do you think?' Domino ventured, the thought tormenting her that her enemy might even now be waiting, ready to make another attempt on her.

'Apparently…' and Flora drew in her cheeks at the thought of the news she had to impart '…the Regent has advised his friend to go abroad for a space. Lying low, I call it. He should be in prison.'

'And all this has happened while I've been asleep.'

'Yes, indeed, miss. It's like you were under some kind of spell, but it's so good that you're back with us again.'

There was a gentle tap at the door and Alfredo looked into the room, his face drawn, but when he saw Domino sitting up in bed and sipping her morning chocolate, a wide smile lit his face. Flora quietly slipped away.

'How good to see you looking yourself again, *querida.*'

'I'm sorry I gave you such a fright, Papa. But as you see, all is well.'

He came to the bedside and enfolded her in a stifling bear hug. Her tears began to fall again and he pulled back, his face once more anxious.

She put her hand in his and squeezed it reassuringly. 'I am well, so you must not worry, but I cannot seem to stop crying.'

'You have had a terrible shock, my dear. I am not surprised you are deeply upset. When I think what could have happened!'

She would rather not think but she was desperate to know from him what had passed at the Pavilion. Had her father learned anything of the shameful history that existed between herself and Moncaster? She prayed not.

'Do you know why Lord Moncaster tried to abduct me,' she asked at last, 'for I presume that is what it was?'

'An abduction indeed. It makes my heart heavy

to say this about any man, but he is evil through and through. And the Duchess of Severn is no better. She was in on the plan, too, it appears. I always thought her an indelicate woman, but I had no idea that she could sink to such wickedness.'

He fell silent as he considered the two miscreants.

'But what was their plan, and why should they plot against me?' she probed.

'Why they should do so, I have no notion. As for the plan, I do not think you need to know it.'

'I want to know, Papa,' she said stubbornly.

'My dear, how will it benefit you to know the depths of their villainy?' His voice was filled with misgiving.

'I have to know, Papa. I have to know the truth.'

He gave a heavy sigh. 'Leo Moncaster planned to hold you overnight in a house that the duchess owns in Worthing, just a few miles down the coast. He would have kept you there some days and allowed the gossip on your whereabouts to flourish. Or so I have learned from the Regent.'

'But how would that have served his purpose?'

Her father's face grew grimmer and his mouth tightened into a thin slit. He could hardly bring himself to speak the words.

'When Moncaster released you, he intended to publish to the world that you had voluntarily stayed with him as his mistress. It would be his word against yours and as a notable member of the *ton*, he expected to be believed. Even if he were not, the mere suggestion that his words might be true would ensure that your reputation in England would be shattered forever. No doubt he would spread news of your supposed affair as far afield as he could.'

Her mind swiftly processed this information, but she said nothing.

'Do you know why he would do such a thing, Domino?' her father ventured at last.

'I believe the duchess is for some reason jealous of me,' she extemporised. 'Perhaps Lord Moncaster has feelings for her and he planned this dreadful attack on her behalf.'

That, at least, was partially true. Charlotte Severn must suppose her intervention at the theatre had failed and she would be eager for the abduction to destroy Domino's reputation and make her a social outcast. The way would then be clear to seduce Joshua all over again.

'The crime seems out of all proportion to the cause,' Alfredo was saying thoughtfully.

Moncaster had his own reasons to hurt her, Domino knew, but she was not about to explain them.

Her father was still following his thoughts. 'But then these people cannot be understood by any normal standards of conduct, so perhaps we should not look too far for a motive.'

She closed her eyes, suddenly very tired again, but Alfredo had not yet finished. 'Lady Veryan would very much like to see you when you feel able to receive her, my dear. She has been much disturbed by this terrible business and is wishful to be a comfort to you if she can.'

She nodded wearily. 'I should like to sleep a little longer but later perhaps we can take tea together.'

'I will tell her,' he said softly and took a seat by the bedside. It was evident that her father intended to keep watch as Flora had done through the night.

She sank back on the pillows and closed her eyes. But it was not to sleep for almost immediately a procession of shadowy figures began to dance across her vision. Blurred images of Christabel, her father, the Regent, Moncaster, and in their wake memories of Joshua: Joshua fighting for his life, Joshua fighting for her. Why had he been there? Why had he intervened? On that dreadful morning by the sea, she had rejected him, told him starkly that she never wished to see him again. But last night he'd ignored her dismissal, intent it seemed on proving that he could still cause her passion to flame: they had only to dance together. The shaming truth had been plain for all to see and in her anguish she had ruthlessly snubbed him and left him to face public humiliation.

Yet that had not weighed with him. He had continued to watch her, to watch out for her. He must have seen those brutal men waiting as she walked heedlessly into their trap. And he had gone into the fray with no more weapons than his own two fists. He could so easily have been killed. Moncaster would have denied all knowledge of the crime, glibly blaming it on the shiftless men who occasionally inveigled their way past the guards and into the Pavilion gardens. Such unsavoury people gather around the palace these days, she could almost hear him say. She would have lost her reputation but Joshua would have lost his life.

As if sensing that she did not rest easily, her father spoke again, his tone hesitant. 'This is a delicate matter, *querida*, but you owe much to Mr Marchmain. I understand that your—hmm, friendship—is at an end, but it is still right that you should see him. A few minutes only, sufficient to thank him for his bravery in your service.'

Her heart was beating too fast. She acknowledged how very much she owed Joshua but how could she meet him again, knowing that he had risked his life for her, but that she must still spurn him. The dreadful events of last night changed nothing. He was still the man who had deliberately betrayed his best friend, deliberately seduced Christabel Tallis. He was not the man she had hoped for, the man she had invested with her dreams.

'You will see him?'

She opened her eyes and saw her father looking anxiously down at her. 'It will be for a few minutes only,' he repeated, stroking her hand reassuringly. 'I can be with you. Or Lady Veryan if you prefer.'

'No!' She almost shouted the word. Her father looked astonished.

'I mean, Papa,' she said in a quieter tone, 'that it is I who owes Mr Marchmain such a debt of gratitude and it is I who should thank him. I will see him alone.'

'Very well, my dear. I will send a message asking him to wait on you tomorrow if that is convenient.'

Domino closed her eyes again. She was safe but not at peace. Tomorrow she must see Joshua and offer him her heartfelt thanks but still stay true to herself. It would be difficult. No, it would be utterly painful: to see his dear face, to look into his loving eyes, to desire his beautiful form and be unable to touch. She groaned inwardly. The pain was almost physical. But she was tired, so tired. Her eyes shut fast and sleep overcame her.

It was evening before she woke again and Christabel was standing in the doorway with a small tray in her hands.

'You've missed tea, my dear, but I've bought a little supper. Sleep is an excellent restorative but you need to eat.'

Her friend placed the tray on a nearby table and drew up a chair at the side of the bed. She bent down to kiss Domino's cheek and a subtle scent of roses filled the air.

'How are you, Domino? Such a fright you have given us!'

'So I understand. I'm sorry I have caused such consternation but as you see, I am fully recovered. Almost fully recovered,' she amended as Christabel's face registered doubt.

'I could hardly believe my ears when I learned what had happened. It is almost impossible to comprehend. Lord Moncaster is the most wicked of men. I understand that the Regent has banished him from Court for some time. That is mild punishment. He should be in prison.'

Christabel's normally gentle manner had given way to one of hot indignation, causing Domino to smile. Lady and lady's maid were evidently in agreement.

'It's so good to see you smile,' her friend cheered. 'You will be back to your old self in no time.'

Domino thought otherwise but she had no intention of admitting Lady Veryan into the deepest and darkest of her secrets. Lady Veryan, though, it seemed had other ideas.

'And it was Joshua Marchmain who came to your rescue! I have not seen or heard of him for an age and then he appears out of nowhere, your very own guardian angel.'

Domino held her breath.

'I must tell you,' Christabel said a trifle self-consciously, 'that I was acquainted with Mr Marchmain in my youth.'

Her companion's face assumed an ignorance of the fact.

'It appears that he forms part of the Regent's entourage and that you have been in the habit of meeting him regularly. You never mentioned it.' There was a gentle scolding to Christabel's tone.

'I've met many people from the palace this summer.'

Her friend ignored the dissembling and continued blithely, 'I understand that he is to come here tomorrow. It will be good to meet him again.'

Alarm at these words was clearly written on Domino's face and Christabel offered a hasty amendment. 'Naturally you will wish to see him alone. You must have much to say to each other. But I would like to exchange a few words with him before he leaves the house. An opportunity to lay the past to rest comes seldom, you know.'

Domino felt her tongue stilled and her face freeze. She eased herself into a sitting position and looked directly at the visitor by her bedside. What exactly did this lovely young woman intend for the morrow? Whatever it was, she feared it could only make her meeting with Joshua even more tormenting. The air between them prickled.

In an attempt to diffuse the uncomfortable mood, Christabel spoke again.

'I should explain, Domino. As a young woman, I fell into trouble. I mentioned something of it when we talked yesterday. Mr Marchmain was involved and I fear that in the end he suffered unjustly for his part in our small tragedy.'

'And you wish to see him again?' Domino's chagrin fought with jealousy. Were these two old lovers to be reunited and under her roof?

'I turned out to be a very bad mistake for him. I would like to make my peace,' Christabel said simply.

Joshua threw down his brush in annoyance. He had been standing before a blank canvas all morning and getting nowhere. Normally his studio was a blessed retreat and painting a path to serenity. But today the magic was not working. He looked gloomily through the long glass windows into the garden. Since midnight the rain had been incessant and its dripping from the ornamental roof beat a repetitive tattoo on the gravel beneath. The world looked drear. The Regent had risen betimes, sending a collective shudder through the household, and Joshua had been summoned to his presence before the great ormolu clock in the Long Gallery had struck even ten. A lengthy interview had culminated with the Prince's command that Moncaster leave the Court immediately. His lordship was swift to make preparations for France and at Steine House the duchess was organising a hasty departure to London.

That was all very satisfactory, but this was not: he was unable to paint. If he were honest, he had been unable to paint for days. Ever since Domino had made plain that he was not her future. He wondered how she was faring after the frightening events of the previous evening. She was tough, he concluded, she would survive happily enough once the immediate shock had receded. As for him, he had a few bruises from the tussle with those ruffians, a few aches and pains, but in days he would be as new. His rawest ache was something that would not heal so easily.

His offer of marriage had stemmed from guilt at ensnaring Domino so badly, but once she made clear that he was the last man on earth she would consider marrying, any guilt should have vanished. After their disastrous meeting on the beach, he'd told himself that he could resume his old life with equanimity. He could feel free once more. But last night at the ball he'd known himself to be anything but free. He had wanted to master her, wanted to prove that she was not indifferent to him, no matter how much she might wish it. And he had succeeded so well that she'd fled without warning and left him looking a fool, alone in the midst of the dance floor. He had watched her storm from the room, watched her met by a liveried servant he did not recognise. That was strange in itself. In a furious mood, he had begun to follow her. He wasn't sure why, perhaps it was simply an inability to let go. But thank God he had. When she had taken the little used passageway, his instinct for danger had been alerted. How right he had been!

Two burly thugs had set upon her as soon as she'd emerged from the palace and following close on her heels, he saw what they intended almost immediately: a coach and pair stood waiting in the shadows beyond. He hadn't seen Moncaster, the third villain of this blackguardly trio, but it would not have mattered if he had. Two men, three men, he would have intervened in any case. He would have intervened on behalf of any woman so threatened, but his blood had run cold when he saw it was happening to the girl he loved. And he did love her, he knew that now. His wish to marry had stemmed from love, not guilt. He had pretended otherwise, but after all the excuses, the justifications, the weasel words he'd told himself, he loved her. The minute he had seen her threatened he knew that she had all of his heart. But his case was hopeless: she would not change her mind. She was adamant that she could not forgive him.

He had been surprised, therefore, to get Alfredo's message asking him to call at Marine Parade. Unsure, too, whether or not he should obey the summons. The thought of seeing her again made his heart jump, yet it could mean nothing but distress for them both. Pride had strengthened his resolve that this unlucky love affair would not destroy him and a meeting would call on every ounce he possessed. Anger had proved useless. He had tried stoking it against her, telling himself again and again that she had dismissed him for no good reason—a past misdemeanour that had no currency in the present. When last night she had fled so precipitately, his wrath had reached its highest pitch; he had felt furious beyond belief. Furious that a chit of a girl should do this to him! But his rage had died the minute he had seen her in danger and he knew that for once in his life, his feelings were not playing him false. Whatever she did now and in the future, this was a woman he loved, truly loved.

His meeting with her tomorrow would be an elegy, a melancholy closing of the one good chapter in his life. The Court was busy packing for London and the leaves in the Pavilion gardens were already turning gold. It was a time for endings, and his own ending that would have no new beginning—for him at least.

He would see her on the morrow, feel the turn of the knife once more, and walk away. He would return to his bare canvases and his bare life. He should not repine. This was the path he had chosen when he had betrayed his friend and seduced the girl he was to marry. From there he had gone from bad to bad. For a brief moment this summer he had glimpsed a different life, but that was at an end. He must not repine.

'Flora, lay out my cream figured muslin, please.'

The maid stared in surprise. 'The cream muslin?' she questioned, thinking she must have misheard.

Domino nodded. 'And the deep red satin ribbon we bought the other day in Barthlomews. I shall wear it threaded in my hair.'

'Are we going somewhere important, Miss Domino?' the maid ventured.

'We are going nowhere, but I am to have a visitor today and I wish to look my best.'

Why? she asked herself. It mattered not how she looked when Joshua came to call. She planned to be with him a few minutes only before he disappeared forever. It was mere whistling in the wind. A façade to cover her misery, a boldness when she felt fatally weakened.

Flora scurried around laying out underwear, stockings and the figured muslin along with matching satin slippers. She could see that her mistress was hardly herself but that was not to be wondered at. Such a dreadful experience she'd gone through. And now this Joshua Marchmain coming. She supposed it was right that Miss Domino should thank him prettily for his rescue but the man meant trouble in Flora's view. Ever since

Miss Domino had met him, she'd been on a wild carousel, first happy and exultant, then cast down with dejection. It would be better for all of them once they were free of Brighton and free of him.

Domino dismissed her maid as soon as she could. She wanted time to collect her wits before Joshua arrived. She had formulated the words she needed to say. He had only to respond in similar vein and their ordeal would be finished.

But when an hour later she faced him across the drawing room, the words died on her lips. He looked a picture of quiet elegance, his clothes as always moulding themselves to perfection around his athletic form. The dark blue of his coat set off his shining gold locks and a waistcoat embroidered with small grey and blue flowers worn over dove grey pantaloons completed a more than alluring picture. But his eyes, that familiar colour of melting honey, held a reserved expression.

'I am delighted to see you so well.' His tone was neutral.

'Thank you, I am well,' she managed and then as a scattered afterthought, 'and you?'

'I've suffered no lasting damage—at least from the fight,' he offered drily.

She tried to keep her mind on the words she had rehearsed. 'I am so glad you were able to call, Mr Marchmain. I wanted very much to thank you.' Her voice began to break as she met his shrewd gaze.

She tried again. 'I must thank you for your bravery', and then finishing in a rush, 'and of course your skill.'

'It's comforting to know that my experience in Italy

has proved useful at last.' He fingered his scar and his voice sounded a caustic note.

'If it had not been for your intervention,' Domino doggedly followed her script, 'I would be in a sorry case.'

'We must not think of that.' He brushed aside her thanks. 'You are well and safe and that is all that matters.'

She felt stupidly annoyed that he seemed determined to make light of his rescue. How nonsensical of her. She should be glad that he was willing to pass over the event so quickly for it could only mean that his visit this morning would be mercifully brief.

'But still,' she persisted, 'I am conscious—my father and I are conscious—that we owe you a great deal.'

'You owe me nothing, Domino, unless it's a fair hearing,' he said harshly.

The interview was not going the way she had imagined. Why had she ever thought it would? A painful silence filled the room for what seemed an age but when he spoke again, his voice was deliberately indifferent.

'May I ask what your plans are?'

'I am to go first to London and from there I will travel on to Spain. Carmela will accompany me.'

'Ah, yes, to Spain and the unknown suitor. I imagine he has been resurrected.' They were back on dangerous ground and his gaze was derisory.

'There will be no suitor,' she said shortly.

'How can that be?' His eyebrows rose in mocking question.

She decided to fight back, to call his bluff. 'Surely,

Mr Marchmain, you of all people should know the answer to that question.'

'But I don't.' His eyes had lost their sardonic amusement. 'If you no longer intend to marry, it isn't because you love elsewhere. A week ago I would have said differently. I would have said you had sought and found an abiding love. But now? I think you want only the illusion of such a love.'

She was desperate to end this dreadful conversation but was stung into exclaiming, 'You are unfair, sir!'

'I think not. You don't like reality, Domino. You prefer illusion and when the real world comes too close, you retreat. Your love for Richard Veryan was empty emotion. And now your love for me has gone the same way. You don't want a flesh and blood man with all the good and bad that that implies, you want a man that doesn't exist, a fantasy lover. Veryan filled that role until he inconveniently married. My tenure was even shorter. I fell from my pedestal almost immediately.'

For a moment the breath went out of her and she looked as though she was about to collapse.

'If it's not to be the unknown bridegroom, then what?' he asked as if he had not just uttered the most wounding words possible.

Wasn't that the question she returned to endlessly? What *was* she to do once back in Spain? Once they knew she was not intending to marry, her aunts would be eager to suggest a convent.

'A convent, perhaps?'

She stared at him. 'Well, isn't that one of the few acceptable choices for a virtuous Spanish girl? The altar or the cloister, or so I understand.'

Rage fought with tears. How dare he predict her

future? What she did was no longer his concern. But suddenly his voice was soft.

'Don't choose a convent, Domino. You were not made for such.'

He began to walk towards her and she seemed paralysed to move. But before he reached her, the door opened and Christabel walked into the room. Domino had thought this encounter could not get worse but she had been wrong.

Joshua stared blindly at the vision that had entered. Though well into pregnancy, Christabel was able still to stun any man who crossed her path. But Joshua's mesmerised gaze was not for the woman he saw before him, but for the one he had long ago bid farewell.

'Christabel?' he queried in amazement. 'Christabel Tallis!'

'Christabel Veryan,' she corrected him gently.

'Of course. Lady Veryan, my apologies, and my very good wishes on your marriage.' He bowed politely. 'And on your forthcoming happiness,' he added, smiling at the noticeable bump Christabel carried.

'Thank you, Mr Marchmain. You are most kind. And I am delighted to see you again.'

Domino remained silent and unmoving, hardly able to believe the turn of events. It was as though she was watching a play enacted, with herself the sole audience.

Christabel continued unperturbed, 'Domino told me you were to call today and I was hoping that I might speak with you.'

He looked enquiringly and she said with hardly a pause, 'I am sure she has thanked you profusely for the service you rendered her. But I would like to add my own thanks. Your courageous action saved her from the most dreadful fate.'

He nodded an acknowledgement but she had not yet finished and her quiet voice seemed to fill the room. 'There is something else. I wished to thank you for the service you rendered *me* many years ago. I know that as a result you must have suffered harm.'

Joshua was looking dazed—as well he might, thought Domino, burning with righteous anger.

'If you had not intervened in my life so dramatically,' Christabel went on, 'I would have wed Richard, but for all the wrong reasons. I would not have the happy marriage I have today. I needed to find out where I truly belonged, and you did that for me.'

His expression was wry. 'You are most kind, Lady Veryan.'

'I speak only the truth. But what of you, Joshua? I hope you, too, have found where you belong.'

'I thought I had but apparently I was mistaken,' he said curtly.

He picked up his gloves from the small table beneath the window and bowed to each of the women in turn.

'I believe it is time I left. Christabel, Lady Veryan, it has been most pleasant to meet you again. Domino, my very best wishes for your future happiness.'

And with a brief nod, he was gone. The front door shut with loud finality and Domino could no longer maintain her veneer of detachment. Careless of what Christabel would think, she rushed from the room and up the stairs to her bedroom, locking the door behind her.

She sank down on her bed. She was out of reach of friends and family alike, but not out of reach of torturing thoughts. The carefully scripted encounter had gone very wrong. All she had to do was express grateful thanks for her rescue. A few words on either side would have sufficed. Instead, what had happened? Joshua had not wanted to be thanked for his endeavours. He had wanted her to know that her priorities were wrong. The rescue was unimportant; what she did with the rest of her life was what mattered. He had brought home to her in bald terms just what her choices were and she had not liked them. And he had chopped her into the smallest of pieces by claiming that she had no idea what love was; that all she was capable of feeling was a pretence of love.

And then there was Christabel greeting him as a long-lost friend, behaving as though they were meeting at some dowager's tea party. She had clearly astonished Joshua with her words. She had absolved him, Domino thought savagely, so that he no longer need feel a shred of guilt for his past sins. She had even come close to praising him!

The churn of thoughts flooding her mind brought her to her feet. She could not rest and began aimlessly to pace the polished floorboards. Joshua had done a dreadful thing; he had almost destroyed the man she once loved. According to him that love had been nothing but illusion—and he was right. She had recognised that weeks ago. But he was so very wrong about this love. The love she felt for *him* was no illusion. He had taunted her that she didn't want a flesh and blood man. If that meant that she didn't want a man who carelessly inflicted hurt, then he was right. Yet both Richard and Christabel were happy now. Their baby would soon be with them, an added joy in the life of love they already shared.

And what of her, Domino de Silva, heiress and sad, sad girl? What was to become of her? Just a few days ago her world had been full to overflowing, then Charlotte Severn had dripped poison into her ears, and suddenly her life, her future, was changed forever. The duchess had won their battle of wills.

But why should she? She was allowing her to win—no, willing her to win. She was behaving exactly as Charlotte Severn had anticipated. The woman had judged her correctly to the last inch. How mortifying to be the duchess's creature. But if she were to defy Charlotte's malign calculations...

She paused her restless wandering and gazed out of the window. For several long minutes she stood there, watching the waves endlessly tumble to shore. Joshua Marchmain was a fallible man, a man who had lived a far from perfect life. But it was a life that had given him strangely little happiness. She remembered how puzzled she'd been that someone who seemed to have everything could be so bored and discontented. Yet from the moment they'd met, he had appeared quite other. Was it really possible that his days of philandering were over, that with her he'd finally stumbled on fulfilment?

She rested her forehead on the cold glass of the window pane, thinking, thinking. Minutes ago she'd heard him say that he thought he'd found where he belonged but that he'd been mistaken. But he hadn't been. He did belong with her and she belonged with him. Not with an unknown husband, nor behind a veil. She belonged with him, a strong, tender man who had once been an unloved child. He'd lost sight of where he belonged and before he'd properly matured, had committed the fatal error determining his life's path. Why couldn't she accept that?

There was no reason, no reason. She snatched up her bonnet and pelisse. The wind was blowing strongly and dark clouds threatened the return of an early autumn storm, but she took no heed. In a minute she was tripping down the stairs as quickly as she had run up them. Flora was crossing the hall and made to speak to her. She held up her finger for silence and slipped out of the front door.

The wind sent her skirts skirling but she bent her head against its force and pushed on towards the Pavilion. The guard on the gate recognised her from previous visits and though surprised at her solitary state, allowed her through into the gardens. She quickly found her way around the side of the palace, making for where she knew Joshua would be. Where else but in his studio?

He looked up as she appeared in the open doorway. The wind had whipped colour into her pale cheeks and her dark, dishevelled curls framed a luminous face. Her graceful young figure was silhouetted against the stormy sky outside and she looked heartbreakingly lovely. He drew in a sharp breath but resisted the impulse to reach for her. He had no idea why she was here. It was yet another confusion in a vastly confusing day.

Meeting Christabel after so long had been astonishing and his mind still grappled with her sudden arrival. He could make little sense of it except that her presence had forced him to be circumspect. When she'd entered the room, he had been in a fair way to forgetting his resolve to remain coolly polite. He'd wanted to grab Domino, shake her, make her see the foolishness of her decision. He would have done it, too, if Christabel had not opened the door at that very moment. In the end he had been forced into a cold, mechanical farewell: a fitting end for a doomed love affair.

But now here she was, teetering on the threshold of his studio, her face wistful, her eyes shining.

'I had to come,' she said simply.

'And...' A small flicker of expectancy started deep within him.

'I'm sorry. I was wrong.'

'About?' he prompted, the flicker growing stronger.

'About everything. I've been obsessed with what happened all those years ago. You behaved very badly but so did Christabel. She has forgotten the bad memories, Richard too, and you—all of you have forgotten. I don't know why it became so important to me.'

'Perhaps because I was not the man you imagined.' His voice was guarded and he remained standing aloof from her.

'I have been very stupid.'

She walked further into the studio, moving closer to him, her gaze clear and unwavering. 'I don't know why I got it so badly wrong. I started out thinking you were the worst kind of man, a thorough rake, irredeemable. But then I fell in love and thought the world had wronged you and treated you callously. You became the best kind of man there could ever be. I placed you on an impossible dais.'

'And now you know that I am neither?' For a moment he looked tired and brushed away a lock of hair which had fallen over his forehead. Her heart stirred in tenderness.

'I know that you're the only man I ever want to be with,' she said with a catch in her voice.

He was beside her in a step, his tiredness forgotten. He held out his arms wide and she walked into them.

'Is that true?' he breathed into her ear.

'I've never stopped loving you, Joshua. But for a while I lost my trust.'

'And now?'

'Now I've come to realise that your past is truly dead and I was wrong to doubt you.'

'Does that mean you still wish to marry?'

'I do with all my heart—though what Papa will make of it, I cannot begin to imagine.'

He smiled down at her, the familiar glint back in his eyes. 'And not only Papa,' he mocked gently. 'How will Carmela survive the news?'

Domino pulled back from him a little and said in a considered tone, 'I think perhaps we should wait until she is back in Spain before we formally announce our betrothal.'

'Then let us make her travel arrangements as soon as possible.'

She gurgled with laughter. He had thought he would never hear that sound again and pulled her close, holding her fast against his body, his suppressed longing overtaking prudence and destroying the carefully forged restraint. The palace was full of interested observers and the studio doors stood wide open to the garden. It mattered not.

He tipped her face to his. Her dark eyes were radiant and filled with love for him. This is where they both belonged. Gently and insistently he began to kiss her. Over and over again, at first soft and exploratory and then demanding, ever more demanding. Blind to everything around them, they crashed a path through the studio until they came to rest on the well-worn couch pushed against its rear wall. Laughingly they disentangled themselves and surveyed the carnage. Canvases were scattered here and there, an easel had been overturned and paint streaked the floor and soaked though their footwear.

'We seem to have managed a pretty good demolition.'

'Since we've made such a satisfactory start, perhaps we should finish,' she suggested, her full mouth curving into a provocative smile.

In response he folded her tightly into his body. 'Do you not think we should wait until you have a wedding ring on your finger?'

He was nibbling delicately at her ear but she detached herself sufficiently to take him to task for such heresy. She ran a finger lovingly down his face.

'I would never agree to such a foolish notion.'

'How foolish?' He kissed her eyebrows one at a time.

'Unbelievably foolish! Every girl knows that once she's caught her rake, she must make it impossible for him to escape!'

'Is that so?' His hands were making light work of the muslin's fastenings. 'I've obviously left it far too late to save myself.'

'I fear so.' Her voice faded into a sigh as she felt his limbs pressing fiercely against her, imprinting her with his form.

'Sadly your beautiful gown is like to be ruined,' he

lamented as the crushed dress was swiftly undone and cast to one side. Shirt and breeches soon went the way of the muslin.

His lips were moving across the bare skin of her neck in sweet, fiery kisses. She heard her breath coming fast as his mouth reached her breasts, tasting them, teasing them, moulding them into sharp pinnacles of desire.

'I cannot think of dresses just now,' she panted, small groans of pleasure emanating from somewhere she had never before known.

'And why would you?' he murmured, his body hard and hot. 'While I am so very close, what need have you of a gown?'

Epilogue

'*Las Meninas* has to be the most flawless picture ever painted.'

Joshua was squinting at the large canvas, trying without success to detect an imperfection. The young Infanta Margerita, surrounded by her entourage of maids of honour, bodyguard, two dwarfs and a dog, looked out at him from a room in Philip IV's palace.

Domino smiled knowingly. 'It depresses you.'

'Only a very little. Nothing so perfect can depress me for long. Do you see Velázquez himself in the painting, just behind this group here, working at his canvas but looking out at the viewer. He's mocking me for my very poor efforts.'

'He's greeting you from across the centuries,' she said consolingly. 'You must have seen the picture many times before. I remember your saying how much you loved coming to the Prado to see Velázquez. Does he always have this effect?'

'Far worse. I'm finding the painting much less dispiriting today. That's because you're by my side.'

'*Las Meninas* looks different with me?'

'Everything looks different with you.'

'You are a shameless flatterer', and she held his arm more tightly. 'At least I assume that was a compliment.'

'It could be nothing else. I feel as though I've been walking on clouds for the last six months. I want to paint the most exquisite picture which will say everything I feel for you. But Velázquez reminds me how far I am from achieving that.'

She smiled up at him, her face aglow with happiness. 'Whatever you paint for me will be better than anything hanging in the Prado, for it will be done with love.'

'An understatement, my darling.' And he dipped his face beneath the brim of her bonnet and kissed her soundly.

'You shouldn't do that! No London manners here! And I am fearful that any time soon you will come down to earth with a bump.'

'I am almost sure that you're wrong. I find that married life is exactly what suits me.'

Their fellow visitors shuffling their way around the white-walled room stopped for a moment to glance with curiosity at the couple. A tangible lustre surrounded them and everyone in their vicinity felt its warmth.

'Only almost!'

'I cannot allow you to get too puffed up,' he teased, adjusting the rose-satin ribbons of her villager hat and surreptitiously slipping his arm around her waist. He squeezed her tightly and an elderly lady wrapped in black glarcd at him through her pince-nez. In response he smiled sunnily back.

They began to move away from the picture that had taken their attention for so long, strolling slowly through each succeeding salon, their bodies brushing as they walked together, side by side, over the thick red carpet. In this fashion they made their way to the huge polished wood door guarding the front entrance. Domino could see ahead the fresh blue of a spring sky. Beside her Joshua's flaxen locks glinted in the sun's rays as they penetrated the gallery's long windows.

'Madrid in spring is heavenly.'

'The city has made a perfect end to our journey,' he agreed. 'But now it's time to head home—to my home, rather.'

'My home, too,' she reminded him.

'You will miss your father.'

She looked a little troubled. 'We will miss each other. We have had such a short time together but he is very happy to have been posted to Spain. I think he found London life a deal too complicated. And he will visit us in England for sure.'

'And your aunts?'

'It's strange,' she conceded, 'but I will miss them too. I never thought I would say that but they have been so welcoming. It must be your charm, you've won them over completely.'

'But not Carmela, I fear.'

He reached over to take their outdoor coats from the attendant and helped his wife into her rose velvet capote, shrugging himself into a greatcoat with upwards of a dozen capes.

'You never will,' Domino said sagely. 'For her you will always be the dangerous rake. But she is happy enough in Santa Caterina. The convent is where she has always wanted to be, you know. Brighton was a horrible deviation and I am sure she wishes to forget that she ever visited the town.'

He took her hand and guided her down the long flight of steps. 'That's something *we're* not likely to do, I fancy.'

'Forget Brighton? No indeed, though I don't think I would ever wish to return.'

'But why not? In the end everything came right, and since we found happiness there, the town should have a place in our hearts.'

A shiver prickled the surface of Domino's skin as they began to walk slowly along the wide pavement, the trees on either side sprouting their first greenery of the season.

'The place has as many bad memories for me as good,' she said as easily as she could. 'Lord Moncaster, for instance.'

'He need never concern us again.'

For a moment they were forced to abandon their conversation in order to negotiate a path round a group of chattering acquaintances, intent on enjoying the mild sunshine and blissfully unaware of the obstacle they presented.

'I received an intriguing message yesterday,' he continued once they had rounded the group. 'I forgot to tell you—it came from an old friend at Carlton House. The duchess has married Moncaster!'

Domino looked shocked but said with some spirit, 'They deserve each other. But it is very soon after the duke's death. Only a few months. Surely that cannot be right.'

'Charlotte has never been one to spend too much time observing the proprieties,' he said wryly. 'I imagine she was desperate to find another husband—marriage gives at least the semblance of respectability—and Moncaster was free. She grabbed him while she could.'

Domino remained silent, watching the stream of stylish carriages making their way along the wide boulevard at a smart trot, but with her mind far away.

'And they are in London,' she said finally, the strain in her voice betraying her anxiety.

'Don't fret, my darling. They may be in London but that's where they'll stay. Being close to power is all that interests them and now that Moncaster has been allowed back into Court, they will be eager to resume their places in the Regent's entourage. They're sure to hang on to George's coat tails forever and we're just as sure never to see them again.'

'Norfolk is not that far from London,' she reminded him, still anxious but willing herself to be convinced.

'It's far enough, particularly in the depths of winter. The climate can be inclement and the roads sometimes impassable. I only hope you won't find it too quiet.'

That galvanised her and she turned impulsively towards him. 'I am so looking forward to seeing Castle March and setting up house with you there.'

'It will be a house for someone else too,' he reminded her, gesturing lovingly to the gentle swell of her stomach.

'Indeed. It will be the perfect place for children and the perfect place for us.'

'No chance there of falling back into my wicked ways, you mean.'

She nudged him playfully. 'You know I mean nothing of the sort. I am very sure that your wicked ways, as you call them, are long dead.'

'You should be sure. It's you that has tamed me.'

'I doubt that', and she blushed at the thought of the night they had just spent together. 'Not that I would want to!'

He bent to kiss her full on the lips, ignoring the scandalised glances of their fellow strollers along the broad walkway. 'Together we'll make Castle March a real home, Domino. At last I can hang my da Vinci. It's the very first thing I shall do. Actually, the second,' he corrected himself. 'There's a small matter of carrying you over the threshold.'

'You must make sure that you don't drop the pair of us!'

'I will be taking the greatest care of you both.'

He looked at her blooming cheeks and shining dark eyes. 'You are more beautiful than ever,' he murmured and then stopped short and pulled her to himself, almost roughly. 'I think we should be thinking of quite a large nursery.'

'Do I get any say in that?' She smiled roguishly up at him.

'Not a word. It's already decided. But I do need your advice with something that has me in quite a puzzle.'

Domino, still smiling, raised her eyebrows.

'It's a matter of the greatest importance, so take care before you answer. Where exactly *am* I to hang the Leonardo?'

* * * * *

MILLS & BOON®

The Rising Stars Collection!

1 BOOK FREE!

This fabulous four-book collection features 3-in-1 stories from some of our talented writers who are the stars of the future! Feel the temperature rise this summer with our ultra-sexy and powerful heroes. Don't miss this great offer—buy the collection today to get one book free!

Order yours at
www.millsandboon.co.uk/risingstars